Mother of Pearl

Doug Booth

Mother of Pearl

Copyright 2008 R.D. Booth

Mother of Pearl

To Robert and Gladys,
The two classiest people I never knew

Mother of Pearl

Part One

One

Saturday, August 31, 1957
Up-State New York, NY

Mary Fletcher would never run away. She could never run away. She had nowhere to go. She had no family that would take her in and no money of her own other than a few crumpled bills she had secreted under layers of soiled clothing in the family laundry bin. All she possessed in life was her little girl and her mother's favourite ring.

She didn't mind the beatings. They were an integral part of her life, her lot in life for being what she had become: nothing. The beatings were also her destiny, her constant reminder that she was his to honour and obey until the good Lord would one day see fit to take her away. And then what would become of her daughter who gave her reason and determination? Her daughter who kept Mary alive against her will. No one and nothing mattered more than Pearl.

Mary told herself a hundred times that if Jack Fletcher ever hurt her little Pearl she would bash in his face with a shovel or put a match to his bed. She would watch him bleed or burn and then she would walk away. Each night she relived the same elusive dream as she lay by his side listening to his noises and smelling the pungent odour of a hard day's work.

She would never run away. However much she dreamt of leaving, of being free. She would never run and Pearl would grow up to be no different than she had become: too afraid to leave and too afraid to stay. There was the truck, but Mary had never learned to drive. She had no friends, their few neighbours knew to stay away and Jack Fletcher would chain her to a wall without so much as a blink if he suspected for a moment she would leave him.

He worked sawing lumber at the mill. She stayed home to cook and manage her garden. She had learned to kill and dress chickens, gut fish for their meals, to tear the feathers from ducks and to smoke the venison he would bring home in the fall. She had learned to knit and to sew, to darn his frayed pants and socks and to pray in silence for her daughter's well-being. She prayed each day that he drove Pearl to school and brought her home at night, after the girl walked the four miles to the mill. He ate supper each night at six, not a moment later, and then he would go to his workshop where he drank until he needed sleep while Mary did her best to help Pearl with her lessons.

There was never enough money for extras, not since the baby was born. Mary looked old beyond her years. She felt ancient without the comfort of wisdom and wore a long braid of hair that had long since lost its sheen. Her face had lost its radiance; her eyes were always tired and circled with the dark hues of desperation and defeat. The single mirror in the house was Fletcher's for shaving and she was happy for it. She didn't want a mirror. She had seen her reflection in the lake one bright afternoon the year before, or the year before that. She couldn't remember. Time no longer had meaning. What she did remember was sinking to her knees in tears, promising herself that one day she would truly be beautiful, like her daughter, and that her skin would glow and her eyes would sparkle, if only in heaven.

She hadn't looked at herself since. Seeing her calloused

hands and sinewy arms each day that were dry and rough from labouring in the house and in the yard were sufficient reminders of what she had become. She hadn't dreamt of romance in years. Romance was harsh and cruel. She would often bleed or wake up bruised. Whenever she whimpered or blurted out a gasp he would give her all the more reason as he breathed his laboured and foul breath into her face. She never refused him. She did once and never would again. Pearl was thirteen and that worried Mary the most.

Mary's mother was born in Sicily in 1903. She arrived at the Statue of Liberty in 1918 to live a difficult life of drudgery and sickness, held back by the dark olive colour of her skin and a frail body. She died miserably of typhoid at the young age of forty, amidst the poverty and destitution she never escaped, and with only the warmth of Mary's young trembling hands to comfort her.

Mary's memories of her mother were not the weakness of her final breath, the moment she watched her mother die, so despairing and wasted, struggling not to close her eyes one last time, wanting to see her wonderful daughter another moment longer. What she remembered was the fading shroud of agony and disease yielding to an unmistakeable aura of serenity and peace everlasting, her single keepsake a perfect black pearl mounted in a tiny and intricate silver shell of Florentine swirls.

Her father had come by the next morning, not expecting to deal with a dead wife. He had no money with which to bury her and explained to Mary what that would mean for her mother. She would be buried by the town in a pauper's grave along with others, with all due respect in accordance with the laws of God and the township. His responsibility as a husband ceased with her death. She had departed to a better place. She was beyond earthly woes and would not care not in the least whether her spot on earth was marked with a crude wooden cross and not a marble stone. She was dead. She was in a better place and at peace. That's all anyone could expect when all was said and done, he insisted.

The afternoon Mary's mother was taken away to be buried Mary had no one to call, no one to bid her mother farewell. Her mother was number four, fourth in a line of cardboard boxes supported by two narrow strips of roughly hewn timber. Mary stood in shock as the planks were laid over the open grave and two men with their foreheads and necks roped with sweat-stained neckerchiefs came together at the head of the coffin. They hoisted the planks in unison, dragging them backward until the opposite ends hung freely over the small excavation. Ever so slowly they tilted the planks downward, pulling them away as they did so, until Mary's sole guardian disappeared into the ground.

That morning Mary washed out the Sunday dress her mother hadn't worn in years. She had no pretty dresses of her own and stuffed her mother's oxfords with toilet paper to make them fit. Her father stayed away. He was looking for work, and when Mary collapsed onto her knees in tears no one was by her side to care or to comfort her. The year was 1943, the date was July 08 and Mary Bingham celebrated her eighteenth birthday alone and afraid.

Not long after his wife's death, and feeling free to leave, her footloose and out-of-work father joined the army. He was the first of his division to fall in Europe at the battle of what Mary would always regard as the Battle of Comeuppance. He left her with nothing, telling her the time was nigh for her to marry, to be a good wife and to let a good man take care of her. He had raised her as best he could. Now she would be someone else's burden. His final words as he climbed onto the bus were to tell her to choose well. A girl with her looks wouldn't take very long at all to wed, he insisted, what with nature's generosity towards her natural endowments.

He said nothing else before turning his back on her and when she heard of his death weeks later she spoke to her mother in a whisper and smiled. Her father always doubted Mary was born of his doing. He'd been gone from home often in the early years and she looked nothing like him. She was curiously dark and that Mary's mother was born in Sicily meant nothing to him.

All her young life Mary Bingham wanted to be a nurse. Helping those in distress was all she ever wanted. She wanted so much to help people not to die, to make a difference. She wanted to travel, to see Chicago, New York and Europe. She dreamt of moving to a big city where she would have lots of friends, be invited to parties and go to fine restaurants.

That day at the bus station, when she said goodbye to her father, she knew the day would never come, that her dream would never come true. She had little education and didn't know very much about life or the world around her. She left school while in the eighth grade to stay by her sick mother's side and now she was alone with no job and very little money. She searched desperately for work each day, each day no better than the one before. She had no skills and no experience. She was frantic, until three weeks later when she noticed a Help Wanted sign in the window of a roadside diner.

As a young girl Mary had long copper-coloured hair, thick brows over deep, penetrating eyes and a strangely exotic olive complexion. To most of the town folk she was not quite white and not quite black. They didn't know what she was. When she was small she had always looked as though she needed a good scrubbing and often she did. Though, as she grew older she evolved into an alluring young woman. She was beautiful despite her handed-down clothes. They were faded and the fabrics were worn from too many encounters with a washboard and buckets of cold water and coarse detergents that chafed and dried her hands.

The way she looked was fine with the owner of the diner. She would be good for his business. She would work behind the counter serving meals or cleaning tables for her room and board. She could have one of the rooms over the diner and any tips were hers to keep. The job was hers if she wanted, and she began the same day. To Mary the job meant a new beginning. She could move out of the rooming house, which would help her to save, and she had looks. She knew that would help too.

Very few days later a young travelling vendor from another town came in for his Friday dinner. The attention he gave Mary instantly captivated her. He became a regular, coming in each Friday and eventually asking her out. She said "yes". She'd never been on a date, let alone with an older man. He wasn't debonair, not sophisticated like the men in the movies, but he paid attention to her and promised her the world. He told her she was beautiful. He couldn't think of any other woman, he began to bring her bouquets of flowers he would pluck from behind white-picket fences along the street and very soon Mary began dreaming of being Mrs. Jack Fletcher.

One Friday night he came in as the diner was closing, too late for the movies and too late for dinner. He was exhausted after a long and wearisome week of dusty travel and his home was too many miles from the restaurant to drive safely in such wicked weather. He needed to rest. He hadn't been able to phone for a motel room so he thought he might sleep behind the diner in his truck and have breakfast with her before continuing home the next morning. Mary was distraught. Heavy rains had begun and she agreed for fear he would be injured or worse. She would rather see him safe behind the diner than driving in such wretched weather, when he could barely keep his eyes open.

Unable to sleep for worry, Mary sat in bed as bolts of lightning lit her small room, explosive bursts of thunder making her feel vulnerable, making her shudder. She leapt from her bed and ran to her window. She moved her hands in tight circles to rub away the condensation and peered into the darkness. She could see the dark outline of the truck, nothing more. She worried for him. The weather was worsening beyond what she had heard earlier on the radio, deteriorating into a torrential downpour and the dark parking lot appeared like a skating rink or shallow pond.

Another deafening clap of thunder shook her body and startled her as lightning illuminated the sky. Then she saw him. She pressed her face against the cold pane, waiting for the next bolt that would let her see him, and when the sky brightened he was so retched and pathetic huddled against the truck's unforgiving door and window. Then he was gone, engulfed once again by darkness. She hurried to him in slippers and a thin robe with her coat held over her head and flapping wildly in the violent wind. She splashed across the short distance between them and stretched herself onto her tiptoes to bang her palms against the wet glass, doing her best to hold her coat in place over her head.

Half awake, he jumped. He could come up to her room, she yelled into the raging wind. He could sleep on the floor with warm blankets, but he had to promise to be a proper gentleman. She was drenched, soaked to her skin, when she stepped back to let him push open the door.

He promised her, and they ran up the stairs laughing and giggling. Mary was dripping wet, shivering with cold. She scurried into the bathroom to change and comb her wet hair. When she came out Jack Fletcher was sitting on the floor by his blankets. He waited until Mary turned off the lights and leaped into bed before he removed his shoes and his shirt. She listened intently to the rustling noises, a little aroused and feeling wickedly sinful at having a man in her room. She was quite excited, and when at last she found the courage to speak with him there was no reply.

The next morning Mary opened her eyes, feeling a strange burning sensation between her legs. She looked to the floor. Jack Fletcher had gone. What she saw was her underwear. She pushed aside the blankets and pulled her nightdress to her waist to see herself. Her thighs were tinted with rose-coloured stickiness; her secret place was puffy and red. She throbbed there. The feeling was unpleasant, not like the invasive tingling she had come to enjoy when imagining herself in the arms of the handsome and gallant gentlemen in her magazines or in the movies as she drifted to sleep. She smelled in a way she never had before. Her wrists were coloured with faint bruises and her buttocks felt red hot as though she her skin was severely scalded.

She flinched, pushing her nightdress to her knees, embarrassed when the bathroom door opened without warning and the six-foot frame of the burly Jack Fletcher stepped out. His face under a week-old black beard was beaming. He wore slacks and a singlet. His hair was still wet, her towel slung over his broad shoulders. She had no time to speak. He told her he loved her. He wanted to marry her and take her away. What happened between them was too exciting for him, for both of them. He wanted to be with her forever. He couldn't imagine himself with any other woman and he promised to return in two weeks to take her away. She could quit her job at the diner and go north with him into the country. They could be married and find a place to live, a new home, and they would never stop being happy.

Mary lay motionless in her bed, watching him dress. She remembered his fingers against her lips, his quiet words, his lips pressing hard against her mouth, his strong hands at her shoulders. How long had he lain beside her, she wondered, his hands gliding over her body, teasing her so brazenly in her sleep, arousing her in her dreams until she awoke to the heat emanating from their bodies. She remembered the warmth of his hands squeezing her shoulders, pressing into her back. She remembered how she squealed as he first pressed an open palm against one ample breast, then the other, plucking at their dark crowns until each one responded and he could pinch them between his fingers.

She was embarrassed, and she was ashamed. She was excited and afraid. No one had ever touched her breasts. She enjoyed how she felt inside and out and she wanted him to like them. His caresses were different from her secret touches, not what she ever imagined. His were urgent, not as tender as her own delicate explorations, though her mother never told her what to expect.

She remembered how he tugged at her nightdress the night before, how she let him, how she wanted him to be like the men in the movies, and how she thought she would awake in the morning feeling like a princess with bright sun shining through her windows. She remembered how he pushed the hem higher and wrapped his arms around her. He pulled her closer and kissed her as he kneaded the soft mounds of her buttocks. She remembered how she gasped when he slipped his hand under the elastic of her underpants, pushing downward, and how she closed her legs tightly together to make him stop.

He did stop, leaving his hands where they were, bringing his mouth to her breasts and kissing each one before laying his head against them. Her skin was hot, her chest heaving under his weight. He heard her heart pounding. She brought up her hands and stroked his hair. She was desperate to see him, yet her eyes were shut tight. His hands were rough against her bare skin. She thought they should be. He was a man, she was becoming a woman and she opened her legs willingly. She was embarrassed, exhilarated, and locked her fingers into his hair as the flimsy material of her underpants was pushed to her knees and pulled away. Still she was afraid to open her eyes.

Then his hands came away from her and she remembered how she had felt cold. She remembered feeling him between her legs, staring down at her, and how she moved her hands to cover herself. She remembered the pressure of his hands over hers, the warmth and the waiting. She remembered the pain, but she had never been with a man before and didn't know whether the stinging hurt would ever go away.

He didn't stay for breakfast and for the next two weeks Mary Bingham floated on air. Her face glowed. At night she dreamt of Jack Fletcher and the romantic honeymoon amidst the fall colours of the Poconos he promised her. Friday night she stood outside and waited on the steps of the diner because she didn't want her new dress and coat to smell like grease or for the gravel from the parking lot to ruin her new shoes. Jack Fletcher arrived at 8:00, wearing the one suit and the one pair of shoes he possessed.

He greeted her as though in a hurry, tossed her small suitcase into the back of his truck, climbed in behind the wheel and reached over to swing open the other door for Mary as everyone in the diner peered from their windows. An hour later, in a small chapel on the outskirts of town, and in a moment lost in time, a vulnerable and naïve Mary Bingham gave herself away.

Their first night together was spent at a dank motor lodge off I-87 in the Catskills and they ate dinner in the motel's brightly lit restaurant. They would have time for the Poconos later, he promised her. He was so eager to show her their new home that he knew was perfect for them, a property he recently came across in his travels, not many miles from where they were staying. The owner had given him the key. The man was old and was moving away to be with his son in the city. He was willing to sell the place furnished, with all his tools and a rowboat. All the young couple would have to do is move their personal belongings into the private lakefront property which sat on forty forested acres, ideal for young lovers. Mary believed him.

The modest house by the lake was available for immediate occupancy and Jack Fletcher had saved enough to pay the man outright. He left Mary alone to roam the property without the slightest indication of what she should do as he went to meet with the old man to transfer the deed before he changed his mind or raised the price.

She strolled along the narrow dirt trail embedded with ancient pebbles and lined with tall, wild grass on either side to the private, crescent-shaped beach to wait and gaze out over the lake, her lake. When he'd been gone what she thought must be two hours or more, she decided to explore her new home.

She went to the old shed and swung open its crooked wooden doors, startling herself when the hinges shrieked. She peeked in, afraid to venture further. The inside was dark and damp and smelled of oil and gas. She didn't want to go into the house without him. Instead she walked cautiously to the back of the shed to discover what was there. At the corner of the weathered building she stopped in her tracks, standing still to study a much smaller ramshackle construction which appeared on the verge of collapse. She'd never seen one. She wondered what its purpose might be. She tiptoed to the other side, instantly causing a noisy commotion of fluttering wings and a frenzied melee of chickens colliding with chickens. She tripped backwards, crashing blindly into the unyielding arms of a wheelbarrow and onto the ground.

She stayed as she was with her legs sprawled apart, and a moment later she thought to raise them. She brought a hand up under her dress and pressed into the apex of her thighs. He had hurt her as much the night before as he had the first time with what she assumed was ardent fervour. She pressed harder. The pain was subsiding with only a mild burning sensation remaining, as he had promised. All the same, the warmth of her hands felt soothing. She looked again at the chickens. She had never seen live chickens and wondered why the old man would possibly have so many. They would have to go. They were dirty and they smelled.

She wondered what was taking her husband so long. She wasn't anxious to return to the motel, but she would for him. He seemed to enjoy himself and had paid for the two nights.

She didn't want to disappoint him. The motel wasn't what she had imagined and the room was much smaller than her room over the diner.

She suspected Jack would want to do it to her again, he seemed to like it very much and the noises he made were not the same as hers. She seemed not to hurt him the same way and she wondered why. She had no one to ask. Perhaps she would have to actually touch it to find out, but she didn't know how to or when. Each time he finished, after he hurt her the most, he rolled onto his side and soon fell asleep. After the first time she had stayed beside him, not knowing what to do, though on their wedding night he told her to cleanse herself in the bathroom. She obeyed, not understanding why she should as she closed the door behind her. She didn't need to pee, though she did feel something and when she peered into the bowl her stomach constricted and she forced herself not to be sick.

She grimaced and put the thought from her mind. She picked herself up, dusted the back of her dress and walked towards the house, her new home. So why couldn't she go in by herself? The place needed work and a good cleaning. She didn't care. She was at home and the vista surrounding Deep Lake was magnificent. She knew she would be safe when he travelled for his work and soon she would get to know her neighbours and have friends.

She went from one small room into another making a mental list of improvements and repairs he would attend to as soon as he could, as soon as the honeymoon was over. When she sauntered into the main room, which also served as the kitchen, he was standing with both suitcases by his side and large bags of groceries in his arms. He had bought the house and he saw no need to spend good money for another night in a motel room when she could just as well cook him a meal at home.

She was delighted. She gazed at the small fireplace and pictured glowing logs flickering amidst orange flames, as he held her in his arms. She could not have been happier until, at six-thirty, when his meal was done, he went to the shed. The honeymoon had lasted one night and the fireplace remained cold. On the Sunday she began cleaning and Jack Fletcher left her for the second time in as many days. She knew he had no family. She knew he was an orphan and had been living in a boarding house several miles away. He told Mary he needed to gather his few possessions, settle his account with the landlady, and would be home by 6:00 for his supper.

Monday morning he went to work. Mary had been up for hours making his breakfast and preparing his lunchbox. He told her he'd be spending the week locally, wanting to be at home with her at night to make up for the honeymoon. And she was so happy. When he did return home late Monday afternoon, he waited until dinner was done and Mary was set to do the dishes to tell her he had lost his job. Business was failing because of the war in Europe and he was the one laid off, but he'd spent the day looking for another position and was taken on at the sawmill.

The pay wasn't as good as selling, he explained, but the work was steady and would give them a good living. He was twenty-six, weeks away from twenty-seven, and with hard work he could be a supervisor by thirty-five or forty. And Mary believed him. She gave birth to her daughter eight and a half months later, feeling the back of Jack Fletcher's hand for the first time for not having given him a son. He left her in a daze on the floor of his four-room cottage and strode to the lake, away from the baby's wailing.

During those first months Mary worked hard at being a good wife. His home was always clean, his meals were always ready for him and she never denied him his right. Her daze continued through the night and when, for the first time, she did deny him, she learned a difficult lesson and throughout days that followed she began surreptitiously to

17

learn about her new husband. He was never a vendor of trinkets and household goods and her new home had always been his. He was thirty, not twenty-six, and had worked at the mill for fourteen years. Then she began to doubt whether she had ever been married. Mary Fletcher, nee Mary Bingham, was trapped and that single doubt erased her dreams and her fantasies in one fleeting moment.

From that day forward the baby was asleep by dinnertime each night and daily traces of Mary's curiosity were meticulously removed. She put away her mother's ring, afraid he would one day take the heirloom from her, telling him it had come off while she'd been doing the washing down by the lake. He called her stupid and slapped her, warning her never to expect fine trinkets from him. His money was too hard-earned to be thrown into the lake or into the woods. Mary's single pleasure became the time spent at the lake with Pearl, bathing and enjoying the privacy, and Pearl knew from a tender age never to tell her father.

Beyond counting the months, the weeks and the days, Mary paid little attention to the passage of time. Thinking of her past, she often hated her father more than the deceit and the pain she suffered at the hands of Fletcher. One day, she promised, she would give Pearl a good life. Her daughter would no longer have to stay awake at night listening to the sounds of slapping and whimpering or see her mother bruised and despondent in the morning.

At Christmas, Mary knew to expect extra money to buy each of them a practical gift, at Easter, extra money for new clothes. Though on her birthday Fletcher would take the wife and daughter to the mill for the July 04th corn roast and barbeque, which was close enough to her birthday to count. There was no better life for little Pearl, except on her birthdays when she would open whatever Mary was able to make for her, or coloured ribbons Pearl would wear in her hair when they were alone, ribbons from shop owners who always had a few inches to spare.

Pearl was becoming a young woman. Her body was changing its shape and her clothes were fitting differently. Her favourite times were still when she bathed with her mother at the lake. Now those happy moments were limited to summer vacations when Jack Fletcher worked at the mill. Those special times for mother and daughter were times for talking, times for listening. She loved her time at the lake with her mother, listening to stories of how one day they would wear fine clothes and become fine ladies.

Pearl wouldn't be a nurse, she maintained stubbornly. She would be a doctor, or maybe an FBI agent. Some of the girls at school often let her borrow their mystery books to read on the way to the mill and Pearl knew all about the FBI and how they pursued war criminals. That's what she wanted, she decided. She would spend her life tracking down bad men and kill them, especially the ones like her father who made her mother cry.

At the time Mary had smiled and hugged her daughter close, yet that night she lay awake thinking her of daughter's innocent words. From the mouth of babes so much truth is borne, she thought. A single tear trickled onto her pillow. Mary was thirty-two and prayed each night to die in her sleep, waking to each new day for no other reason than Pearl. Deep in her heart she knew, but for Pearl, she would have died long ago.

Labour Day weekend, 1957, began like any other. The forest had begun to change from shades of green to hues of gold and red. The evening air began to lose its summer warmth and preparations for another long, bleak winter were soon to begin. Jack and Mary Fletcher had gone to town to purchase supplies for the coming cold, dark months and school supplies for the girl. The day was unseasonably warm for the last day of August and her parents would not be home for hours, at least not until dark.

Pearl was tall for her age, and mature. She had the highest marks in her class and she spoke like a young woman, not a girl. Mary always insisted that Pearl read out loud as she walked to the mill each day, and whenever they had time alone she spoke to her daughter as an equal. In front of Jack Fletcher, however, the young girl knew to revert to what she actually was.

At first she was shy bathing in front of her mother at the lake as her body began to blossom, though Mary was her friend, not her mother, and soon her shyness evaporated. The midday dips were once again a natural part of them. She loved her mother deeply, as she had always wanted to love her father, the way she never would. She hated him for what he did to Mary, to her friend, and often thought of what she would do to him if she were with the FBI.

She knew the Indian boy at school had often looked at her the year before, though she never looked back at him. She had read in magazines the other girls let her borrow how proper women never appear eager. He lived at the other side of Deep Lake, his name was Billy Stream, he was Iroquois and Pearl believed he was the bravest of them all. He was tall and strong, handsome with black hair, deep black eyes, and even though he was a senior he still looked at her. He was so handsome. All the other girls envied her and she loved him with all her heart. He did things to her in her dreams and she wanted to be with him. She wanted to be held tenderly in his arms and to feel his hot breath on her lips. That was real love, she knew.

She hadn't seen Billy all summer and wondered how she would feel seeing him on her first day at school. She often imagined him wearing cowhide chaps without a shirt and long eagle feathers hanging from his beautiful black hair, or rowing his canoe to her secluded beach and stepping out with only little cowhide flaps to cover his magnificent body.

Pearl never looked before taking off her clothes at the lake. There was never anyone to see and her mother was always with her. This was the first time her parents had left her alone, one of her last times to swim before the water began to chill. Her work frock fell to the ground and she squirmed from what was once Mary's brassiere. The thing didn't fit her well and she hated it. She wanted her own. She threw the thing to the ground, then her underpants that were plain, not anything like the pretty ones in the magazines at the drugstore where she always went before walking to the mill. Hers had no frills. They were cotton and functional. She hated them as much.

She strolled into the water, fixated by the rippling image encircling her knees. She could see the difference. Each day her breasts were fuller, each day her pubis thickened more with dark curls and each day she felt differently about Billy Stream. The water was cool. She splashed herself and watched her body react. She walked to where the water swirled at her waist and dived in, surfacing a few feet away with her hair dripping, her youthful contours glistening in the sun, her youthful body titillated and excited. Being alone in the lake wasn't at all the same as being with Mary. The sensations were inexplicably different, suddenly heightened. She waded toward the crescent shore and sat gazing dreamily out over the glistening lake. The sun's warmth felt exquisite on her body and she lay back on her roughly woven blanket, letting her mind travel to wherever it wanted to go.

She had recently begun understanding the sensation. Her first time was several weeks earlier, when she had cried out, quickly calling to her mother that she had stubbed her toes in the dark. Mary suspected otherwise, grateful Jack Fletcher was sleeping and snoring contentedly, sorry her little girl was becoming a woman. What she didn't know was that her daughter was now lost in reverie, heated by the innocent passion of youth and summer's final warmth as her Onondaga brave stepped from his war canoe to take her in his arms and carry her away to distant shores. What Pearl didn't realize was that her girlish fantasy had come true.

Billy Stream absorbed every inch of the young girl as his canoe glided silently towards the shore. He had seen pictures of naked girls in his older brother's books, mostly white girls with brown hair or blonde, but this was different. He was so close to her. He couldn't believe it. He could see Pearl's stomach rising and falling, her young breasts and the dark hair between her legs. She was real, not a drawing in a book, and he wanted to see more. He liked her since the first time he saw her. She was cute, and didn't seem to mind like the other girls that he was an Indian. He never told anyone how he thought of her every night, not even his brother. All he wanted was to see more of her and he quietly paddled from shore, careful not to cause the slightest ripple.

Pearl opened her eyes. She turned to let the soothing heat warm her back. She squirmed into her blanket, raising her hips to trap a small hand between her body and the coarse cloth, thinking how wonderful his skin would feel to her touch. She didn't want to move. She wanted the feeling to last forever. At night she learned to put her face into her pillow each time her body went rigid and shuddered, but now she was alone with no one to hear. She felt the crescendo happening, she felt her body ready to convulse and she raised her hips from her blanket as the intensity shot through her and her body jerked uncontrollably. She cried out and sank to the ground.

She lay still, depleted, unable or unwilling to move. Billy Stream leaned against the trunk of the huge maple tree, also depleted and wanting her. He never imagined anything could excite him as much. He'd never seen anything so enticing. Her skin glistened, skin darker than his, the colour of gold mixed with green to match her hair was that was the colour of dark sand mixed with obsidian black. She was incredible to see through the binoculars, watching as her face expressed the strain of her arousal, grimacing as her body trembled, collapsing onto her front, squirming. He'd never heard a sound like the one she made.

When she stirred Billy moved quickly and stealthily to behind the tree, his view of Pearl unimpaired as she pushed herself to her knees. He felt as though he could reach out and touch her. She sat straight and stretched, groaning, then she reached for the bar of soap by her side and stood. Billy had never imagined anything as exotic as she went in and out of focus.

She walked thigh-deep into the water and crouched, wetting herself. The water felt cold and invigorating against her heated skin. She began washing herself, dreamily coating her young contours with thick lather. She felt totally free, completely alone. She felt like a woman, she was a woman. She dropped the soap, covered in white froth, looking at herself as her hands caressed each curve with youthful rapture. She was learning.

Looking into the sun, the pristine water was black to Billy, coated with millions of sparkling diamonds. Pearl was standing perfectly still, bathed in a golden hue, looking like an exotic young nymph as an island of white foam spread out from her legs, and Billy Stream made the worst decision of his young life. He stood naked by the tree as he watched her, waiting for her to dunk herself or begin swimming. When she did, he slipped into the water and swam towards her, towards the girl whom he knew was the most beautiful young maiden on earth.

The sun was beginning its slow descent towards the western horizon and Pearl dived in once more. She would have time to dry, finish her chores and start supper for her mother and father. She swam back and forth, trying not to think she would soon be at school and that the lake would not be hers to enjoy for another year. Then she screamed and twisted her head from side to side.

She was terrified. He was not an illusion. He was smiling, standing right there in front of her in shoulder-deep water. She thought of everything and thought of nothing. He was with her, not in her fantasies. He was there. What had he seen? How long had he been watching? She wanted to die. She yelled at him to go away. He didn't, so she splashed water at him and yelled again. She was furious. Still he did not budge. He stood fast, grinning stupidly. Then he told her the lake was his as much as hers. He lived on the other side and she could always swim to shore if she wanted to be alone.

He pointed to his canoe, explaining he felt like a swim and didn't expect to see her. She was the one who surprised him, and he was glad. He introduced himself and reached out his hand. Pearl kept her hands by her side and yelled at him to leave. She told him how she hated him. He asked how she could hate him when she didn't even know him. She did hate him, she insisted, knowing very well she loved him. He was so handsome. She looked around, searching for a way out. There wasn't one. She called him a pig. He shrugged, smiled, and stepped towards her, causing Pearl to trip as she jerked away, flailing her arms as she disappeared below the surface.

Seconds later she splashed into sight, coughing and sputtering. Billy was a few feet closer. He wanted to tell her how beautiful she was. He wanted to tell her he'd watched her at the shore and how aroused he was. He wanted to hold her, to feel her strangely coloured skin. He wanted to touch her. He wanted to be touched by her. He looked into the pristine water. He could see all of her, his new expression telling her so. She swept her hands to her breasts and yelled at him again to leave.

Billy Stream was seventeen. He forced himself to look away, giving in to a temptation that was too great. He apologized with a smirk, telling her in the same breath that he didn't see anything. She called him a liar and he shrugged again, insisting he was telling the truth. But if he had seen her, he knew she would be the most beautiful woman in the world.

"I'll go after one little kiss, if you want me to. I know you like me, Pearl. One little kiss before I leave you alone and die a happy man."

He was a man: young and virile. She knew he wanted to kiss her and he knew her name. How many nights had she lain awake kissing her pillow and pretending? And now he was real. He had to be real. She was shivering with cold and in her dreams she was always warm. Her stomach constricted and her heart raced. She swallowed hard.

"Close your eyes, Billy Stream. If you want to kiss me, you have to close your eyes." Billy did. "And put your hands behind your back, Billy."

He did. Pearl urged herself forward, knowing if she didn't she would stay where she was forever and drown. She was standing face to face with him, eye to eye. She leaned forward touching her lips to his, her stomach twisting into a tight knot and she thought she would die.

"That was nice. Now can I open my eyes?" he asked.

"No, you cannot. And why are you laughing like a stupid idiot?"

"My sister kisses me that way. I was expecting something more, you know, the way a girlfriend kisses a boyfriend."

She was going to die. She splashed water into his face, he splashed back, and without warning they were wrestling and shrieking and laughing until, as abruptly, they stopped and he kissed her again the way she knew a real man would take his woman. She was dizzy with joy, confused and afraid. She was pinned against his body, held in his arms, her bare breasts pressed against his chest, telling him what she could not, her legs floating freely against his.

Her mother had told her about them on several occasions, and all the girls in her class talked about them, although none had ever seen one. She could feel that part of Billy changing, wanting to wedge between her thighs. She

25

wanted to reach down and push the thing away, afraid because her mother had told her what they were for and how much they hurt. Instead, she hung there swaying in Billy's arms.

She let his hands explore her back, waiting until he began moving one hand towards the tight space between them to push him away and look at the sky. The sun was disappearing behind the trees. She pleaded with him to leave and he shook his head. She begged him to leave, or turn around, and he agreed. He would swim away, after he watched her wading to shore.

He laughed when she slapped his face, then he did promise to close his eyes. She made him swear that he would and he did, until the sound of her thrashing at the water was far enough away and he opened them to see her scurrying with her arms waving and her legs kicking out in every possible direction. He whistled and called out that he'd never seen anything so wonderful, that he would always remember her as a naked angel, dripping wet, even when they were married. Then the young man froze where he stood.

Jack Fletcher was charging down the hill as fast as he could, raging, his face distorted into a horrible scowl. He didn't slow his pace, slapping Pearl to the ground as he lunged into the water to chase after Billy Stream. The sheer momentum behind the violent impact hurled her several feet. The canoe was too far away, mere seconds ticking invisibly until Fletcher raised an arm into a wide arc with deliberate precision. Billy never saw the crowbar crash into his shoulders. His body arched up and out of the water, he screamed a sickening gurgling sound and whirled around with his arms raised in defence to face the enraged Fletcher. He heard each limb shatter, unable to scream again in terror before the bar crashed into the side of his head, smashing his temporal bone and murdering him.

Fletcher let go of the limp body and heaved the crowbar as far as he could into the lake with a guttural howl. He swung around to see Pearl sprawled on ground and pushed his way through the water as he stomped wildly to the shore. She was crying hysterically, her head was spinning and she gave no thought to the fact she was naked in front of her father. She stared at him, horrified, screaming as he yanked her to her feet and smashed his fist into her face. He threw her to the ground and kicked at her buttocks, her hips and her arms before jerking her to her feet once again by her hair, grabbing her throat and shaking her.

Pearl's arms and legs flailed defencelessly. She was crying copious tears and trembling. She was being killed and all she could do was stare into his wild, maniacal eyes. He was shouting at her that no daughter of his would be the town whore and with his other hand he drew his belt from its loops. He coiled half its length around his hand and raised the menacing lash high into air. Pearl tried with all her strength to break away, to run, squealing at the searing heat as the first lash whipped at her breasts. She covered them with her hands and he whipped her back and her buttocks, leaving cruel welts. He dropped the belt and stepped in closer, grabbing her hard between her thighs, squeezing and shaking her with savage fervour. He was screaming at her, demanding to know if she liked it, if the Indian kid liked it, if it felt good, if she liked being a whore. He threw her to the ground where she instantly coiled into a ball, covering her face. Screaming frantically for her mother was all she could do. Then there was quiet, an invasive stillness, tender hands and comforting warm kisses to her face and her shoulders.

Mary whispered to Pearl over and over again that he had gone away, that he would not come back, that she had no more reason to be afraid. She stroked her daughter's hair and helped her to stand, holding her close and telling her with a firm voice to look straight ahead. Mary assured her the boy was fine. He might have had the scare of his life and possibly a few bruises, though nothing more. He was able to swim away. He was fine, and so would Pearl be.

They made their way to the house where Mary poured a bath for the girl and brought her a cup of steaming broth laced with brandy. When she finished the toddy Mary put her to bed, put salve to the fresh welts and waited with quiet uneasiness for Pearl to fall asleep. Clutching her hands together, she kissed her daughter's cheek and walked outside to live the worst part of her favourite dream.

Jack Fletcher lay dead at the bottom of the hill, the shaft of the hammer protruding from his skull like some macabre ponytail. She left it there, thinking how ridiculous he looked. Dusk had arrived. The sun had set, leaving a faint afterglow to illuminate the evening sky. She looked out over the dark water clutching her stomach and throat as she retched several times at the sight.

What looked to be a clump of grass attached to a narrow floating log were Billy Stream's head and outstretched, broken arms. The lake she had always thought was so calm and serene was eerie and threatening to her and the peaceful forest of tall trees where she had strolled so many times with Pearl made her feel small and afraid. A pang of fear and foreboding shot through her, disappearing in an instant. She rubbed warmth into her arms, breathing deeply and running her fingers through her hair. Then she purposefully undid the buttons of her dress and willed herself to be strong for her daughter as she walked from her small bundle of clothes and strode naked into the dark and sinister water.

Billy Stream's body had drifted farther out, pushed by a gentle breeze beyond Mary's 5'3". She swam with measured strokes, praying he wouldn't sink before she got to him. All she could see was his head and she knew that was how she would do it. As she came to him she reached out to lock her fingers into his hair, but as she pulled him closer her legs touched his and she thrashed away from him in a panic. She screamed inwardly, the high-pitched sound scaring her all the more. She looked toward the shore and the dim lights of her home, images of Pearl racing across her mind, then to Billy, whispering that she was sorry as she grabbed a fistful of hair.

She breathed a deep sigh of relief when her feet touched the bottom. She dragged the body to the shoreline and left him half in the water where she could later manoeuvre him with greater ease. Looking down to see a young man, not a boy, and seeing Pearl's housedress and underwear a few steps away, Mary imagined the worst. She would ask her daughter the question. She had no choice. She had to know the truth and prayed Billy hadn't harmed her daughter in any way.

Even though she had expected the boy to be naked because Pearl had been, the thought had not occurred to her that Billy would have hidden his clothes somewhere. Mary had often seen him canoeing on the lake and had often thought to wave. She never did. Everyone knew of Jack Fletcher, even the other children at school, and no one ever bothered them. She waded back into the water to gain a better view of what lay around the tiny peninsula that had always made the little crescent-shaped cove so private. The canoe was there and she stopped for a moment to think. He certainly would not have undressed in the canoe, she thought. He must have sneaked up on Pearl to watch her bathing. Billy had been watching her daughter from the trees and that is where she would find his clothes.

She pranced to the shore as fast as she could and ran towards the narrow foot path she knew would lead her to the canoe. The fallen leaves were still damp from the morning dew and felt strange against her bare feet. She slipped once, landing hard on her back and cursing aloud. Crawling to her knees and pushing herself to her feet, she closed her eyes to all that was around her, controlling herself, telling herself she was in a dream and soon she would wake up in a new and better life.

With her eyes open and her heart beating normally, she slowed her pace, doing her best not be scared by branches seeming to grab at her and rustling leaves that had given up their vivid shades of late summer to ghostly dark shadows.

The boy had discarded his clothes quickly, strewing them recklessly around the maple tree. She stooped to gather them and put each piece one by one into the canoe. Satisfied, she stepped in herself, pushed from the shore and paddled to where the rowboat was tied to a tree. She dragged the canoe from the water and ran as fast as she could to the shed, ignoring her own pile of clothes, repeatedly reminding herself not to panic. The handsaws were too big or too heavy so she settled for an axe and ran to the shore, taking a full fifteen minutes to smash the canoe into workable pieces which she stacked over logs with Billy's clothes soaked in kerosene.

With the jerry can empty she threw the match and ran to the house to check on Pearl who was sleeping peacefully. She went to the kitchen to fill a glass with brandy. She swallowed as much as she could in one gulp. The unfamiliar harshness of the cheap liquor warmed her and stole her breath.

She scanned the room. She would never miss a house that was never her home. She had never met Billy's parents, though she prayed for them anyway and asked their forgiveness, not for what her husband had done, rather for what she was about to do to their son. She looked in on Pearl once more and hurried to the shed to search for anything light enough to carry and heavy enough to sink, deciding on Fletcher's iron toolbox with as many tools as she could manage.

She stumbled her way down the hill, barely able to lift the box over the side of the rowboat. She tossed in Billy's binoculars, testing the lock to be sure the tools would never fall out and ran for a length of chain which she looped through the handle and fastened in place with the padlock from the shed. Finished, she went to Billy. She dragged him into waist-deep water and pulled him to the boat, talking softly to comfort him as she put a rope around his neck and secured the other end to a rear cleat.

The fire had been raging for thirty minutes when Mary untied the boat and stepped in. The morbid jerking and twisting of Billy Stream's body with each stroke of the oars hadn't occurred to her, nor did the possibility the limp body might roll over. Several times his head collided against the low, wooden transom with hollow-sounding thumps beyond her sight, making his torso, arms and legs appear all the more ghastly. She rowed several hundred feet to where she knew no one would ever swim or fish. That the depth was over 200 feet was all she needed to know as she brought Billy to the side and tied the chain around his neck with a brass hank. She kissed her fingertips and put them gently to his head.

He was killed for being a curious teenager. She might have hated him in life for what he did to Pearl. In death, she pitied him and cried for his mother who would never see him again. She untied the rope from his neck, whispered goodbye and struggled on her knees to throw over the iron box. She didn't look as Billy's head was snapped into the water and his lifeless legs kicked water into the air.

At the shore the canoe was disintegrating. She added more logs, threw in the broken oars and stirred the embers. She ran to the house to look in on Pearl, gulped another mouthful of brandy and hurried into her bedroom for one of Fletcher's heavy work shirts and her own winter gloves. She ran to the shed for the small fourteen-pound hammer she knew lay on the workbench and his hunting knife.

She doubted Billy would ever surface. The lake water was cooling with the arrival of autumn and by the coming summer what the lake fish hadn't nibbled from his lean body would be well-anchored. Fletcher was another matter.

31

If he were to break free and be found with a hammer stuck in his head, even the local sheriff would believe he'd been murdered… if they were able to identify him.

She put the knife into the glowing embers and knelt beside the head. The eyes and mouth were open, showing surprise. So what, she mused. She had promised herself Fletcher would never touch Pearl. She would have killed him anyway for beating her so maliciously, then, to see him so cruelly groping between her legs, her own father, she instantly enjoyed killing him.

There would be no more beatings, no more oppression and no more unfeeling intimacy. She was free, Pearl was free. Mary shivered. She was still naked and her hair was wet. She chuckled at how she must look: a small, naked and bedraggled woman tugging and jerking a corpse twice her size with a hammer stuck in its head to the water's edge.

She left it in knee-deep water and went for the shirt and the hammer. She checked on the fire and threw in more logs. She stoked the embers, looked toward the house and went to the water. She put the heavier hammer on its chest, pushed it out to where the water was up to her waist and covered its face with the shirt. Then she took up the hammer and pounded its head until the sharp sounds of breaking bones became the dull thuds of mashed tissue and cartilage.

She reached between her feet and let go of the hammer. She rolled over the corpse, grasping the convenient handle and swiped its mouth forcefully with her gloved fingers. Seconds later she felt the teeth sprinkle across her feet and she stirred the silty bottom for several seconds more. She let go of the corpse, reached for the hammer and dunked herself before wading to shore.

She ran to the shed to find more chain. At the shore she crisscrossed the body with the entire length and tied the ends together with another brass hank. She ran to the fire where steam wafted from her wet glove as she closed her hand around the knife. The blade glowed red in the dark as she ran to the body to sear each fingertip, oblivious to the sizzling and tiny puffs smoke. When all ten fingers were done she cooled the knife in the water and ran to the fire where she threw in the shirt after checking that nothing from the head had stuck to it. The night air and her time in the water should have chilled her. She wasn't. She was heated with adrenalin and excitement.

This time she brought the boat to the face-down corpse. She secured it to the side by its feet and its neck and pushed the boat into deeper water before crawling in. The small boat was tilted and she sat closer to one side for the oar to reach the water, the increasing wind making her task more difficult. Her arms ached. She rowed for thirty minutes until she was satisfied the once Jack Fletcher was far enough out. She stopped, cut the lines and said farewell with a smirk as he disappeared from her life.

At the shore Billy's canoe was gone, converted to heated ashes, though she stoked the embers once more and added more logs. She gathered her clothes and threw them in with her shoes and gloves. She did the same with what Pearl had been wearing, she walked to the shed to replace the hammer and the knife and she went to the house to check in on her daughter. She poured another brandy and went to the fire where she sat looking over the lake. How she hated Jack Fletcher: wife beater and killer of children. She took a sip of her brandy and laid back, enjoying the heat from the flames and glittering stars.

She was thirty-two. She looked at the length of her small body, remembering her once youthful shape. She wondered whether she would ever marry again and knew she would not. That was Pearl's world, her universe. All Mary knew was that no man would ever again beat her daughter. She added more logs, shivered with the cool evening air and walked into the water to be reborn.

She had bathed in the lake a thousand times and never felt as rejuvenated. She hadn't felt so alive in years. Looking into the water, the moon was curtained by thin clouds and her image was vague, but Mary remembered. She ran from the water to the house as fast as she could, talking to herself all the way, and laughing. She looked in on Pearl and skipped into the kitchen, strangely elated; half crying, half laughing as she cut through the top of the three-foot long copper braid.

She hurried to the lake and threw the coarse remnant into the flames with a casual fling. She dived headfirst into the water and floated face-down with her legs and her arms spread wide, truly reborn until she thought her lungs would burst and she ran to once again sit by the fire.

Warmed, she went to the house for her robe and worked late into the night, expunging any and all traces of him. She burned his clothes as she gathered his papers, and she burned them, keeping the bills she found in his change purse. She found his shotgun and rowed once more into deeper and darker water. Done, she burned what clothes she had left, and Pearl's, keeping aside what she laid out for their journey. The outfit she once wore for her wedding was next to burn. Then she burned the laundry, hoping the 110 dollars she had managed to squirrel away over thirteen years, along with his meagre offering, would see them through the coming weeks.

Her final task before letting herself sleep was to take her mother's black pearl and silver ring from an old soup can secreted in the pantry and slip it onto her finger. In the morning Mary woke beside her daughter and told the girl precisely what took place the night before: Billy's parents came by the house. They were very sorry for what their son did to Pearl while she was swimming, and would certainly reprimand and punish him for his behaviour. They explained how he liked Pearl very much and, well, he was a boy. Though Billy had sworn to them that he did nothing to hurt Pearl, that he hadn't touched her that way at all.

When Pearl seemed not to understand Mary reminded her of their summer talks by the lake, of what a man could do with a woman when they were that way and how exactly men came to be that way. Pearl crossed her heart and hoped to die. Nothing like that happened. They were wrestling in the water, splashing each other and playing. Mary searched into her daughter's eyes for something, for anything that might have changed, and saw nothing beyond girlish innocence and Pearl's own penetrating search.

As for Jack Fletcher, he returned to gather his clothes and told Mary he was leaving forever. He was taking a job in another state and should never have married her or given her a child, even though he regretted what he did to his daughter. When Pearl asked her mother what she meant, Mary held her daughter close and didn't answer.

Later she let Pearl trim the ragged edges of her hair. She told her daughter to pack a small suitcase before making them a hearty breakfast and Mary left her daughter alone. She gathered the clothes she would wear and went to the water's edge where the fire had crackled late into the night. She worked with a purpose. She stirred the cold embers. Not a single strand of fabric remained. She reached in for the half-melted buckles from his suitcase and his belt. She threw them far into the lake and she shovelled the still moist puddle of blood that had come from his head into the lake. She examined every inch between where she killed him and the shore, searching the nearby woods for whatever she might have missed of Billy's.

At the rowboat she hiked up her robe to walk around it, retracing her steps to the shed in search of anything she might have dropped or overlooked. She was satisfied. The previous night didn't happen, though she lit one more fire all the same and tossed in her robe. She bathed in the lake one last time and when she was finished she threw the soap into the woods and stood by the fire to dry herself and dress.

They each wore their prettiest dresses and nicest shoes. They stayed at the house not a moment longer than was needed to eat breakfast and for Mary to verify mother and daughter were taking the barest essentials. Nothing was left that would later turn up to haunt her.

As they were leaving, Pearl asked her mother about the raging bonfire and about where they were going. The bonfire was Mary's way of saying goodbye, she responded. They were going to a wonderful city where women wore elegant clothes and spoke French, where the men were handsome and charming.

The words made Pearl think of Billy and how much she would miss him as she stood by the side of the road waiting for the bus that would take them to the next town and from there to the border. She was so happy her father hadn't hurt Billy. She would never forget him or the way she felt when he lifted her into his arms.

Part Two

Two

Paris, France
Tuesday, July 04, 1972

Pearl Bingham did forget Billy Stream. She never knew that Billy's mother never gave up hope that her son would one day come home, or that the Fletcher home had one day been sold by the state for unpaid taxes. She eventually forgot her father, how much she had hated him and how secretly pleased she was when he abandoned his wife and daughter. She never thought of him, not any longer, though she did live through many years of bad dreams and fitful sleeping before those few violent minutes by the lake were forgotten.

So much had happened in her life since that fateful night, though not once did she think of her new life as a new beginning. She was with her mother, and little else was worth remembering about her first thirteen years. At the time she hadn't thought of leaving one country for another as escaping, or as a defining moment the way her mother did, because the days that followed were all so exciting and she had asked her mother a hundred questions.

Mary was very afraid the day they crossed the border into Canada fifteen years earlier. She had never travelled very far, occasionally to neighbouring small towns, certainly never to another country and she worried that somehow the immigration officers had heard of the killings. They hadn't and three years later, standing before a federal judge and a clerk from the State Department, mother and daughter hugged each other with green-on-white citizenship certificates grasped in their hands.

Mary worked hard during the day and at night she attended classes. By the time Pearl completed her high school, Mary was the top salesperson at Feldman Cosmetics and one year behind her daughter in her studies. She had recaptured her youth. Her dark eyes sparkled and her olive skin glowed. By the time Pearl received her undergraduate degree Mary was two years from a business degree and was vice-president of the company. By the time Doctor Pearl Bingham celebrated her twenty-eighth birthday, her mother owned the company.

Mary never remarried, not certain she ever had been married. Her life was her daughter, Feldman, her charities and her benevolent work. The latter two were clearly defined, distinct, and Mary soon became well-known as a leading philanthropist, boasting a repertoire of important contacts in every level of government and profession. Anyone who was anyone knew Mary Bingham. She was invited to any and all parties of consequence, galas, balls, yacht clubs and important fundraising dinners. She danced and dined with politicians, important clergy, high-ranking military and chiefs of industry.

Throughout those earlier years Pearl studied hard. She spent her weekends working in Feldman Cosmetics' shipping department to save toward her medical college fund, believing she was helping out her mother even though the need had greatly diminished, to say the least, and during her four years of pre-med she volunteered as a candy-striper. She had boyfriends, though never anyone serious until her second year at college, regretting that her first experience wasn't at all special and that she wasn't able to tell her mother what she had done. She never forgave him for phoning the next day to tell her he'd found someone else, and now the moment she once thought she would always remember was so long ago and so unimportant apart from the lingering animosity.

Pearl also forgot she once dreamt of joining the FBI to kill bad men and, at twenty-five, with pre-med and four years of medical studies behind her she began her residency where she met the love of her life during her second year, one Braxton Averly.

She visited her mother as often as she could, though Mary began travelling more frequently for business and their schedules often conflicted. Pearl studied every waking hour that wasn't taken up with observing and listening to those who knew more than she did. She wanted a general practice. He wanted to be a surgeon and now, at twenty-eight, she was dressed in black and holding her mother's hand as she stared tearfully into Braxton Averly's silk-lined coffin.

Their life together had begun as though in one of her childhood fantasies. They met by chance at one of Mary's fundraisers. He was the son of an industrialist who was one of Mary's many supporters and they spent the evening dancing and laughing. He was in residency at another hospital. He was tall and handsome; he didn't want kids and didn't believe in marriage. Neither did Pearl, whom he treated like a princess, and six months later they moved in together.

He was charming, debonair, and urbane. He was amusing and he liked to party. He brought her flowers and candy, he never forgot an occasion, and was always a gentleman. What counted most to Pearl was that Mary had liked Braxton at first, if not his bon vivant view of life which gradually became more self-evident and cause for her to be concerned and begin to dislike him. She hadn't approved of them living together, although she reluctantly accepted that a new era was emerging, one which she had little control over.

He had never so much as said a bad word to Pearl, although he hadn't worked a day in his life, nor had he studied to the extent required to excel beyond the most modest academic achievement. Everything in life came to him on a silver platter, including the family annuity, the continuance of which was conditional upon the successful completion of his residency with optimum scores.

No one had ever thought to curb the cavalier lifestyle he'd always managed to camouflage as his characteristic charm. Then, one week after her twenty-eighth birthday, Pearl nervously opened the envelope from the Board of Examiners and read in black and white that she was a physician. Dr. Pearl Bingham was looking at her license to practice as Braxton Averly opened his to read he had failed the final examination. He would have to confirm without delay his intention to reapply for his final year of residency the following year, the letter stated. The next morning Pearl found him on the living room floor, propped up against the sofa, the empty bottle of rum upright between his legs, the empty glass in his hands.

He laughed when he leered at her through blurred eyes. He called her Dr. Doctor and asked if she could prescribe something for his fucked-up life. She answered that he should fix his own life and that losing a year wasn't the end of the world. He shouldn't have failed, she admonished, and she expected him to deal with the setback like a man. He was too good not to reapply, if being a doctor was what he really wanted. And, she added tersely, successful surgeons did not need annuities. When she arrived home later that evening he was on the floor, insensate, a second rum bottle laying empty on the carpet. She went to Mary's to spend the night.

The third night, when she arrived home after her shift, he was sitting on the sofa waiting to tell her he'd been accepted by a newly created ambulance firm. He was to begin his paramedic training the following week. She laughed abruptly, not meaning to, not believing he could say or do anything so absurd, not thinking he would spring from the sofa to slap her with such ferocity that her body would stumble backwards onto the floor. When he did her mind leapt instantly back to those dark nights in her bedroom when she would cover her head with her pillow to block out the haunting sounds of slapping and her mother falling. He stood over her, watching as she crawled to her knees, then to her feet to stare at him in disbelief, searching his eyes for the slightest regret. She went to bed and cried through the night.

Braxton Averly avoided her for the rest of the week. Monday morning he was gone when she went to wake him. He worked days and soon began drinking at night to forget the shootings, the stabbings and the mutilated victims of car accidents. When he worked nights he drank during the day. They began arguing about his excessive consumption and his increased interest in porno which became an obsession beyond the weekend enhancement they once enjoyed together. Magazines and strip clubs became routine, cruel rejections meant to humiliate and diminish her. The second slap came a few weeks after the first and left a large bruise on her face which, she explained to Mary, had come from an agitated patient who had unintentionally struck her.

The couple needed time apart. Pearl needed to think and he needed to stop drinking. He needed to reapply to medical school and to stop feeling sorry for himself, she lectured. Pearl needed time alone, she needed to get away. She arranged for her work schedule to conflict with his over the coming weeks, each one avoiding the other and when she was ready to talk she called him at home from the hospital.

She left work early to prepare a gourmet meal which she served without wine, what he interpreted as an obvious rebuff. The initial tension was palpable and Pearl was the first to speak. She missed him. She wanted him back, though as a doctor. She was fine with his decision, if he actually wanted a career as a paramedic, though she knew differently. What he wanted was an easy way out, she chided, and that was not acceptable to her or his family. Braxton Averly listened quietly, and when she had her say he stood to leave the table. He took a bottle of Bordeaux and a crystal goblet from the cabinet. He uncorked the wine in front of her, neither one saying a word, sitting across from her when his glass was filled.

His becoming a doctor wasn't going to happen, he began. He was beginning to enjoy being a paramedic. Why would he suffer through another residency, not to mention the humiliation of kowtowing to those who had been his peers the year before and taking orders from interns who would never be as good as him? Besides, no one in the squad was better trained and the company was already thinking of making him a supervisor and instructor.

Pearl could only stare unblinkingly. She asked him with a calm voice whether he was serious, or whether he was toying with her, punishing her for having avoided him over the past month. He snickered and finished his wine before answering. Yes, he was serious. He had a good job and a regular annuity. He didn't need the aggravation. So what was her problem? He refilled the glass and slammed the bottle onto the table. If she was embarrassed about being seen with a medic, he continued, that was her problem. He reminded her caustically they weren't married, that she could leave anytime and not expect him to run after her. He would have no trouble finding plenty of other women, real women, not stuck-up bitches.

Pearl stood and poured her own glass of wine, ignoring him. She faced away to leave the room and told him to get out, to go home to his mother who had more experience dealing with a spoiled child.

Pearl hadn't told her mother of the first time Averly struck her and the second time she lied about the violence.

This time she would have to confess everything. There had been no time to react to the wineglass shattering across the floor before he grabbed her loose-fitting raglan sweater and swirled her in circles until she collided with the floor on her hands and knees. He grabbed her hair from behind, jerking her head violently until she was able to claw his forearm with both her hands. He dragged her to her feet, driving his knees into her buttocks, smacking the side of her head with one hand while holding her with the other.

Still in his grasp, Pearl twisted with surprising agility and speed to face him and when she tried to fight back with flailing fists and bare feet he struck out viciously with an open hand. She kicked him as hard as she could, which he returned with several more slaps and punches, cutting her lips and scarring her face with bruises that began to show.

She tried too late to escape. Her wrists were firmly gripped in his hands. He was swinging her in circles, half-dragging, half-lifting her until she tripped and landed hard on her knees. Still he wouldn't let go. Holding her close he kicked the front of her legs repeatedly, driving his knees into her stomach and Pearl cried out instinctively for her mother as he began shaking her like a crippled marionette. He tugged hard at the neck of her sweater until she was left half-naked and began thrashing her with it, ridiculing her and laughing derisively.

All Pearl could see was a thick leather belt and the crazed eyes of her father. She cowered on the floor, curling into a ball to protect her breasts and her face, whimpering each time he whipped her shoulders and head or kicked her legs and hips. She was a doctor. So what, he taunted, sneering and waving his arms. She was the one crawling on the floor. He was the man and that would never change. He was the man, not the famous doctor crying for her mommy, her precious and arrogant, goddamned mother.

She nodded, sobbing, agreeing with him until he stopped and she asked him for water. He shook his head, disgusted, and walked away. When Pearl heard the water running she grabbed her sweater, snatched up her purse by the door and ran out into the hallway. Her subconscious took over. She hung her purse over her bare shoulders as she ran toward the stairwell that would be faster than the elevator and bounded down the concrete steps a few at a time until she crashed through the emergency doors and into the fresh evening air. She struggled into her sweater as she raced as fast as she could for her car. Several blocks later she pulled to the curb where she adjusted the mirror to see herself and burst into tears.

When Mary saw her daughter she fell against the door, horrified by the cuts and bruises to her face. They were at the ER within minutes, met by the Chief of Surgery and Chief Resident who would never think of refusing Mary Bingham. Not that Mary's influence was of great importance at the moment. Pearl was one of their own, but where Pearl was concerned everything mattered to Mary. She stayed at the hospital with her daughter throughout the night, and the next day to watch over her. No bones had been broken. The discoloration to her face would diminish in several days, the contusions to her hips and thighs would make walking painful for several weeks and eating would be an unpleasant ordeal until her lips healed.

Mary waited until Pearl was discharged before telling her of Averly's arrest and that she had arranged for her daughter to spend a week at an elite spa for privileged ladies in Vermont. During Pearl's week away Averly's father called Mary to offer his profoundest apologies for his son's uncharacteristic actions. Mary assured him the incident would have no ill effect on their own future relationship unless, of course, his son were to attend any of Mary's future fundraising events, adding that she intended to seek an injunction preventing his son from ever coming near her daughter again.

When Pearl arrived home from the Green Mountain spa

her condition was much improved. She argued adamantly that she was fine, that she was ready to return to work, though Mary wouldn't hear of such foolishness. In fact she had engaged the hospital's compliance. They were in full agreement, irrespective of Mary's annual seven-figure donation. Pearl was not yet fully recovered, they agreed. She would undoubtedly benefit from another few weeks of rest and relaxation before returning to her duties. Mother and daughter were going to France, despite Pearl's objections to the contrary. The flight was scheduled to depart early the next morning and Pearl had no say in the matter. They both deserved and needed the time away. Mother knew best. She always did.

Pearl did have to agree her mother was right once again. She did need to escape. She hadn't taken any real time for herself since their trip to the Bahamas a year earlier, which Mary had insisted was the perfect and most idyllic place to study for her upcoming examines and, not for the first time, she was the envy of every other intern, though she never flaunted her mother's position or wealth.

Being in France also meant Pearl could make up the time she hadn't spent with her best friend, and from their first day Mary limited herself to one business call to keep abreast of daily activities at Feldman Cosmetics. As she did, Pearl was no less secretive about her daily update. Yet, the first week seemed to fly by as mother and daughter stood sipping cognacs and looking out over the gardens of Paris and the majestic Eiffel Tower. Pearl had wanted to treat Mary to dinner at one of the more elegant restaurants along the Champs Élysées, disappointed by her mother's preference for a quiet dinner together in her suite.

When the phone rang Mary answered the call without the least surprise or hesitation. Her secretary at Feldman was calling with horrible news. Braxton Averly had been found dead earlier that morning, murdered on the grounds of Montreal's historic Mount-Royal. He'd been robbed and stabbed once in the back. His blood-alcohol level was extremely high and the authorities suspected he'd also been doing drugs. Worse, the police had no witnesses and nothing to go on.

Mary displayed no emotion as she sat with her daughter to recount the news. She spent what remained of the evening consoling Pearl while reminding her why she went to the Vermont spa and why they were in Paris: Braxton Averly was sick, deluded, and his death would never erase the fact he had brutally beaten her. In any event, what was doing on the mountain?

They would, of course, do what was expected of them and when Mary was alone in her room she phoned the older Mr. Averly to offer her deepest sympathies on the shocking death of his only child. The funeral would be held in three days and Mary promised to attend with Pearl. Ending the brief conversation, she poured another cognac and reclined to ponder what string of events might have led to Braxton Averly's murder.

Mary was very aware Averly could easily have killed her daughter, that he'd been given no more punishment than a slap on the wrist because of his father's influence. She pressed a fingertip against the black pearl on her finger, remembering her mother laying on her deathbed and the ne'er-do-well scoundrel who deserted her. She remembered her promise to her daughter years ago by the lake, a promise she had broken. The ring felt cool to the touch, its iridescence more like liquid mercury than black nacre. The one was poisonous, she mused. The other was the result of nature protecting the otherwise vulnerable mollusc. Mary laid her head on her pillow and stared into the black mother-of-pearl, reflecting on what the ring had come to symbolize.

She fell asleep, content.

Three

Montreal, Quebec
Thursday, June 29, 1972

The young woman uncrossed her legs as Braxton Averly climbed from his car for his usual coffee and doughnut breakfast before starting his shift. His father had called him a few days after Pearl had run out, after she'd run to her mother's instead of talking through their troubles together. His parents would need time to recover before once again welcoming him at the family estate. His mother was in shock knowing her son was such an ogre. He had humiliated his family. He was behaving reprehensibly and there would be no more free living, his father declared. If indeed Braxton believed himself to be a man, then the time had come for him to act the part.

At the time he thought nothing of his father's instructions to settle in full the outstanding obligation of his joint lease with Pearl without delay, and in the presence of the family attorney who would issue a one-time cheque for the exorbitant amount. By mid-afternoon the same day Mr. Averly called again to acknowledge the transaction. He reiterated his disappointment in the strongest terms, adding without the slightest hesitation or regret that, as previously stated, his son's annuity had been cut off for failing in medicine. He was also expected to make suitable apologies to Pearl Bingham immediately upon her return or face measures being considered by the family to distance themselves from his deplorable behaviour. His father was saying in one breath to be a man, in the other to grovel. That, Braxton Averly promised, would never happen.

He was adjusting to living alone, despite the stumbling block of no longer enjoying the generous annuity which had previously covered all his expenses. He'd get by. As long as the effects of the booze wore off before his shift, what else mattered? He wasn't the only one who had a few daily shots to get by. Screw Pearl and her self-righteousness. Screw his family and the annuity. He didn't need them. The luxury downtown apartment would be his for another fifteen months, he had his car and he was confident the company would soon announce his promotion that would give him more pay. He knew more about medicine and the human body than any of them would ever know. As for the broad with the hat sitting in front of him with her legs wide open, what she didn't seem to know wouldn't hurt her.

She saw him coming from under the brim of her hat. She looked up briefly, long enough to make eye contact from behind her dark glasses and flash a double row of bright white from behind full and pouty lips painted bright red. Then she looked down at her book. Crowd or no crowd she would do it, yet she was happy all the same that no one was on either side of her. At the very worst she would stop traffic and make some guy's day. She'd seen him the day before and decided at once how they would meet. He was good looking, 5'11" and looked as though he'd be the perfect catch for any woman. She was the perfect catch for any man, and she needed no one to tell her.

He didn't wear a ring and she noticed the day before how he looked at anything in a skirt between sixteen and sixty. She would have to treat him differently, not like the others. He was barely a few feet from her when she let her elbow touch the edge of her purse. He wanted her, she knew he did, and she wanted him as badly. What they were about to share would be so good.

She was petite. She might have been twenty-five or eighteen, maybe seventeen. Who knew? Averly didn't care. He liked the idea of dating younger girls. He remembered most of them from high school and college. The young ones were easy. They were impressionable and would do anything once they knew how much he loved them.

The mid-summer weather was excessively hot for nylons. Her legs were bare and her mini- dress was the shortest he'd ever seen. She was sitting alone and seemed to have no idea how much she was showing. She was reading and didn't look as though she was expecting anyone. He whispered under his breath so she wouldn't hear, begging her to make eye contact with him, smiling at her when she did at the very moment her purse toppled from the bench and startled her. She dropped her book and sandwich by her feet, leaning away from him to reach too late for the purse, inadvertently flaring the hem of her dress to reveal more than he could have hoped for and practically sliding from the bench.

Braxton Averly rushed to help her. He stooped, groping for the book as his eyes locked onto her panties and the lower curves of the buttocks that were practically bare. She hadn't seemed to notice him and when she did the young woman gasped and tugged hastily at her hem, a deep crimson blush flooding across her face.

Averly smiled, holding out the book and sandwich. "I didn't see a thing, I swear. And if it helps, miss, I'm a doctor."

She looked at him and chortled. "And I'm an astronaut. I've just returned from the moon, doc. Now, would you mind very much getting your eyes out from under my dress?"

He stood, humbly, and sat beside her. "I am a doctor. I graduated this year, though I still have a few years before I specialize."

She read the name tag on his jacket. "You're an ambulance driver and believing you're a real doctor makes you nuts."

"It's true. I am a doctor. Doing this is like paying my dues. Actually, I'm helping to train the guys in the new service. We're all expected to do time with them to make sure the wannabes are good enough and the reason I'm wearing this thing is to blend in and not appear as though I'm better than they are, which I am. And I can prove it. Besides, how many ambulance drivers have you seen driving around in red Corvettes? Can you prove you're an astronaut?" He looked at her legs. "I would say you're more like a model or actress. I mean, who wears hats and sunglasses to match their dresses?"

"I do." She stated demurely, biting into her sandwich. "Actually, I'm a secretary. Dull stuff, but one day I'm going to be a famous actress or a model. I think my body's good enough." The young woman hooked one leg over the other, seemingly oblivious to his blatant staring. "They're my best asset, at least that's what people tell me. So for now I type letters and get coffee."

"I bet you do a great job."

"Pretty good, but it's my legs and dresses they're really interested in. Whatever works, right?"

"I guess. I have to admit the combo's working great for me. I'm hoping you haven't got a boyfriend. I don't like cutting another guy's grass. It's not cool."

"I'm not into dating right now, if you have to know. No boyfriend."

Averly looked at his watch, then to the doughnut shop.

"Listen, I'm a little pressed for time. I only have another fifteen or twenty minutes. Will you be here when I get back or should I get one coffee?"

She thought about it. "You can bring two coffees if you want, as long as you don't think I'm your doughnut." She paused. "At least not until I see your license. I already have a doctor who enjoys his work and I'm not looking for a free examination." She waited until he was standing, beginning to walk away. "What's your name, doc?"

"Braxton, what's yours?"

"Not so fast. Let's see what happens. A girl needs some secrets and I think our coffees are waiting for you."

Averly stayed with her as long as he could. She refused him when he asked for her number, saying instead that he might see her at the same place the next day. He did, and they had their coffees sitting in the park under an ageless oak tree. She kicked off each of her shoes with the opposite foot as she opened her bag and sat to one side. He wanted to compliment her dress, which he was absolutely certain was shorter than the one she'd worn the previous day, stopping himself with the thought of how she might react to such an obvious line.

She gazed across to the Corvette, his eyes darting to the small patch of pale mauve covering the tiny V at the very edge of her hem.

"So, you really are a doctor," she said, taking a moment longer before making eye contact. "I'm impressed."

He nodded. "Dr. Braxton Averly at your service. I have ambulance duty for another week. Then it's the lab coat and stethoscope all the way."

"And you're going to be a surgeon?"

"No, I'm specializing in geriatrics. It's a relatively new field and I enjoy working with old people. They're the most vulnerable and need the most care."

"That's so sweet, and makes my job sound so lousy. There must be something better than sorting papers and pouring coffee all day for a bunch of dope heads who think I don't see them trying to see up my dress or watching me when I bend over. Jerks."

"If you've got it, flaunt it. That's what they say."

"I don't flaunt anything," she retorted, sounding annoyed.

"I'm sorry. I didn't mean what you think. Your dress is fantastic and from what I've seen so far, they pretty much redefine mini." He glanced downward, discreetly.

"I want to look nice. What's wrong with that? I won't get noticed in jeans or old lady clothes and I'll never be a model or actress if they don't notice. Sometimes at lunch I drop off copies of my portfolio at different agencies. They won't look at me twice if I don't dress like this, so I'm sort of screwed."

"I'd like to see it sometime, the portfolio."

"Sorry, strictly confidential. One of the guys at the office saw it one time when I was away from my desk and he opened it. I was so embarrassed, him seeing me that way. The guy was a real jerk about it, like he'd never seen any T and A in his whole life."

"As in bare T and A?" he asked, grinning.

"As in artistic," she countered. "Since then they try even more to see something, as though they think I'm not wearing underwear. They think being a widow makes me easy or something."

Averly lurched forward, sincerely shocked. "You've been married?"

"Yeah, for a couple of years. Then, about a year ago, he responded to a three-alarm. The roof he was standing on caved in."

"He was a fireman?"

"Yeah. That's pretty much why I don't date."

"Too many good memories?" he prompted.

"No. The marriage thing wasn't so good. Guess I was too young."

"I'm sorry."

"Don't be. Anyway, most guys just want to get into my pants and forget my phone number."

"That's disgusting. There's no way I'd forget you and I certainly wouldn't want any guy treating my little sister with so little respect. Though, I can't say I'd blame them for trying. She's almost as pretty as you are and, believe me or not, we're not all bad."

"How old is she?"

"Late teens," he lied, "kind of a dangerous age." He noted them time. "I still don't know your name. How can I ask you out if I don't know your name?"

"You don't listen very well for a doctor."

"Like I said, we're not all bad."

She giggled. "Okay, because you are a doctor and you seem like a nice enough guy. Pearl, my name is Pearl." Averly reacted with a sudden spasm, splashing his coffee over both their legs. "That's not a very good start, doc."

Pearl used her napkin to wipe her legs dry. Averly stayed as he was, inert, and felt the hot liquid penetrate his slacks.

"I'm sorry. That was clumsy of me. I wasn't expecting …I used to know someone called Pearl. She died recently."

"Was she your girlfriend?"

"My fiancée. She died last summer in a boating accident. We were supposed to get married next month. It's been long year."

"Now I'm the one who's sorry." Pearl hesitated, unsure of herself. "Listen, Braxton, I haven't been into dating either since the fire, not that I don't think about it a lot. Why don't we have dinner Sunday night, Dutch treat, and a walk on the mountain?"

"I'd love to take you out. Do you live near here? I'll pick you up."

"Thanks anyway, doc, but that's a bit fast. I'll take the bus and you can meet me here at 7:00. Don't be late because I'll be gone at 7:01 and you might want to wear different pants."

Four

Montreal, Quebec
Sunday, July 02, 1972

Sunday afternoon Beverly Price lowered her convertible top for a leisurely drive along chemin Remembrance to the lookout atop Mont-Royal. She strolled around Lac-aux-Castors watching boys sail their wooden ships with their fathers and girls playing mother with their dolls while the real mother made sandwiches and fussed over the picnic blanket. Uppermost on her mind was Braxton Averly.

She hated being there. The venue was one of convenience. Inviting him to her apartment was out of the question and to have suggested his apartment would have seemed too forward. Though she had no doubt he would have agreed to a weekend away or a hotel room for the night, which was problematic in itself. She found the perfect spot, kicked off her shoes, sat on the soft grass and pulled her dress to the top of her legs to enjoy the warmth of the sun's rays. She stood an hour later and walked to the bus stop.

Despite not having dated in a very long time, Beverly Price knew what men liked. And what they liked when she was around them was to look at her and dream the impossible. She was twenty-three and could pass for a teenager. She was a talented architect during the day, taught structural design at night, and was lonely most of the time despite having a body anyone would describe as perfect.

She dressed in the latest fashion to the delight of men and the envy of women, changed her hairstyle each week, drove a modified Mustang and vacationed in exotic locations when most others settled for redefining mundane charters to the West Indies.

That was the Beverly she had become, not the woman she once was and never wanted to be again as she sat at the vanity in her bathroom putting final touches to her make-up for the evening ahead. She wore garters and a dress she knew would ride to the playful butterfly clasps holding her sheer stockings in place. She wore panties and a bra she'd bought downtown at one of those "dirty stores", her high heels were high, her auburn hair flowed loosely over her shoulders and her hazel eyes shone like semi-precious gems in the mirror. Lastly, she removed her ring which was given to her following the sudden death of her husband.

She had few friends. She never dated and had learned to take one day at time. She glanced over the case study one last time before shredding the sheets with her fingers, though for no particular need. She knew him and she looked forward to the evening. He wasn't her first and wouldn't be her last. She stood, went to the toilet, raised the lid and flushed.

*

Pearl was at the park when the flashy red sports car drove up. Braxton Averly came towards her with an armful of roses, thinking she was gorgeous. He could have dropped dead, if not for the fact he was certain he'd be doing to Pearl later in the evening what he'd thought of doing to her all day. She had no idea he was behind her as she bent to tighten the ankle straps of her shoes.

He whistled dry air through his lips and kept walking. The evening was going to be a long one and worth every minute. "It's quarter to," he said. "There's no way I was going to be late. I'm tempted to say you look beautiful at the risk of repeating myself. You were beautiful this morning. I'm not quite sure a word exists to describe the way you look this very minute, except maybe fantastic."

She blushed on cue, taking the flowers and smelling them. Her eyes were piercing, her lips curving into a thin smile. Words were inappropriate. She was a woman and she knew how to make a man feel like a man.

"You're very handsome tonight, Braxton." She studied his face, her eyes dropping to his chest from where she could appraise him entirely. Outwardly, anyone knowing him would wonder why he had become such a loser, how he had fooled so many for so long. "That's so much better than a purple windbreaker and wet pants. I'm impressed and these flowers were not necessary. Thank you. They're lovely."

"I hope you like Italian. I had no way of knowing." His lips pursed together for affect. "I thought French might seem too much like expectations of things to come and I don't have any. Chinese or steak seemed too sisterly, so I went with Italian. I should have asked."

She breathed in the scent of the roses. "I love Italian. It's my favourite."

"And what I'm seeing is fast becoming my favourite. I can't believe how lucky I am."

"Do you like it?" She slid an open hand down the length of her dress.

He wanted to say "no shit." Instead he blew a slow "yeah" from his mouth.

"It's been a while, I wasn't certain. I wasn't even certain you'd show."

"I'm here, right now, and I'm starved. So let's get you into the car and get out of here. It's a twenty-minute drive."

Pearl looped an arm into his and smelled the roses again.

"Don't let anything happen to my flowers. They're gorgeous. Now I know why all mothers want their daughters to marry doctors. Thank you."

56

Their dinner was romantic. Braxton Averly had called ahead to the maître d' to set the stage. They spoke about everything and nothing. They danced well together and often she touched his hand to help set the mood, which he correctly interpreted as a sign, the approbation he'd hoped for and had expected. He had penetrated her comfort zone according to plan. Pearl had told him she once enjoyed romantic walks on Mont-Royal, better described as a huge hill in the middle of its metropolitan namesake. The moment he was waiting for had come. He had a blanket, cushions, a bottle of champagne, and crystal glasses. He hadn't overlooked a single detail.

"Thank you, Braxton. This is all so perfect. I love it."

Pearl scanned the dark sloping grass and city lights. The spot was once her favourite place, what she thought would last forever, a place of romance, until the night her husband beat her there, until the night he broke her jaw, her arm, and almost killed her there. She didn't remember the crowd or the police, or the ambulance. She remembered going home from the hospital and seeing him after his few days in detention. She remembered leaving him, hearing his repentant words and tearful promises. She remembered her two weeks in the country and the day they told her how he'd been found dead. Until then the mountain had been her favourite place.

"Close your eyes, Braxton."

"If I do, I won't see you."

"That's the point. I want to take off my stockings."

"Come on. I'm a doctor. I see women's legs all the time."

"Not like this, you don't. Close your eyes."

He did, until he was certain she'd turned her head. She wasn't looking at him as she undid the front clasp at one thigh, then the other before leaning to one side, then the other to undo the clasps at the back of her thighs. She had no need. She knew he was ogling her. She wriggled, adjusting herself so that she was sitting on the hem of her dress before she pushed her stockings one at time to her ankles and away from her feet.

"That feels so much better. I hope you don't mind. For us girls it's like a guy taking off his tie." She prompted him with a nod. "Go ahead. Take it off."

He did, and reached for the wine. She took the glass he held out to her and pulled her knees to her chest. He lay on his side, propped on an elbow.

"I've lived here all my life," he said, "and I've never seen the city like this. I always came here during the day with my parents when I was a kid, doing the picnic thing, never like this. And I'm pretty sure my mother never looked quite like you."

Pearl giggled. "I know. It's special, the city I mean. Most people don't stay late enough to see it this way." She looked around. "See... absolutely no one. It's so unfortunate. They don't know what they're missing. Look at the view, honey. Isn't it...?" Pearl clamped an open hand over her mouth that was wide-open wide with shock. "I'm so sorry. I didn't mean that. It must be the champagne."

Averly showed no concern. "It sounded real. Actually, I sort of liked it. And you're right, the view is spectacular." He poured more champagne. "Here's to the most gorgeous girl on the mountain."

"I'm the only girl on the mountain."

"You're all I need."

They sipped quietly, each one thinking the other would speak first.

"I think I can get back into this dating thing, Braxton. It's been a while."

"I couldn't agree more." He waited for her to take another sip and took her glass. He set it behind him and lay back, hoping she would do the same. "Check out the stars. The night couldn't be more perfect and these cushions were a great idea."

She ignored him. Instead she shivered and Averly reacted as expected to remove his jacket and cover her shoulders. When he eased to the grass she leaned beside him, crutched on one arm and reaching for her evening purse with the other.

"Listen to how peaceful the night is. Close your eyes for a moment and listen." He did and Pearl reached for the bottle, filling his glass first, then her own. "You know, Braxton. I'm beginning to think we should try a second date. Would you like that?"

He opened his eyes and sat to toast the evening that just became perfect. He owned the night. "Do you even have to ask? Yes, I would, whatever you want, wherever you want."

She giggled again, putting aside his jacket "You know Braxton, I used to like giving massages, I used to love giving massages. I was pretty good. Finish your wine and lie on your front. You might want to keep the cushion under your head, though. This ground is pretty hard."

He drained his glass, stroking the side of her head and staring into her eyes. He had her. He eased backward, absorbing every inch of her bare legs as she sat to straddle him.

"Flip, please."

"Shouldn't you start with the front? I think that's the way it's done."

"Not in this dress, pretty boy. It'll ride to my waist. So it's flip over or nothing. It's a one-time offer."

"Do I get to reciprocate? I'm told I've got a pretty good set of hands."

She hesitated. "Sure, why not? Besides, no one's around."

He twisted onto his front. She straddled him with a single movement without touching him with her body as she knelt onto one knee and braced herself with a foot planted firmly by his other side. She ignored her dress riding to her waist and pushed the bottom of her palms along his spinal column. He began moaning under the increased pressure, working with her fingertips and thumbs. She stopped for moment to reposition, pressing a single forefinger between two ribs.

He asked with a drawn out sigh what she was doing and she answered matter-of-factly that she was killing him. He chuckled into the cushion, telling her not to stop, that he never thought being killed could feel so good. Then she told him why she was killing him. His entire body lurched sideways in response, unwittingly helping her bury the slim blade of the pearl-handled stiletto into his back and into his heart. She twisted once. He was dead on the count of one.

She put on a pair of cotton gloves and on the way to her Mustang she'd parked earlier in the day on the other side of Mont-Royal, Beverly Price tossed the bottle and glasses she'd sanitized with champagne into the man-made Lac-aux-Castors along with Averly's wallet and keys. When she arrived home she removed her shoes at the elevator, all her clothing once inside her apartment and luxuriated in a hot shower as the stiletto reposed in a bottle of disinfectant. Then she dressed and went out to discard each item and the cushions separately, which was standard procedure before calling Director Rita Brennan to confirm another successful facilitation.

Five

Montreal, Quebec
Saturday, July 08, 1972

Pearl took Mary to dinner the night before to celebrate her mother's forty-seventh birthday and neither woman spoke a word of Braxton Averly. Not so much out of respect for the dearly departed Averly as for her wish not to spoil Mary's special day. Pearl felt inexplicably as though Averly never existed and part of her wondered whose funeral she would actually be attending. For Mary, his premature passing was a godsend and she couldn't have wished for a better birthday gift other than the cameo brooch Pearl had wrapped in Mary's favourite colours of midnight and Mediterranean blues: colours which had years earlier become her signature.

Saturday the attendees arrived in a procession of rented limousines, the chauffeuse who stepped out to open the door for Mary and Pearl was Mary's personal driver. The church was overflowing with the who's who of society, their faces sullen and their words of condolence chosen to demonstrate a compassion which, for the most part, was missing. Very few of the pseudo-mourners had met Braxton Averly. Being there was simply good politicking and no different for Mary. Mr. and Mrs. Averly stood at the door to welcome each visitor and when Pearl arrived with her mother, Mary extended her hand and her sympathies to both parents. Pearl did the same, unable to assume the role of a grieving girlfriend. She wanted to be anywhere else.

As much as she felt herself ready for what she was about to see, when the couple in front of her stepped aside she was gripped by a whirlwind of conflicting emotions she hadn't anticipated. He wasn't supposed to be dead, he wasn't supposed to beat her and she wasn't supposed to be seeing him for the last time lying lifeless in a coffin. Braxton Averly wasn't the one with his crossed hands knotted in place, his lips painted pink, glued to appear pursed, his eyes seeming to squint. Someone else had taken his place, a stranger, the man who beat her, not her lover who once gently caressed her and made her feel special. Laid out in front of her was a man who had ruined his life, a man who'd been found dead on the mountain with a dozen red roses on the backseat of his car and traces of illegal pharmaceuticals in his blood, not the man who promised to love her forever.

"I don't understand, mother. How could everything have gone so badly between us, so quickly?"

"Who's to say it did, darling? It may seem that way at the moment because these situations never become apparent to us when we find ourselves temporarily blinded for whatever reason. At first we refuse to believe, then we fail to accept, which is not the same at all. I blame myself for not being more prudent when we first met him."

"Who could have wanted to kill him? He could have been such a wonderful surgeon. It's all so meaningless."

"He chose not to be a surgeon, darling. The choice was his, not yours. Then he chose to hate you for it, to blame you for what he did to himself." Mary lowered her head. "He did this to himself. Who held the knife really matters very little. He did it to himself."

"We could have been so happy." Pearl groaned, stifling a tear. "None of this would have happened if he'd passed the exam."

"You mean, if he hadn't failed his exam because he thought more of his fancy suits and fast car than he did of his career, or you. He failed himself and, in doing so, he failed you. He would never have made you happy, darling. "

"It's such a horrible way to end a life."

"You've already seen much worse, darling. I'm sure.

"This is different, mother."

"The police told his father he died instantly."

Mary slipped her arm into her daughter's to guide her away as Braxton Averly's father stepped behind them.

"Mary," he took her arm, "thank you so much for coming. We would have understood entirely had you decided not to. And, Pearl, I have no words. I've worried all day as to what I would say to you and I still don't know. Forgive me. If you can't forgive him, and you should not, please forgive me. You must live with the memory. I must live with the shame. However, he was my son and I will always love him, not to imply I must enjoy my memory of him or honour him. His ill-treatment of you was unforgivable and we'll never know why. I'm sorry. Mary, forgive me."

"Ernie, we have nothing to forgive. What happened is in the past. My daughter will survive and move on. Unfortunately your son will not. I grieve deeply for you, we both do."

"I blame myself for what became of him, for what he did to Pearl. He mishandled a pampered life with far too few restrictions. He never appreciated his good life," Averly gave his attention to Pearl, "or how good a life he might have had. I am truly sorry. I would like to believe that, if we cannot be family, we can at least remain on good terms."

Pearl glanced into the coffin. "I don't feel sorry for him, Mr. Averly. The pain I feel is for you and Mrs. Averly. When he hurt me, he hurt both of you as much, and thank you for taking care of the apartment for me. Mother told me. I won't be moving back in. Please let me know the amount and …"

Earnest Averly put up a hand, putting an end to such talk. He bowed imperceptibly to each woman and walked away leaving mother and daughter alone.

"Come, darling. Let's walk to the vestibule where we can talk privately. I have something for you, something very special I want you to have and I believe the time is appropriate." When they were seated Mary reached into her purse for a little black and silver velvet box. "It never occurred to me that such a frightful thing would happen to you twice in such a young life. I'm very sorry, darling. I once made a promise to protect you and I failed you when you needed me the most. Now this has happened." Her eyes trailed along the plush carpet between the pews to where the Averlys stood alone by the casket, "I want you to have this…my way of making you feel happy again, darling. The happiest moment of my life was when you were born. I never thought I could be so happy nor have a baby so beautiful. You know I love you very much."

Pearl held her mother's hand. "I know, mother, and I'm fine. You've always taken care of me. Still, I'm a little confused. Today is your birthday. Why am I getting a gift?"

"When they asked me at the hospital what name I had chosen for you, I couldn't tell them because I came to believe I would have a son and not a wonderful little girl. I was quite beside myself, then I saw my ring and I knew right away. It's always been my favourite. I have never worn another."

"I always thought you threw the other one away."

"There was no other." She patted Pearl's knee. "Let's not revisit the past, darling." Mary pulled the lid from the box.

"Mother, it's exquisite."

"It comes from the Persian Gulf, darling."

"It's exactly like yours."

"It's identical…and very exclusive. I wanted to give you

something special and the black pearl is very special to me. I do hope you like it."

"It's so precious."

"Yes, and so are you. That's what the nurse said to me the night you were born, that you were precious, and how you came to be called Pearl. You were beautiful then and you are now. You must always remember that and from this moment, when you feel in danger, wherever you are, you must remember this day and call me right away. You must never again wait until it's too late. This pearl is more than a ring, darling. It's an important symbol."

"A symbol of what, mother?"

"That we are never alone, darling, that we must never allow one another to be hurt."

"We've always taken care of each other." Pearl smiled. "We always will."

"Yes, darling, we will. Nevertheless, I meant to imply a far greater reciprocity."

Pearl furrowed her brow. "I don't understand."

"You will." Mary paused. "Come. Put it on. Let me see how pretty it looks on you."

"It is lovely, mother. I'll never take it off."

"I'm not quite certain your Chief Resident would agree with you, darling. If you can't wear it when you're being a doctor, at least do so when you're not dressed like one and remember that what happened to you will never happen again. I have but one simple request of you. Your ring must stay with you when your time comes to cross into a better world. Promise me."

"I promise mother. I do."

Mary and Pearl stood as Braxton Averly was carried past them into the dazzling sun. The sky was clear, the air warm and fresh, making the entourage of mourners appear all the more sepulchral and morose. Pearl was certain she would never see the Averlys again and she saw no rationale in witnessing their son being lowered into his grave. Her most recent memories of him had expunged all the good that had gone before, nothing remained for her to remember. He no longer existed to her, though she knew to expect more restless nights until he would cease to invade her dreams and leave her in peace.

She put her arm around her mother's shoulders. She marvelled at how Mary had transformed her cosmetics firm into such a notable and enviable success. Often she would think back to the first days and months alone in their new home: how they went from a dingy one-room flat to a two room apartment with noisy neighbours, then to a midtown apartment where she at last had her own bedroom. She remembered the first Christmas when all Mary could afford was a silk panty and bra set for her daughter and since then she hadn't worn anything but silk.

Now, fifteen years later, she was a doctor, they each had a lavish home, imported cars, and Mary's company was constantly expanding. Pearl had no real idea how wealthy her mother had become. Her company was privately held and such information was unavailable to the public, though Mary had a domestic staff, a chauffeuse, and had made the unconventional decision the previous year to purchase a corporate jet. All that said something, apart from a whimsical trip to the Bahamas aboard the new jet and their impromptu French excursion.

Mary watched impassively as the hearse led the funereal convoy away from the curb. She did what was expected of her. She would do no more. She would not attend the late afternoon wake at The Plaza, nor would Pearl. Averly's death was a good thing. He was a bad apple, rotten to the core, which Mary believed was an irreversible condition of nature and, had she known, she would have gladly plunged the knife hard and deep to his core a day or a week before.

When she saw her daughter that horrible night, slumped at the door and crying, bruised and swollen, her fervent hope and her prayer were to see him dead. Wealth and position were of absolutely no consequence, she mused, if one could not live their dreams.

Part Three

Six

Quebec City, Quebec
Thursday, August 02, 2007

Dina Becker was a good cop. She had been since joining the force at the age of twenty. She had been the only woman and the youngest cadet at the academy when she graduated at the top of her class, now she was thirty-nine and Captain of the Special Victims Unit. She loved her job. She loved helping those who needed her most. What she hated was always being an hour or a day too late. She had been too late to help her sister, too late to arrest her murderer, too late to kill him.

Prior to her sister's brutal murder she had not thought of marriage, seldom dated, and when she did she would inevitably find more disappointment than love. After the murder she dispelled the thought completely from her mind, preferring loneliness to heartache.

She was tall and attractive with chestnut red hair and a deep voice that exuded sexuality as much as projecting authority. Many of the men in her division had tried hitting on her over the years, always losing the wager, and to a man they had all at one time or another imagined the impossible of being with her for a night in Shangri-La. Each one knew the answer and each one anxiously awaited the annual

Christmas Party when Captain Dina Becker became the very sultry Dina Becker in high heels and something either very short, very low, or both, much to the feigned dismay and rolling eyes of their wives as she danced with each man and gave them sisterly hugs and kisses before leaving the party alone.

Most of the time, she was all business with a near perfect arrest record. She possessed an aura none could define, she dressed for the job in Armani suits, tailored blouses, Ferrari shoes or Gucci boots, and carried Herrera handbags. She never wore dresses on the job, not since Nancy's death. Standard issue were 10mm Glocks, she carried a Berretta 9mm 92FS on her hip and the smaller 84FS Cheetah on her ankle. She travelled to Monaco each spring and to Saint-Tropez each fall, while others went to the cottage or the in-laws. She drove a bright red Jaguar XKR, she wore an IceLink watch no one could discover the price of, she lived alone in an upscale neighbourhood, she had no pets, and she had no one to love. What she did have was deep-rooted passion.

Some years earlier her lifestyle had been questioned by Internal Affairs after the death of her sister and, very soon after, the man who instigated the investigation was severely reprimanded by the commissioner himself, summarily instructed to stay away from the then Lieutenant Becker of Homicide. She was a good cop, beyond reproach, who happened to have friends in Europe to visit and her clothes were all designer knock-offs. Enough said. When the detective persisted by asking the top cop how Dina Becker had managed to come across a BMW knock-off, his suspension for insubordination lasted a week.

She was a mystery, an enigma, yet every Friday night she would buy the first round at Le Flic. Then she would leave them alone and go home to her nineteenth-century mansion bequeathed to her by her wealthy investment banker father and corporate lawyer mother who had died together in a plane crash when Dina was fourteen and her sister Nancy was eight.

The girls' godfather, Claude Jordan, had taken charge of them from then on and had raised the girls as his own. He sent them to Europe for their higher education, insisting they come home at every opportunity, and at the age of twenty-one, one year after her graduation from the police academy, he gave over the mansion to Dina with a cheque for four million dollars which she decided to invest in the Swiss banking system. She wanted a reputation as a good cop, not a spoiled heiress with a hobby. Nancy would receive her inheritance six years later.

After nine years on the force Lieutenant Becker had at long last surrendered to the plaintive pleas of the predominately male homicide division for her to attend the annual summer picnic, an annual event created that same year with that specific purpose in mind. The event had been mind-altering. The men no longer needed to imagine themselves in Shangri-La. Now they would know. She had arrived wearing safari shorts, a starched white shirt with the collar up, white bobby socks, and tan desert boots. The day had been hot and sticky, the lake cool and inviting.

To a man they stood waiting, eagerly anticipating, anxious to compare their stored mental images of her with the real thing, each one silently praying not to be disappointed. The men of the division had always treated her like a sister, they were protective of her. She was Dina and not one of them had ever believed for a moment the day would come as she casually raised one foot, then the other, onto a seat of the picnic table, undid both sets of laces, pulled away her boots and socks, and stood sipping her wine.

They clapped their hands together loudly and hurried for their cameras, yelling back at her to wait. She shrugged nonchalantly, sipping more wine and exchanging wicked grins with the other women who hadn't come to the party completely uninformed. Her belt came away one loop at a time. She tugged at her shirttails and undid the buttons one by one with agonizing and alluring slowness, as though she was daydreaming. She bared one shoulder, and then the other, letting it fall away from her back. The tiniest possible triangles shimmered in red and yellow, highlighting the fullness of her perfectly shaped breasts. She undid the bow at her back to a chorus of howls and redid the knot. She sipped more wine, oblivious to the cat-calls and flashes. Her hands went to her half-open zipper. She tugged at the front of her shorts, making sure everything was in place before moving her hands to her hips and pushing the shorts to her ankles in one smooth and effortless motion.

The howling had been deafening, male praise of perfection in a sparkling red Rio with bright yellow side ties. She leaned forward from the waist with sultry slowness to reach for her lotion, keeping her legs straight. She did one arm, then the other, before doing her stomach, her chest and the swell of her breasts. She raised one leg, coating the front from her hip to her toes and the back from her ankle to a firm and tanned cheek peeking out from its small covering. She did the other leg, she pulled at her strings she had already double-knotted and reached behind to lotion her back, which was difficult and she stopped. Pouting, she scanned the open-mouthed admirers. She needed help to do her back. She walked towards them, stopping and shaking her head. It wouldn't be right, she murmured loudly enough to be heard. It would be too much to ask of them, she decided, and she changed direction to walk towards the women.

One was dressed in her own small bikini and held out her hand. She took the bottle from Dina and stepped behind her. She drew a line down one side of Dina's back from her shoulders to her bikini bottom and up the other side, massaging in the lotion with long, seductive strokes as Dina gyrated her hips and the two girls moaned.

71

Cameras continued to flash. The men were going insane, begging the women to pose. They did, mischievously, and then they ran together laughing and dived into the lake. The other women stood by and shook their heads in stride as their men raced one another to be the first in the water. They knew what their husbands thought of Dina. Each one would give his life for her and not think twice about it.

The picnic had been a great success. Each man had gone home with a memory that would last forever and photographs that would fade with time. Photographs destined to be buried and forgotten in drawers or cardboard boxes and never seen out of respect for their lieutenant and friend, and the memory of her dead sister that would never fade.

Dina pushed the memory of Nancy from her mind. She had to be focused. The evening was misty, wet with a drizzling rain and dark with an eerie stillness. A thickening fog defused pale amber halos that shone from widely spaced lampposts that did little to illuminate the street and she had to be certain. She would have no second chance. Her wig itched, she wanted to rip the thing from her head, and the humid air made her face feel thick with cheap make-up. Her vinyl bolero jacket revealed most of her bare abdomen and her electric orange push-up bra gave an exaggerated fullness to her breasts. Her jean skirt was shamelessly short and covered only the curve of her buttocks with narrow garters connected to dark nylon leggings she knew would draw attention to her bare thighs.

She already looked years younger than her thirty-nine years and the make-up gave her a mid-twenties appearance. Had she bought the costume from some trendy uptown boutique in a more discreet palette of colours she might have appeared to be a young woman out for an evening of sophisticated clubbing. However, she bought the outfit at a discount clothing mart and she looked more like a young hooker looking to earn enough for one more hit or a cheap room for the night. Her own team would not have recognized her, which was precisely the objective. She had no purse, nor a gun. Neither was required for what had become her life's passion, what she did best.

Dina Becker had reviewed the case study, memorizing each detail before destroying it. She had seen the man up close on three previous occasions. She had committed each detail of his dour face and body language to memory. The possession of photographs or case study information was always strictly forbidden during facilitations, always destroyed beforehand. She had committed every facet of the man to memory. He was a devout catholic, he attended church regularly, he went to the same strip bar every Thursday night, and he had been evaluated by the Directorate as a level two for immediate facilitation.

De Beaufort worked late most Thursdays, usually stopping in for a drink at a nearby strip bar before going home to his wife. Dina knew of the bar where the waitresses were either too old or too scarred by life to work in mainstream bars along le boulevard de l'aeroport or the busy downtown bars where more nubile creatures were beginning their careers without thoughts of where they would end their lives: cheap motels and leaning through car windows to give ten-dollar BJs.

The fact his wife had left him without a word and was refusing his calls had made little difference to his week, other than his Thursday night diversion, and he had begun to stay longer and drink more. Dina Becker's watch read 8:30 when she saw him disappear into the bar. She sauntered across the street and strolled to where she knew he had parked his car. The area was a deserted business park and those who usually belonged there were either at home or inside the bar that always closed promptly at 11:00. Extremely narrow timing she didn't like. What she did like was that the other customers still in the bar would stay until the very end.

At 10:40 she walked a few steps in the opposite direction and stepped into a doorway, looking out on the half-minute to watch for him. Like clockwork he exited the bar at 10:45. She inhaled deeply, stripped away her jacket, and stepped out onto the sidewalk where she felt a deep disdain invade her. Jacques de Beaufort virtually jerked to a stop. It was the reaction she anticipated as she continued closing the distance between them.

To de Beaufort she was a vision. She was erotic and seductive. She seemed to be gliding towards him from out of nowhere, from behind a surreal curtain of muted yellow and swirling white mist. Her hair hung down over her shoulder in damp, dark strands. Her bra was bright orange against her skin that seemed to glow with moisture from the mist and he wanted to consume her. As she came closer she stumbled, dropping her jacket. De Beaufort stopped again as she positioned herself sideways and leaned forward from the waist to retrieve the bolero and examine her shoes. He was so close. He strained to see more, not realizing he had stopped breathing.

He could hear her cursing, standing upright and seeming to adjust her garters. De Beaufort hurried forward, propelled by a sudden impetus that was urgent and unfamiliar to him. He tried to think clearly, not yet completely acclimated to five or six gins and tonic in one night. He knew he would never again have such a perfect opportunity to see such a striking woman shamelessly wearing so little. He could see her fingers working at the garters. Their eyes crossed and she smiled.

She wanted to laugh, and might have at any other time. He had brown hair, he was wearing a brown suit, a beige shirt, a beige tie, and his shoes were brown. His belt was brown and so were his glasses that had a string hanging down from each hinge. She already knew his eyes were brown and she could see his beige socks between the cuffs of his pants and his shoes. She wanted to scream out geek, jerk! She could see the way he was looking at her and where he was looking. Creep.

He returned her smile as he knelt in front of her. She was several inches taller and he could see the V of her orange panties as she arched her back slightly to look behind her. He stared, opening his eyes wider as though he might see more of her. He thought a hundred, maybe one-fifty. That's as high as he would go. The question was where, where could they go?

Seeing her like that wasn't like seeing a used-up stripper. She was clean and young. In the bar they were all bruised and slovenly and didn't wash their hands whenever they were finished in the men's room with a customer. This one was a real woman in real panties that looked clean.

She was being obvious. He knew she wanted him to see her, to show interest in her, to pay for her. He was so close to her, close enough to smell her. He had no reason to get home any time soon and he knew she wanted him to ask as much as he wanted her to say yes. He clutched the jacket as he stood openly captivated by her breasts. He let her take it with one gloved hand as her other thrust the slim blade of her pearl-handled stiletto easily into his throat and twisted once.

Dina Becker retracted the blade and slid the dagger into the top band of her nylons. She put on her jacket as though nothing had happened and confidently walked to her car to drive home. Once the garage door had closed she stepped from the Jaguar and undressed methodically, beginning with the gloves she had worn from the moment she had taken each item of the temporary wardrobe she had chosen for the de Beaufort's facilitation from their respective shopping bags. Each piece was put into separate plastic bags and accounted for before she padded into the bathroom and stood for several minutes under a hot shower to shampoo her hair and wash away the cosmetic mask before drawing back the curtain to do a visual inspection of her body. She had overlooked nothing and liked how she looked, wondering who the next person would be to see her naked after so many years alone. So many years had gone by, she thought, but who could she trust enough to love.

She sat naked on the rounded edge of the Victorian tub to comb out her hair, enjoying the lingering steam, asking herself why not; telling herself there was only one reason: She was afraid. She had thought about going a hundred times over the past year and had always come up with the same justifiable reason not to go. Besides, what would she wear and how would she explain the gun that was an indispensable part of who she had become. The notion was ludicrous. How desperate could she be, and how many more nights would she lie awake in turmoil? How many more mornings would she wake up alone?

In her bedroom she dressed in designer jeans, an open-knit sweater, and low heels before strapping the compact backup weapon to her ankle. Then she went into the kitchen to verify her prized red abalone mother-of-pearl stiletto was perfectly sterilized and returned it to the silk-lined case. She made one call from her disposable cell to advise that her case study had been successfully facilitated and left home to dispose of each plastic bag several city blocks apart.

When she had completed the requisite final phase of the facilitation she sat outside the bar, watching from a block away, not knowing whether to feel happy and excited or sad and desperate. At least she would finally know and, more importantly, no one else. She twisted the key in the ignition and pulled slowly away from the curb, stopping between two valets who had seen her drive up and had already flipped the coin.

When she arrived home a few hours later she laid awake musing upon her evening, not certain anything had diametrically changed in her life apart from the diminishing need to question herself. She drifted to sleep content with the promise she had whispered into her pillow and wondering what she would wear the next time to Le Discrèt.

Dina Becker awoke Friday morning to a freshly brewed coffee and breaking news of the year's eighteenth murder. That was Homicide's problem. Her concern was for Marie-Ève de Beaufort whose file would be closed and shelved in the SVU storeroom. Her dead husband's file would be stored elsewhere and would never be revisited.

Seven

Toronto, Ontario
Friday, August 03

Miranda Stevens stepped onto the private patio of her nineteenth-floor luxury condo with a morning coffee and her comb, a ritual she began as early as mid-April each year and continued until the chill of autumn's morning air became unpleasant and the dew felt cold to her feet.

The privileged few who might ever possibly see her standing outside so unabashedly naked on weekdays, combing out her long, golden hair would be the early morning traffic reporter whenever he might convince his pilot to cut the power and glide a mile or two. Or the curious captain of a Great Lakes freighter who might zoom in on what would appear to him at first sight as a miniature, glistening figurine as Miranda stood still and gazed out over Lake Ontario.

It was 6:00 AM and the sun had begun to cast a wide blanket of amber across the huge body of water. Absorbing the early morning sun or feeling the cool mist of a light summer rain against her skin was her sole enjoyment. That morning the sun's warming rays were particularly revitalizing. She had been up since 5:30 and awake since she had gone to bed.

She threw her head down, letting the damp and tangled mass of golden strands cascade to her knees before sweeping it straight with long strokes of the comb and throwing her head back to reverse the particularly feminine process. She was five-ten, thirty-two, not that her age bothered her, and saw the world through piercing blue eyes. She was slim, toned, and her body had not the slightest blemish to mar the pale hue of a perfect tan.

As the rotors of the helicopter grew louder she stepped inside, exiting with fresh coffee when the distinctive whooping sound faded into the distance. She let her mind drift to the coming Sunday evening, her first date in well over a year. They had met the day before while Miranda had been finishing a fast lunch before going to trial: tall, perfect teeth, a good dresser, and a senior city administrator. What else could she ask for? They had agreed to meet for dinner on Sunday, exchanging non-committal cell phone numbers on their way to the courthouse, neither one wanting to exhaust possible topics of conversation for their evening together. Miranda had suggested eight o'clock at an unpretentious restaurant where she was unknown, claiming an early courtroom appearance on the Monday, and had instantly regretted not suggesting a lunch or a drink in a bar.

Her last date had gone badly, ending before the entrées were served and she had been left sitting alone at a table encircled by lovers and curious expressions. The time had come, she hoped. She was nervous and had told herself a hundred times that, no matter what the outcome, she would sleep alone in her own bed. She owed that much to Morgan whose picture she had spoken to throughout the night.

Miranda leaned in to the railing, peering down over Lake Shore Boulevard and the lake. Morgan had been dead ten years and three months and would understand her loneliness. A month following the brutal murder she was introduced to Pearl who came to be such an important part of her life, and a few months had passed since they had last spoken to one another. She knew Pearl was concerned for her well-being, wanting her to achieve some sort of balance in her life, and her boss was no less anxious to see her do more than simply feign happiness. Throughout her years at the prosecutor's office he was the one person who had ever been privy to the real Miranda. She stepped back, closed her eyes, and inhaled a deep breath with her arms outstretched. The sun felt so good. She had nothing to lose. She was going on a dinner date, not to the end of the world.

She put down her cup and finished combing her hair. When she was satisfied with whom she saw in the reflection of the bay window she tossed the comb onto a deck chair and spread a thin layer of lotion across the supple curves of her body. When she was done she went inside and dressed for the day. Sunday evening would come soon enough, whether she worried or not. Until then she had three full days of legal briefs and arguments to prepare.

Miranda Stevens could not know how drastically her chance encounter at lunch the day before would forever alter her life and the lives of others after learning of a man she was yet to meet.

Eight

Quebec City, Quebec
Saturday, August 04

Jacques de Beaufort was laid to rest Saturday morning in an ordinary pine box and a plot closest to the lane that meandered its way between lush manicured gardens and groves of tall trees. Such had been his written request years earlier. The frugal accountant had never understood the need to squander hard-earned money for the sake of being remembered as a corpse with a perfectly good suit ripped down its back and stuffed between his body and the silk lining of an exorbitantly priced box. Nor did he want to pay for the privilege of spending eternity under the shade of a tree or overlooking a city he would never see. Such was the stuff of romance novels and wasteful in the extreme. He would be dead and the dead had no appreciation of hillside vistas.

His death had been an unexpected tragedy at the age of forty, stabbed in the throat on his way home from the office Thursday night. There had been no blood other than a small amount absorbed into his collar, no indication of a struggle, no weapon, no witnesses and no suspects: a dead end. He would not have cried out. De Beaufort had died quickly and efficiently, for no apparent reason, and his distraught wife wept believably as she told the police she should never have gone to her sister's, that if she had stayed home he might not have been killed. They had no comment. When they had contacted her she had wailed into the phone, inconsolable, and her sister spoke with them to confirm Marie-Ève had been staying with her for the past week or so, information they would verify with the airline and her credit card company.

All they had were questions that had no answers. Marie-Ève had no idea why anyone would kill an ordinary and quiet man such as her husband, but they did. The police report would indicate a 'random killing', and would remain one, despite their supposition that Marie-Ève had sufficient motive to kill her husband. The investigating detective had a copy of her medical file on his desk. He told her the investigation would not be pursued and she knew to believe him. De Beaufort was dead and the murder scene had not produced so much as a drop of blood or a strand of hair.

The presiding cleric had appeared dutifully sad throughout the ceremony, though he wasn't sad at all. He had another funeral scheduled for 3:00 PM, on the other side of town, and on the Sunday he was to marry yet another joyous young couple who would live together in harmonious love till death would tear them apart.

Jacques and Marie-Ève de Beaufort had been devout Catholics, which meant the priest had always known more about de Beaufort than the dead parishioner would have wanted. Her infrequent and brief moments in the cramped confessional had been Marie-Ève's sole salvation. For the priest, maintaining the sanctity of those sacred meetings made him as guilty as the man he was consigning unto heaven, despite his belief that he was blameless by virtue of divine absolution.

De Beaufort had been a devoted and loving husband, an accomplished citizen of the community, and would be sorely missed, the priest had lamented with practiced despair. Marie-Ève would never again see her husband. The cleric had looked her way frequently throughout the service, his expression kind and compassionate. He knew that for the first time in so many years Marie-Ève could be truly happy and he knew with absolute conviction that the peace everlasting which was soon to be refused her dearly departed husband would be hers to enjoy.

The hillside cemetery was coated with early-morning dew glistening on freshly mowed grass, rows of grey marble stones stood like silent sentinels guarding the dead as the few obligées gathered at the grave watched with little emotion as stone-faced men in black methodically and indifferently lowered Monsieur de Beaufort from memory. His widow, masked by black mesh and the brim of her hat, felt the warmth of tears trickling down her bruised and discoloured cheeks. She was free at last. Her youthfulness and her beauty would soon return to her and never again would she be afraid. Her years of torment and fear were at an end.

Their last evening alone had been the worst, three weeks earlier, when he had beaten her for the last time. The hospital had called the police immediately, to no avail. Marie-Ève had refused to admit what had happened. She had fallen. She had been careless and had she had fallen down the stairs. Her husband wasn't even at home at the time, she had explained to the police, and he wasn't. He had gone back to a local bar.

The next day at home had been a different matter. The police had come to her door asking relentless questions, women officers under the command of Captain Becker, trained to understand, persisting in what they knew to be true. They left feeling frustrated and angry, though a few hours later another woman had come to her home to change Marie-Ève's life forever.

The woman was refined and looked to be middle-aged. She was elegantly dressed, as though she had been attending a garden party of socialites, and carried herself with grace. Jasmine Leclerc was also a widow who had not remarried since her husband's death twenty-six years earlier. Her life was her children, her grandchild, and her valued work as an Enabler within a non-profit agency which was clandestine, incredibly wealthy, and whose membership was earned by the admission of one's own pain and suffering. She felt passionately about her important contribution and her devotion to Pearl had not wavered for twenty-six years.

Pearl demanded blind faith out of necessity: during her first ten years as a Facilitator and subsequent years as an Enabler Jasmine had only ever met infrequently with her two directors whose names she had never known. For Jasmine, it was enough to know Pearl had once saved her life unconditionally.

Her case study was Marie-Ève de Beaufort, nee DuPont, who resided at 3200 rue Saint-Vincent and who had been released from hospital that morning. She was currently unemployed, she had aspirations and dreams of one day owning her own real-estate agency, and she was married. She was French-speaking and college educated, which had made her unwillingness to press charges or leave all the more difficult to understand. She should have known better than to stay with an abuser. De Beaufort pulled in sixty K a year. She had been earning double that amount before he had begun to transform her face into something too unattractive to succeed in the looks-equals-success-oriented real-estate industry. Jasmine prayed with all her heart that de Beaufort would very soon make his wife three million dollars richer. She put her finger to the doorbell and prayed to succeed. She had come for one specific reason: to enable Marie-Ève. The young woman was about to be freed. All she had to do was answer the door.

When Marie-Ève did come to the door after long moments of doubt she opened it as little as possible and lowered her head. She was wearing a flannel hoodie in an attempt to conceal most of her face. She need not have bothered. Jasmine knew what to expect, she had seen the photographs. Her voice was calming, her eyes commiserate. She had come to help.

Marie-Ève allowed the woman into her home without knowing why, feeling as though she had known the stranger for a lifetime and that, at long last, she could cry out for help or understanding. Moments later she understood why. Jasmine followed Marie-Ève into the living room and wrapped her arms around the young woman when Marie-Ève pulled back her hood.

"Marie-Ève, please understand. We know about you. There are no secrets. More importantly, we care about you very much and you are no longer alone. We know he beats you and that you have been to different hospitals several times over the past few years, each time for the same reason: falling down stairs. You probably believe going to different hospitals means different reports. You're wrong. You have no secrets and no one believes your explanations."

Marie-Ève was stunned. "You said we. Who are you and why would you possibly care about me?"

"That doesn't matter for the moment. What does matter is that one day very soon he will use a hammer or a knife, not his hands or his fists. He will kill you. That is what we care about, nothing else."

"No, you are wrong. He would never do such a thing. I know how it must look. Believe me. It is not that way at all. It is not his fault. It is mine. I'm holding him back. He tries so hard, but it's not always easy. He has been losing clients and I'm not working. Also, he has always blamed himself for not giving me children and I have often been less than a perfect wife."

"His becoming a failure in business has had nothing to do with you. His coming up short as a family man is also his problem, not yours, and who amongst us is perfect. All you must realize is that one day soon you'll be dead: cold, lifeless, and dead, a corpse in the ground. At least the pain will be over. Is that what you want, to be dead?"

Marie-Ève shuddered and clasped her hands together between her knees. She began sobbing and shaking her head. Jasmine remained stoic, her compassion would come later.

"I am truly sorry, Marie-Ève. Sometimes we must be shocked into doing what is right for us. Please understand, one day he will kill or maim you. The only question is when."

"I'm sorry. You must leave. I should not have let you in."

"I will, very soon, after you have heard what I have come to say. You have come this far, don't turn me away now." Jasmine paused, taking a moment to collect mental data of what she saw around her. "Marie-Ève, I'm a survivor. Like you, I was beaten for years and, like you, I did nothing about it. Until one night, the last night, he beat me so badly I did not wake up until after my surgery. The police arrested him. They held him until I was lucid enough to deny he had beaten me and a month or so later he was dead."

Marie-Ève hesitated. "Was it suicide? He was angry with himself for what he did to you?"

"No, it wasn't a suicide. It was prevention."

"You killed him?" Her mouth and eyes opened wide with horror. "Did you kill your own husband?"

"No, I would never have had the inner strength to be that brave. I didn't, though I had wanted to for the longest time. Down deep, I had always regretted marrying him." Jasmine shrugged. "Unfortunately I was so young and stupid. What I thought was love was an entirely different sensation and not very good if memory serves. We did what everyone else was doing. We were children of the seventies, free love and all of that. We actually ran away to get married."

"Why did he beat you?"

"Marie-Ève, as I have said, we know everything about you. He beat me for no reason other than what was in his own mind, a sick and distraught mind I was never privy to. He never sought help and that made the problem his, not mine. In short, I never did anything to deserve waking up in a surgical ward wondering why I was alive, wondering why I was defending him, as you are doing now. Tomorrow, my dear, or the day after, you will be the woman I once was. You will open your eyes through bandages and wish you had listened to me."

"He loves me. He does. We are both still young. I remember when he used to hold me and love me. I remember how it used to feel. I tell him all the time how things will get better, that one day I will own my own company. One day my dream will happen."

"He's forgotten how to love you. He loves having you. He loves how he feels when he's striking out at you. He feels like a man, he feels empowered. That is what he feels, not love." Jasmine paused for affect. "Did you know his father had a history of beating his mother, before he died? It's a matter of record."

The colour drained from Marie-Ève's face.

"No, I did not. He was found at bottom of stone steps with his neck broken, a terrible accident. That is what I know. It happened many years before I met Jacques. His mother never recovered from the loss."

"Yes, it was horrible for her," Jasmine answered, thinking back to a night so many years in her past, "until he was taken from her. From what I understand he was a cruel man. Curious, isn't it? Even as your husband grew to be his father's equal in size he did nothing to stop the violence. However, you are wrong on one point. She has recovered and is happily remarried to a wonderful man."

Marie-Ève shivered. "You know her? You know maman de Beaufort?"

"No, I do not. I have never met her. All I know is what I've been told, nothing more. Nor does she know of me."

Marie-Ève clutched her sides and leaned forward,

87

feeling desperate. "He doesn't mean to hurt me. He cannot help himself. One day he will stop, one day it will get better."

"No, it won't, not without intervention. One day he will simply be arrested for manslaughter or murder, second degree. He'll get out in ten or twelve years, probably less and you will still be dead. Are you aware he goes each Thursday night to a strip club to ogle desperate and naked women whose daily existence depends on him, and men like him, seeing them in their most vulnerable state?"

Marie-Ève seemed not to hear. She sat straight and asked: "How did your husband die?"

"He was killed one night, very unexpectedly. There was no pain. The police never did find the killer or killers. I suppose it's what they call a cold case."

"Do you miss him?"

"No. I miss the early years, or what I remember of them. Frankly, I never think about it. The fact is the first time was so good, I never remarried." Jasmine paused for affect and Marie-Ève misconstrued. She thought she had awakened a dark memory and suddenly felt sorry for the lady, until she felt Jasmine's hand over hers. "I don't want the same for you. I want you to be happy. I want you to have whatever you want out of life. Most of all I want you to live. I won't stay much longer, Marie-Ève, though before I leave I want you to tell me what you didn't tell the police this morning. I want you to tell me very succinctly that you are afraid of dying, that you are afraid of being beaten again tonight or tomorrow. I want you to tell me it's alright."

Marie-Ève was more afraid than she had ever been. She was crossing over and she knew it. The stranger sitting in front of her was as warm as she was cold, as empathetic as she was unyielding in what was about to unfold.

"To do what, that it is alright to do what?" she asked.

"To make you free, to make you feel whole again'"

Marie-Ève felt tears welling in her eyes, her heart was

beating erratically. "You did kill your husband. You murdered him."

"No, I did not. However, I am very glad they did. Perhaps relieved would be a better word because I am certain he would have killed me. What's worse, he would already be out and almost certainly beating his second wife."

"Did you arrange his death?"

The woman smiled. "No, I did not, although I did nothing to prevent the event. And, yes, I do know who they are, which is why you will never be allowed to know me. I am also very happy. I've never been happier or freer because of them."

"And you want me to do the same. You want me to let them kill my husband."

"Yes."

"That is insane."

"More insane than him killing you? Go onto the Web, Marie-Ève. Research the statistics. He's going to kill you, if you don't kill yourself or him first. And what would either solution prove?"

A spear of cold froze Marie-Ève to her very core. She felt her body convulse, yet the woman beside her seemed composed, unaffected.

"Leave me alone. Please, leave me alone. You are talking to me about the murder of my husband."

"No, I am not, and I understand your inner turmoil. You must understand I am not talking about murder. I am talking about premeditated self-defence. Murder is what he will do to you. Marie-Ève, listen very carefully to me. You will never be involved and you don't really have a choice. You can decide about yourself, you cannot decide about him. However much you believe you know him, you do not. When he remarries, after he buries you, he'll mistreat his second wife the very same way. It's who he is, a learned condition. We intend to break the chain, pro bono if need be.

Though we would prefer not to, those cases are generally restricted to known pedophiles, rapists, and the underprivileged."

"I will call the police."

"I realize right now you are struggling very hard to believe that. I responded the very same way until I came to realize my reality. Finally, I did not call them and I'm so very happy because I'm still alive. Not calling them saved my life." Jasmine stood. "Marie-Ève you don't have to be afraid anymore. He won't hurt you again."

"I am afraid. I am afraid of you. You're scaring me. What do I tell him, what do I tell the police? I cannot even say who you are."

"You won't tell him. You don't have to see him again." She paused. "Tell the police and we'll go away. We will know when and if you do. They'll do the job for us if you're honest with them, then he'll be out in a few months and blaming you for how his new friends will have turned his rectum into an amusement park. It will be status quo and, if you think it's bad now, wait. You're thirty and could pass for late forties. Is that how you want to die, old before your time, because he will kill you? " She paused. "Let us help you, Marie-Ève. Be young and pretty again. Be happy again. Find someone else and be happy."

"They will arrest me. I cannot do this. I cannot think of doing such a thing. I will go to prison for what you are suggesting."

"No, you will not." Jasmine responded with vehement conviction. "You will go to your sister's. You must travel by plane and you must tell her nothing beyond the obvious. You won't have to explain why to anyone. Everyone will know why, even him. Be very guarded in what you say and when you're there you will use your credit cards once a day at least. You will know when the time is right to come home. Don't worry. You will know."

"The nurses at the hospital told me to leave him, to go to

a centre for women."

"They were right. However those centres serve short-term needs and are terribly overworked and under-funded. At least you went to the hospital. That should have told you something, including that you have gone too many times." Marie-Ève nodded, wringing her hands. "The decision must be yours, Marie-Ève. If you sincerely what this to continue, if you sincerely believe he is not an out-of-control animal, you will have an opportunity to say so. All you need do when the phone rings this evening is to say no, or not pick up. Not answering will make you free. Be very aware of that fact. Not answering the phone will make you free. Do you understand me?"

"I want to be sick."

"You have been sick. What you need now is to be well. You won't ever be alone, Marie-Ève. You will be free of guilt, entirely, which does not mean free of obligation. The usual fee is ten percent of the man's life insurance, nothing else. In your case we would suggest three hundred thousand, payable within three months following the release of funds. Talking about payment sounds mercenary, I know, although we all find the fee quite equitable. Some of us are wealthy to say the least. Others are less fortunate in varying degrees. We are concerned about saving you, not your money. If you decide not to contribute, so be it. No action will be taken against you, although contributions do help us to sponsor important pro bono work for less fortunate women. I must also caution you that telling the police about this part of our conversation won't matter. We are essentially invisible to those around us. They won't believe you. In fact the one you might speak with could well be one of us, at the highest levels, or your banker, or your dentist."

"Who are you?" Marie-Ève began crying. "Why did you even come here? I'm nobody."

"You are Marie-Ève. You are in grave danger and we want to help you. Let us do what we do best. We've been doing this for a very long time. You are not the first. Believe me, and believe in us. We won't let you down."

Marie-Ève's face contorted. She was frantic. She wanted the strange woman to go. "Who are you?"

"My name is Pearl, and when I call you later this evening, do not answer the phone. I implore you not to answer. Your life will be so much better very soon."

That was a month earlier and Marie-Ève wasn't home to answer the phone. She left that afternoon for the airport, leaving a message for her husband that she had gone to spend time with her sister. She had not seen Pearl at the funeral, wishing somehow the woman would have been there to comfort her through the day as the priest and well-wishers returned to their cars.

There would be no festive reunion to remember the defunct de Beaufort with amusing anecdotes and kind words. Everyone had gone. All she had in the backseat of a limousine was the memory of her last few moments with Pearl who had given her a gift to cherish: a beautiful ring and a promise she would never be alone.

Sunday Marie-Ève booked a fourteen-day trip to Puerto Vallarta and bought an expensive bottle of wine which she drank while modelling scanty bikinis in front of a mirror she had ignored long enough. Not until late Sunday evening did she stare with disbelief into the iridescence of the lustrous black pearl set in silver. Her body shuddered with cold. Jacques' mother wore one exactly like it.

Nine

Montreal, Quebec
Sunday, August 05

Alicia Kendall's head snapped backward, away from the vicious blow. The left side of her face radiated a cruel shade of pink and her right cheek was pale with terror. She felt nothing. She was numb, afraid of what he would do to her little girl and unborn baby. She knew his rage and the violence would soon subside. They were the ephemeral culmination of his sporadic dark moods. She had lived through them before and knew this would not be the last time. The beatings would get worse and become more frequent.

She braced herself for another stinging slap that flung her petite frame against the wall, suspended in space and time, waiting, protecting the roundness of her belly that had recently begun to show. Cringing in fear did no good. Standing for as long as she could was her way of fighting back, until he stopped, when she would crumple to the floor. Blood trickled from her nose, forming a tiny ridge of dark red that seeped into her mouth. She willed herself not to swallow, to remain inert. She would not cry, not ever. He hated to see her cry. He loved her and hated to see her sad. It was over. Nothing else mattered, for the time being.

When would she ever learn, was all she heard him mutter under his breath. He did love her, she knew, when he was sober. He walked away, cursing her. He was incoherent, the smell of his sweat and beer lingering behind like some vile and suffocating shroud. She had stopped listening. She had heard endless times before how she had to understand, how he was doing his best to make things right, to make their life together the way it used to be before she had become such a burden and his life such a mess. Why did he even care? What was the use?

The clock on the kitchen wall struck midnight. Alicia Kendall's twenty-seventh birthday had come and gone. She stayed on the floor, counting her breaths. There were no more tears to count. What had she done this time to trigger his mood, she wondered? He should have been overjoyed by the news, ecstatic, yet he wasn't. He had always wanted two little girls and now all he could think to do was blame her and beat her. A tiny explosion of pink spittle burst from between her quivering lips. What had she ever done other than try to understand, until understanding had become too difficult?

She had been downsized from her job a few months earlier, which she had thought of as an opportunity to search for something better. To him the downturn was an opportunity to berate her and punish her for letting him down. She didn't mind that he had forgotten her birthday. She never did. This time she had been too excited about telling him of the special gift they both would soon share. She ran her hands over her stomach, pressing with a mother's gentle touch.

The early morning sun would have wakened her through the kitchen window, but she hadn't slept. Sleeping would have meant forgetting for too short a time, sleeping would have meant dreaming of what they once had, before waking to a reality irrevocably forming in her mind. He would never let her go, she knew. He had said so a hundred times without passion or the ardent glint of young, adoring eyes. She belonged with him.

The night air was heavy and damp with mid-summer heat. Her cheap muslin shift clung to her body and the ringlets of her jet-black hair hung down in the matted clumps he had formed in his tightly clenched fists. The kitchen curtains fell straight over open windows, blocking out the darkness, and she wondered who had heard, who had ignored her muffled shrieks and the loud echoes of his rough palms against her once pretty face. She tried to move. She knew if she didn't that one day soon she would be found by her daughter, dead.

Her body ached and she felt cold. Her head throbbed and all she heard was the pounding of her heart. She was shivering uncontrollably, cuddling into herself, trying desperately to rub away the chill of dark foreboding. She searched her mind to understand the tumultuous juxtaposition of fond memories and vivid fears. As she did she stared up at the kitchen drawer, feeling an inexplicable sense of relief, an infusion of warmth and well-being that was foreign to her. In those fleeting seconds she realized what she must do. She summoned all her strength and pushed herself from the floor. He would never beat her again. Now her single most important reason for living was to save her daughters.

Ten

Toronto, Ontario
Sunday, August 05

Miranda Stevens pushed herself from her chaise-longue on her patio at 5:30 to shower and dress for her date. She was as excited as she was afraid. She hadn't been on a date in over twelve months and by seven there were more clothes laid out on her bed than hanging in her closest. She finally settled for a pleated cream-coloured linen miniskirt, a matching double-breasted blazer, and an embroidered, three-quarter yellow bra with blue rosettes to match her open-toed sandals sans nylons.

She liked how she looked in the classic ensemble, so did her favourite doorman who had parked her silver Aston Martin V8 Vintage at the front entrance of the exclusive high-rise. She was sexy, yet didn't seem flirtatious or easy. She might have worn the same outfit at an after-hours cocktail party and no one who knew her would have been surprised. She was Miranda, and all who knew her knew she was synonymous with the unexpected.

The doorman had put the top down and opened the driver's door for her, wishing he was thirty years younger and millions richer, though Miranda had never made him feel anything but special. She was his only tenant who cared about his birthday or missed him during his vacation, and when she drove onto Lake Shore Boulevard he waved into her rear-view mirror.

Miranda had no expectations, although she wanted so badly to make a good impression, and did to anyone fortunate enough to see her en route to the restaurant where the couple had agreed to meet at 8:00. Leaving the European import with a valet she walked directly toward the hostess' lectern, who led her to their table with the indifferent impersonality inherent to most of the city's restaurants and the evening deteriorated from there.

The couple's initial conversation was banal and easy, neither one talking about past loves or future expectations. Their careers soon became safe ground after discovering quite different tastes in wine, travel, and an obvious disaccord in what was currently fashionable, each one trying to suppress first-date jitters. When the dessert menu came Miranda suggested a nightcap at a nearby bar, sensing the distinctive signs of a pending disaster.

The already tenuous evening disintegrated from the moment their drinks were served as Miranda listened incredulously to the proposal and mindlessly swirled the crushed ice in her glass, thankful for something to do. She was not interested in being with someone who wanted her only for the occasional dalliance whenever the novelty of a beautiful woman trumped a traditional and mundane home life. She wanted a commitment, a partner and lover, not to be someone's weekend love toy.

*

"Thing is," exhorted Charlie Preston across the bar to his buddies, "who hasn't dreamt of getting rid of the wife at least once in his life? They can't arrest us for thinking. Shit, think about it. They never have enough of this, never enough of that. They need money for this, money for that. They don't like staying home so they get little jobs and then complain about having to keep the frigging house clean. Their clothes are never good enough, we never take them out. And no goddamn wonder. Once that frigging white dress comes off nothing else ever fits right, and the goddamn kids. Not that I don't care about them, but shit, what is it now, one-eighty, two-hundred K before we can kick the little fuckers out and not have them slipping back in to suck us dry." He downed his beer. "Tell you the truth; I'll be working till I'm a goddamn hundred. It makes a man think. Shit does it make me think."

"Only ever hit the wife once," the second man volunteered, "after she smacked me for whatever I said at the time. Sort of like her tits for tat. She hit me, so I hit her." He paused to moisten his throat. "Okay, so maybe a little harder, oops." He grinned. "It doesn't mean I don't love her. Fact is, a guy has to do what a guy has to do and I had to make a point. It was a lesson learned and she's been good ever since. Anyway, it was years ago. It's water under the bridge. It's like anything else. Do it right the first time and forget about it."

"Women don't ever forget that kind of shit," a third man answered. "They might act like they do, believe me they don't."

"So what, as long as it gets the job done. Now we get along fine, man and wife."

"You think so. I'm telling you, they never forget. The biggest problem isn't getting so pissed off that you have to smack them around a little. The biggest problem is getting married in the first place for the sake of a little tail," the third man shook his head, curving his mouth into a mocking grin, "the same tail, year after year after year. Me, I spend a couple of extra bucks when I'm away from the office and get serviced the right way: always a different menu du jour, different flavours, and sometimes a double serving if you catch my drift. I've been doing it that way for twenty years with nothing older than mid-twenties and never the same one twice. They go home, I go to sleep and come home to a …"

"To a dry weekend and a sore hand," the fourth man cut

in. "My brother-in-law, big Italian shit, he told me once if I ever hurt his little sister he'd kill me and, I tell you, he fucking meant it. The guy's a fucking lunatic, but it was too late to back out. I'd already done her fifty different ways and he would have killed me for bagging her. So what the fuck, what can I say? I adapted. The funny thing is, now she's bigger than me."

"Always check out the mother first," the third man continued. "It's like looking into the future. They all look great when their young, but shit does everything fall fast, some faster than others," he paused, "and there's nothing dry about my weekend. My neighbour works weekends." He chortled and leaned back, loosening his belt. "I've been doing his wife for the past four years. Saturdays and Sundays like clockwork on the patio, in the rain, in the park, on my car, in the snow, in the pool. The broad's a nymphomaniac, pure and simple, with no lovey-dovey shit, no flowers, and no candy, just hot and heavy good times. No holds barred. I caught a glimpse of her sunning her naked buns one Saturday, then again on the Sunday. I must have taken a hundred close-ups of her. The next week it was the same thing, buck-ass naked."

"So, what, you jumped the fence and asked her for some, just like that?" asked the fourth man, not believing a word.

"No, I needed a reason. I damn near ran to the liquor store, bought a two-four of coolers, and carried them over, just like that. I got my breath under control, walked straight through her gate, and stood there. All she did was drag a hand towel part way over her bare ass and say 'thanks, are they cold?' I said I was sorry and looked away. Told her I didn't expect to see her... that I only wanted to welcome them to the neighbourhood. I put down the coolers, then the next thing I know she's standing right beside me covering her titties and not much else with her towel and she's popping two of them open. I spent the afternoon. Then she was twenty-five, hubby was twenty-six. Now she's twenty-nine, as tight as ever, and hasn't talked about divorce once. She loves the dumb-ass. She just can't get enough. True story, guys, and I've got the photos to prove it. Something else she likes. I could start my own frigging porno site."

"He knows," the second man offered. "The guy knows."

"He doesn't know shit."

"Yeah, he does, and he probably gets off hearing about it."

"I don't get that lucky in my dreams and tonight's going to be a bitch when I get home." They all laughed and Charlie Preston took a large swallow of his beer." I gave mine a good one last night, thought I broke her goddamn jaw. Never thought I would. Shit. It happened before I could stop myself, a knee-jerk reaction to all her bullshit. You wouldn't believe the goddamn noise she made." He took his hand away from his mug and opened it towards them. "The damn thing still smarts."

"No, shit," the fourth man said. "It's crossed my mind a few times, got to admit. The one thing stopping me is her freaking brother."

"First time?" the second one asked.

"Yeah, first time," Charles Preston answered. "Before it was pretty much showing her the back of my hand and letting her know not to push it. This time she pushed. Guess I always knew it would happen one day."

"What she do to piss you off?"

"Found her going through my suitcase, smelling my goddamn clothes if you can believe that shit. Somehow she found out about my last trip and she wouldn't shut up about it. I told her I couldn't even remember the broad's name, that she was a fluky one-time piece of pussy, a one-time thing. She wouldn't shut up about it. I swore it was the first time. She just kept on and on, throwing anything she could grab. It was like a frigging hurricane." The foursome laughed into their beers. "Then she started with the kids, telling them she wanted them out. I had them on the phone for an hour yelling into my ear. Jesus. She can't even take care of her own goddamn kids."

"Walk out," the third man suggested, countered by the second.

"No way, don't do it. You'd lose your shirt. I knew a guy once who thought he could walk. He walked straight from riches to rags in a matter of months. He ended up on the street and got kicked to death one night over a frigging park bench. The wife didn't even go to the funeral. What kind of woman doesn't go to her husband's fucking funeral? My advice: don't leave. Stick it out. It could be a lot worse. They got laws about abandonment shit these days. It's all about them and who's to say your kids wouldn't plaster your face all over the net. You'd be screwed inside of a month with no job, no house, and no money. Stay with the occasional one-nighter. It's a better ride and it's cheaper."

They drank their beers in unison, each one in another world until Charlie Preston broke the quiet.

"Ever think it would be worth it, ever dream about it?" All three looked at him. "You're right. I should have walked out years ago, before the goddamn kids, but she wanted them. She had to have them, and now she can't wait to get rid of them. Shit, I want out so bad I can taste it. She never shuts up. Sometimes I see her dead in my dreams, just gone. Thing is, I always wake up." He chuckled. "Life is pure shit, guys." He shook his head, snapping his fingers for another round. "Could be it's time to stop dreaming about it. With a good lawyer I'd be out in eight to ten with a million or more in insurance. Shit, compounded, it could be as high as one-five."

The three-man audience nodded their heads in agreement. They had to, they were men and none of them thought Charlie was serious as the clock struck midnight. In the darker months, Sunday was their hockey night at the local arena when ice time was cheap. During the warmer months they had played their hands at poker at the same cheap hotel for the past six years. Sunday was the perfect day of the week with a rotating bar tab.

None of the four spoke with the others during the week and over the years Sunday evenings had become sacrosanct. Rare absenteeism derived from vacations or Christmas and New Years. They were sales reps, all travelled extensively, all were late forties, and all were immune to the rigors of late hours and hard liquor. They were overweight and balding, none as much as Charlie, they all hated their jobs, and each of them knew change for the better would never happen. Each one worked for food, clothes, extended mortgages, for Christmas, birthdays, and college. None worked for satisfaction or for light at the end of the tunnel. There was none.

Their lives were cul-de-sacs with no room to manoeuvre. They were trapped and they knew it. Their sole escape was Sunday evening when, for a few hours, they could forget for a few precious hours. However, this Sunday in particular, Charlie needed to erase the worst week he could remember and was ready for that habitual one drink too many.

For the others the time had come to once again face their personal ruts. Not because they were drunk. Municipal budgets restricted roadblocks to Fridays and Saturdays and the foursome seldom appeared to have exceeded the limit. Most times their biological clocks kicked in with Swiss precision when other corporeal and cerebral mechanisms began to malfunction. Yet for Charlie the night was still young. Simply put: he didn't want to go home to her. He wasn't afraid. He was fed up. He knew what was waiting for him. By now the kids would know, the sister-in-law, and God knows who else. The argument hadn't been his fault and what ensued was an involuntarily reaction to pent-up frustration. Screw conjugal violence, he thought. What about all the bullshit he had put up with all those years. He knew he hadn't hit her very hard, that had been for the sake of male bravado, for the benefit of the guys. At least he had managed to shut her up. If only she hadn't over-reacted.

He should have walked away years earlier. He had been right about that much at least, thinking back to a better time when life had all been about image, about keeping up with the Jones, and getting married. Everyone got married. They got laid first, then they got married, and the need to be first didn't stop there. The race continued for the first kid, the best car, the biggest house and what they thought was the passionate love-making of youth soon became an infrequent and inconvenient responsibility of middle age.

Now all he wanted was out. He wanted the Caribbean, a yacht, a red convertible and the blow-your-mind blonde halfway down the bar. He felt their slaps on his back and chortled into his fresh beer. No, he assured his departing friends, he wouldn't be killing his wife anytime soon. Anyway, where was the gain? He'd do the time and the kids would walk away with the insurance. So what was the point?

Alone, he eyed the blonde. She was whispering into her cell phone and looking into the mirror in front of her that was behind an uneven row of half-empty bottles along the bar. He wondered with whom. The hour was late, too late to call a husband from a bar. She had come in an hour earlier with another woman who had left abruptly without finishing her drink.

At first he thought flight attendant or nurse, though not the way she was dressed. He had seen similar clothes in high-end fashion magazines and was quite certain what she would be wearing underneath her skirt. He didn't have to imagine, he could see her bra. He fantasized anyway. He knew exactly how she would look without the short skirt and blazer. She was all leg, small on top, and probably knew she had a killer ass. She was thirty, tops, and light years away from where he was sitting. He wouldn't spend for clothes in a year what she would have paid for that one outfit. Anyone wanting to do her would do so in their dreams and need an executive's expense account and a five-star hotel room. She was big time. He wasn't.

He filled his lungs slowly and blew the air loudly from his mouth, the way people do when their vital organs seem to constrict with anxiety and when any combination of clumsy words seem pedestrian and trite. She looked at him and smiled as she snapped her cell phone shut. He smiled back thinly and drank more of his beer. The barman freshened her drink and halted as he went to place the glass in front of her, not quite believing what the young woman had said to him.

The barman knew Charlie well and placed the woman's drink by his stein with a wink and a sly grin, still disbelieving Charlie's good fortune. Charlie's friends had chosen a propitious moment to leave. She was walking towards him. Shit. His cheeks flushed instantly and his throat dried. He wanted to run a hand through his hair, stopping himself, thinking he would draw attention to his receding hairline and patches of grey.

She was gorgeous; the drop-dead kind of gorgeous most men would willingly give their lives for, if only in their dreams. She was really hot. Her hair was thick and more golden than blonde. He let his mind wander. Women like her had pride in themselves. Her jacket was intended to show her embroidered bra. The affect was exotic, the French way, and he looked for as long as he dared at the swell of her breasts.

He knew she wore a matching thong, which he imagined was sheer and alluring. He undressed her, seeing an unblemished nude as she walked towards him. His wife wore cotton briefs, knee-highs, and needed a steel-reinforced brassiere to keep her breasts from swaying recklessly under his company's monogrammed polo shirts or fleeces. This one was shapely and five-ten. His wife was five-six and he seldom saw her shape, knowing her size was double-digit was enough for him.

The woman's mouth opened in a wide smile as she came nearer, the sharp clicking of her heels resonating against the tiled floor.

"Now how stupid would it be for me to sit over there and for you to sit here? You wondering about me, what I'm doing in a place like this, and me trying not to look at you so as not to give you a false impression."

Charlie chuckled. "I was sort of wondering why you came in here so late."

"I'm a corporate lawyer. I put in a ninety-hour week a few blocks from here and most times that means weekends. Usually I go somewhere on Fridays to find some balance." She laughed. "This week, I seem to need a little bit more. The lady I came in with is my partner. She had to get home. Mind if I sit?"

He fought the urge to look down. He wanted to see her legs, her thighs. He wanted to see all of her. He knew he should have stood, at least stepped from the stool. He didn't. He was five-nine and the barstool helped to eradicate the perceived imperfection. Instead, he pulled back the one beside him and waited. "Not at all, and whatever you're drinking, it's on me."

"Thanks, I'll buy my own. That way I won't feel bad when I go home alone tonight. It's nice to talk with people, though. Don't you think so? Sometimes we get a little caught up in ourselves." She climbed onto the barstool without adjusting the hem of her skirt and Charlie swivelled in his seat to face her. He did look down, not disappointed. "So, what is a nice guy like you doing in a place like this on a Sunday night?"

"I met up with some guys from my graduating class. I haven't seen them for years. We got together for a few beers and some guy talk."

"I should do more of that. All work and no play isn't good for us girls." She sipped her drink. "I am curious though."

"Curious about what?" he responded.

"About what you said earlier to your bar buddies, about your wife." Charlie furrowed his brow. It was the last thing he would have expected her to say. Why would she care about his wife? "About getting rid of her," she added.

"You heard that?" She nodded, her expression taking him as much by surprise as her sitting there talking with him. She was being flirtatious and condescending, conveying a message he was at odds to fathom. "I'm sorry you overhead. Really, I am. It was all guy talk. I didn't mean any of it. It's been a very bad week and sometimes people say stupid things. I'm not like that. I wouldn't hurt a fly."

"I know. I can tell. You don't have to explain. Believe me, I'm a good judge of character. I recognize ego-centric and domineering male assholes when I see them." She shook her head. "I don't see you that way and it does get lonely always being out of town. I empathize with you. I know exactly what you go through."

"Thanks, though it sounds strange coming from a woman."

"Having said that, you were wrong about the eight-to-ten time frame. You would be sentenced to more like fifteen to twenty and, talking about assholes, your first few months in prison would not be very pleasant. So you'd be better off forgetting your dream and taking your friend's advice about one-nighters." She swirled the crushed ice in her glass and sipped her Ultimat through the straw. "What's your name?"

"Charlie."

She laughed. "Listen, I'm strictly corporate, nothing to do with the criminal mind unless it's wrapped in a white collar. Now, what's your real name?"

"Charlie, Charles Preston, my final answer."

106

They spoke for another hour. She knew what he was thinking. He wanted her in bed and, despite the fact that was the reason she had joined him, the thought made her noxious. He knew she was leading the conversation. He didn't care. She was sitting with him, which was enough for him and all she needed to know was Charles Preston was not going home to his wife for a little while longer.

At 1:45she pushed away her empty glass. "Charles, you're a nice guy and it's been fun. However, 6:00 AM comes early for some of us. I'm not a pro at this late night drinking thing."

"It has been fun. I hope I'll see you again."

Her eyes caught the light and seemed to sparkle. "You will see me again, Charles. Count on it."

"You never told me your name."

"You never asked me."

Her retort was glib. He acquiesced.

"I was intrigued. What can I say? I'm sorry. I never thought you would stay this long. So, how do I remember you? How do I call you next time I see you?"

She slid from the barstool, letting her pleated skirt ride before she turned to face him. She knew men. She could see in his eyes that Charles Preston wanted to see her naked and had she met him on Friday or Saturday she would have stayed later. She had him. She paid her bill with a fifty and waved away the barman. She smiled at Charles with her mouth, not with her eyes, though he didn't notice. Her breasts were too compelling.

"Goodnight, Charles."

"You're stunning. I'd be remiss not to say so. And, please, tell me your name."

"Thank you for the company, Charles. You're certainly good at making a lady feel good about herself. I think I'll have to try this Sunday thing again, perhaps even here, next week, although nowhere near this late. A girl needs her beauty sleep."

He grinned, stupidly, wanting to appear nonchalant. "You mean I should dump my friends?"

Without warning his face flushed, his eyes twitched, and his brow creased for the briefest instant. He wondered if she had recognized the faux-pas. His mind raced erratically, searching for words too deeply suppressed by the late hour and beer. Her expression had not changed, she had not noticed, he was still good to go.

"I mean I enjoyed this part of my evening," she said.

"So did I. Sometimes I'm alone for supper on Sunday. Maybe I'll eat here next week. The food's pretty good."

The young woman smiled coquettishly. She did know men, men had become her speciality. "Goodnight, Charles."

"Let me walk you to your car," he tried.

"I don't drive in the city. I take taxis."

"No, not so soon," he seemed to plead. "You haven't told me your name?"

She smiled, blowing him a playful kiss. "My name is Pearl," she whispered. "Don't forget me, Charles. I won't be forgetting you."

She was amazing with deep blue eyes, voluptuous red lips, a perfectly tanned complexion, and breasts that were taunting and inviting. He watched her saunter to the doors without looking back, letting her disappear onto the sidewalk before exchanging quizzical glances and a thumbs-up with the bartender.
*

Miranda Stevens had never been to the bar in her life. Her legal career kept her busy beyond the normal nine-to-five of most career women and she hadn't been clubbing in years, let alone barhopping. Outside she checked her voice-mail, smiling contentedly, pleased her intuition about the married woman's expectations had been right and that she had suggested a drink.

The urgent case study she had in cryptic Pearl-speak soon after her date had left the bar had been conditionally approved. The proposed facilitation had met the most important criterion: Preston had beaten his wife and had said he wanted to kill her. The nightcap had been intended as a convenient way to end a disastrous evening and would now serve to save a woman's life. What more could she ask?

What Miranda Stevens did not already know about Charles Preston she would before their second and final meeting one week later and she was anxious for the moment, dispelling him from her mind as she walked back to the restaurant and climbed into her waiting Vantage, hoping in the meantime that Preston would not harm his wife.

Eleven

Montreal, Quebec
Monday, August 06

Rick Kendall opened one eye, then the other. He pressed his head into his pillow and coughed hard several times. He wiped his nose and eyes with the pillow case and reached for the fresh beer to wash away the acrid taste of stale beer and whisky. He let the empty bottle fall from his hands, cursing aloud. It was as though she continually went out of her way to irritate him. She knew he enjoyed a morning beer, a stimulant for the long day ahead, and this wasn't the first time he had awakened to an empty bottle. He yelled out her name and coughed again into his pillow.

There was no need to look over his shoulder or to reach out for her. She wasn't there. She never was following another ruined evening. She would be in the kitchen, staring at the floor, making him feel guilty, or in the kid's room coo-cooing over her precious Brianna or pouting. He hated her pouting the most. He looked at the alarm clock and kicked away the sheet, still half-dressed. He would be late for work, again, her fault, and how would he explain that to his shithead boss, again. She knew Mondays were the worst for him. When would her carelessness ever end, he muttered? When would she ever learn? This time her name resonated throughout his house as he stormed down the hall into the kitchen.

Alicia's birthday cake lay inverted and crushed on the floor and Kendall kicked it away. He slammed the fridge door violently, making it bounce open and he slammed it again and again. He swallowed several gulps of the cold beer, wiping his mouth dry and taking a deep breath to calm himself before walking to their daughter's room. He felt his rage intensify at the mere thought of seeing his wife standing with slumped shoulders and looking so impassive, as though she had done nothing wrong. Bitch. That's what she was: a goddamned selfish bitch who never thought of anyone but herself and the kid.

She wasn't there, neither was the girl. He screamed out her name in a howl and hurled the bottle into the wall. The clock read 8:30 on a rainy Monday morning and his leg hurt like hell. The pain was always with him and unbearable on wet or humid days, not that she had ever fucking cared, he screamed into the empty house. He knew that much about the selfish bitch. He wasn't even a real soldier. That's what she said the day he came back to her, crippled. He was a mechanic, not a soldier. He should never have enlisted. He should never have gone to fight. He could have been killed, and then what, she cried as though being wounded had been his fault and now all he could do was spend his days changing filters and banging dented rims back into shape.

He looked down at the ragged scarring on his leg. He was twenty-nine and would walk with a limp for the rest of his life. He hadn't held a job for longer than a year since his discharge and he was running out of options. He had signed up for an education and a future. He had signed up to make something of himself, to carry an assault rifle, kick down doors and get the job done. Now he couldn't kick a balloon. He had signed up for action, to be a sniper or Special Services. Then what? Then they had shipped him out as a mechanic to get shot up by a brain-dead twelve-year-old in rags with an AK-47. He had been discharged after less than a month of scorching desert heat. No one wanted a crippled

111

soldier, not even her. He could see what she was thinking each time he looked into her eyes, each time he looked at her, from the moment he looked up at her from the stretcher.

That was four years ago. Four years of constant nagging, four years of never feeling good enough, four years of never being good enough. He went to the kitchen and poured a double shot of whisky before calling in sick. He'd be waiting when she got back from wherever. This time there would be no excuse, no pouting. This time she had gone too far. He would teach her for once and for all. It was his goddamn right.

At 9:00 AM the doorbell rang and for the first time he saw the chef's knife Alicia had tossed on the carpet by the door. He reached for it, cursing. Rick Kendall would never see his wife or daughter again.

Twelve

Montreal, Quebec
Monday, August 06

The night duty nurse had seen the hurt and the suffering so many times before. Each time another broken soul came into emergency she prayed there would not be another, yet week after week the violence and the hurt continued. However, this victim was different. This young woman wanted help and Nurse Murielle Laplante would make certain she was not forgotten. She encircled the young woman with her arms, careful not to hurt her, and when she went to let go Alicia hugged her all the harder.

When at last she was able to extricate herself Nurse Laplante went to the nurse's lounge with the Kendall file to make a call from her cell phone with complete confidence at a few moments past midnight. Her reputation spoke for itself. Murielle Laplante had never been wrong about someone in need. The case study had been approved with no more criterion than her past success. When she was done she called the police who arrived thirty minutes later.

Alicia had come back from radiology moments before the detectives walked into the examination room. They were SVU. The woman was soft-spoken, her first words were convincing and compelling as she took Alicia's limp hands and sat beside the distraught young victim. Her partner's face creased, showing his disgust. Right then he wanted

113

nothing more than a few minutes alone with the guy who had abused her so brutally. He had a daughter Alicia's age and he became more livid as Alicia spent the next hour recounting details of the years she spent in hell.

When Alicia had finished she told them about the Browning pistol and the knife she had taken from the drawer. She remained calm and composed when they told her Rick would be arrested within a few hours. He would be spending three or four days in custody before being arraigned and, as a first time offender, he would likely get off with a temporary restraining order while undergoing mandatory counselling.

When she told the detectives without feeling that her husband would refuse counselling and would not stay away, the detectives answered that he would then be arrested and do time for contempt of court. She laughed and asked what arresting him a second time would prove. He wouldn't care about a few days in jail. He would become worse, more determined and more violent when he learned she had pressed charges, she told them. She asked how much time she had and when they asked her for what she answered: to run... and to hide.

They left the hospital room assuring Alicia she would be safe if she wished to return home any time after noon with her daughter. Kendall would be in custody at least until Thursday and she would be notified of any change to his detention. Nurse Murielle Laplante stayed beyond her regular shift. She gave Alicia a tight hug and told her not to worry. She wanted to assure the young woman that the police would help, that things would work out, and that people cared about her. She couldn't. To do so would have been a direct violation of the covenants.

Alicia left the hospital at 10:00 with her daughter, not believing in anything or anyone. She had bathed at the hospital and had left wearing the same clothes she hated so much.

Alicia had always put most of her paycheque into the joint account when she had been working, but Rick Kendall had never known about her savings account. By mid-afternoon Alicia's black hair had been cut short and was auburn, she and her daughter had new clothing, new suitcases, and the joint bank account had been emptied. Even though the street was quiet she told the taxi driver to stop several houses from the address she had given him. The soon-to-be Alicia Stone would not let herself feel safe for a very long time.

The police had been sincere, though Alicia knew they would always arrive after the fact, and that one day they would be too late to help her, Brianna, or her unborn baby. Kendall would be back for them, soon or later he would show up and he would kill her. She saw her caring neighbours and ignored them, she despised them. They weren't important. She knew they must have heard her the evening before. She would take her best clothes and her best jewellery, which wasn't good at all, and she would take her photo album to sort through, to one day cherish the good memories and expunge the bad.

She had been about to leave when the doorbell chimed. Her heart stopped beating. She called out her daughter's name and ran through the house to find the little girl. The doorbell chimed again. Alicia was frantic, gripped with fear. She hurried to the phone to dial 9-1-1, knowing they wouldn't arrive in time. Her finger had pressed the nine when she heard a woman's voice call her name. The woman tapped the door again and waited until the door opened as far as the chain would allow. Alicia's face was cloaked behind dark glasses.

"I'm a friend, Alicia. I am here to ask for a small part of your afternoon before you begin your new life." She eyed the chain. "However, I would prefer if we could speak inside."

"Who are you?"

"I am a friend who is able to help you, who can make you safe. Please, undo the lock."

Alicia closed the door, undid the chain, and stepped back. "I don't know you."

"Friends have sent me, Alicia. I assure you, there is no immediate need for concern. We have time. We have as much time as we need to talk." The woman looked down at the little girl. "Hello, Brianna. I am so glad I can be with you and your mommy this morning. You look so pretty, so much like my little girl. She's going to be six and she's so excited about starting school." Then she looked at Alicia.

"Who are you?"

Alicia stepped back to study the woman. She could have been anywhere between thirty and forty. She was so attractive, her skin was flawlessly smooth and her brown eyes sparkled. She spoke like a lady, wore a hat and gloves, and carried a big shopping bag from a store Alicia could never dream of visiting. She was lovely. Her purse was made from real leather and her shoes were so stylish. Alicia knew she would never own a pair as fine and suddenly she wanted to cry.

She knew then she wanted so much to look like the woman, to look like a real lady, to be pretty and sophisticated like the lady, something she knew she would never be. Her eyes glazed over and without warning the woman reached out and touched Alicia's shoulder. Noelle Barton knew everything pertinent about Alicia Kendall of 82, chemin des Bois-Francs. She had studied the urgently transmitted dossier while waiting in her car from the moment Alicia had left the hospital: She was twenty-seven and English, her French was a street dialect known as joual, she had no job and no known aspirations. Her husband had no insurance worth mentioning and she was to be enabled pro bono. Alicia Kendall's lucky day had come. The nurse had been right. People did care. Noelle Barton most of all.

Noelle let Alicia serve them coffee, in fact she had

asked for one. In the meantime she had ingratiated herself with little Brianna by way of a plush teddy bear not much smaller than the girl. When the coffee was served the little girl was in another world where all creatures great and small were cuddly, soft, and warm. That hadn't been Alicia's world for a very long time. She looked at the bear and wondered how much the lady must have paid. She wanted to tell the lady to take back the stuffed toy. Then she looked at her daughter.

"Why are you here? You don't look like the others, or like the police."

"I'm not with the police. I'm a friend and I have been sent by others who are also your friends. We're going to help you leave him." Noelle Barton looked across to the suitcases by the door. "We're going to make certain he doesn't find you and that he doesn't hurt you. You cannot run, Alicia, not these days. Although with a little help you can walk away and never look back. You can walk away and never be afraid."

Alicia looked around her small home. The furniture was all second hand, none of the curtains matched and one of the lamps was missing a shade. The television was missing a knob and the carpet was threadbare.

"Do you have a home, a nice home?"

"Yes, I do."

"And your daughter has nice clothes like yours?"

The woman smiled sympathetically. "Yes, she does. She's very fortunate, so am I."

"This is all I know. It's all my daughter knows." She shrugged. "I want more for her. I looked in the mirror when I got home and knew he was right. He called me stupid while he was hitting me, and he was right. I was stupid. I don't want to be stupid anymore. I want a nice home, with nice furniture, and when I look in the mirror I don't want to look like this anymore. It hurts."

"It's going to happen for you, Alicia, everything. You're

twenty-seven. You're young. The bruises will fade and, very soon, so will the hurt. There's time," Noelle looked down at Alicia's stomach, "for all the three of you."

"I hope what you're saying is true. I used to be pretty. I don't think I ever will be again because of him. We've been together since high school. I never knew anyone else. He should have been a year ahead of me, but he never studied, and when he failed a second time he dropped out to learn a trade. After graduation I got a pretty good job in a music store and Rick got his certificate to be a general mechanic. My family never liked him and it was difficult for us until I was eighteen. There was always arguing at home, mostly about him."

"Did he let you see other friends, other boys?"

"No, and I never wanted to. He was a bad boy," she smiled, "and at the time I liked it. He was different from the other boys who were all too immature. Rick was already working and acting like a real man. Staying together seemed like the obvious thing to do at the time."

"Did he beat you back then?" Noelle asked.

"No, never, and for the next four years our life was wonderful. We moved in together. I put something away each month for our wedding and Rick did the same for the honeymoon and his dream car, but when the big day arrived we didn't have enough to pay for everything. We were both so disappointed." Alicia let her mind drift into the past. "There was no exotic trip to an all-inclusive and his new car had already been someone else's for five years. He did let me have my dress." Her weak attempt to chuckle sounded more like a whimper. "I can still remember how much I loved putting it on and how much I hated taking it off. I looked like a princess, like you, with only twelve more payments. At the time I didn't think anything about it. We went home after going to a restaurant..."

"With your families?" Noelle prompted, sipping her coffee.

"No, they didn't come. We pretty much went by ourselves. Rick invited some guy from the garage to be his best man and I invited a girlfriend from the store. We don't see them anymore."

"Because of him?"

"I suppose that's part of it. We don't go out very much, not since the army accident. I go to church once in a while, for Brianna. Everyone likes her, but I know they talk about us. I can tell. Sometimes they ask us to lunch…"

"The money thing?" she asked. Alicia frowned and Noelle smiled. "Don't worry about money. Your circumstances will change very soon." She sipped her coffee. "Is that when things started to go bad, after he was wounded?"

"Yeah, I guess." Alicia paused. "Yes. After the wedding the first eighteen months were okay, until Rick lost his job at the garage and no one wanted to hire him. We had no savings and his unemployment cheques didn't make up the difference between what I brought home and what we needed to live. We started looking for cheaper places to live without much luck. They were all pretty slummy looking, worse than this place, and six months after Rick lost his job he went to a recruitment centre without telling me."

"And he got in."

"Yeah, he got in. I begged him to go back, to tell them he had made a terrible mistake. He refused. He said enlisting was his chance of a lifetime to finish his education and do better for himself, maybe even get a job at one of the big three dealerships when he got out. We argued for a week."

"And he started beating you?" Noelle asked.

"No, the beatings came a little bit later. He looked good in his uniform. It suited him, though I always thought he was prouder of the way he looked than of the uniform itself. He always liked doing physical things and he always liked people looking at him like he was different. Then he'd complain about them staring. The good thing is we didn't have to move. His training was local, he came home most weekends. I remember how he loved the training, especially the guns. When he signed up he told them he wanted to train as a sniper. It never happened. Then he signed up for active combat, I think because he wanted to look good for me. They refused him. I remember the night he came home to tell me. He was furious. He wasn't going to see combat. They were sending him over as a mechanic. He would have a weapon, some sort of regular rifle for self-defence. He went on about it all night." Alicia looked at Noelle. "He wanted to wear a real gun, like they do on television. He wanted to kick down doors. He said he wanted to feel the rush, you know, adrenalin." She sighed. "Less than a month later he was back home."

"WIA," Noelle said, already knowing the answer "was he wounded in action?"

"I guess. He was wounded by a stray bullet from a young boy. They told me he was coming home. I met him at the base. I couldn't believe it. He looked so different lying on the stretcher. He wasn't a bad boy anymore, just an angry man. He started yelling, really loud. I wanted to look good for him so I wore new patent leather shoes," she looked down, "not expensive ones like yours, and my favourite short dress which really wasn't new. To tell the truth, it's old. I wore it because he always liked it. When I went to kiss him he turned his head." She shrugged. "I started crying. He was so angry. I even remember the horrible words he used."

Alicia was quivering. Noelle Barton hugged her close and asked whether there was anything stronger in the house. She stood to go into the kitchen and came back with two glasses of cheap brandy. She sat and put an arm around Alicia's shoulder to comfort her, taking the young woman's hands in her own.

"Take your time, Alicia."

"What an unusual ring," Alicia remarked.

"Thank you. It was a gift from Mother," the woman answered, "after my husband was killed. I have another like it."

"I'm sorry... about your husband."

"Don't be. His death was my freedom day. When I heard the news I cried, although not for him. I cried for the happiness that lay ahead of me. I wasted no tears on the past. His death was a godsend."

"He beat you?"

"Yes, he did. I barely survived the last one."

"But you're so beautiful."

"I don't think of myself as beautiful. Thank you. It took a while, and a surgery. When they asked me at the clinic how I wanted to look, I said like myself, and I gave them a photograph of how I looked before the beatings began."

"I'm sorry."

"Don't be. I'm remarried and have a wonderful life."

"Do you see her very often, your mom?"

"No, I don't, not very often. She's very old. Now, tell me. What is it he said to you? What did he say to you from the stretcher?"

Alicia hesitated, nodding when she felt the reassuring squeeze.

"He said: "They almost fucking killed me, they made me a fucking cripple, and you're wearing a fucking party dress." Alicia burst into tears, convulsing. "All I could do was look at him. I couldn't believe he could say such a thing. Even the men carrying him looked away. I guess they didn't care."

"They couldn't exactly drop him, Alicia. I'm sure they did care in their own way."

"It was the first time he ever slapped me, when we got home. I thought I would feel the pain forever, it hurt so much. I was three months pregnant with Brianna. A month later he was a civilian again and he began rehabilitation."

She shrugged. "He never finished. He started drinking instead. Since then he's had trouble holding down a job, he controls the money, the spending, and pretty much me. I could never buy new clothes and we could never plan a vacation. He never wanted neighbours in the house and he never let me spend even a little on a new hairstyle or make-up. It's been hard, especially since I lost my job. I was terrified to come home. I knew what would happen. I knew this time what happened was my fault. I should have quit months ago, on my own. I don't know why I waited so long. Now I'm pregnant again. That's why, when it happened last night, I knew I would have to run. I stood by his side of the bed, praying he wouldn't open his eyes. I took the clothes I needed and then I woke Brianna. I made her warm and went to the front door in bare feet so he wouldn't hear me. Before leaving I dropped the knife on the floor. I ran to the corner and kept running until I saw a taxi that brought me to the hospital. I've never been so afraid. The driver was nice. He knew exactly where to go and when I went to pay him he smiled and walked away. He looked sad, like he was sorry for me. The nurse was very nice to me also, so were the police."

"This is the beginning of something new, Alicia, something good. Do you have anywhere to stay for the next few weeks, perhaps with your family?"

"No, we're not close. We haven't spoken for a very long time and I don't have any real friends."

"And your current resources are somewhat low. I believe your current balance is twelve hundred in the bank and five thousand available on your card."

"How could you know that?"

"As I said at the door, Alicia, there are people who care about you. I'm one of them."

"I withdrew all the money this morning, to buy some new clothes and the bags." She put a hand to her hair and tried to smile, her exhaustion showing. "Do you like it?

Brianna had hers done as well, for the first time ever."

"You are very pretty, Alicia, and Brianna is delightful. Your lives are going to get better, starting right now." Noelle held Alicia's hand once again. "I'm afraid my time has come to leave you. May I ask where you do intend to stay?"

Alicia hesitated.

"Alicia would you like me to recite your mother's name, your father's, your SS number or the one on your driver's permit? Our research is very complete, Alicia. Please tell me where you intend to stay?"

"The east coast, Peggy's Cove, where I used to go with my parents on vacation. It's nice. Brianna's going to like the ocean. I haven't given her very much so far. It's time."

"That's wonderful. I love the coast. Now, listen to me very carefully. Travel by bus and pay cash for your fares and your hotel rooms until you arrive. You'll be more difficult to track. Keep your ticket stubs and receipts. Once you arrive use your credit card for the hotel and use what is left of your money for food and incidentals for as long as it lasts. Stay in one that has a good restaurant and spoil yourself. Eat in the restaurant each night until you know you're safe to come back. Do you understand me?"

"No, I don't, not at all. He'll never find me. I'll keep running, for as long as I have to. The money won't last forever, but I'll find work somewhere. I'm not stupid."

"No, you are not, and the money will last long enough, Alicia. Don't worry about money. Money is the least of your worries and please do remember what I said about running. You cannot run. What you can do is walk away. It's not as easy to disappear as so many people believe, not these days, Miss Stone. You do intend to use your maiden name, do you not?"

Alicia was struggling to maintain her sanity. The woman was so kind and her calm voice with its soft accent was so comforting. She felt defenceless. If a complete stranger knew so much about her, what chance did she have? "Yes."

"Do as I have asked you the moment I leave here. Use cash until you arrive. Then pay by credit card. You will understand when the time comes. You're smart. Soon this will all make sense to you. You will be fine, Alicia, the three of you. I promise you. Three or four days after you come back you will find an envelope in your mailbox. Check each morning. Don't forget. It's very important for you to do so."

"For what?"

"It will be little something to get you by, a gift, something for a rainy day or to begin a new life. Buy Brianna something special. Buy something special for Alicia Stone and do not, under any circumstances, deposit the money into a bank." She paused, letting Alicia absorb what she had said. "I've enjoyed meeting you and your little girl. We won't see one another again, Alicia. That doesn't mean we will forget you. We never forget our friends."

"Thank you for the teddy bear ..."

Noelle laughed quietly. "What is in a name, Alicia? Years from now you will remember my visit, the bear, and this. You won't remember my name." The woman leaned to one side and brought a small box wrapped in midnight blue foil and Mediterranean blue ribbons from her purse. "May I give you something very special and very personal, Alicia, something for you to remember me by?"

Alicia stared at the box until Noelle Barton had to prompt her to take it. Inside was a smaller black and silver box and Alicia couldn't stifle her loud gasp when she opened it. "It's so perfect. It's like yours. You said your mother gave it to you years ago."

"No Alicia. I said 'it was a gift from Mother.' And yes, it was years ago."

"It looks so perfect, and so expensive. I can't."

"It's yours. It's a black pearl and, yes… quite rare. More importantly it comes from our hearts and you are worth every penny." Noelle stood.

Alicia felt awkward. She had no way to thank the woman. She sat with her head down, awestruck by the ring.

"Goodbye, Alicia. I won't wish you good luck. That's already begun. I know you don't believe me right now, but you will soon see I am right and do not forget the mailbox."

"I won't forget. I promise. I'm going back to school. It's time for me to stop being stupid."

"I'm glad, and I'll be telling all your friends." Noelle leaned forward, saying goodbye to Brianna and the bear. "Alicia, may I ask one small favour of you before I leave?" The young woman nodded eagerly and stood. "Would you give me a big hug, a tight one? It would make me feel so good."

Alicia slid into Noelle's open arms. Murielle Laplante had told Pearl on the phone how Alicia had not wanted to let her go.

Thirteen

Montreal, Quebec
Monday, August 06

That morning Rick Kendall hurled himself toward the front door. His eyes were wide with fury and his face was still purple with rage. Within seconds his head was pinned to the floor of the front porch and his hands were clamped together behind his back. Two uniformed officers jerked him to his feet, escorting him into the house where they threw him onto the couch as the detectives who'd been with Alicia at the hospital followed and began a thorough search of the rooms.

When he saw them again they looked pleased, one of them holding the Browning. The man did the initial questioning while his partner photographed Kendall's face and hands. She swabbed the kitchen wall, photographed the blood stain, the splattered cake and the knife which Alicia Kendall claimed she'd thrown onto the carpet. When she was done she worked the blade from the wall with a gloved hand and sealed the knife in a bag as her partner stayed with Kendall who was handcuffed and seething, mocking them and telling them his wife couldn't stay away forever. At some point she would come home and learn to do what she was told.

They read him his rights, advising him to shut his mouth, and when he didn't the detective's foot inadvertently made contact with Kendall's wounded leg. They'd seen Alicia at the hospital. What else had to be said? Though she was right, they conceded. He wouldn't stay away. He'd be more determined. Alicia Kendall was a woman in jeopardy. She would have to run.

The cops took twenty minutes to search the home and drag Kendall to his bedroom, ignoring him as he finished dressing. When they took from the house he was handcuffed, escorted with purposeful slowness to the squad car where he was left in the backseat as the detectives and uniformed officers talked amongst themselves and curious neighbours lined the street, shaking their heads or peering out from behind windows or doors. Rick Kendall was under arrest, charged with aggravated assault. They read his rights once more, this time with a louder voice, before the squad car drove away with its lights flashing to make a point as the detectives began interviewing eager bystanders. All the cops could do for the moment was make a spectacle of him and wait for the courts to release him.

Fourteen

Toronto, Ontario
Monday, August 06

Alicia Kendall was fortunate. She was young and vital. She still had a future. She could move away, change her name, study, work hard and become somebody. She realized at the hairdresser Monday morning she wasn't a silly young woman dreaming. She'd been formulating a plan, her plan, and the pretty lady who came to her house hadn't laughed at her or looked down at her.

Such was not the case for Ann Preston some three hundred miles to the west. Ann was forty-five and a mother with two boys in college. She worked at home a few hours each day for a telemarketing firm and knew very little else. She was unskilled and unaware.

Her reprieve from a mundane existence came when her husband travelled for business and she could escape into the quixotic world of cheap romance novels. Those nights she could imagine who she wanted to be or forget who and what she was. When he was at home with her she was ignored, for which she blamed herself as much as she did her husband. She was not the woman he married and she didn't care. She was overweight, she was frumpy, and she despised looking into a mirror. She was no longer firm, her skin no longer elastic. She had lost her slim shape and her flat belly that had once excited him and made her so proud years ago was now soft and round.

Her cute and chiselled belly had become a gut, her breasts streaked and sagging monuments to her past, her once tight ass now functional and dented buttocks. She had a slight bit of hair on her chin, a few dark strands protruded from her nipples and she seldom attended to the sparse growth at the back of her legs that were no longer smooth. Why would she? He never paid attention. He was never at home and, when he was, he farted, he scratched everywhere and he belched during every meal.

He was balding, each year at Christmas she bought him a belt one size larger, and what little passion was left in her to give were disgust and resentment. He had transformed from a sleek young lover to an overweight and uncaring husband: a prick. He wasn't even a husband, he hadn't been for years and to Ann he had become less than a man which was worse. Over the years he stopped caring, so had she. She'd gone from short dresses and skirts with sheer blouses to shapeless sweats and Dockers and had not changed her hairstyle in years. She hated him, yet she knew she should hate herself even more for doing nothing to make her life better.

She had been told repeatedly by her mother, her grandmother and her married girlfriends. They hadn't been wrong. Men were pigs. Men wallowed in the comfort of their foul habits, they told her, and she didn't believe them. She'd been in love with the most wonderful man possible. He was gallant and thoughtful, courteous and caring. None of those other women had ever known true love and Ann remembered feeling sorry for them at the time. Now she knew. They were right, though none of them had ever told her she would one day wake up in a hospital.

She had wanted a college degree. She had dreams to fulfill, dreams she shared with him until the kids came along and she succumbed to being his wife and not his lover as he imperceptibly evolved into an ordinary and inattentive man like any other. He was the one who wanted children, insisting Ann stay home. They hadn't been married a year before the first one, the second a year later. Now the boys were twenty-four and twenty-five, she still cooked their meals and their clothes hampers were constantly full. They both worked part-time, they had girlfriends and quite often Ann noticed money was missing from her purse.

She refused to let the girls sleep over. One Friday night in particular, when Charles hadn't yet arrived home, the contention grew to become dangerous as the girls waited at the door with backpacks, smirking as they witnessed one of the boys ending the heated debate by shoving his mother against a wall. Ann had remained adamant. The girls would not stay the night and despite the abuse she went on to say that if they didn't agree with her rules they could pack their belongings immediately and find somewhere else as a convenient bordello.

Charles was furious; arguing that he saw nothing wrong with allowing his sons to entertain in their own home, when Ann knew perfectly well what he meant to say was he saw nothing wrong with seeing whatever he could see of the girls the next morning.

They hadn't been a real family in years. The boys were out constantly, she knew they did drugs and drank, and they were treating her as badly as Charles through neglect and verbal abuse. They constantly yelled at her and called her names. Whenever she approached Charles for support he would answer that she must be exaggerating, and defend them, telling her they were going through a phase that was no big deal. She knew otherwise. They were learning the intolerable behaviour from him and how they acted towards her was a big deal. They weren't boys anymore, they were men being taught by osmosis to act like boys and one day the yelling would escalate into something she was afraid to imagine.

For months Ann had thought of leaving them, of divorcing him and letting him deal with his sons. She desperately wanted to escape, trapped in a home she hated. Their savings were dismal because of the kids and she knew she would incur heavy legal costs. She also knew Charles would sue her for child support, for children who should have left home. She felt entirely lost and defeated.

All she had ever done was sell appliance insurance for a department store. She was trapped. She was unskilled and would have to be retrained, yet she had no idea for what or where to start. She was too old for university, she would never qualify for assistance and she had no real savings of her own. Starting over without him would take money, and money was Charles' domain.

What she did know was that she was overweight, she hadn't danced in years and the last time he thought to buy her flowers she was young and pretty and Charles hadn't begun cheating. He'd cheated for years. At first she had wanted to confront him. Then she had thought better of it. At least she had him, she thought at the time, and she believed that once he got his indiscretions out of his system he would stop. He was charming and debonair, a ladies' man and he always came home. Now she wanted him never to come home.

She had expected him back from his last trip late Friday night, instead he called to explain how a meeting had run into overtime and he'd missed his flight. He would be home sometime Saturday afternoon, he promised, and arrived well after the dinner hour.

The boys were out, Ann had begun preparing dinner and Charles poured a beer he half finished before reaching the bedroom. He heaved his suitcase onto the bed, emptying the bottle before taking a shower. When he came out Ann had been standing over the open suitcase smelling his shirts and checking the collars.

Charles exploded instantly into a furor. They argued for hours: Ann accusing, Charles denying. He had always been faithful, he shouted. He would never think of being unfaithful, of doing such a thing, and searching through a man's luggage after twenty-six years of marriage was unconscionable. Even if he had been with another woman, she was a thousand miles away, so what was the goddamn problem, he screamed. He spent more time away from home than with a family who treated him like shit, her included, he went on.

She called him a liar and began throwing his clothes across the room. She tore at his shave kit and when the zipper wouldn't open she threw the thing at the mirror. She was crying, ranting on about how pathetic he was and wanting to know how much he paid his whore, how much he paid for her dinner when he hadn't taken his wife to a restaurant in ages. He was bald and overweight, she yelled, he hadn't been in shape for years and she was supposed to believe he just happened to be with another woman. His need to screw around when he was away was disgusting enough. She wouldn't tolerate him fucking someone on a Friday night and coming home late on the weekend to wake up and go drinking Sunday night with his worthless cronies. She wanted to know how many times he'd fucked other women behind her back while she was at home trying her best to raise the children alone and watching them gradually become disappointing clones of the cheating failure of a father.

The blow was so brutal Ann lost consciousness, flung over an ottoman and sprawled across the bedroom floor. He left her as she was and went to the fridge for another beer, waking Sunday morning after several more to stumble along the hallway from the living room, his head aching more than his hand. He had tried to erase the scene from the night before from his mind, when staggering into the bedroom all he could do was stare at her in disbelief. She hadn't moved. Her chest was heaving and her sighs sounded pathetic. What the hell had she been thinking?

He had to get out, he muttered. He needed to breathe. She could smell his goddamn shirts all she wanted, he yelled. Nothing would change what he had done. He made a one-time mistake because she let herself fall apart and he needed to relive the past if only for a night. Whatever he might have done was her fault, he persisted. He would never have gone looking for someone younger and prettier, he accused, if for once he could come home to someone who took pride in herself. He pointed to the floor and told her to get rid of the broken glass. Then he dressed and went out to spend the day alone until the time came to meet his friends.

Ann Preston remained on the floor until she heard the front door open and her sons walk in. They called out to her and when she didn't answer they went into the kitchen for a beer. She took her time crawling to the side of her bed, dragging herself up. Her shoulders and arms ached. Her head throbbed and at the same time felt numb. She had not been struck once in her life and the sensation made her want to be sick.

She had believed for a long time that one day he might hit her, though she never imagined the horrible feeling. She stayed all night thinking, wondering. She had to do something. She took a deep breath and pushed herself from the bed, padding her way to the kitchen where her sons were laughing and drinking.

"Why are the two of you drinking? It's not even ten o'clock?"

"It's a hangover cure," the younger one said. "Last night went on for fucking ever. So it's like still night time for us."

They never called her mom or mother. They never called her anything. They clashed their cans together and guzzled what was left. Each one belched.

"Anyway, there's only three left," the other added.

"Who does the shopping around here now? The old man's going to be righteously pissed when he sees you fucked up."

"There was a full case yesterday and your father's already gone out."

"To buy more?"

"To drink more. I don't think he'll be home until tonight. Sit down. I want to talk with you."

"Later, we've got to crash. We told the ladies to pick us up at two. That's too few zs after what we've been through. We had a rough night."

"So have I."

"Yeah, you look like shit," the younger man said. "You guys party a bit too much."

"Your father beat me. Now sit down and listen."

The younger one stayed as he was, his brother went to the fridge and tossed him a beer.

"Put those back and sit down."

They didn't.

"What's got you so pissed?" asked the older.

"We're cutting off your expenses at the end of the month and we want you out of here. You're on your own, the two of you. So I would suggest you start looking for a place to stay."

They laughed. "No fucking way," one said. "Does the old man know about this? Is that why he smacked you, because you pissed him off again?"

"He'll find out when he comes home and from now on you're buying your own beer and food even if I have to eat in restaurants for the month."

"We have school. You can't throw us out."

"Your tuition is paid and you can find an apartment together, or with those girls. I don't care. I've had enough. I want you gone. We both do. It's time you both stopped being children."

The older one finished his beer and threw the can in the

sink.

"No way. This is shit."

The younger one threw his can and missed. "Like, hello. There's laws, lady. We've got rights. We'll leave when we're ready." He went to the fridge for the last beer. He pulled at the tab, sneering. "Not a fucking chance, no way." And when he stomped from the kitchen he ploughed past her, pushing her against the wall.

His brother followed, stopping in front of her. "He's right. So just get the beer and forget this shit."

Ann waited, not reacting to the reverberation of the front door being slammed shut. She went into the bathroom and faced into the mirror. She burst into tears and brought trembling hands to a swollen and tender face. One eye was blue-black and one corner of her lower lip was cut. She tightened the belt on her robe and sat on the toilet seat until she stopped crying.

The shattered bedroom mirror remained on the floor. She had no sense of time as she stood to lock the door and remove her robe and nightgown before stepping into the shower. She pampered her face, letting the hot water sting until gradually the uncomfortable tingling dissipated and she felt good. She applied what little make-up she owned and phoned her sister who she thought must be at church. She hung up without leaving a message. She would call later. She had more important things on her agenda.

She returned to a home she despised by 4:00. By 6:00 she was a much different woman. She showered once more. She disposed of the empty skin care containers, the depilatory creams and the shopping bags. Her hair was self-styled and her new dress and heels felt strange as she went about preparing a dinner for one. She was still awake at 2:30 Monday morning when Charlie Preston stumbled through the door.

His wife was sitting in the living room, wide awake, which made him appear all the more drunk. He wanted

135

desperately to avoid her, suddenly feeling disgust. "Don't start with me, Ann, don't frigging start. The boys called me. What the hell were you thinking?"

"I was serious. It's not as though I can go anywhere, so they have to, and as soon as they're gone things around here are going to change."

Charles ignored her. He walked past her into their bedroom and bellowed her name. Ann stayed as she was. He shouted her name again and she remained immobile as he charged down the hall.

"I told you to get rid of the frigging glass, goddmamnit."

"And I chose not to. You caused the mess, you clean it."

He glared at her.

"That won't work anymore. As I said, things are going to change." She stood. "This afternoon I went shopping. At first I went out for make-up to cover what you did to my face," she forced a smirk, "then I began a shopping spree. I can't tell you how good I felt being in real stores, buying real dresses and skirts instead of shapeless pants and sweatshirts. I'm doing the same next week and the week after. I also joined a gym and this morning I'm enrolling in college night courses. You can do what you want. You can join the gym, or fuck around, or fuck yourself. It's your decision Charles. I want and I need something more. I accused you last night of having affairs. I was wrong. I'm sorry. I'm the one you've been fucking all along. You've held me back and the other two have dragged me down. I want more and I'm going to get it. Come along if you want, or go away. I don't care either way."

His face was purple with fury. He started giggling stupidly, wiping spittle from his mouth, and walked past her into the kitchen. Moments later the fridge door banged shut. Ann's heart was beating wildly, she was as afraid as she was determined and stood her ground as he rushed at her. He grabbed at her dress, ripping the front to her waist, scraping her chest and pulling away her bra in the same violent movement.

"You spent all afternoon fucking around stores, spending hard-earned money on clothes you don't need and you forgot something as simple as beer. How stupid can you be? And college?" he shouted. "Do you think so? Do you think it's that easy? You've been gone from school thirty years and you weren't the brightest bulb at the time. It's far from easy. Don't forget, I know."

She chuckled. "For two years. You were at college for two years. You tell everyone you graduated, you didn't. You dropped out." Ann jerked away from him, holding up the front of her dress. She shrugged. Her smile was insolent and she prayed her lips would not quiver. "You could simply have said you didn't like my new dress, Charles. Thank you. Because of you I won't be waiting until next week. I'll be shopping again this afternoon, and dropping by the hairdresser, as I will every week from now on until I'm happy with myself. And I will get into college. I'm also quitting my job today. I can do better for myself. I want to meet and be with people. You can do what you want. Screw around all you want." She chuckled; surprised at her defiance, at how her voice was not failing her. "I suppose I should feel sorry for them, for anyone who lets you into her body for the sake of a free meal or a few dollars. You're pitiful."

Ann didn't feel his fist crashing into her face or the dental bridge flying from her mouth. When she woke three or four hours later he was gone. When she was able to crawl to her knees she remembered her torn dress and saw the blood that had leaked from her mouth onto the carpet. She ran her tongue around the inside contours of her mouth, not understanding the sensation at first. Then she saw her teeth on the carpet. She laughed hysterically and went to the bathroom to face the mirror. She was hideous. The previous day's bruising was dark, her nose was swollen to grotesque disproportion and her toothless smile was brownish-red with hours-old blood.

She kept laughing and went to the phone to call the police. She didn't feel endangered. The danger had passed. She knew he would be in Quebec City the entire week for a sales meeting. Of greater importance was her long-term survival. She had new reasons to live and she sat on the couch with a knife in her hands until the police arrived cautiously through the door she'd left ajar.

Fifteen

Quebec City, Quebec
Monday, August 06

Charles Preston should have known to stay away. He left his wife motionless on the floor while he packed in a fluster. He stormed from the house without looking at her, without seeing the damage he inflicted. He arrived at Person International an hour before his co-workers, ready for the annual sales meeting the management had decided to hold in Quebec City and cursed aloud.

It was 5:00 AM and the line had already formed. He hated waiting in line, printing his own tickets, his own baggage claim, his own everything. His face was flushed, his blood pressure threatening to burst at every pulse point. He looked volatile and he was. He could feel the breath of the guy standing behind him on the nape of his neck. The air around him smelled of decay and he thought the woman in front of him must have fallen into the perfume bottle. He wanted to vomit. The man behind him coughed and sniffled back what sounded like thick phlegm. Then he heard the man gulp and gasp for cleaner air, and the woman wasn't moving ahead into the ten-foot gap in front of her. The so-called ticket agents were waving their hands without looking up and when he got to the counter he knew the three questions she would ask him, reciting the answers before the agent asked. She ignored him, holding out her hand for his passport, his tickets and his baggage claim and still she wasn't looking at Charles Preston. When she did acknowledge him she asked the three questions.

"Yes, yes, no", he answered. "Yes, yes, no. Yes, yes, no. The same as last week and the same as next week: yes, yes, no."

What was there about his elite flyer status she didn't understand, he wanted to know.

She was sorry, she had to ask. He should know that, she insisted, telling him not be nasty or she would call a supervisor. He knew she wasn't sorry at all. Neither were the clones at security, his real weekly treat: anything in your pockets, any coins? Anything metal in your pockets? Take off your shoes. Step to the side and wait. Come this way. Buzz, buzz. Stop here. Spread your legs. Raise your arms. Turn. Spread your legs. Raise your arms. Undo your belt. We're doing this for you, sir, for your protection. Fold down your pants. Thank you. Don't forget your shoes, sir. Enjoy your day, sir. At least this time he didn't have to deal with cross border interrogation.

When he was done he went directly to the Prestige Lounge for a light breakfast consisting of one four-ounce tonic water and few generous shots of gin, over easy. He said "fuck it" and poured a fourth. No one attending the meeting would care. They would all have the same first meal of the day, everyone except the snotty-nosed new kid. That was the true essence of sales meetings. No one cared about fiscal growth, percentages over margin or little gold performance buttons at the end of the year. Bullshit. For years he'd been the one to win the coveted prize, now he couldn't remember where he'd put them. That was fodder for the new kids who didn't know better. The ones who went to the office each day with mouths open wide, ready to please the boss, or for the one guy every company had who wanted to be the boss at any cost.

140

By the time Charles set himself up at his usual armchair, his glass was empty and he went for a refill. The others joined him within the hour and they finished breakfast together in time for the final boarding call. The CRJ-705's wheels folded in at 7:30 en route to Quebec City: ETA: 8:50

The mood onboard was jovial, lightened by mild intoxication, particularly for Charles Preston who was beginning to relax. He knew he'd be spending an extra couple of nights in Quebec before returning to Toronto on Sunday and from the airport he would go straight to the bar to the meet the blonde. He had no idea what would come after. What he was certain of was being with someone other than the wife Monday morning. Ann had gone too far this time and he would have to do something about her erratic behaviour.

There was nothing to see as the pilot lined up for a final approach into Jean-Lesage. Heavy rain zigzagged horizontally across the blurred windows. The Saint Lawrence appeared dull and flat, the normally majestic nineteenth-century Château Frontenac with its stone façade and pale-green, oxidized roof more as a neglected monument to a forgotten time.

Monday was set-up day, Tuesday through Thursday would take care of business and Friday the others would depart. Night time was designated party-time, expensed within reasonable limits, and they'd been told Quebec had some of the finest female talent anywhere. They were set to go. The wheels touched down and the jet taxied to the gate where the attendant spoke first in French, telling everyone to remain seated, followed by English. She spoke in French again. For as much as Charles Preston knew he might have landed in Paris. He was going to have one hell of a good week, until the attendant repeated what she had said in English.

"The captain requests that all passengers remain seated

until the passenger seated in 16-C clears the cabin. Passenger Charles Preston is requested to come to the forward cabin with any luggage."

Each of the other seventy-four passengers stretched in their seats to see the man in 16-C, straining their necks or leaning sideways to see forward. The men sitting beside him looked on with ridiculous grins.

"Forget to kiss the wife, Preston?" one asked.

"Yeah, Preston, what's up? You didn't leave the wife smiling. You got to leave them anxious for more, man."

Charles Preston sat paralyzed. The captain had left the flight deck and was standing by the attendant's side. The companionway was open and they were talking to someone he couldn't see. Heads were bobbing, the attendant looking at him as she reached for the mike.

"Passenger Preston, please come to the forward cabin. We need to disembark the aircraft."

His face was beat red. He was sweating profusely and the cramped cabin space was becoming suffocating. He saw their faces. He saw the same curiosity in everyone's eyes. He was amongst the last to board and his briefcase was closer to the rear of the cabin. They were all staring at him as he sidestepped along the narrow aisle and reached into the overhead bin. His hands were shaking and his mouth was bone dry. He had no moisture to swallow. He left the bin open and looked blindly into the gauntlet of peripheral stares. His boss leaned into the aisle, asking what was going on. Charles Preston had no answer. He shook his head and kept walking. He saw them at the very edge of the galley.

"Monsieur Charles Preston?" one officer asked.

"Yeah, that's me. What's this all about?"

"Monsieur, please step out from the aircraft." He did, his eyes focused straight ahead, seeing nothing. "Monsieur Preston, you are being arrested. The charges are aggravated assault and sexual assault."

"That's crazy. I just got here. This is stupid."

"Monsieur, your wife is in the Intensive Care of the Hôpital Général of Toronto. Put down your case and put your arms behind you."

"I never hit my wife. There must have been an invasion or something. I've never hit her."

The officer brought up a gloved hand, grabbing Preston's right wrist. "You did hit something, monsieur."

"There's no proof. I know my rights."

"Yes, monsieur, and to be sure we will explain them in detail as we are walking." The second officer stepped behind Preston, cuffing one wrist to the other. "Your wife also has rights and she has implemented them. Allons. Let's go." The officer spoke to the captain and flight attendant. He thanked them with a few words Preston couldn't understand and tipped his hat.

They walked at a good pace, the officers guiding the prisoner by his arms. Preston saw nothing beyond the feet beside him and those around him. He asked about his luggage. He had more to worry about than his luggage, they answered. He wanted to ask another question, but his throat was burning and none came to him. He saw a flash and was startled, jerking, everyone was staring and some were pointing cell phones at him. He dropped his head. He wanted to collapse. He felt as though he was walking on air, as though he had no control. He felt trapped, the steel against his wrists was cold and he began to cry.

Then they were outside where the air was heavy with a steady rain, the sky was dark and all he could see were the red and blue flashing lights. They guided him into the rear seat with a firm hand at the top of his head and slammed the door. He was sitting on his hands, staring at the door panels that had no handles. In front of him a heavy-gauge metal lattice was bolted to the floor and ceiling. He was caged.

Rainwater was dripping from his hair onto his knees, the radio was crackling and emitting foreign voices, there was a shotgun beside the radio and he was terrified. He was being arrested and had no idea what that meant. Would he be fingerprinted? He didn't know and was afraid to ask. Would he spend the night in jail for something he didn't do? That's all he knew. He hadn't touched his wife. He knew that much. He was innocent until proven guilty and they had no proof. He needed to talk to her. Whatever she did to herself, whatever happened to her was not his fault.

The cops were in the car. One was seated behind the wheel, waiting while the other spoke into the mike on his shoulder. They were talking about him, he knew it. His head hung down, his shoulders were slumped forward and he saw that his legs were shaking. He wanted to wipe his nose and his face. He strained to see through the rain-beaded window. Everyone was looking at him as they hurried by, his boss and the division manager peering out from behind the airport's plate-glass façade and through the downpour. They were talking, their expressions serious. They were talking about him. He was in a nightmare. He was still onboard or at the bar. He was in a horrible dream that was unreal. He would wake up and be onboard. Everything would be normal. Instead the dream became worse. More men he knew joined the onlookers at the window, none were smiling, and his boss began speaking into his phone.

Charles Preston wished for someone to kill him and twenty minutes later he had more worries than ticket agents and airport security. At the precinct they said nothing to him and when he tried to speak with them they ignored him as though he'd gone to a foreign land. They removed the handcuffs and led him to a counter where they tagged and confiscated his briefcase, adding his wallet, his money and his pens to the envelope along with his tie, his belt, his watch and his wedding ring. They put him in a room and left him alone without saying a word and he had no idea how much time passed before he called out.

"Hello, hello." He waited, and no one came. "Hello...

anyone… hello." His eyes went to the door handle.

"Monsieur," the officer said.

"Bathroom, I need the bathroom," Preston replied.

The officer had no reaction. He closed the door and left Preston alone once more. Sometime later the door opened again and two other officers walked in and told him to stand. One took him by the arm, leading him through the door and down the corridor. The sign on the door read "homme", which meant nothing to him until he went through and he saw the urinals. They released him and leaned against the sink to wait.

Preston stood looking first at the urinals, then at the cops.

"Allez, monsieur. Pissez," one of them said, nodding toward the urinals.

Walking to the wall, Preston thought he would collapse. His legs were weak. He unzipped his pants and reached in to tug at the front of his underwear. His pants were sagging without his belt and his shirttails were hanging out, forcing him to spread apart his legs to keep his pants from falling. His penis was shrivelled and he needed both hands to free the diminutive member from his pants. He was too nervous. His mouth was dry, his heart was racing and his breathing was laboured. He stood staring at the wall, waiting. The men behind him were talking, speaking meaningless words.

He shifted his weight from one foot to the other. He moved his head backward and stared at the ceiling, trying to concentrate, taking in a deep breath, and after what seemed an eternity he felt relief. Then he grimaced, biting down hard on his teeth. He was dribbling, a warm wetness sprinkling over his hands and he leaned in closer to the lip of the ceramic bowl. He was dribbling, feeling a penetrating burning sensation and he stopped breathing. He stopped urinating and let go of himself to adjust his grip and start over, breathing out as the stream became stronger.

When he was finished he adjusted himself and looked at

the floor. Shit! His pants were blotched from his zipper to his knees, urine had splashed onto his shoes and his hands were wet. He wanted to kill himself. He wanted to go home to kill Ann and kill himself. He inhaled another deep breath and faced them.

The officers straightened, expressionless. He wasn't the first and wouldn't be the last prisoner to mess himself. They stepped from the sink and when he'd washed his hands one cop pointed to the paper dispenser and Preston's shoes. When he finished, he stood, his face flushed with a deep purple tint as they led him along another corridor and into another room with a dozen or more people.

"I know my rights. I want a lawyer, one who speaks English. I want an English lawyer."

"One is coming. He will be here soon." A woman wearing a white lab coat said something in French as she typed information into a laptop. "She is telling you to hold out your hand for your fingerprinting."

"You can't fingerprint me. I haven't done anything."

"Do as she says. Start with your thumb of the right hand."

The woman didn't wait. She pulled on silicone gloves and pinched Preston's right thumb between her thumb and forefinger. When she was done with his right hand, she did his left and closed the electronic scanner. She typed more information and spoke for a few moments with the officers. They nodded and moved him into a corner, positioning him between a camera lens and a white screen. When they were done with the head shots they photographed his hands, they escorted him to the first room and sometime later a woman came through the door. She looked like an executive. She was tall, attractive and confident. He felt like a dishevelled indigent. Somehow she made him more nervous as she pulled out a chair, sat, and arranged her papers.

"If you're my lawyer I didn't do anything wrong." When she didn't respond Preston spoke again, raising the tone of his voice. "I need an English lawyer, an English one. I did not do anything wrong."

"I'm not a lawyer, Mr. Preston. I'm a detective. My name is Dina Becker. I'm Captain of the Special Victims Unit. Normally I wouldn't process you, however you're from another jurisdiction and your crime wasn't committed here, so we're giving you special status. How about that? And, congratulations, you're officially a criminal. You have a police record, Mr. Preston: fingerprints, a personal photo shoot, the whole nine yards. You know all the stuff you see on TV, all that cool shit. Well you're in it, right up to your little cojones. So here's how it's going to play out. First, your wife came out from surgery a few minutes ago." Charles Preston's eyes flared open. "Yeah, apparently they had to put her teeth back in her mouth, the ones you knocked out." Dina Becker opened her file and slid a series of photographs in front of him. "This is what you did to her. When the officers arrived she was sitting waiting for them with a kitchen knife in her hands. I suppose you should be happy you didn't forget anything for your trip."

Preston blocked out the grotesque enlargements, shaking his head. "I didn't do what you're saying."

"Yes you did, twice, and she's pressed charges."

"It's her word against mine."

"I see your point. She punched out her own teeth." Dina Becker grimaced. "Stop it. Here's what's going to happen. Your lawyer should be here in about an hour. He or she will get you into court sometime tomorrow for an arraignment and will get you out on bail, if not you'll be in here until the Toronto guys come for you. In either case you're in here tonight, in a cell with all the modern conveniences. You'll have a toilet, a sink and company."

"On what charge?"

"For the time being, one count of aggravated assault and one count of aggravated sexual assault, though the Toronto police might have other charges by the time you're in their

147

custody."

"Now she's saying I raped her?"

"You stripped her. She was naked from the waist up, with scratches on her chest from your hand."

"She's lying. She's always lied."

"To herself for quite a few years, but not about this. You're screwed, Preston. You're going to jail. One for our side, you lose" Dina Becker pushed her chair from the table. "I'll be back when the lawyer gets here. In the meantime I'll leave you the pictures. If I were you I'd spend the time thinking up a good story. Be as creative as you want. We already know the ending."

Charles Preston's legal counsel arrived moments before noon. They spoke for an hour before Dina Becker stepped in with a tape recorder and an hour later his statement was typed and signed. By 4:00 the lawyer was back, the arraignment was set for ten the next morning and Charles Preston was returned to his cell. He spent the night huddled into the corner, sitting on a hard mattress with his arms wrapped around his knees.

There was a toilet with no seat, a sink, a paper cup and a cot. The room was six by nine, stark, with no window and a wall of steel bars. He needed to urinate but the man in the cell facing his would see him. The man was standing with his hands by his side, behind his own bars, staring in. Then Preston's head and face began to dampen with sweat at the thought of the next morning. What would he do in the morning? He shifted his eyes to the toilet and saw the small roll of paper. He groaned, bringing a hand to his mouth, and bit into the loose web between his thumb and forefinger, his eyes blurring with tears. Where would he dress? Where would they put his clothes? Where would the man across from him be and when would he stop staring in?

Preston didn't sleep and he forgot one thought as soon as another entered his mind. He thought of Ann, he wanted to kill her. He wanted to see her dead. He thought of the sales meeting and how they'd be talking about him in a strip bar somewhere. His thoughts drifted to the blonde in Toronto and he wondered if he would ever get to have her. The cell was warm, but he was cold, the kind of cold brought on from fear and lack of sleep. He thought about what would happen in court the following morning, he wondered if he would spend the week in jail or whether they would take him to Toronto in handcuffs, humiliated for the entire world to see. He wondered if he would miss Ann when she was dead. He wondered how he would feel killing her.

The cell block was noisy and no one had dimmed the lights. He buried his head into his knees for darkness; still the noise didn't go away. People were talking, other prisoners. They were speaking French and he understood not a single word. At one point he thought he would lose his mind. He pressed his palms against his ears and yelled at them to shut up and they laughed. The man across from him was leering at him and laughing. Charlie Preston, the man of the hour most Sunday nights, had nowhere to hide, no hole to crawl into. He was not adjusting well to his new life.

At 6:30 Tuesday morning his cell door opened along with thirteen others. They would all be appearing in court the same day. The shower room had a long bench, twelve shower heads and no changing rooms. The air smelled dank. The female prisoners had been in before them. He felt ridiculous in his paper slippers and orange jumpsuit. Most of the other prisoners were younger by decades, in their twenties or thirties. Many were in for DUI or disorderly conduct. Others were in for felonies. They looked as though they could hurt him and he believed throughout the long night that they wanted to. He didn't belong there.

Charles Preston was the oldest and he stood out. The others pulled off their suits easily, he struggled. Naked bodies were walking past him, sitting beside him and standing in front of him. Many of them were tattooed with designs that made him afraid. They were all stronger than him. He didn't want to stand. He was embarrassed. He'd never been stark naked in front of other men. He was shapeless. His buttocks were flat, he had pronounced breasts, his skin was pallid at the end of summer and his scrotum looked like a pimpled cushion for its diminutive companion.

The others were laughing and joking, Preston thought at his expense, and when he stood he covered his genitalia with his hands. He faced into the wall letting the water spray over him, afraid to move. When the water shut off he hurried to the towel bin to dry himself as discreetly as he could. He sat on the suit to pull on his underwear, then on his slippers to pull on the legs of his suit. He put on the slippers and stood, keeping his eyes focused on the grated floor, avoiding those around him who were applauding and mocking him. He hadn't dried himself properly, making it impossible to finish dressing as one prisoner tugged at his collar that was halfway up his back and another took hold of a sleeve that was dangling by his side. He wanted to scream at them as they paraded to the cellblock. Instead he left his loose torso bare and let the coveralls drag from his waist as he wrapped himself into his arms, lowered his head and whimpered.

Breakfast was at 7:00: cereal and coffee. The lawyer arrived at 8:00. He'd been to the airport the night before and came with Preston's suitcase. Each piece of his clothing was checked before he was instructed to dress in his cell. He asked for privacy, the immediate response a curt "no", forced to change into a business suit to the accompaniment of lewd whistles and jeers. The others cared nothing about him. They needed something to pass the time. Jail anytime was a boring place.

He was allowed to shave in the men's room while handcuffed and at 9:00 he was herded into a van with half a dozen others at the very moment his division manager was calling the meeting to order. At 10:00 he was told to stand, before which he was instructed to plead not guilty, to be calm and to call the judge Madame. The hearing lasted eleven minutes. Bail was set at twenty-thousand dollars and the prisoner was released with a court order to surrender his driver's permit, his passport and surrender himself to the Toronto authorities within twelve hours of his return.

Furthermore, until his departure from Quebec, he would present himself each morning and evening at the downtown precinct and, once in Toronto, he would not contact his wife, nor return to his house or place himself within a thousand feet of her. Contravening the restrictions would find him in contempt of court and he would be arrested at once. Leaving the courtroom his lawyer cautioned him to do nothing foolish. He was a first-timer. At most he would get a year, six months with good behaviour, and serve easy time doing community service or wearing a leg monitor, although the counsellor was unfamiliar with Ontario law and could not be certain.

Preston walked away from the man who dropped him off at the police station without saying a word. They kept his permit and his passport, treating him as though he'd become invisible. They didn't see him and all he wanted was out. Going to jail for killing the old bitch would be easy for what she did to him. He could kill her, he thought. The tough part would come later that afternoon: the bosses. He was ready for them. First he would go to his room, order room service for lunch and drink as much as he needed in order to prep himself for the most important presentation of his career.

Had he glanced over his shoulder before climbing into the taxi, Charles Preston would have seen a beautiful woman with lustrous red hair and very sad green eyes cocking her thumb and forefinger into an imaginary gun and shooting him in the back of the head.

Sixteen

Quebec City, Quebec
Tuesday, August 07

Preston arrived at the Château at 1:15. He saw nothing as the taxi drove along la rue Grande-Allée, not the people scurrying in the rain from the doorways of fine restaurants to parked cars, and not the centuries-old architecture. He was focused on the minutes and hours ahead and, when the driver pointed out that they were passing through the arched gates of the oldest walled city in North America, he wasn't interested. He would see the city at night, he hoped. The taxi driver tried to make conversation, Preston thought to tell him to fuck off. What was with that stupid accent? Why did every person he came into contact with have a fucking accent, he wondered? The whole fucking country was loaded to overflowing with fucking foreigners.

After his lunch he wasn't quite drunk enough, nor was he quite sober enough, which meant he was ready and fully prepared. Charlie Preston was always ready. He was the quintessential salesman, the best. There was none better, albeit from another era, an increasingly apparent reality which he was comfortable ignoring. Ever since he could remember he'd practiced answering theoretical questions not yet asked. He always appeared spontaneous and honest, that was his life: spontaneous and honest. This was no different. He'd been through hell and survived. He would survive the real inquisition. He walked through the double doors of the Salon Jacques Cartier as though nothing untoward had happened.

The room was lighted solely by the rainbow beam emitted from the projector. One man was standing facing him, the others sat facing away. The new divisional manager was speaking and didn't miss a beat. "Preston, we missed you at dinner last night and you're late. The meeting began at nine. Is there something you'd like to share with us?"

"Peter, they made one huge mistake, more like a misunderstanding," The CEO stood to flip the light switch, "and everything's taken care of. I got a lawyer, but the guy couldn't come before this morning."

"So you spent the night in jail."

"Yeah, though it's not what you think. I wasn't behind bars or anything like that. They gave me a small room with a shower and a bed. Not quite like this place. Anyway, what can I say? I survived, and the misunderstanding was cleared up by eleven when I had to go back to the airport for my suitcase. I got here as fast as I could."

"So what was the deal? What happened that you were met by police on the plane?"

Preston went to the podium. His hands were shaking, his knees ready to buckle. He scanned the faces around the conference table and looked over to his direct boss before acknowledging the man beside him. He chuckled.

"Peter, you can't even imagine. When those cuffs go on, and you're sitting in the rear of one of those cars, it's a whole different world. I was imagining everything from never seeing my little Annie again to lethal injection. Then I saw you guys in the window and, I have to tell you, I felt like shit. I was worried about what you must be thinking, me being taken away like some sort of criminal. Then they told me about my Annie and I couldn't believe it. I couldn't even speak with her and they wouldn't let me go until I could."

"What happened to her?"

"She tripped, goddamnit, on the goddamn stairs, after I left for the airport. She knocked herself out and lost a tooth. One of my boys found her a few hours later and called the cops. When she woke up in the hospital she was still dopey from what they gave her. She wasn't making any sense, telling them what happened was my fault. She was reacting to the drugs. However," Preston raised his open hands, "guilty as charged. What happened was my fault, for not fixing the top step. I kept putting it off. If I'd fixed the damn thing all this wouldn't have happened. That's pretty much it. Case closed. I spoke with her this morning." He focused his attention on the CEO. "Tony, she's fine. Can't say she's not a little pissed at the moment, but she'll have a new tooth by the Christmas party and we'll be laughing about it," he chuckled, "once I fix the step. She's fine. So am I, if she doesn't kill me when I get home. The lawyer spoke with the doctors and the cops and everything's fine." He turned to the divisional manager. "Peter, I'm sorry about disrupting the meeting this way."

The man nodded. "It's more important the situation has been corrected. Give our regards to Ann when you see her. What time is your flight out?"

Preston shrugged his shoulders. "Hopefully Friday, with you guys, after we wrap up here," he answered. "I did change my flight this morning to be with her tonight, before I spoke with her. The boys are with their mom and she wouldn't hear of me going home early, letting down the team. She knows it's important for me to be here and she insisted I stay. Problem is, when I went to change my flight back to Friday nothing was available so I booked for Saturday. I'll keep on top of things in case there's a change."

"Good. Then read through the morning presentations this evening. Get caught up. Now, go find your seat."

"Thanks, Peter, and thank you, Tony."

Preston chose an empty chair beside his boss. He slapped the man's shoulder and smiled to ingratiate himself. At day's end the meeting adjourned and the men went to their respective rooms for raincoats and a quick precursor to a night of drinking. They understood Charlie needed to call his wife and speak with his distraught boys. He would join them later for dinner, a few to many drinks, and he would once again become the man of the hour.

He hated retuning to the police station. They hadn't looked at him once during the minute he spent signing in and the officer walked away without saying whether he should go or stay, so he walked out. The week would cost a small fortune for taxis, a cost he would have to absorb, not to mention Saturday night.

When he returned to the hotel he went to the ATM and withdrew a few hundred, not noticing the woman until she stopped at the wall beside him to rummage in her purse. She was somewhat taller than him, slim and blonde, and she was wearing a wide-brimmed linen hat. She reminded him of the blonde in the bar Sunday night but her hair was longer and a few shades darker, pulled into a ponytail and she was wearing glasses. His eyes trailed from her hat to her ankles. Her blouse was tapered. He could see her bra strap and her skirt came to above the crease behind her knees. When she twirled around he was still staring.

"Charles, I don't believe this. How crazy is this?"

He stood gawking at her, speechless. She was directly in front of him, the blonde, looking so different. And what the hell was her name?

"I thought you said you travelled to the States," she said.

"I do. I'm here for a company meeting. What are you doing here? You're the last person I expected to see."

"No kidding. I just happened to be thinking about our date on Sunday and here you are."

"You look great. The hat and the glasses, they add

155

something. How did the hair get so long?"

"It's magic, part of a girl's bag of tricks."

"Can I buy you a drink?"

"I'm sorry, I can't. I promised some colleagues I would meet up with them for dinner. I only came here to check out the architecture and a few boutiques. When in Rome, right?" He was lost for words. "We're here until Thursday, meeting with new clients." Miranda Stevens examined the carpeted floor, her smile radiating real warmth. "Listen, if you don't have any other plans, why don't we meet up tomorrow night and do the tourist thing around six. We can have drink, see a bit of the town and have a late dinner. I've been here for since early yesterday and haven't seen a thing."

Preston couldn't believe it. He didn't believe the woman would show at the bar Sunday night and now she was in front of him, asking him out. Proof positive she'd be with him on Sunday if he played his cards right. "If I did have plans I'd cancel them, and dinner is on me." Then a thought flashed across his mind. "On second thought, seven would be better, if you don't mind. The meetings I'm attending never finish on time and I wouldn't want to keep you waiting. So, you're not staying here?"

"No, I'm staying in a boutique hotel on the rue Saint-Louis. It's quaint, like stepping into another more romantic time. The beds are massive, Charles. They take up the entire room." She looked at her watch. "Seven is fine. Right now I have to run. Sorry. So, it's a date?"

"Yeah, it's a date."

"Great. Why don't we meet by the funicular over on the Dufferin Terrace?"

"I don't know the place."

"Walk out and turn right. I'll be wearing a tan dress and my hat. You know what Charles? I think I'm going to enjoy our time together. I know I will. See you tomorrow."

As she walked across the cavernous hall Charles Preston

thought of her naked. Why else would she tell him about her bed? Miranda Stevens glanced behind her and waved at the very moment she disappeared around the corner. She would indeed enjoy her time with him. She had seen the horrific photographs of Ann Preston the night before.

Seventeen

Quebec City, Quebec
Wednesday, August 08

Miranda Stevens called her office first thing Tuesday morning. She needed unexpected personal time and would return to work the following Monday. Her files were up-to-date and what work had to be done by her could be done remotely.

The cryptic call came late Monday evening, much sooner than she had expected. Permission was granted. She had thought the facilitation would happen Sunday night, after a fast dinner and a few drinks to dull his mind. She imagined doing him in his car, in a parking lot or a suburban motel, and had made a mental note of her wardrobe for the event. She hadn't expected the change of venue. Preston hadn't mentioned Quebec City in the bar. She was to travel by plane to Montreal and continue on to Quebec City in a rental car. She was to stay in the South Shore city of Lévis and do what was necessary to facilitate the case study by Thursday night, latest.

She spent the night studying the brief profile. Ann Preston had pressed charges. Good. Battered wives seldom did or they waited until time ran out. Charles Preston had been arrested and released on bail. She knew where he was staying, that he changed his flight and had to report to a police station twice each day. She knew he had two million worth of personal life, an additional two million were he to become the late Charles Preston while on company business, and that Ann was about to begin a new and happier life.

To be assigned beyond their sectors was unusual. However, Miranda had argued special privilege. She was the one to overhear him in the bar Sunday night, the one to call her director to initiate the case study and the fact Preston had been arrested meant nothing.

He would serve token time, and then he'd be released to mistreat his wife again. He would lose his job, he would blame her for what happened and he would beat her again. That Ann intended divorcing him was irrelevant. Why would he care? He would lose the house, half of everything, and he would find someone else to abuse. Men like him always would. They ran from big dogs, kicked the little ones, and beat their chests with bravado outside the office while prostrating themselves to placate their bosses at work before going home to beat a defenceless woman. Miranda wanted him dealt with. She wanted him dead and she presented her case to the Directorate through her director as effectively as any court case she had ever tried and won.

She walked to the bottom of the hill after leaving Preston in the lobby. The damp air was gradually dissipating after her supposedly unexpected encounter with Preston. She wanted so much to stroll along la rue Saint-Anne or sit at a café-terrasse and watch everyone enjoying the warmth of the early evening sun. She wanted to amble down the cobble-stone slope of the crooked and dark alley where artisans were selling their crafts and their paintings, sketching caricatures of one lover as the other looked on under a quilted and ancient-looking canopy of big and small wooden overhangs decorated with art. She wanted to ride a horse-drawn calèche and hold hands with someone she loved. Instead, she cautiously descended the steep and humid stone steps lining the walls of the vertical cliff General James Wolfe once scaled centuries past with five-thousand British troops to conquer the French as they slept. From there she boarded the ferry to cross the three-quarter mile expanse of the Saint Lawrence River to Lévis where she left her car. She drove to her hotel, ordered room service and fell asleep without finishing her meal. In the morning her pillow was stained with shades of blue and black and she lay there remembering Morgan.

She knew the time had come, not to forget, rather to go forward. She had thought on two or three occasions over recent years the right one had come along, yet each time what she longed for was not to be, coming to realize she'd been confusing being with someone with loving them, happy never to have cheated on Morgan's memory.

Each time she had fallen into a deep depression concealed with false smiles, long hours and more intense investigation into her cases files than any of her colleagues. The time had come to move forward with her life and dispel her fears. She wasn't afraid of what her office might think. They all knew what happened to her ten years and three months earlier when she was out with her best friend celebrating their graduation from law school. Her co-workers were constantly after her to find a new friend. They were concerned about her. They wanted her to be happy, though her boss often admonished her that when she did find a special someone he would not tolerate being callously relegated to second place. In response, she would smirk and pat his cheek in a way she knew annoyed him, or so he wanted everyone to believe.

Not a day went by that she didn't think of Morgan and being in Quebec City with its romance and je ne sais quoi joie-de-vivre made her time alone all the more painful. She spent the beginning of her second day reviewing legal briefs by the pool. She had nowhere to go. She wore a boring two-piece swimsuit when years ago she would have worn a thong or Rio with a tiny top. She hated that lost part of her life.

She tanned easily. She was thirty-two, not sixty-two, and she wanted to feel young again. She left the pool and the hotel, crossing the river dressed to kill for an afternoon of shopping. She ate lunch without wine in a charming out-of-the-way bistro and thought of what she would buy first. Liquor of any kind was strictly prohibited by the Directorate within twenty-four hours of any facilitation, excepting necessary subterfuge, and by five o'clock she was in her room dressing for the evening ahead. She knew Preston's meetings began precisely at 8:00, that he would have been to the police station to sign in and she could imagine him drooling from the mouth while thinking of his evening with her.

She was pleased with herself for not spending her day lounging by the pool, anticipating another day of shopping in Vieux-Québec for lingerie she would never find at home. So what if no one would be with her to tell her she was beautiful and sexy. She would know.

She sat on the edge of the bed and slipped into her silk tap pants and bra. She stepped into her patent leather pumps and stood in front of the mirror. She longed for someone to see her that way, sexy and young, not as some lonely lesbian desperately wanting someone to love.

She was satisfied with her appearance. She would be alluring to him without being obvious. She would undo the top buttons of her silk shirt dress to reveal the detailed trim of her bra and the lower buttons to show more of her bare thighs. Her objective was for him to want her and he would. He would imagine more than he could see, and feel empowered.

She remembered the previous Sunday when she walked from the bar, convinced she'd left Charles Preston to have another beer and fantasize about her. Being a senior Crown Prosecutor at such a young age was rewarding, she thought. She was good, with an almost perfect conviction rate and one day she would sit on the bench. Yet being a Facilitator was that much better and she was certain one day she would sit as a member of Pearl's elite Directorate.

She was one of the city's top trial lawyers. Incredibly lucrative job offers continued coming her way from the city's top law firms whose clients she was sending to prison. They wanted her on their side; though for Miranda the law wasn't about money. Being a Crown prosecutor was about the dregs of society, putting them away and not back on the streets.

She was delighted to have met Charles Preston, increasingly anxious to meet with him again. He might have been the one who got away, but she was in the right place at the right time. She was anxious. She held the pearl-handled stiletto in her hands. Most organizations recognized significant achievement with insignificant bonuses or meaningless plaques. Pearl recognized achievement with six-figure deposits into foreign accounts and elaborately designed daggers. At thirty-two Miranda was a few dollars shy of a four-million-dollar portfolio. She didn't have to continue risking her life and her career. She could stop anytime, but what she was doing was never about the money.

Morgan had been dead for over ten years, ten Christmases, ten Thanksgivings and ten vacations. Morgan was never coming back. They began their life together with such vitality, such passion and were together throughout most of their time at law school. They were each other's first lovers, each other's best friend. Miranda graduated at the top of her class. Morgan came in a close second and together they began to plan a law partnership and future together.

They had been to the on-campus pub a hundred times before and were making the most of their last night to drink a little too much and be carefree. The next day they would be leaving campus, going home to nervous families and new careers. Miranda's family had never met Morgan and

Morgan's family had never met Miranda. How completely foolish their parents were at the time, Miranda thought as she dressed. But for the parents' meaningless social inhibition the girls might not have gone to the pub that dreadful night and Morgan might still be alive.

She dropped onto the hotel bed. She knew her memories of Morgan were the impetus that drove her forward, her raison d'être for all that she did. Those precious memories made her a quintessential Facilitator and she knew she would never stop making the world a better place. She was born to kill bad men, to kill men like the four who gang-raped her and killed Morgan.

*

They were returning to the dorm from the bar, jubilant, yet sad at leaving their friends. The night was pitch-black, but they were on campus and felt safe and secure, as though they were walking in their own backyards, until without warning cruel hands clamped over their mouths and they were dragged behind the cover of bushes and pushed to the ground.

Two of the men punched them viciously, dazing the girls, and held them in place, fondling their breasts while two others pulled off their skirts and their panties before ripping away their sweaters and bras. They tried to scream, unable to, and Miranda never forgot the face of the man who kneeled between her legs and pushed down his pants. She had never felt such pain. She strained to see Morgan, but her head was clamped between the other man's thighs. The pain was unbearable. She heard Morgan's muffled screams. She knew Morgan was calling her name and she struggled to do the same. She remembered the second brutal punch to her face when the first one finished, before he changed places with the man who'd pinned her head between his knees. She remembered waiting for the horrible pain to begin again, crying out to her friend and lover from under a vicious grip.

At dawn the next morning security guards heard the sorrowful sounds of a girl crying coming from behind nearby bushes. What they found was a dishevelled Miranda sitting in her torn clothes with Morgan cradled in her arms, her skirt pulled across her middle, her sweater draped across her breasts. The ambulance arrived within minutes and the girls were rushed away. Miranda didn't stop talking to her all the while and when they wheeled Morgan into intensive care Miranda had to be restrained.

They sedated her and administered an ECP. Twelve hours later they woke her to give her another. Her first thought was of Morgan and she enquired anxiously, too fraught with emotion to understand the nurse's empty promise to find out and come back. The nurse never did. A doctor came in her place, telling her with professional empathy that Morgan hadn't survived her injuries.

The following morning the police arrived and Miranda painfully relived each moment of the crime. She visualized their faces and their shapes, she remembered their clothing and their voices, she remembered the one called Sammy who had told his buddy to shut his mouth and she remembered looking up at the scar on his chin. She told the officers how she hoped the four would resist arrest and when they asked why she answered that she wanted to see them dead. One officer commiserated, confessing she wanted the same, adding that unfortunately prisoners seldom resisted arrest. Men, she had told Miranda, always became surprisingly tame in handcuffs.

Within a few days the police tracked down the four and arrested them. Their parents hired high-powered attorneys and they were released on bail the same day, the day of Morgan's funeral. The judge believed flight risk was minimal and saw no need to remand. Instead, they each spent the summer at home awaiting their trial date.

The evening of the funeral Miranda lay in her dorm room hugging Morgan's pillow. She knew the law and knew all too well what the eventual verdict would be. She wanted them dead, nothing less would suit the crime. She knew their names by then and she'd determined that very soon after she would know everything about them.

The next morning a senior partner of the law firm where the girls were to begin their careers called to delay her start date, giving her time to heal. She thanked him very much for his thoughtfulness and consideration, informing him in the same sentence she'd decided not to join the firm. She would practice law, she told him, albeit from what she then believed to be a more consequential perspective, and in the afternoon she went to the provincial justice building where she was interviewed by senior prosecutors. They had been very interested in her months earlier during the annual career day at the law school, however at the time she had decided in favour of a more lucrative offer from private practice and they had necessarily made other arrangements. Young Miranda Stevens was without a job and without a home.

When the trial date arrived in late September the judge heard how the four men had been partying, how they had consumed intoxicants without knowledge of the potentially mind altering effects of alcohol when combined with other stimuli. Attorneys for the defence argued their clients never planned to hurt the girls who'd been provoking the boys, claiming the girls were provocatively attired, brazenly flaunting their young bodies and their sexuality during the course of the evening. In effect, the girls encouraged the event and the boys had ultimately succumbed to poor judgement and immaturity. They were taught to respect women of all ages, they had sisters and their actions, as deplorable as they were, were completely aberrant to their natures.

When Miranda was called to testify she held her own against them, shocking some in the courtroom when she told them in a vindictive and cutting voice that they didn't flaunt themselves, that her past was not their business and that Morgan was her first and exclusive lover. A long list of willing witnesses for the Crown confirmed the relationship was strong throughout the girls' time at law school and several more reluctant witnesses were subpoenaed by the Crown to testify how they themselves had each been intimate with as many as all four boys, many of them being passed from one to the other and, in the days following, shunned or rejected by all four.

The trial by judge ended with the two seventeen-year-olds sentenced to one year less a day in a minimum security facility and the two eighteen-year-olds to three years on charges of aggravated sexual assault, forcible rape and involuntary manslaughter.

Miranda remained in the courtroom and cried. Mrs. Stevens had been called as a character witness and was the last to leave after expressing her shame. Knowing the neighbours were talking about the girlfriends was embarrassing enough, now the whole world knew about her daughter and her disappointment in knowing she would never have grandchildren. She couldn't understand why Miranda stayed away all summer, refusing to apologize for the sordid affair with a person who obviously hadn't been well, refusing to seek counselling to correct the damage she'd done to herself before all hope was lost.

Miranda reminded her mother caustically that her weak husband was more interested in his neighbourhood image than his only daughter, so humiliated by her so-called shamefully sinful and lewd conduct he refused until the day after the funeral to leave his home. She moved out the evening of the funeral without regret, slapping his face with as much vehemence as she could muster for having denigrated Morgan. She would never see him again, nor would she ever forgive her servile mother for not understanding, and in the deserted courtroom she told her mother to join him in hell. She would do very well on her own. She had worked in the school's library throughout the summer and would one day sit on the bench. She would never see either parent again and soon after she stopped remembering them. They would one day die alone and Miranda would neither know nor care.

Leaving the justice building a woman approached Miranda as she was about to step into the footwell of the bus. She called Miranda Miss Stevens and asked for a moment of her time to discuss a legal matter of some importance. The woman seemed to be from a bygone era. She was dressed in a long cashmere coat, a fur-trimmed close-fitting hat and fine leather gloves. She wore sunglasses and Miranda had no idea how old she might be. She was well-educated and poised, her voice was soft yet commanding and she linked her arm into Miranda's who was at once intrigued and compelled by the woman's demeanour.

She had been in the courtroom, the woman explained, and found the verdict despicable. The four murderers should have paid a higher price for their crime and they would one day.

"How do you mean?" Miranda asked. "Two of them won't even have criminal records after their release. Part of me would shoot them in a second and spend my life in prison. Another part knows killing them won't bring Morgan back to me."

"I appreciate your logic. She was such a pretty thing, and so are you. You'll find someone else to be with when the time is right."

"My mind can't go there right now."

"I understand, and to be rejected by your family must be especially hard. You know the law firm would have taken you back when the province denied you. Pride goeth before the fall, Miranda."

"I know you learned my name in the courtroom." Miranda stopped. "Tell me how you learned about my family and my job…and why?"

"Oh, I suppose I'm nosier than most. I know quite a bit about quite a few people, including those four killers and their families."

"Money got them reduced sentences, pure and simple."

"Yes, sometimes the power of money is ill-spent, though not always, not always, my dear, as you may soon see."

"I wouldn't know. I'm running a little low these days. Sorting law books was never my idea of a lucrative legal career and the basement I call home isn't quite the luxury I was dreaming of about a year ago."

The woman chortled. "When I was your age I was living in a small two-bedroom apartment with seven other girls. There were two beds, so four of us slept in them one week and the other four got to sleep in them on alternate weeks. The rest of the time we used sleeping bags and air mattresses." She pulled Miranda in a litter closer. "You'll do fine, which brings me to my reason for meeting with you, dear. I have a proposition for you."

"Are you hiring?"

"Let's say I'm recruiting."

"For what exactly?" Miranda asked. "You haven't even seen my academic history and we've never interviewed."

"I possess a complete copy of your academic standing and your achievements and we are interviewing now. I was not in court this week to witness judicial injustice. I was in court to watch you. The sentence handed down is irrelevant."

Miranda pulled away. "Irrelevant!"

"I don't mean to imply in terms of Morgan, dear, I mean irrelevant in terms of the four killers and rapists. Now, give me your arm. We haven't finished… interviewing."

Miranda slid her arm under the woman's sleeve. "What firm do you represent?"

"Oh, I'm not a lawyer, dear. No, no. I was a teacher

168

when I was younger, for a little while, until something happened to redirect my life. Now I'm what might be called a private investigator of sorts, an enabler you might say. My job is one of helping people find themselves and, every so often, I am called upon to assess certain of those people and offer them a position, albeit not on my own. You were studied this week by several people who see a promising future ahead of you as a prosecuting attorney."

"The job's been taken. I'm on a waiting list. They said they'd call when someone leaves for a bigger and better offer. I'll be dead by then, killed by a falling book, or maybe I'll hang myself from a shelf when I can't take all the excitement of a new edition. Ooooh"

She woman covered her mouth and giggled. "I believe otherwise. In fact your career will flourish quickly, Miranda." She flagged a taxi. "Let's take a ride. I have a good deal to tell you and a good deal to show you. I hope you're good with numbers."

"Where are we going?"

"To the island park where we can talk without all this noise and confusion. I'm sure the driver won't mind waiting for us."

The taxi pulled in to the curb. The woman asked Miranda to climb in first, claiming Miranda was younger and more limber, following with surprising litheness and closing the door. During the drive to the ferry Miranda understood by the woman's manner to keep the conversation facile. On the ferry, and free to walk around, they spoke about Morgan and once at the island park they stopped at a quiet and private cluster of trees where the woman asked the driver to come for them in time for the second return ferry.

The woman let Miranda speak more about Morgan until she deemed the time was proper to address in more detail her purpose for approaching Miranda. She opened her briefcase, revealing several white folders of photos and data.

Also in the briefcase was an envelope containing twenty-five thousand dollars, a blue folder containing travel information, a red one with enlarged photos of Morgan lying dead in the hospital's pathology lab and a small black velvet box trimmed in silver.

Miranda looked at the black pearl ring, listening to the woman tell her of its symbolism, how the black pearl in a miniature silver shell represented women helping women and that she should think of the ring as a constant reminder that Morgan's violent death had not gone unnoticed and would not be forgotten or ignored. The woman prompted Miranda to slip the ring onto her finger.

Miranda asked the woman why she was being given a gift and what she meant about Morgan not being ignored. The answer stunned her. She listened to the statistical data and saw heart-wrenching photographs of anonymous women in IC wards and morgues. She listened, her mouth agape, to what the woman guardedly had to say and when the woman told her of the invitation to spend several months overseas, and the objective, she bolted to her feet and ran away.

The taxi came back and the woman stood to advise the driver she would require another half hour. When she returned Miranda was standing to one side of the park bench staring at the graphic imagery of her murdered lover. She was crying and shaking. The woman explained that once Miranda accepted there would be no going back. Once she stepped from the plane she would have no idea of her location and no communication with anyone other than her keepers and guardians who would subject to a barrage of psychological and physical tests. If she passed she would become a Facilitator. In the eyes of the law she would be a killer. Others would either not care or be thankful for her good work. She would be well-trained by experts in their respective fields. In the previous forty-one years no Facilitator had ever been discovered. She would be trained to be invisible. She would be introduced to a director whose real identity she would never know, she would be well-paid and she would have the job in the justice department. However, if she failed any part of the testing she would be sent home not knowing where she had been and within the next three years she would be contacted with instructions to leave town for two weeks, which she would obey without question.

When Miranda asked why she would be asked to leave town the woman responded in such a peculiar fashion that Miranda couldn't resist smiling.

"Because, dear, the four darlings are going to be facilitated immediately upon the release of the two oldest and we want you far away. Then you will be left alone to carry on with your life and your career without intervention of any kind." She saw confusion on Miranda's face. "They have up to three years left to live, dear. The decision is irrevocable. Once a case study is approved, the process is unstoppable."

Miranda looked at the photos as the woman began to gather them. "I'll do it."

The woman showed no surprise, giving Miranda the envelope of hundred-dollar bills, instructing her to rent a safety deposit box. If she were to put the money in an account she would do so in reasonable and irregular increments. She handed Miranda the blue file folder with travel instructions and wished her bon voyage. They would not see one another again.

The woman had one final remark, one which would be repeated constantly throughout Miranda's training: Do not fail an assignment. Failure was not an option. No Facilitator had ever failed. Resigning was understandable, failure could be fatal.

Miranda left the country a few days later and was gone for eight months. Twenty-two months following her return, as she was walking to her car one evening after another exhausting workday, a sophisticated and middle-aged woman wearing a long coat and hat appeared from nowhere to walk behind her. The woman had pre-dialled Miranda's number and covered her mouth as she spoke into her phone. The conversation was succinct: Pearl was to leave the country by week's end.

Miranda knew not to ask why. As a result of their fathers' deep pockets and the persistence of the defence lawyers the oldest of Morgan's murderers were released earlier than anticipated. She booked her trip the next day, unaware the same woman followed her to the entrance of the travel agency where she could watch her young operative closely. When she was satisfied Miranda Stevens was leaving the country as instructed the director stood and left the mall.

Miranda flew to the Caribbean with two-piece swimsuits in her suitcase and Morgan on her mind. When she returned her boss called her into his office at the justice department and poured two plentiful cognacs. He had good news to share with her. The four punks who raped her and killed Morgan had been murdered on the same day in four different parts of town. One was shot, two others stabbed and the fourth was found with his neck broken. According to the police the killings were contracted. There was absolutely no evidence whatsoever. Of course, the cops had come to the office looking for Miranda. She was the prime suspect in the four murders, the one person they had singled out who would have motive, other than Morgan's family, and they had left shaking their heads upon hearing of her well-deserved vacation in St-Martin. Morgan's family on the west coast had also been discounted as possible suspects.

Miranda cried in Troy Torrington's office for an hour and asked for the rest of the day off, insisting she would make up for the time lost. She had something to do. He stood and gave her a tight hug. He gave her the cognac

172

bottle, a glass, and ample money for taxis as he admonished her not to drive and not to come back to work until the cognac wore off.

She took a cab to the grave to spend the afternoon talking with Morgan and getting drunk. By dinnertime she finished the bottle and fell asleep. She remembered waking in the dark, unafraid. She would never be afraid again. She could defend herself expertly and kill a man with ease. In the months since her return from the overseas she had employed her new skills on six occasions. Four met their fates by way of the pearl-handled dagger that was delivered to her from a mythical woman few people had ever seen. The other two were found with twin nine-millimetre holes in their foreheads.

The next morning Miranda Stevens was sitting in her office smiling when Troy walked in at 7:00 AM. She gave him a hug, blamed him for her atrocious hangover, and shooed him out to begin her day. She had said goodbye to Morgan. She would never forget her best friend. They would be part of one another forever. Her boss had been right. The time had come to find closure and move on, yet seven years later she hadn't forgotten, she hadn't moved on, and she was dressing to lure another man to his ironic end. He was cheating on Ann with the woman who was going to facilitate him, his wife surreptitiously doing to him what he had dreamt of doing to her. And Miranda intended for him to know.

At 5:30 she adjusted her fall and put on her hat. She knew Preston's meeting had already wrapped up, that he was likely en route to the police station. She would arrive at the Terrasse-Dufferin well ahead of him. She took her stiletto from her clutch and verified the mechanism. She reached for her gloves and left the room.

She arrived at 6:30. Tour buses lined the château's curved driveway, dozens of excited Japanese tourists were taking pictures of other excited Japanese tourists taking pictures, couples were strolling hand in hand, singles were reading in the park and the café-terrasses were overflowing with patrons coming together for the time-honoured cinq à sept.

She sat under the gazebo where she could see him arrive and be ready for him, without being seen by him. He climbed from the cab at 6:40, searching the immediate area for a tan dress before hurrying into the hotel. Miranda waited for a moment and walked to the high railing at the edge of the historic precipice. She undid the top few buttons of her dress and leaned forward to undo the bottom few. A warm breeze wafted up from the river to play with the silk edges and she looked up at the muted sound of a camera clicking. She smiled coquettishly, waving a scolding finger at a senior gentleman dressed in beige polyester pants, a matching windbreaker and pure white running shoes. He beamed widely, exposing a row of perfect porcelain teeth and walked away with the best souvenir of his trip. She was ready.

She looked at the impression her ring left on her finger and wondered what Ann would think of hers. Wearing it during any facilitation was forbidden. She had seen the photos of Ann Preston and had never forgotten the photographs of Morgan placed on a park bench a lifetime ago. Only once in her career had she seen another pearl ring like her own. Pearl existed everywhere, yet they existed nowhere. They were invisible. They had one unique agenda and she had no idea who might be a sister Facilitator.
*

The woman had been walking past Miranda in a grocery store one rainy Saturday morning and grabbed her arm without warning. She told Miranda she didn't have very long to talk. She had at last seen the ring she'd been searching for on the hands of strangers for so many months and her husband would soon be joining her. He had gone to the bank for grocery money.

174

"Where did you buy your ring?" Miranda asked coolly. "Mine is supposedly unique, yet they're so much alike. Excuse me for asking... is yours real?"

"Yes, it must be. It was a gift many years ago from a stranger, a lady. I never saw her again, but I do remember how elegant she was. She told me her name was Pearl. All I know is very soon after my husband had a terrible accident. He was killed. He died one night in our garage when I wasn't home. Somehow he came home very drunk and didn't shut off the engine. I moved away and started a new life. I never told my new husband about my insurance money, I didn't want it to be the reason he married me. It's over two million in all because of interest and when he found out he went crazy. He works coaching football and basketball at a local college. He makes fairly good money and we had an okay life, but when he discovered what I had kept from him things at home changed. I never wanted all that money."

"Why are you telling me this? Tell the police. Leave him."

"No, the police won't do anything. He has no previous record and I can't leave him. It's my house and my car. He moved in with me. I also have a twelve-year-old daughter."

"Has he hurt you? Has he hurt your daughter?"

She nodded. "It started about six months ago when I decided she should be going to a private school. He began laughing at me, saying there was no way and asking me what I was thinking. When I told him how wrong he was he didn't believe me at first and started thinking I was making fun of him. He got pretty upset. When I finally told him about the insurance, how I was left more than the house and car, he started drinking and storming around the house mumbling about all the times he wanted to go on vacation, about the car he always wanted, about a lot of things. After a while he punched me in front of my daughter. He never said he was sorry and soon he started talking about his rights, insisting fifty percent was his. He's wrong. I've checked with a lawyer. He even went to the bank trying to transfer part of it into his account. I want all the money for my daughter."

"She's your daughter?" Miranda asked. The woman nodded. "How often does he hit you?"

"It's sort of strange. He doesn't always hit me. He's always bumping into me and saying excuse me, but he's over six feet and weighs two-fifty. Or he he'll stick his foot out in front of me when I'm walking by and I trip quite often. I know that's what he wants. He wants to look down at me, to see me on my knees. What I don't know is why. Sometimes he holds my head under the bathwater, pretending he's joking when I know he isn't. He wakes me up in the middle of the night with toys, you know, adult stuff, and he's started going into my daughter's room without knocking. She's twelve. It's not right. The other night we got into a big fight about it. I heard her crying and when I went to her room he was spanking her under her nightie." The woman raised her sweater to show Miranda the bruises on the small of her back. "The ones on my shoulders are fading. I went through this before with the other one. I can't take much more and now I'm afraid for my daughter. The next time he touches her, I'll kill him. I swear" The woman looked at Miranda's ring. "I'm sorry for bothering you. It's just that the last lady was so much like you. I had to take a chance. No one else in here this morning is wearing such nice clothes or looks so pretty. I came right over to you, hoping, and I noticed your ring. I'm sorry."

"I'm sorry for you. I'm sorry this is happening to you."

Miranda saw a shift in the woman's eyes. "He's coming. I have to go. Goodbye."

"Goodbye."

The woman walked away and Miranda strolled with her cart in the opposite direction. She went to the cashier and left the store. Several minutes later the man and woman came out. Neither one noticing the car cruising slowly past them or the woman who was dictating their car's model and tag number into her mini recorder.

Her phone call had been answered without delay and her request for a case study was granted. She would learn of the decision by Monday, Tuesday latest. Weekends had no relevance for Pearl, nor did times zones, seasons or borders. Miranda watched the couple drive away and returned to finish her shopping.

The following Tuesday morning the response she expected came via a cryptic message. The facilitation was approved. The couple had been married barely three years. He was forty-seven and a college coach with a decidedly poor record. He was previously married and his current wife was wrong about his not having a record. Her predecessor had been treated at the hospital twice in two years. The first incident involved a broken nose, the second a dislocated shoulder. No charges were laid and his wife filed for divorce a few days later. Both times the explanation was a playful free-for-all, both times the patient's history sheet had been stamped "abused", a notation indicating the daughter's grades had suffered over the previous several months.

There would be no Enabler sent to Lillian's home, no black pearl in a black velvet box and Miranda was ordered to be somewhere else for the coming week with a well-documented history of her absence. She was also instructed to do whatever was necessary to avoid future contact with the woman. Miranda put her condo on the market the next morning and left town for a week of relaxation, much to the chagrin of her superior who had nothing to say about it. He was well aware of her standing in the legal community and that she hadn't taken a vacation in over a year. He made her promise to be back by the following Monday and walked away espousing his views on the younger generation.

Thursday Lillian Spencer sat on the sofa in her living room while her daughter slept peacefully in her room, waiting for her husband to come home from a pre-game strategy session with his team. Friday morning the college phoned to ask where he was, if anything was wrong, and Friday afternoon the police came by to tell her they had found her car abandoned in a no-parking zone. The vehicle had been towed, which wasn't the reason for their visit. They'd found something else. The keys were left in the ignition and a typed note was found under the visor. The officer read it, feeling sorry for Lillian: No more lost ball games, no more Saturday morning groceries, no more searching for the one perfect pearl. Good luck. You will never see me again. The officer left satisfied that further investigation was not warranted. There was nothing unusual about a man deserting his wife and worse crimes were on the books.

Lillian Spencer knew without the slightest doubt the woman in the grocery store with the pearl ring had known what to do. Lillian would never discover her husband's fate and she would never care. She knew he would never come home. She thought about the young woman in the store, and the enormity of what her black pearl ring must represent. How could anyone so quickly and secretly alter another person's life?
*

Miranda saw Preston exit the hotel and faced away before he could make eye contact. She raised a foot a few inches to the lower rail and let the wind sweep away her dress to reveal a tanned inner thigh. She adjusted her hat and looked at her watch.

Preston came towards her along the railing, taking in every bare inch of her exposed thigh. He stopped five or six feet away and leaned against the railing, absorbing the slight swell of her breasts before he spoke. All told her clothes couldn't weigh an ounce, he thought.

178

"As usual, you look great."

"Thank you, Charles. How was your day?"

"As usual we ran into overtime, happily with minimal casualties. I barely had time to change. How was your day?"

"Successful. So, are we ready for a drink?"

"You bet we are. I hear pretty well every place is good, except the one on the corner where the guys from the office go to bird-dog the babes."

"Nice term. They sound like wonderful men." She filled her lungs with the warm evening air. "So let's walk a little and you can tell me about yourself."

He was forty-three. He graduated with a degree in education, deciding on sales as a career for the better money and the travelling. He had been with the same company since his graduation and had climbed the ladder to National Manager. He was thrilled to have met her on the Sunday and since then he thought he was living a lie. He was having his marriage dissolved and had spoken with his wife by phone over the past few nights who was in full agreement. The divorce would be amicable, the best solution for both of them. He hoped Pearl would still be joining him for dinner on Sunday. She answered that she was looking forward to dinner and how surprised she was when they ran into each other the previous day.

It had been a gruelling day, she continued. She was looking forward to a cocktail, a light dinner and perhaps a calèche ride. She spoke a little about her work as a corporate lawyer, clearly showing more interest in his life. Frequently, while sipping her drink on the crowded terrace, she needed to place a hand where the front edges of her dress came together and she had no doubt by the time they left for dinner that Preston wanted to see more than a tiny patch of puffy white silk.

Before going into the restaurant Pearl insisted she pay half the bill. He wouldn't hear of it and she graciously accepted on condition he would allow her to pay for Sunday's dinner. He agreed and, caught up in his euphoria, failed to notice as the evening progressed that she had scarcely touched her wine and had left her cocktail glass untouched as she chuckled inwardly at the power of panties.

The calèche carried them to the Citadel and the Plains of Abraham, where Montcalm died in battle the day after his adversary James Wolfe in 1759, clacking along North America's oldest street built in 1615, la rue Notre-Dame, on their way to the harbour where Pearl seemed uneasy.

"What's wrong?" Preston asked. "That looks like a business frown."

She smiled in response. "It's not. I assure you. Listen, I was thinking. I've enjoyed my evening very much and I wondering ..." She let her words trail off.

"About what, how this nag is going to get us back up the hill?"

"No, not exactly. I was thinking we should go somewhere for a nightcap, somewhere not too noisy. I have some vodka in my room, but it's a boutique hotel and I'd hate to run into people from the office. You know how some people are." She paused, crossing one leg over the other and folding her arms. Her dress separated across her bare thighs and her crossed arms made her breasts seem fuller, all the more inviting, achieving the desired effect.

"I have an en suite and room service. I can order up bottle of vodka or cognac or whatever you want."

"I'd like that very much. Vodka with crushed ice would be a perfect ending to the evening. As long as you kick me out if I stay too late."

"The night's still young and this beats being with the guys hands down."

"I believe bird-dogging is the term you used."

"They're all talk. If any of them ever did find a real woman like you they'd be up the creek, sans paddle."

Preston laughed, Pearl smiled demurely. He wanted to

jump from the carriage and flag a taxi. He couldn't believe he was going to have her. She couldn't have been more implicit. He'd finally see the tops of those long legs wrapped in panties he would yank to her ankles and run his hands all over that perfect ass he couldn't stop thinking about since first seeing her.

The ride seemed to take forever. Outside the hotel he handed her a spare key and gave her the room number, asking her to wait a few minutes as he strode away. Once in his room he ran to the stack of laminated info sheets to check the bar menu, then he all but passed out. Who gave a shit, he thought? He was going to bag her and she was hot. All his past one-nighters had seen their best years and looked their best in the bar or in the dark. This one was close to half his age and he was getting her for free. So who cared about a few hundred bucks for a bar bill when most of it could be expensed?

He called down to order the liquor and crushed ice as he scanned the room. His en suite was a standard bedroom with a small alcove containing a sofa-bed and a table. He dimmed the lights and set the television to a pay-per-view movie he knew contained partial nudity. Moments later Pearl walked through the door as though returning to her own room and went to the window to see the spectacular view. She saw the harbour lights, the green and red navigation lights of freighters passing in the night, people strolling and a million sparkling stars. The whole setting was charming, romantic, and she turned from the window with a feigned start when she heard the discreet knock at the door.

"Charles, before you open the door let me go into the bathroom. Apart from the requisite decorum of the moment, I would like to freshen myself." He pointed towards the bathroom door. "And don't forget, I take lots of crushed ice. We don't want the evening to end too soon, do we?"

"Hell, no. That's the last thing I want."

He waited until Pearl closed the door before opening the other to the waiter. Preston had never signed a more expensive chit. He didn't care. He was moments away from fucking the best looking thing in the city. He poured the drinks and angled the television towards the alcove. He would take his time and not show how anxious he was. He'd wait until they watched a few nude scenes and put down a few vodkas and gins. Then he would take her hand or brush his against her leg. Her dress was as thin as a veil, he felt his excitement grow and he wondered what was taking her so long.

Pearl came out looking good. Her hair was combed straight. She had retouched her make-up and hadn't closed a single button. She reached for her drink and sat into a corner of the sofa in the alcove. She kicked off her shoes, crossed her legs and Preston sat beside her as the movie began. Nude scenes came and went, which she seemed to enjoy and he had served her a second and third drink within the first hour. He stood to serve her a fourth.

"Charlie, can I ask you something?"

"Ask me anything."

"Do you mind putting on something a little more exciting and would you mind if I took a shower?"

Hallelujah, the deed was done.

"There's a spare robe in the closet if you want something to wear until it's time to leave."

"Let's see what happens."

Pearl took her purse. She locked the door and put on surgical gloves before she began. She wiped off her newly purchased make-up as the shower was running, she flushed the toilet, dampened a towel which she tossed over the edge of the bath and she put on the robe before returning the gloves to her purse and checking her fingernails. Fifteen minutes later she emerged revitalized.

"Wow."

"What a great idea. I feel so refreshed. Thanks, Charlie.

I feel like a new woman." She placed her folded dress on the bed and took up her refilled glass. "I left some hot water for you. Go on. Don't tell me you're not screaming to wash off the day."

"That's probably not a bad idea. Give me a few minutes."

"Go. I'll be here."

Preston went, glancing at her dress on the bed to see whether she'd left off her panties and bra. He couldn't tell and whether she was wearing them or not was moot. He grabbed the second robe and disappeared into the bathroom. As soon as Pearl heard the water running she strengthened his drink and poured hers into the sofa as she had done with the previous three, then she increased the volume on the second movie.

The scenes were explicit to say the least and she watched for a moment. The couple looked silly and disinterested. The woman was on her hands and knees, lurching back and forth, trying to see behind her as she whistled endless short and long "ahs" through lips Pearl thought had lost their ability to close. The man was grimacing, his lips squeezed together and he was groaning. Pearl giggled, thinking he seemed to have a high tone for in and low tone for out. She didn't believe any human would naturally make those noises, despite believing for years that penises belong in pickle jars. She wondered how much the woman was paid, whether they were a couple, or whether she was promised the world by some no-name, sleazy film director. She had another idea of love-making and she wasn't missing anything.

Preston came out ten minutes later with his hair dried, combed over, and his robe cinched and knotted at his waist.

"You were right. I feel great."

She nodded at the screen. "Apparently so do those two. Charlie, have your drink and pour me another. I have a suggestion."

Preston's eyes were glued to the screen. He whistled and downed his drink in one gulp before refilling both glasses, swallowing the better part of his refill and topping off what was left. "What's your suggestion?"

"Well," she began coyly, "it is a little late and I have had a little to drink. I think a little too much. Would you mind if I stayed the night and left first thing in the morning, say six or six-thirty. I've enjoyed my time with you. I haven't had this much fun in a long time."

"I was hoping you would say that. I didn't want to sound as though I was using you to help me get over my upcoming divorce. I want you to stay and I want dinner with you on Sunday."

"God, I'm so horny watching this stuff. Let's cut to the chase, Charlie. I like you, you like me, and we want to fuck each other like monkeys. So let's do it." She grabbed for her purse and stood. "Give me a couple of minutes and be ready for the best rodeo ride of your life, cowboy."

Preston stood. "Two minutes and counting. Go."

By the time Pearl was halfway to the bathroom Preston had tossed aside his robe and thrown back the covers. By the time she came out he was covered to his mid-chest, waiting for her to drop her robe, disappointed when she darkened the room.

"Let's watch a bit of this movie first, Charlie. Maybe we can show them a thing or two. I think she's hot, don't you." Pearl almost choked on the words. The woman on the screen looked as though she'd been up all night with a collegiate football team and their horned mascot.

"No kidding, but nowhere near as hot as you."

"I'm hot? Do you really think so?"

"Baby, you are very hot. Believe me. I know hot when I see it."

"That's nice. Thank you, Charlie. I tell you what. Close your eyes and lie flat. I want to try something on you that some guy showed me once on vacation. I think you'll like it.

184

He was ecstatic when I got the hang of it. I remember he told me I was one of his best ever." Preston closed his eyes like an obedient schoolboy and slid down as she clambered onto the bed. She dragged a pillow over his knees, wanting to avoid body contact, and crawled over him as his hands came up to push away her robe. He wanted to fondle her breasts, he wanted to see them. She said no, first things first and she took his arms by the wrists and placed them by his pillow. "Are you ready, Charlie? I promise you're going to want to scream. It'll be that good." She spread her hands across the sheet covering his bloated abdomen, eliminating the loose folds and despising the feel of his body

"I am so ready. Do it. Whatever you're doing, do it before I explode."

Pearl reached inside her hotel robe and grasped the extended stiletto she'd taped to her thigh. She ran a hand along the sheet to the base of his rib cage and pressed in with her thumb. She looked at him thinking he was a shapeless troll. She had facilitated men on the street, in cars, in hotel lobbies and in theatres, never in a bed. He was disgusting. She wanted to retch, and the thought flashed across her mind that anyone Ann Preston would find to replace him would be better than this overfed baboon.

Straddling the pillow, she rocked to and fro to tease him and asked if he was ready for the trip of a lifetime. He said yes, he was ready. Good, so was she. She shifted her weight to one knee, telling him to arch his back and place his hands behind his head. He obeyed her. He looked absurd, like a bloated sea mammal. She asked with practiced coolness how he felt as a man when he left his wife lying on the floor, bleeding and without her teeth. His eyes opened wide as she drove the eight-inch blade in under his ribs and through spongy flesh to his heart. She twisted the blade once, wiping it clean as she pulled it through the sheet. The last thing Charles Preston saw was Pearl staring into his eyes. The last thing he heard was "from your ex-wife, Ann.

Goodnight Preston." He coughed once and died.

Preston filled the room with putrid air from under the sheet as Miranda Stevens put on her dress and verified the room. She put on silicone gloves before washing her glass, the key card, the bathroom doorknob and the TV remote. She rinsed her stiletto and buried the blade into the pearl handle that she put into her clutch. She rolled the robe she'd worn over her lingerie, added the twin strips of tape and put the bundle into the plastic hotel laundry bag. She took his wallet from his jacket, his watch and his wedding ring, and searched the room once more. She turned off the television, put on her shoes and her hat, and checked her purse once more for the dagger before leaving the room with the laundry bag swinging by her side.

Not looking up in public places had been drilled into her head a thousand times. Do not look up and always wear a hat when acting on behalf of Pearl. She left by a side door and walked several blocks to where she parked her rental car. Along the way she emptied the contents of his wallet into various gutters. She kept the three hundred in cash, pushed the robe into a public garbage receptacle and a few blocks later she tossed the bag into another. Driving across the Pierre Laporte Bridge, named to commemorate the Labour Minister assassinated by the FLQ in 1970, she lowered her window and tossed the watch and ring onto the deck.

Charles Preston expired at 12:05. By 1:00 AM Miranda Stevens had showered thoroughly, sanitized her knife and placed her long hairpiece along with each item she'd worn into separate plastic grocery bags. She organized the small pile by the door and punched a phone number onto her cell's dial pad. There was seldom a response and her message never changed: Facilitation confirmed. Then she forgot him, poured a bar brand vodka from the mini bar and lay on the bed to watch television and formulate a shopping list.

She didn't set the alarm and woke late, at the very moment four police officers pushed through the doors of the Salon Jacques Cartier at 8:30. The precinct had called Preston's room minutes earlier with no response. Peter and Tony explained that Preston was seldom late for meetings, though he did unexpectedly run into an old school friend the previous day and went out for a few drinks immediately after the meeting. Tony had also called his room and assumed he was in the shower.

The cops already had everyone's attention, but when they explained the court order and the reason for his arrest, Charlie Preston reverted to being the pathetic image they witnessed behind the rain-streaked window of the police cruiser Monday morning. Everyone realized Preston's portion of the sales meeting had abruptly ended. Ten minutes later the same held true for all of them.

They gathered in the lobby to watch the commotion. Hotel managers were talking with detectives and nodding their heads, uniformed porters were nodding with uniformed cops, video tapes were being confiscated and the twelfth floor was cordoned off as a crime scene. 1218 was being searched as one detective with a digital camera compiled a graphic file of Charles Preston's wide-eyed corpse lying oblivious under a blood-stained sheet in a noxious mixture of his body's excretions.

Outside, Japanese tourists snapped photos of smiling wives and frowning mothers standing in front of a backdrop of flashing red and blue lights.

Eighteen

Toronto, Ontario
Thursday, August 09

Ann Preston learned of her husband's murder later Thursday morning. Hearing the nature of his death she shrugged her shoulders and thanked them for coming to the hospital to tell her. She would be fine, she told the police, and when they offered to relate the news to her sons she accepted and thanked them again. Her release papers were signed at noon.

She sat in the taxi looking at her home that seemed so cold and empty, devoid of warmth and memories. She snorted, thinking of her dead husband. When whoever the person was killed him, they also killed the mortgage and the car loan. She pressed her lips together and nodded. She would put the house up for sale in the afternoon, she would rid herself of her deadbeat sons and after dinner she would trade in the car for a model that didn't remind her of a taxi or a cop car.

She realized in the hospital how much she didn't like her sons. Worse, she didn't love them. Her sons had never heard of the insurance policy and would not. The time had come for them to get out. Her time had also come at long last. She would give each one ten thousand and tell them to get lost. Then she would get lost. She had wanted for the longest time to live by the ocean and she would. She would sell everything and leave. She would start over. She would drop weight and she would buy a new wardrobe each month until she was happy with herself. She would get the education she had always wanted and she would get a real man.

By dinner time the For Sale sign was planted, she cashed in two savings certificates and gave each son a cheque with a warning on their way out not to come back or she would call the police. Then she sat and cried. She had kept her promise to herself and the salesman promised delivery of the new car by noon the next day.

She gathered all his clothing along with whatever she didn't need of his in the short term. She emptied the fridge of beer and swept the shelves in the family room clean of photo albums which went into green garbage bags to be left and forgotten on the curb. She stripped the bed, put on fresh sheets and put whatever would be of interest to his company in a cardboard box which she would send the next morning by taxi. By eight o'clock she had pretty much expunged Charlie Preston from the house when the doorbell chimed.

Ann opened the door, appearing agitated. She was running on nerves, caught up in her own hectic whirlwind. Her legs and her feet were bare, her blouse was hanging out from the waist of her skirt, her face was discoloured, still somewhat swollen, and her hair was a scattered collection of bobby pins. The woman on the porch was ten inches taller in heels, she wore a linen dress with a matching wide-brimmed hat, her sunglasses and purse reeked designer and she couldn't have been more unexpected or unwanted. Ann could not have felt more like Ann.

"Good evening, Ann. My name is Pearl. I realize you have been through a difficult time following your husband's death. However, I would ask for a few moments of your time. I have a small gift for you."

"Are you from his company?"

"No. I never met him. Although, I do know a good deal

about him and I would like to share certain information with you, if I may, information I hope might make you feel better."

"I already feel better."

"Then you will feel fabulous. Please."

"The house is a mess. I've been making a few changes."

Pearl grinned, seeing the cluster of garbage bags. "Yes, I know, and I understand many more are to come. I sincerely wish you success."

"Success at what?"

"Your new life, which is the reason I'm here."

Ann felt like a scullery maid beside the woman as she stepped aside to allow Pearl inside. She felt ashamed in her own home. She found herself wanting the woman to see how she would look in a month when she would be living on the west coast or in a year when she would be in college and feeling smarter. She woman spoke with such eloquence. Ann wanted the same. She wanted to be a lady like the one sitting beside her.

"I want you to listen to something, Ann."

"How do you know him? How do you know me?"

"We've known him for no more than a few days. We met him fortuitously and took an immediate interest in him, and in you."

"Why? What was he doing?"

"He was explaining to his friends that he wanted to kill his wife. Please believe me when I say, if we had thought for a moment he would beat you Monday morning he would never have made his way home."

"I don't understand. What is that supposed to mean?"

"I want you to hear something Ann, something recorded a few hours before you last saw him, before he beat you." Pearl reached into her handbag for the micro recorder and pressed play:

Thing is, who hasn't dreamt of getting rid of the wife at least once in his life. They can't arrest us for thinking. Shit, think about it. They never have enough of this, never enough of that. They need money for this, money for that. They don't like staying home so they get little jobs and then complain about having to keep the frigging house clean. Their clothes are never good enough, we never take them out. And no goddamn wonder. Once that frigging white dress comes off nothing else ever fits right, and the goddamn kids. Not that I don't care about them, but shit, what is it now, one-eighty, two-hundred K before we can kick the little fuckers out and not have them slipping back in to suck us dry. Tell you the truth; I'll be working till I'm a goddamn hundred. It makes a man think. Shit does it make me think.

Only ever hit the wife once, after she smacked me for whatever I said at the time. Sort of like her tits for tat. She hit me, so I hit her. Okay, so maybe a little harder, oops. It doesn't mean I don't love her. Fact is, a guy has to do what a guy has to do and I had to make a point. It was a lesson learned and she's been good ever since. Anyway, it was years ago. It's water under the bridge. It's like anything else. Do it right the first time and forget about it.

Women don't ever forget that kind of shit. They might act like they do, believe me they don't.

So what, as long as it gets the job done. Now we get along fine, man and wife.

You think so. I'm telling you, they never forget. The biggest problem isn't getting so pissed off that you have to smack them around a little. The biggest problem is getting married in the first place for the sake of a little tail, the same tail year after year after year. Me, I spend a couple of extra bucks when I'm away from the office and get serviced the right way: always a different menu du jour, different flavours, and sometimes a double serving if you catch my drift. I've done it that way for twenty years with nothing older than mid-twenties and never the same one twice. They go home, I go to sleep and come home to a ...

191

To a dry weekend and a sore hand. My brother-in-law, big Italian shit, he told me once if I ever hurt his little sister he'd kill me and I tell you he fucking meant it. The guy's a fucking lunatic, but it was too late to back out. I'd already done her fifty different ways and he would have killed me for bagging her. So what the fuck, what can I say? I adapted. The funny thing is, now she's bigger than me.

Always check out the mother first. It's like looking into the future. They all look great when their young, but shit do things fall fast, some faster than others...and there's nothing dry about my weekend. My neighbour works weekends. I've been doing his wife for the past four years. Saturdays and Sundays like clockwork on the patio, in the rain, in the park, on my car, in the snow, in the pool. The broad's a nymphomaniac, pure and simple, with no lovey-dovey shit, no flowers, and no candy, just hot and heavy good times. No holds barred. I caught a glimpse of her sunning her naked buns one Saturday then again on the Sunday. I must have taken a hundred close-ups of her. The next week it was the same thing, buck-ass naked.

So, what, you jumped the fence and asked her for some, just like that?

No, I needed a reason. I damn near ran to the liquor store, bought a two-four of coolers, and carried them over, just like that. I got my breath under control, walked straight through her gate, and stood there. All she did was drag a hand towel part way over her bare ass and say thanks, are they cold? I said I was sorry and looked away. Told her I didn't expect to see her, that I only wanted to welcome them to the neighbourhood. I put down the coolers, then the next thing I know, she's standing right beside me covering her titties and not much else with her towel and she's popping two of them open. I spent the afternoon. Then she was twenty-five, hubby was twenty-six. Now she's twenty-nine, as tight as ever, and hasn't talked about divorce once. She loves the guy. She just can't get enough. True story, guys, and I've got the photos to prove it. Something else she likes. I could start my own frigging porno site.

He knows. The guy knows."

He doesn't know shit.

Yeah, he does, and he probably gets off hearing about it.

I don't get that lucky in my dreams and tonight's going to be a bitch when I get home. I gave mine a good one last night, thought I broke her goddamn jaw. Never thought I would. Shit. It happened before I could stop myself, a knee-jerk reaction to all her bullshit. You wouldn't believe the goddamn noise she made. The damn thing still smarts.

No, shit. It's crossed my mind a few times, got to admit. The one thing stopping me is her freaking brother.

First time?

Yeah, first time. Before it was pretty much showing her the back of my hand and letting her know not to push. This time she pushed. Guess I always knew it would happen one day.

What she do to piss you off?

Found her going through my suitcase, smelling my goddamn clothes if you can believe that shit. Somehow she found out about my last trip and she wouldn't shut up about it. I told her I couldn't even remember the broad's name, that she was a fluky one-night piece of pussy, a one-time thing. She wouldn't shut up about it. I swore it was the first time. She just kept on and on, throwing anything she could grab. It was like a frigging hurricane. Then she started with the kids, telling them she wanted them out. I had them on the phone for an hour yelling into my ear. Jesus. She can't even take care of her own goddamn kids.

Walk out.

No way, don't do it. You'd lose your shirt. I knew a guy once who thought he could walk. He walked straight from riches to rags in a matter of months. He ended up on the street and got kicked to death one night over a frigging park bench. The wife didn't even go to the funeral. What kind of woman doesn't go to her husband's fucking funeral? My advice: don't leave. Stick it out. It could be a lot worse. They got laws about abandonment shit these days. It's all about them and who's to say your kids wouldn't plaster your face all over the net. You'd be screwed inside of a month with no job, no house and no money. Stay with the occasional one-nighter. It's a better ride and it's cheaper.

Ever think it would be worth it, ever dream about it? You're right. I should have walked out years ago, before the goddamn kids, but she wanted them. She had to have them, and now she can't wait to get rid of them. Shit, I want out so bad I can taste it. She never shuts up. Sometimes I see her dead in my dreams, just gone. Thing is, I always wake up. Life is pure shit, guys. Could be it's time to stop dreaming about it. With a good lawyer I'd be out in eight to ten with a million in insurance. Shit, compounded, it could be as high as one-five.

Any natural colour drained from Ann's face, leaving her complexion a hideous yellowish-blue mask.

"That's horrible. He was laughing and talking about killing me."

"Yes, he was."

"How did you get that?"

"Very much by accident…or happy coincidence."

"You said he would never have made his way home."

"That's right. Had we suspected for a moment we would have facilitated him on the spot, not last night."

"What?"

"The term is a trade euphemism. We are responsible for what happened to your husband. You may be interested to know that the facilitation was performed by a woman he invited to his room for sex. Of course, the rendezvous was orchestrated by us and things didn't quite work out for him as he had anticipated." Pearl reached into her handbag for the little jewel box. She pulled back the velvet lid and showed Ann the ring. "We would like you to wear this, Ann.

It will tell many people you will never know or see who you are and what you have been through."

"The bastard was actually talking about killing me. He was at the bar on Sunday, wasn't he? He was talking with those horrible men about killing me and they were laughing about it."

"He's not laughing anymore. I don't imagine any of his bar cronies will either, once they see the six o'clock news." Pearl placed the little velvet box in Ann's lap. "Your combined insurance is four million, Ann. Most times we request ten percent for our services, although in your case we acted without your previous knowledge or consent and, for that reason, the case study was pro bono."

"How could you know about the insurance?"

"We know, simply said. The ten percent is never mandatory, although no one has ever refused."

"Is the money a fee for the killers?"

"We prefer not to call them killers. The woman last night did what she did to save your life. I have never met her and never will, though at one time she was in a situation similar to yours. It's the unfortunate commonality we share, and I am certain she wears her ring with pride. Nor will you ever know her, though she has seen you by virtue of your recent photographs, the ones taken without your teeth. To answer your question, she does receive compensation for her service, though not the full amount. What she does is very dangerous and if something were to happen to her we would have no way to help her. However, the greater part of the fee is put towards administrative costs and pro bono work which we undertake for various reasons."

"Ten percent doesn't sound like very much for somebody saving my life." Ann took the ring from the box. "He's never given me anything as lovely as this." She laughed softly. "A pearl from a Pearl which, I assume, is not your real name."

"You're quite correct."

"Did he suffer?"

"I would think not. Facilitations must be carried out extremely quickly and with precision to avoid a struggle and possible failure. We do what we do out of necessity, not pleasure, although some case studies are more gratifying to us than others. We simply don't fail, one reason being we maintain a high degree of objectivity."

"And the woman who did it, will she ever get caught?"

"No. There's absolutely no way to discover who she is. It's not like television. No one will see a hair from twenty feet away or a trace of blood on a shoe one week after the event. Even if those things were to happen, and they don't in our world, the person doesn't exist to anyone but herself and a very privileged few."

"Where do I send the cheque?"

Pearl shook her head. "It's not mandatory."

"I disagree. Knowing someone cared so much about me makes it mandatory. Besides, I'm selling the house. I'll still be very well off."

"Thank you. If you're certain, we accept. Another person will contact you within three months. It's not at all complicated and done with the utmost anonymity."

"Can you thank her for me, the woman who helped me?"

"I can, through channels. I have no idea who she is, however I will make certain she hears the message. She'll be pleased to hear of your concern for her well-being and your generosity. Thank you."

Nineteen

Quebec City / Montreal
Thursday, August 09

Pearl left Ann to her dreams and her future as Miranda Stevens strolled the narrow and winding streets of Vieux-Québec with a growing number of shopping bags dangling from her hands. Her first priority of the new day was the disposal of the grocery bags from the night before. Her second was to put the three hundred dollars into the Salvation Army jar she'd seen the previous day. She spent a few thousand dollars on European lingerie, dresses and shoes. She had a croque-Madame with a carafe of wine for lunch in a quaint bistro, she did more shopping, found a hairdresser called Henri who actually was French and returned to the hotel for a dip in the pool. She had bought a thong bikini with a daringly tiny top, convincing herself she would dare to wear it if no one else was at the pool, but seeing practically none of her body covered when she stepped in front of the mirror she wasn't sure and she pulled at the strings.

At home she would often steal one or two weekend hours on her private nineteenth-floor patio to tan au naturel and she had no lines, deciding she didn't need the hassle of sex-deprived guys pointing their cell phones at her from the pool or their windows. She tossed the thong into her suitcase, promising herself an island vacation in the spring when she would be seen wearing the bottoms, if not the top. At the pool she flipped through tourist brochures, deciding which of the finer restaurants to visit for dinner, and which bar, before deciding which of her new purchases she would wear.

Rick Kendall, on the other hand, was released from his seventy-two-hour detention on his own recognizance following his preliminary hearing and was working hard at getting drunk. He refused the option of remaining in custody until his court appearance and consequently was ordered not to communicate with his wife, nor to come into contact with her until that time. He was not to remain in the house any longer than was necessary to collect his personal accessories and officers were assigned to ensure his compliance with the order.

As the cruiser approached the home on chemin des Bois-Francs he saw the accumulated flyers strewn across the porch and he knew what she had done. Once inside he hurried to the fridge and reached in for a six-pack of beer, claiming sarcastically the cans were personal items. The cops ignored him and followed him through each room of the house. Her clothes were there, so were the suitcases, but Alicia was gone. She didn't leave a note, the beds hadn't been slept in and the air was heavy and stale from the warm summer heat. He went to the garage. The car was there. Then he thought of the bank account and howled involuntarily. The police watched him leave after relieving him of his house keys and the remote for the garage. They activated the override on the latter and secured the front and back doors before leaving as Kendall raced to the ATM at the corner store.

His balance was a dollar, leaving him no money for more beer, gas or food, and he had nowhere to stay. He called the garage where he worked to say he would be in early the following day. They told him not to bother. The police had gone to see them, they knew all about his arrest and his final cheque was put in the mail on Monday. He slammed down the pay phone and stormed out. At the mailbox he tore open the solitary envelope. The cheque was for two-hundred dollars and change, enough for two or three nights in a flop house, a few cases of beer and some sandwiches if he was lucky. The twelve hundred would have lasted the full three weeks with some panhandling. While in custody he heard what kind of money good panhandlers tallied at the end of each day. His life had gone to shit because of her, so why not go full circle and beg for money.

He went to the bank to cash the cheque and to the corner store where he bought a twelve-pack and a few sandwiches. He would have to go the unemployment centre once again to be humiliated and demeaned, though he wouldn't get a government cheque for a month. That could wait one more day. He blamed her. Everything was her fault. She had no right to run to the hospital and involve the cops. They could have talked. They always talked after an episode and she always understood why he did what he did. She just never learned and because of her they confiscated his gun, he had a criminal record and, if no one wanted him before, they wouldn't want a cripple with a police record.

He went to a shopping mall he knew would be crowded, thinking he might make a few extra dollars. He combed his hair in the mirror. He had one beer and a sandwich, and wondered how he would do as a beggar, what he would say. People were suckers, his cellmates told him, especially women who were particularly easy to con. People give money because they don't want to feel like shit, he was told. Hit on the older women, though not too old, and forget the very young ones, they told him. Look humble and desperate and never look directly at them. Sit on the ground, round your shoulders and never look at them. When they see your eyes they know you want what's up their skirts, not dollars. Women only want eye contact when they're the ones looking for some guy's money, then the skirts don't matter very much.

Kendall opened another can. He guzzled the beer from full to empty in a few gulps and went to the mall's main entrance.

Miranda returned to her hotel with an armful of new clothes.

Twenty

Montreal, Quebec City
Thursday, August 09

First he went into the mall, stopping at the first coffee counter. He asked for an empty cup, saying he needed water to take his pills. The woman behind the counter gave him a medium size filled with tap water and smiled mechanically before serving paying customers. At his car he spilled the water onto the pavement, refilling the cup with beer from the cans he had left. At the entrance he sat on the ground, propped himself against the wall with his legs straight out and waited.

Most people passing by ignored him. Teenagers were the worst. Young girls wearing indecent skirts that flipped up as they sauntered along snubbed him while their brain-dead boyfriends sneered at him. The older shoppers didn't laugh. They hurried by without making eye contact and he realized he hadn't brought anything into which they could toss their coins. He gulped his beer, wiped the white froth from the rim, and set the cup by his feet. He tugged at a pant leg and pushed the sock to his ankles to show his battle scar, telling all who passed he was a war vet and unemployed.

It worked. Within an hour he earned ten dollars from people going in, not enough for a twelve-pack, and people coming out either shrugged with full arms or claimed not to have change. When the younger ones who first taunted him came out he told the boys to screw off in a gruff voice and scrambled to lie flat on his front to look up as the girls passed him. He told them he liked what he saw, especially what the tallest one was showing him, and asked to see more. He asked her name, noisily lapping his tongue in and out his mouth, and when the boys started to mock him and stick out their middle fingers to him he pushed himself to his feet, towering over them. They turned and ran into mall ahead of the girls, tripping on their sagging jeans and shoelaces. The older patrons were appalled by the spectacle, yet did nothing as Kendall scurried with a limp to the cover of parked cars and the security of his own, forgetting his money in the excitement.

No one was coming after him. Security guards worked the mall, real cops patrolled the perimeter and that gave him enough time to think of where to go next, certainly not downtown. The thirty-minute drive would take three times as long in late-day traffic. Instead he drove to a convenience store for more beer and sandwiches, then to a street lined with houses on one side and a park on the other where all-night parking was permitted until the first year's first snowfall.

Twenty-One

Quebec City, Quebec
Thursday, August 09

Snow was three months away and winter was the last thing on Miranda's mind. She loved her boss and everyone in her office. Most weeks she put in seven days to their five or six and fourteen hours to their ten or twelve. There was never a problem with him or friction with them when she needed time for herself.

When she called the office to stay current her boss asked slyly if she had certain news she would like to share with him. She giggled and answered she would not be late Monday morning and that she needed a salary increase because she'd spent a ton of money to make herself look good in court. He asked where she was and she answered she was shopping in heaven. When she closed her phone she tapped the casing as though she was patting his cheek. Troy had become a surrogate father to her as much as friend and she had somehow managed never to lie to him.

Stockings and garters were tempting and completely out of the question. The night air was too warm for even the sexiest buckles and bows. Her panties were black and sinfully sheer, her bra was a sprinkle of Valentino perfume and her Miu-Miu sandals were a black-on-white decadent treat. Her black linen skirt with delicate white-ribbon trim accentuated most of her toned thighs and her décolleté white silk blouse had black patchwork pockets and cuffs. Her new handbag was a bright red Pravda and her hematite earrings, crafted by a local artisan jeweller, were the perfect complement to her ring. When she was finished she dragged over a chair and sat in front of a mirror to cross her legs. Oh yeah, she thought, somebody somewhere had to like that.

There would be no hat and no car. She took a taxi to the beginning of la rue Grande-Allée and climbed out at the corner feeling exquisite. Men and women alike looked at her, not the same way as they would at home, she thought, and she loved the attention. Her restaurant of choice was the Louis Hébert where the most intimate table was reserved for her. The meal surpassed all expectations and the sommelier's choice of wine was superb. Dessert was a small selection of the finest cheeses she had ever tasted, accompanied by a single glass of dessert wine.

Miranda never made a secret of her feelings, neither did she flaunt them. She was characteristically quiet and subdued. Such was her mood on the Thursday as she discreetly queried the hostess in a whisper as to where she might find a lounge where she would not be outnumbered by men wanting to buy her drinks. The woman gave the question serious thought. Miranda could see her searching her mind for an answer. Nevertheless she was unable to think of a single bar, suggesting the maître d' would be more aware, and Miranda was a second too late in raising her hand to halt the woman.

She expected curious looks, or raised eyebrows, quiet murmurs between the two. Instead the elegant and charming gentleman came to her table, stooped slightly to speak with her and suggested what he thought would be the perfect conclusion to her evening. The sophisticated lounge wasn't specifically for women; however, he suggested she might expect a discreet clientele of singles and couples with an appreciation for finer wines and premier spirits that were somewhat a step above.

When Miranda settled the bill he escorted her to the curb, signalled a taxi and gave instructions to the driver. Five minutes later they drove through the gates of the old city and she was saying "merci" in her own cute way to the valet who opened her door at the curb in front Le Club Discrèt. Walking past another man and through the doors he opened for her, she wondered whether she had screamed out "wow!" or imagined she had. She was coming back to Quebec, definitely was. The ambiance was refined and quiet, the lighting muted, the music calming, and the women serving drinks were practically as well dressed as Miranda.

Young couples were lost in intimate tête-à-têtes, sitting side by side in plush and comfy sofas. Professional-looking young men were seated with other au courant young men, beautifully-dressed and professional-looking women her age oblivious to all but their female companions. She had promised herself a hundred times before. This time she was serious. She would learn French.

Two men were sitting in separate worlds, reading, a few single women sat alone, waiting to be served, and one was sitting solo at the bar. A waitress who in no way looked like one came to Miranda to welcome her.

"I'm sorry. I haven't been here very long and I don't speak French."

"This is not a problem, mademoiselle. I do speak English. A sofa, may I suggest, or a stool at the bar?" she asked with an accent Miranda was beginning to adore. "Are you to be joined?"

"I'm sorry?" Miranda questioned, not understanding the pronunciation.

"Will someone come to meet with you?"

"No." Miranda chuckled. "And I'm sorry about that, too."

The waitress' cheeks blossomed into a bright smile. "Then I would recommend to you the bar, which is much more easy to speak with someone, or not." She nodded towards the row of empty cushioned stools. "Take anyone that you want. All are at the same price."

She counted twelve stools. The other woman was sitting three in from the end. Miranda decided on the middle stool closest to her, anything farther might be awkward, she thought. This way conversation would come, or would not come. Either way she knew she would come back to Quebec. She would stay in the old city and she would wear her new little bikini around some rooftop or patio pool. She wasn't driving, she didn't care. Her first vodka led to a second and she loved how she looked and felt.

"Pardonnez-moi, mademoiselle. Puis-je vous offrir un petit verre possiblement?"

Miranda summoned herself from the dream world she'd drifted into, feeling the bargirl's eyes on her.

"Mademoiselle, may I serve you a drink from her?"

The girl behind the bar pointed to the woman sitting a few stools over.

"I apologize. I was lost in another place. I thought you were speaking to someone else. I don't speak French."

"I was asking if I could buy you a drink."

Miranda had studied the woman on her way to the bar. She was taller than Miranda by at least two inches, in great shape and definitely beautiful. She looked about the same age and very much in the ball park, dressed in a midnight blue two piece linen suit and a micro-fibre top. Her shoes were patent leather pumps from Europe, not some local shoe mart. The woman answered her without the slightest trace of an accent and suddenly Miranda wanted to leave. She would leave. Being there was crazy. What had she even been thinking?

"I'm pretty good at reading a person's thoughts through their eyes. It's a drink, not a long-term commitment," the woman joked. "It's been so long since I've enjoyed another woman's company. I work mostly with men, which can be a little one-sided at times. Don't get me wrong. I love them like brothers. I do, etcetera, etcetera."

Miranda chuckled softly. "I have a few of those at home, too." She paused. "Sure, why not? I'd like a bit of girl-time. Like you said, it's been a while. Thank you. "

"So what's a girl like you doing in a place like this?" the woman asked, easing into her barstool completely relaxed. "Are you here on vacation? Your ensemble doesn't look like a work outfit."

"Actually I was here on business. It's pretty boring stuff. I'm leaving tomorrow."

"Did you enjoy your stay?"

"I enjoyed today, until the credit card receipts follow me home."

"Which is where?"

"Toronto." Miranda let her eyes travel the length of the mirror, taking in the couples behind her. "There's nothing like this place at home, not even close. Do you come here often?"

"No. This is my first visit," she lied. "I needed a quiet place to think." She lifted the edge of a travel brochure.

"You're choosing a vacation, lucky you. I can't remember my last time. It seems like forever ago."

"Not a vacation, more like a dream that's a few years away from the real world. I'm considering buying a property on the French Riviera. The problem is deciding between Monaco and Saint-Tropez. I'm leaning towards Saint-Tropez. It's my little piece of heaven."

"Seriously, the Riviera?"

"Yeah, seriously."

"Oooh, that's so sexy."

Miranda paused as the drinks were served, noticing the woman had only one ice cube to chill her Jean-Marc XO. Her taste for the good life was obviously refined. Miranda raised her own old-fashioned of finely crushed ice and Ultimat.

"To women of superior taste."

The woman raised her glass and smiled thinly, taking a sip.

"This is the closest I've ever been to Europe, apart from the French Antilles, years ago. I didn't understand a word, even when they were speaking English." She shrugged. "I'm pretty linguistically challenged. I take it you're here on business also."

"No. I'm local, born and bred."

"Yet your English is flawless. I hate to sound uniformed...I didn't think English-speaking people could work here."

"Not true. They can as long as they speak French. My mother was French. My old man was English with a horrible French accent." She grinned. "Thank goodness I take after my mother." She sipped her vodka, staring into the mirror for a different perspective of the woman beside her.

"I wish I could stay a while longer. Quebec is such a beautiful old city and I'm committed to myself to returning for a vacation. The shopping is great. It's like the whole city is a polyester-free zone."

"Shopping, something else we have in common." The woman raised her glass to the bargirl. "So what is it you do that brings you to Quebec?"

"I'm an accountant and this one is my treat, not that we're counting," Miranda answered, thinking of a name for her firm, confident anyone who was so put together as the woman beside her would be far removed from such mundane matters as spread sheets. "And you."

The woman ignored the question. "Accounting, I always wondered what it would be like to work in an office all day. Are you married?" Miranda shook her head. "Divorced?"

"No, I'm single, not to say I haven't stopped looking for the right one." She sipped her drink. "What about you?"

"I'm single, a career woman all the way with no time for

family for friends. Such is life." The woman eyed Miranda from her shoes to her blonde hair, shaking her head. "No. I don't see you as an accountant. I don't mean this as hit, I really don't, however I do have to say you are stop-traffic beautiful. I can't imagine you crunching numbers in a dusty office."

Miranda was taken slightly aback and very disappointed. "It's been too long since I've heard anything near that, thank you. It means a lot to me. And I don't want you to think I'm saying this to play catch up, but before you spoke to me I was thinking the same about you. And I love your shoes. I don't suppose you're into true blondes with deep blue eyes and no baggage."

"No. I'm about as straight as they come. I experimented once years ago with a high school girlfriend. I suppose we wanted to show our new boobies to someone other than our mothers." She shrugged. "I haven't thought about that historic moment for years. It was innocent play and looking back it must have been very silly. I remember we laughed and giggled. We got naked and then didn't know what to do so we jumped up and down on my bed until we got tired. We kissed a little, giggled some more, and groped each other's breasts which I suppose was as exciting as squeezing tomatoes. Then we couldn't look at each other for an entire week."

Miranda wanted to move closer to the woman. Her voice had a deep, soothing and exotic quality. Yet she seemed so confident and exuded an undeniable aura of quiet and arousing sensuality.

"God, I hope it's better than what you're describing or I'm in real trouble." She sipped her drink to create a social pause. "Listen, I'm sorry. I'm not a hard-nosed dyke. I hope I haven't made you nervous or uncomfortable."

"Do I look nervous? And what is there to be sorry about? You like girls. So what? Life's too short. We both know that all too well. Don't we? And what woman can say she hasn't thought about it or experimented with a little girl-on-girl touchy-touchy. My old man taught me never to ignore a learning experience, though I'm pretty sure he wasn't talking about that exactly, and I wouldn't be sitting in this place if I was homophobic?" The woman paused a moment to sip her drink. "I can't imagine you being single. Are the other girls in Toronto visually impaired, or what?"

"Thank you. I suppose it's partly my fault. Actually it's entirely my fault and a very long story." Miranda inhaled deeply. "So, now that we have that out of the way, I suppose we should introduce ourselves. My name is ..."

"Don't tell me your name. Let me guess what it is." The woman eased from her stool, taking a few steps towards the one Miranda instinctively pulled out. "First let me tell you something about yourself...and about me." She chortled. "I'm pretty good at matching names to faces." Miranda was intrigued. "You know the expression "I would tell you, but then I'd have to kill you." Well, this is one of those moments."

Miranda was intrigued. "So you're a clairvoyant."

"No, it's much worse than that, I'm afraid. I'm a cop."

Miranda instinctively activated her mental defences. "Dressed in designer wear? You're kidding. Where's the Glock. Isn't that what they call them?"

The woman grinned. "It didn't go with my choice of suit, not the same way that beautiful ring on your finger was made for your ensemble and, yes, most of us use Glocks." She reached for her drink with her right hand. Bringing the glass to her lips she sipped slowly, pausing a moment before continuing. "That ring is the widow's black pearl, but somehow I believe you know that. And, if you're not a widow, your cover name is Pearl and you're an Enabler or Facilitator."

Miranda froze, gripping her chilled glass with hands struggling not to tremble.

"I'm sorry, again. I don't know what any of that means.

It sounds so dramatic, but what girl called Pearl would ever spend what I did on all this."

"Your outfit is stunning, Pearl. You're stunning, and if any other woman was sitting here you'd probably have a date by now. Sorry, but what you just said is light years from the truth. Mother would never want to see us any other way and there's only one way to come by the widow's black pearl."

"I didn't realize it was so common. My mother gave to me. It's an heirloom passed down to me from past generations."

"That's very unlikely. The ring is never bequeathed and isn't common at all. We both know the only way to wear the ring is for someone to need help and for someone else to get what he deserves. What you meant to say is Mother gave it to you, Mother of Pearl, and not for facilitating Charles Preston sometime over the past twenty-four hours. He was level-two, wasn't he, Pearl. He was non-anticipatory, wasn't he? He wasn't considered a threat to anyone with your training. You're a Facilitator and you came here to do Charles Preston with one under the sternum. Twist and shout. Ouch. Congratulations on your excellent work. There's one less piece of shit on our sidewalks. Personally, I would have cut his throat or put my stiletto through an eye and into his sick brain."

She was a cop. Christ, Miranda thought. How could she have been so unaware, so blind? "Listen, whoever you are. I'm very sorry. I don't know what any of this means. All I wanted was to have a drink and to talk with someone. Now you're scaring me. I have to go."

"Scaring you? I'm not scaring you. Nothing scares us, Pearl. Isn't that what they drill into us each year at the compound, particularly days six and seven? Which accommodation is your favourite? I prefer the Ruby Suite and my second choice is always the Red Jade Suite." Dina Becker laid her right hand palm-down against the bar to display her own distinctive ring with its Florentine swirls in the form of a delicate shell cupping a black pearl. "So, how complicated is this? Think we've ever been there at the same time?" She took Miranda's hand and squeezed, then brought her hand to her nose. "Good girl, barely a trace of perfume. Perfume to others, to us a lingering trace, a scent to remember us by: evidence."

"Shit. This can't happen."

"This has happened."

"You're a cop."

"Yes, I am, and my day job didn't pay for my outfit either. I'm a Facilitator. And don't expect me to believe you're an accountant. No way." Dina sipped her drink. "Would I be wrong to think, I don't know, a fashion executive somewhere?"

"And your name would be?" Miranda asked.

"Pearl, like you, and like you, I have a director." Dina put her hand over Miranda's, this time without squeezing. "Please, don't go. I've wondered for years when this would happen and here you are. I can't say I'm disappointed. I don't mean the girl thing. I mean meeting another Pearl. It's not as though we have Christmas parties or do the after-hours thing." Dina stopped and leaned into the barstool, "Actually, we are the after-hours thing. Aren't we? You must have pulled some pretty high-up strings to do him here. You did good work. The entry wound hardly showed, and practically no blood. I interviewed him after he was arrested. He was vermin. Between us girls, he pissed himself at the precinct, right down to his shoes." Miranda said nothing in response. "Why you, Pearl? Why here?"

Miranda called to the waitress. "Please, two more. Make them doubles and no ice." She stretched her forefinger away from her thumb to compensate for her lack of French regarding the quantity and stuck her finger into her crushed ice before waving forbiddingly regarding the quality. She turned to Dina who wasn't disguising a wide grin. "And after this one I'm taking a taxi and going home."

"And, let me guess, you're paying cash." Dina sipped her vodka. "Please tell me, why you?"

Miranda felt cornered. She ran her tongue absently across moist red lips.

"I have a difficult job, like yours. It's very time consuming and doesn't leave much opportunity for meeting people, which is not a particular forte of mine. Though most people I work with think girls fall from trees. They don't. Most of the good ones are either attached or gorgeous and straight." She shrugged, wanting to appear urbane and nonchalant. What Dina saw was sadness. "A few nights ago I went to dinner with someone I thought or hoped could become a friend. She didn't work out. She knew before the evening began, so did I, and for some reason we went to a bar to pretend the date never happened or that everything was fine. When she left I hung out a bit longer to make an already disastrous evening less awkward." Miranda's eyes travelled along the mirror and paused to reach for her glass and linger for a moment before continuing. "Anyway, four guys were sitting at the other end getting a little loud and for no real reason I decided to record them. What they were saying was pretty sick. Now I'm here and you know half my life story."

"And Preston isn't here."

"Who would that be, exactly?" Miranda asked. "The name doesn't ring a bell."

Dina squeezed Miranda's hand. "I'm sorry things didn't work out with your new friend. Hey, listen. You met me, albeit not such a good choice."

Miranda dismissed the sympathy, not sounding quite as glib as she intended.

"These things happen for the best, I suppose. What didn't work out for me did for Ann Preston. I had never gone to that bar before, so my miserable social skills sort of paid off big time. They saved Ann's life. Being at the right place at the right time was a complete fluke."

"It always is." The women fell silent and after a few moments Miranda crossed her legs and Dina realized she was staring down at them. When she looked up their eyes locked. "I have a face too, you know. Are you sure you're not into girls?"

"What can I say? Not being a lesbian doesn't mean I can't appreciate killer legs. No pun intended. They are fantastic, objectively speaking of course. Someone's certainly missing out."

"Tell me about it." She wiggled her fingers slightly under the weight of Dina's hand. "You certainly send out strange signals for a straight girl."

Dina withdrew her hand. "Sorry. My mind was somewhere else."

"Yeah, I noticed."

"Blame it on the vodkas."

Miranda checked the time and reached behind her for her purse. "Don't lose sleep over it."

"Listen, I can't remember how long it's been since I've wanted a girls' night. You know, as opposed to a night with a girl. You can leave after your drink and we'll never see each other again, or you can stay and we can enjoy a few drinks and the ambiance. No names, purely a girls' night out to talk about shopping, vacations, live men, girls, or whatever, as long as it's not about babies. No babies and no pearl daggers."

"I've planned to leave the city early. I'm sorry."

Dina nodded, reaching for her drink. "Yeah, so am I."

Miranda uncrossed her legs and brought the glass to her lips one last time. She threw a hundred on the bar and slid from her stool. "Goodbye, Pearl."

"Goodbye, Pearl, and thank you for joining me. Something tells me I won't forget you anytime soon. I hope you find the one you want. You're too beautiful to be alone. It's a waste."

"Do you have anyone?"

"No."

"And you had to be straight, the story of my life." Miranda's voice betrayed her. "Another time, another place, isn't that what they say?"

"Yeah, that's what they say, the lucky ones who don't know what we know. We know, don't we, Pearl? We know what we do must come first." Dina forced a wide grin and raised her glass. "To another time and another place. Regards to Mom. À bientôt, chérie."

"Goodbye, Pearl."

Miranda turned from the hip and walked away. All she wanted was out. Dina remained as she was, feeling a surge of regret. She was a cop and a good one. She never questioned that part of her life. She also knew what else she was and often wondered whether any of her people would ever discover the true Dina Becker, the secret Dina Becker. She hoped not. She was committed to never compromising Pearl and that came before being a cop. And who was the to-die-for woman growing smaller in the mirror, the one who put down Preston, stabbed him under the chest with one of Mother's pearl-embossed stilettos? Dina exchanged shrugs with the bargirl. She would never know.

Outside the bar Miranda tipped the valet as she stepped into a cab. Her heart was racing, pounding. Her head was a whirlwind of confused thoughts. She had been so stupid, so lax and inattentive. What she let happen could have cost her life or possibly caused the end of Pearl and the destruction of so many women. She wondered who the woman could be, whether she was truly a cop.

Miranda couldn't be angrier with herself. She had done everything by the book. She knew she was textbook perfect. She twisted in her seat and peered from the cab's the rear window. She had to know. If she didn't go back Pearl would leave the bar and Miranda would never see her again, she would never know the truth. She told the cab to stop, paid the two-minute drive with a twenty and strode quickly to the lounge.

She explained to the doorman as he opened the door to her how she had forgotten her lipstick in the ladies' room. All she could see of Pearl was the sheen of her lustrous chestnut hair and the dark tapered contours of her suit.

"Pearl, I have to know." Dina swivelled in her seat. "Are you a cop? You could have heard about Preston any number of ways and your mother or sister could have given you the ring."

"Mother did give it to me and, in a way, my sister did as well. And, yes, I'm a cop." Dina raised her left leg at an angle and tugged at the hem of her slacks to reveal the nickel-plated compact. "It's bigger than it looks. Two rounds to the head or chest, but you know that."

Miranda stared at the gun as she spoke. "Nice 84FS Cheetah, love the finish, and I'm not an accountant. I'm a trial lawyer with one last question for you."

"No names," Dina answered.

"No, that's not the question, and I don't mean this as hit, I really don't. But I do have to say you are stop-traffic beautiful and I was wondering, hypothetically, if I were to stay in town a night or two longer, could we maybe do some girl stuff together without any shop-talk?"

Dina coughed into her glass. "You're not serious. Me and you, doing girl stuff?"

Miranda nodded. "Yes, me and you, doing girl stuff. Why not?"

"You are serious." Miranda didn't answer, and Dina's mind was racing. She wanted to say yes and with any other woman she might have. This woman wasn't any other woman. She was a Pearl operative and a lesbian. "What do you have in mind?"

"Not a date if that's what you're thinking. We could go shopping or you could show me the city and we could have a late lunch or dinner. Who else could have more in common with you than me and I promise I won't come on to you?" Dina waited what seemed the longest time to Miranda, trying to rationalize her thoughts. "You know, as my grandmother used to tell me: when in doubt, don't."

"What did she have to say about talking to strangers?"

"We aren't strangers, we're business associates. Sort of."

Dina bit her lower lip and shook her head, knowing deep down she was making a mistake. "Okay, here are the ground rules. We cannot under any circumstances tell each other our names, you can't see where I live and I cannot know where you're staying. It's not the Château, I know that much." Dina pulled out a barstool and Miranda squeezed into the narrow space between them. "But I suppose we could meet somewhere for a breakfast and spend the day together. What the hell, why not? I'm overdue for a vacation. I should have gone somewhere in June, instead I cancelled due to a piece of good news I was waiting for. I'll call in with cramps or some other girl thing."

"Good news that spoils a vacation. The lottery?" questioned Miranda.

"Not quite, although as good or better. Let's say my time may have come. I've been waiting a long time."

"Your boss won't mind on such short notice?"

Dina chuckled. The sound was a soft and warm. "No, she won't mind at all."

"I have until Sunday. Perhaps we can rent a car."

"Sunday? Hey, let's back up a little. I was thinking more like Friday and no, we cannot rent a car. You should know better than to make the suggestion. Who would rent it? Either one of us would know the other's real name within minutes of leaving each other."

"Then I'll settle for Friday. Friday's good and Saturday will take care of itself. Maybe I'll drive into the country."

"Are you always this excited?"

"Are you always this passive?"

"No," Dina replied, "but when I came in here I wasn't thinking a lesbian would be asking me to spend the weekend with her."

Miranda glanced at the other couples in the bar and answered with the popular teenage "duh" inflection in her voice. "Well, hello, when in Rome. Anyway, I can play straight. I'll be on my best behaviour. It's been so long since I've been with anyone that I practically am straight."

"That's too much information."

"Sorry. So where do we meet for breakfast and are we wearing sexy or casual."

"Sexy?" Dina winced. She brought up her glass and swirled what was left of the cube. "I haven't felt sexy in years and shopping is out. I prefer European brands at source. It's how a cop with a pathetic life spends her vacations. Okay, listen. This might be a stretch, but what the hell. I'm thinking perhaps a spa weekend would be good and I know the perfect place."

"A spa, like in being pampered and massaged?"

"Yeah. The place is far from cheap and worth every penny. I can't remember the last time I let it all hang out at a spa. God, what we women sacrifice for our men." They both chortled. It's what they both needed. "We could be there by noon tomorrow and check out sometime near noon on Sunday.

"Oooh. I like the idea. I'm in, but that's longer than Friday."

"I don't think I like that smile or the oooh. Do you always oooh?"

Miranda nodded. "But don't worry. I'll be good. I promise. They'll think we're sisters."

"Sisters?" Dina put her head back slightly and breathed noisily, groaning and not realizing the effect she was having on Miranda. "I know I'll regret this. Your grandmamma was right, though she probably never worked twelve-hour shifts. Let's do it." Dina eased from her seat, swept up her purse from the other barstool and asked Miranda to order another round. When she returned a few minutes later Miranda was beaming with expectation. "We're booked in for the weekend."

"What about names?" Miranda asked.

"No names, we pay cash, we trust each other and we leave our cells in our cars at the airport. No phones." Dina held out her hand to signal the bargirl and scratched the air as though signing a bill.

"So, what do I call you? We can't call each other Pearl, that's sort of stupid." Miranda leaned in closer to Dina. "I'm going to call you Green Eyes, and you are sexy. You are."

Dina half chortled and half coughed. "My name's Green Eyes and I'll be spending my first weekend away since whenever with a gorgeous lesbian who thinks I'm sexy. How weird is that? So, are yours really so blue?"

"Yes, but that's not original." Miranda wiggled teasingly on her stool. "You have to think of something else."

Dina thought for a moment. Then she put an elbow on the bar and a fist against her cheek. "What the hell. Chérie, I'll call you Chérie."

"Oooh, Sherry. You make it sound so sexy. You called me that before, but you have an unfair advantage."

"You're kidding, right?" Miranda shook her head mischievously. "Okay, it can mean darling or honey. In this case it means I can't think of anything else at the moment and we're sleeping in separate beds. Understood? In fact, I should bring my handcuffs."

"And I'll bring my whips." Miranda answered eagerly. "Hey, we can dye our hair purple, wear studded leather and spank each other." The premium vodka in Dina's mouth gurgled through her nose involuntarily and sprayed from the corners of her mouth. "Okay, this time I am kidding. I'll be the very best-behaved lesbian ever, all weekend, wherever we're going. So, how do we get there, Green Eyes?"

"We'll meet at the airport and take the spa's shuttle. We'll be there by noon" Dina hesitated for a brief moment, leaning into Miranda to put a hand on her shoulder and whisper. "Hey, what's with the teary eyes? It doesn't become you. Besides, everyone will think we're a couple of dykes breaking up. Come on. We'll have a fun weekend, not to mention weird."

"I'm sorry. I'm having my first weekend since forever with a straight girl. What's the world coming to?"

"Tell me about it."

They stayed an hour longer and kissed each other's cheeks before stepping through the door. Dina waited for Miranda's taxi to disappear around the corner before giving her parking stub to the valet. At home she pulled off her jacket, kicked off her shoes and unstrapped her ankle holster. She pushed her slacks to the floor and collapsed onto her sofa in her panties and micro-fibre top, asking herself what she had done. For that matter, what had Chérie done, or Pearl, or whoever she was?

She would be spending the weekend being pampered beside the woman who killed Charles Preston, and sleeping in a suite with a lesbian, a woman whose name she could never know, a woman who could kill as efficiently as she could herself, a woman who was an enticing anomaly. The woman was right, she mused. What the hell was the world coming to?

Dina let her eyes travel the length of her body. She cupped her breasts and squeezed, realizing her heart was beating quickly. She looked at her panties. They were the same pale blue micro-fibre as her top and she pushed them down, thinking of Chérie and how she was dressed. Her skirt and blouse must have cost several hundred, she obviously wasn't wearing a bra and Dina was certain that what she was wearing under the skirt was no less chic. And what did they cover? She was definitely a Pearl. All that was missing was the hat, the one she probably discarded or destroyed after completion of the Preston case study.

Dina knew Chérie would never think to spend their weekend together in anything less than what she wore to the lounge. She kicked away her panties and hurried into her bedroom closet. She spent the next few hours deciding and changing her mind. One side of her closet was all cop clothes: slacks, jackets, low-heeled shoes and party dresses she wore once a year and forgot. The other side was wall-to-wall designer-name skirts and dresses, sheer silk blouses, cashmere sweaters, exotic casual wear, shoes for every occasion that were stacked from the floor to the ceiling and drawers filled with requisite accessories. She never wore her bikinis at home. She had no reason and no one to titillate, though twice each year on the beaches of France she was the best and least dressed woman and she wondered whether Chérie, being a lesbian, would wear thongs in spa's pools.

When she was done, what she laid out on one side of her bed were two tiny thongs with Band-Aide-size tops for the pool, silk chemises and teddies for the room and a silk, mid-thigh robe and low-heeled slippers for breakfast. Each item boasted European tags. On the other side lay new panties and a bra, matching crimson garters for a red silk dress she had never worn and a blue panty set without garters for a deep blue-on-black satin pant suit and silk blouse she once wore for herself at home. She thought carefully about Sunday's wardrobe, deciding on a long, white summer sweater and white tights.

She was exhausted, yet too excited to sleep. She modelled the micro-fibre bikinis in front of her mirror, both microscopic, both fitting snugly to her most intimate contours. She frowned, uncertain. Neither thong nor the tops left anything to the imagination other than the inspiration of European men who never succeeded in their quests. She yanked at the side strings, tossed the triangles onto her bed, and went into the bathroom.

She felt like a giddy teenager. She was going for a girls' weekend with a woman she didn't know. She was a cop, the Captain of SVU and she was standing under streams of steaming hot water letting her long, red hair and her body rinse clean for no other reason than to make a good impression on a woman she met hours ago. She was making herself more gorgeous than she was for Chérie, she had selected her clothes for Chérie and what the hell was she doing? She couldn't think straight, nothing she was doing made sense and she knew she had to stop thinking before she went insane. What she was doing was insanity. Chérie was a lesbian and a Pearl. Which one was worse?

She stepped dripping from the shower and coated herself with cream in front of the mirror. She didn't look thirty-nine, early thirties maybe, she told herself, she hoped, and Chérie couldn't be older than mid-twenties. She was going away with a woman at least twelve years her junior. Dina tried to think, to rationalize. Chérie must have been married at a very young age and badly abused. How else could she have become a Pearl Facilitator? They had lied to each other and would throughout the weekend. They had no choice. A straight cop and a lesbian trial lawyer, Green Eyes and Chérie: killers both.

The cream burned her newly sensitive skin with cold heat. The bareness felt good and her body tingled as she padded into her dining room. She poured a straight Jean-Marc XO and went to the bedroom to pack. She threw in her thongs. She had worn similar at the women-only spa on previous occasions, so why not this weekend, and she knew Chérie wouldn't be the first lesbian or appreciative woman to see her in something so skimpy, she justified, not with two trips to the south coast of France each year.

When she finished she put aside her clothes for the morning and stood her suitcase by the door leading to her garage. Her bedroom clock showed 3:00 AM and she had to be at the airport by ten looking good.

She set the alarm for 7:00 and climbed between satin sheets. They felt cool against her skin. She stretched, and curled into herself to imagine. Would she greet Chérie at 10:00 with kisses on her cheek? What would they talk about in the shuttle bus? Would they undress in the bathroom or would that be stupid? Stupid, she decided. They would be together all weekend being massaged and pampered, oiled and smothered in mud baths. They would lie side by side like beautiful nude figurines sculpted from Belgian chocolate, so what would the big deal be about walking around in panties and bras. She hadn't been asked out on a date for so long, longer since she had accepted one. They never worked out and this one wasn't a date. Chérie was a lesbian, Dina was a cop, and only other cops liked cops.

A woman with guns on her hip and her ankle was a definite turn-off. She also knew how hot she was or wanted to be wouldn't matter once she pulled on her panties. Her rare attempts at searching for love prior to her sister's death were never very good. Her dates always found excuses not to see her again and finally she gave up trying, preferring to work. Every female cop lived with the same stigma and the lonely nights. Not that she cared. Being alone was part of her life, but Chérie was hot. Dina sighed. In six years she would no longer be a cop, she could live in France to become something else and someone else. Then she could be hot, too.

She was lost in her past, her future and her weekend. Her eyes opened wide, shocked by the loud grunt from deep inside as her body shuddered and jerked into the folds of the top sheet. Another small pleasure she'd forgotten over time, one that had become too much of a tease, a reminder she had aroused herself and not someone else. She didn't care. She let herself drift until her thoughts and fears, her hopes and her dreams, became one.

When she woke to the calming musical chimes of her clock Dina stretched and luxuriated between the warm sheets. She let her mind wander, remembering the night before, thinking of the day ahead. Then she shrieked and leapt from her bed.

Twenty-Two

Miami, Florida
Thursday, August 09

At precisely 10:00 PM Julia Saunders seated her last couple of the evening at one of the restaurant's few remaining sidewalk tables before going to the ladies' room to change from her white tank top and denim mini-skirt uniform into a form-fitting bra top, micro-mini skirt and stiletto sandals. It's what Eddie Mendez liked her to wear, for him as much as for the others. She was 5'8", a slim six feet in heels. He told her each time they met how proud she made him and how he loved her. He never came to meet her, parking was always difficult, though he was always there for her, waiting for her outside his door after she walked the mile from her part-time hostess job on Lincoln Road to his Ocean Drive condo in South Beach.

Most days she attended theatre classes at the New World School of the Arts, studying diligently between lectures for exams, reciting verses and lines as she waited to greet and seat the next customer, or during the bus ride home from Eddie's to keep from falling asleep. He never drove her home. Why would he when she could as easily take a bus? She understood his logic because she loved him. He was right: driving her all that way through late night traffic would be stupid, especially after he worked all day and waited all evening to see her and to be with her.

She had promised her parents who remained in Cuba that she would study hard, that nothing would get in the way of her success, and she tried her best to honour them. She enrolled in a summer semester to hasten her graduation. She worked afternoons, evenings and weekends, studying when she could without letting down Eddie, yet not disappointing him was increasingly difficult and her summer grades would certainly be below average. He was pressuring her to be with him at the condo as much as possible and to please him she began skipping afternoon classes or leaving campus early.

Julia lived in a small two-bedroom apartment in Little Havana with her two brothers, eight miles and two buses from Eddie's condo, and the stress was beginning to show in little ways. Her brothers noticed the difference in her. She was losing weight, she was always tired and they often heard her crying in her room after arriving home exhausted at one or two in the morning. They implored her to leave her job, to focus on her studies. Money was not the issue. Her future was the issue and they would willingly work extra hours at the hotel to make up the difference. They were stronger than her, they insisted, more resilient, and an extra few hours each week would be nothing at all for them to manage. Each time she refused them.

She had promised to arrive at the Ocean Drive condo at 10:30 and she did. The evening air was heavy and still. He was sitting on the front steps, waiting. She smiled and waved, he raised an open hand in response. She leaned forward to kiss his lips and hug him. Eddie Mendez stayed as he was and noted the time.

"Each night you take longer, chica. ¿Qué haces?"

"Don't be angry with me, Eddie. I am sorry. A lady was in the bathroom at the restaurant and I had to wait to change. Do I look nice enough for you tonight?"

He eyed her from her face to her stilettos. "Chica, you are beginning to look like shit. You were wrong to enrol in these summer classes. We could have done a lot more a lot quicker with these afternoons you are wasting on acting."

"It is for my parents that I do it, Eddie."

"And me?" he replied. "What about me? You know how important this is to me, to us. I love you, chica, you know this is true." He put a hand to the hem of her skirt and pulled upward, his other hand slid under the front of her panties. "This little thing is mine, chica, no one else's. ¿No es verdad? They can see it, smell it and play with it, but it will always be mine. Soon this thing you do will all be over, they will be gone and we will be married. We will put this thing behind us, chica."

"I am doing this for you, Eddie. When they see me that way, I see you, not them. When they touch me, I feel you touching me, not them. I love only you. Your life is more important to me than what I do and I know you love me so much."

"He is waiting for you. He is important to them, chica. Treat him nicely. Do whatever he asks of you." Eddie Mendez pulled away one hand and tugged the front of Julia's skirt with the other. "Soon my debt to them will be over, chica, and we will be as we should be."

"Yes, mi amor. Will you be here when he leaves?"

"No, as much as I want to be with you. They want to see me. I have no choice, chica. I cannot refuse them. You must also be with me tomorrow night. We will have dinner first and later a few drinks together when the guy has gone. It is time we began to make plans. Make sure you are sexy for him, and for me. I would die for you, you know that I would. Many times I wish they had killed me."

"No, do not say such a thing. It will soon be over. Soon your debt to them will be paid." She kissed him. "Goodnight, Eddie. I love you."

She climbed the flight of stairs slowly, the night air was heavy with humidity, a thin film of sweat coated her body and her top was damp. She ran her fingers through thick, chocolate-brown hair, patted her face with a tissue, waited a moment to compose herself and walked through the door unannounced.

The patio doors of the one-room, second-story apartment looked out over bumper-to-bumper traffic. Eddie Mendez' dream was to own a much-envied ocean view condo. He told her countless times. Julia's dream was to share the ocean with him. However, as on so many past evenings and afternoons, Julia would give herself to nameless friends of the man who had agreed to take her body in lieu of killing Eddie for having crossed the line.

The room smelled of city traffic, sweat and salt air. The lights were dimmed and the man lay under the top sheet of Eddie's double bed. She saw his outline. He was very large, which was all she could discern as she put down her purse and leaned against the table to kick off her shoes. She set the stage in her mind. She was on stage acting out a scene in which her body was the prop, she told herself. She was acting, like she did at school, like famous actresses who gave their bodies to strangers and the audience so they could later walk on a red carpet in beautiful gowns and jewels. The same red carpet she would one day walk with Eddie by her side. She knew Eddie loved her, pitied him sitting alone on the steps hating what she was doing, yet unable to prevent it.

She pulled her top over her head, pushed her skirt to the floor and walked toward the man in her panties.

"Good evening."

"Yeah, good evening."

He was American, white, she thought he must be at least 300 pounds, and in the dark she couldn't judge his age.

"Our boy Eddie tells me you're good, that you haven't been doing this very long. That true?"

"Yes, it is true. Eddie does not lie."

"How old are you?"

"I am eighteen."

The man drew in a noisy breath. "Take them off by the doors and turn around real slow, and bend over a little."

Julie padded to the patio doors where street lights illuminated her body. She faced the man to unclasp her panties and tug them away matter-of-factly as she turned to lean slowly forward, bracing her arms against her knees.

"That's very nice, damn nice. You Mexican gals sure have a nice colour to you. You just stay there awhile so I can take it all in." He waited a few minutes, staring at the curves of her buttocks as his breathing grew louder and heavier. Then: "Whew! That's a damn fine set of tight little cheeks you've got, little girl. Face me. Not too fast." She obeyed. "Don't know which I like better, the front or the back. Those sure are nice little titties."

"Thank you."

"Au contraire." His hand dropped to his side. "Looks like I got a little excited. Why don't you go get a shower started for us? Not too hot."

Julia left him without commenting. The bathroom was small and the shower was a three-sided cubicle. When the man limped in to join her, Julia wanted to be violently ill. He was 6'2", more like 350 pounds with bent, veined legs and rolls of sagging pale skin, each one pressing against the other from top to bottom. The lowest hung over a drooping purple scrotum and a penis that had retreated into its dark shroud. His hair was yellowed-grey, his purple-white face was streaked with thin red lines, his nose was bulbous and his eyes were covered over with a dull film. When he side-stepped into the stall she saw his pockmarked and bruised buttocks. His back was blanketed in red patches and, as the hot water rained down on his head, his hair slid to one side and clung to him like part of a gruesome mask.

"This'll be a tight fit, little girl." He reached out, bringing her in. "But first, why not see what you can do about Peter down there. He died a little bit when he was watching you pull off those undies." She couldn't move,

229

pinned between his spongy flesh and his soft arms, naked and vulnerable. "At my age this shit doesn't happen on its own." He sniggered. "Come on now. It's no different than praying. Close your eyes. Think of it as communion without the bread."

"No, I cannot. I have never done such a thing."

"Can't say as I blame you. It's not like I'm some pretty chico Latino. Don't matter. Eddie boy and I have a deal and I'm three bills poorer than when I walked into this shit hole, so say a prayer."

"I don't understand."

"Get on your goddamn knees and bring Peter to life." He gripped his penis.

"No, I will not. I will never do such a thing."

Julia ran from the bathroom to the patio windows clutching her stomach, wanting to cover her body. She leaned from the waist, reaching for her flimsy underwear, yelping at the crushing impact of his knee colliding into her buttocks and the sensation of her body being flung into the air and through the open doors onto the concrete floor of the balcony. A massive hand clamped against her quivering lips, another between her legs, lifting her, throwing her back through the doors. She landed face-down, too stunned or terrified to scream. He grabbed at her hair, forced another hand between her legs and jerked her from the floor to throw her onto the bed.

He twisted her onto her back with one movement and clamped a hand over her mouth before pushing her legs apart and positioning her so that he was centered to her. He was talking, speaking words she didn't hear, telling her how pretty she was, how he liked the little girl look as she felt his other hand pounding furiously against her inner thighs. When he was ready he pushed hard against her, forcing his way, squeezing a hand harder against her mouth until he finished and sank breathless onto his knees.

Her warm tears wet the hand muffling her moans, her

body lay inert and her chest heaved convulsively. She wanted to scream his name. She needed Eddie to burst through the door and save her. Then the hand came away and she was twisted onto her front. Her legs were once again forced apart so that he was kneeling under her and her buttocks were pressed against the flaccid skin of his ponderous gut. He pushed her face firmly into the pillow, until he was ready, all the while talking to her as though they were lovers with a past together, a present and a future.

He began probing her with his fingers, first one, then two, letting her be until his body shuddered and he did nothing to clean her as he hurried frantically to revitalize himself. Julia was sobbing hysterically, struggling in vain against his massive weight. His first lunge failed, as did his second, his third made her scream. The muffled affect sounded gruesome and unreal. She had never felt such pain, pain which would not begin to subside until he pulled away from her.

He hung over her, panting, sweating and trying clumsily to force his hands between the bed and her nubile breasts. Tired of the struggle he brutally smacked her buttocks and manoeuvred from the bed to rinse away his sweat with another shower.

The most delicate parts of Julia's body pulsated and burned. When she moved she wanted to scream from the searing pain. She didn't care, she had to move. She had to tell Eddie. She had to find him and tell him. She had to tell someone. She rolled from the bed onto the floor, dragging herself to her clothes. She pulled on her skirt as quickly as she could, listening intently for the shower to stop.

The man was singing contentedly. She grabbed up her shoes, her purse, and her eyes caught a glimpse of the clothes he'd strewn across the couch. The shower was still running. Eddie would want to know all he could about the man, she rationalized. She hurried to the scattered clothes, frantic and determined. She squeezed the fabric of his trousers, searching for his wallet, feeling nothing. She reached for his suit jacket and stuck a hand into one inside pocket, then the other, clutching the wallet and burying it into her purse without checking the contents as she ran to the door in bare feet.

His roar should have startled her. She should have leapt towards the door without looking back. She did the opposite. He was naked and running at her. He shoved her into the wall and pinned her there with a tight grip at her throat. He squeezed each of her breasts viciously, laughing. He groped savagely between her legs, telling her she was a bad little girl and had to be punished. He grabbed her hair and banged her head into the wall several times. He dragged her to the couch where he pulled her across his knees, pressed hard against the back of her head, yanked up her skirt and began wildly slapping her buttocks until he tired and slouched backward, breathing heavily.

He reached out to pull her closer and roll her over. Julia lay motionless, arched over his legs, staring at the ceiling with one arm between them and the other dangling away from her at an odd angle as she forced her mind to dispel his doughy hands from her body. She thought of Eddie, who would want to kill the man. She thought of her brothers and how ashamed they would be of her. She thought of her parents and tears trickled into her hair.

She began whimpering, telling the man she was sorry. She was nervous, and his rude mauling became long continuous strokes across the length of her body. He relaxed an open palm across her breasts, the other he wedged into the sticky wetness at the apex of her thighs to massage the soft flesh and Julia asked if she could sit up. He held her under her arms, helping her to sit facing him. Straddling his legs she looked between them, checking the urge to vomit. He was old, she was young, and with a surge of will power and determination she brought both her clenched fists into the air and crashed each one with all her strength into the sides of his head. She kicked herself away, flailing her arms, and ran to where a slim ceramic vase sat on a side table. He was sprawled on the couch, dazed from her two forceful blows when she hurled the vase with all her might into his face.

She ran to the door as fast as she could, stooping for her top and purse. In the stairway she slumped against the wall, sobbing. Bruises covered her breasts and thighs, her body ached everywhere and every part of her was trembling. She struggled into her top, reached for her shoes, her purse and hurried down the stairs and onto the street, running several blocks before sitting on the curb to put on her shoes. She hugged her knees to her chest and cried. No one cared. She was in Miami: party town. What did another promiscuous and streetwise Latina teenager count for?

She had nowhere to go. She couldn't go home. Her brothers would learn the truth and would kill Eddie before dealing with her. Nor could she go to the police. They would arrest for being something she was not: a prostitute. She was doing everything for Eddie, for their future together. She had to phone him, to warn him, but he was with the ones who would kill him without thinking. She searched through the man's wallet for his driver's permit. He was Eric Wilder. He lived in Scottsdale, Arizona. He was born in 1937 and was five years older than her grandfather. Julia dropped the wallet onto the street, parted her knees and threw up between them.

People walked past her shaking their heads, male tourists out for a good time yelled out lewd remarks and made obscene gestures, while other girls laughed at her. She stood unsteadily and tugged at the hem of her skirt. Three times she held out her hands for a taxi and three times they drove by, many more times cars stopping to lower their windows and offer her a ride.

She stopped crying and her eyes began to clear. She combed her hair as she walked and thought of what she would say. At Collins and fifth she climbed onto the bus that would take her over the MacArthur Causeway to a connecting bus that would take her to within a minute of Mercy Hospital's emergency room.

She went in timidly and told male admissions clerk she needed to see a female doctor. When he asked whether she had insurance, she shook her head. When he asked what was troubling her she told him she wanted to see a female doctor. There was nothing more to say. To the man she was another rape victim or another stupid teenager who thought she was cool walking the streets of Miami half-naked. Her appearance told the story and when she was taken away he forgot her.

She was examined without delay. They first gave her an ECP pill to prevent pregnancy, searching next for internal injuries before treating her welts and the many abrasions to her hands and knees. She lied when they asked her questions. She explained how she was driven to a party, she didn't know where, and things got out of hand. What they did was as much her fault as his, she persisted. She asked him to try something different because she was curious, they both were, and he got too excited. She begged the doctor not to contact her brothers, to let her go home. All she came in for was the pill, nothing else.

The doctor was adamant: she wasn't going home. Instead they sent her to radiology, let her bathe and gave her a bed for the night with a sedative that would keep her asleep until morning. By the time they woke her for breakfast complete dossiers had been compiled on Eduardo Mendez and Eric Wilder.

Julia was released later Friday morning, wearing new jeans, a white cotton blouse and loafers, left for her anonymously at the Admissions desk. The doctor and nurse frowned when she walked uncomfortably from the wheelchair. When she stepped onto the bus they swept Julia from their thoughts and returned to those who did want help.

When she reached into her purse to search for the fare she blanched and had to be prompted by the driver to pay. The bus was empty, yet the woman who followed her onto the bus sat behind her. Several stops later, when Julia disembarked, the woman followed.

"Buenos días, Julia. Me llamo Pearl."

Julia winced from the pain caused by her sudden reaction. "¿Cómo? How do you know my name?"

"I know. How I know is unimportant. I also know why you came to the hospital, I know of Eric Wilder who did this to you and I know of Eduardo Mendez who allowed this to happen. Julia, you cannot go home, if that is what you are thinking. It's too dangerous."

Julia shook her head. "I do not know any Eric Wilder. I know only Eddie. He is a good man. I am going to marry him."

"So I am told."

"We were playing. That is all. We went too far."

"No, you were with Wilder and he wasn't playing. He did this to you. I have his permit which was found in your purse. He is a tourist from Arizona who left his wife at their hotel and went to enjoy a much younger woman, you. He paid Mendez for you. The going rate is between two and 400 dollars. Although for someone as pretty as you, probably closer to four and when he wanted you in a different way you must have refused him and he did this to you while he forced you."

"No. That is not true. He is one of the bad men, the drug dealers. Eddie is in trouble with him and the others because he borrowed money he cannot repay. Now he is in trouble with them because of me. They were going to kill Eddie if I did not agree to be with them. He has no money to pay them. He has no other way. I am saving him by doing this. I am doing it freely because he loves me."

"How much is the debt?" Pearl asked.

"I don't know. He told me at the beginning he would soon be killed, then some of the men saw me and wanted me. They told Eddie he could live if they could be with me for a short time."

"He told you that would forgive the debt?"

"Yes. He went to see them last night," Julia added, very afraid of the woman.

"No, he did not go to see them. Has he ever given you money, given you gifts?"

"There will be time for gifts after the debt is paid. Until then his love for me is enough."

Piedra Batista sighed. "No es verdad, Julia. None of what he's told you is true. There is no debt and there are no drug dealers. Everything he told you is a lie. You told the doctor he works in a bar. There is no bar. He has no job, yet he drives a European sports car and lives in the Vista del Mar condos with a magnificent view of the ocean." Pearl showed Julia photographs taken earlier in the morning of Mendez sitting in a BMW Z4 with a white girl in her late teens. "Chances are she isn't his sister. Chances are he was with her last night, one of many other girls, Julia. He has many girls working for him. He's a pimp. You're working for him. You are not a devoted girlfriend to him. You're a prostitute who isn't sharing in the proceeds and before long he will convince you to leave school for him. Eventually you will work on the streets with no chance of becoming a fine actress." Pearl grinned thinly. "Yes, Julia, I know about you."

"You are the one who is lying to me. None of what you are saying is true."

"Look at the photograph. You must leave Miami, right now. You are in great danger. What Wilder did is nothing compared to what Mendez will do when he discovers what happened. The time has come for you to stop being foolish and infatuated with a criminal. You left Wilder with a broken nose and very black eyes. He was taken to emergency by ambulance. You did a good job on him, a good job you'll pay dearly for. The drug dealers don't exist, none who care about him anyway, and no debt, just an endless line of johns with their zippers down. Do you believe Wilder could possibly be a drug dealer, that pathetic old man?"

Julia stood beside Pearl as though in a trance. "I must go home. I have school."

"What you will do is go home and pack enough clothes for a few days. Your classes can wait and do not worry about your job. Your life is more important than earning a few dollars a day at a job you are on the verge of losing one way or another. Leaving Miami is the one way we can protect you, Julia. You have no choice, although we would prefer that you leave voluntarily."

"What do you mean?"

"I mean we need you to leave and you will leave."

"I cannot. My brothers will worry."

"You will leave a note telling them you have gone to Savannah for the weekend with a girlfriend from school and her family. Tell them you will be home Sunday night."

"Even if I believed you, I have no money for such a trip."

Pearl handed Julia the small envelope she was holding. "Inside you will find a thousand dollars for your hotel, taxis and bus fare. Keep whatever is left over. I have enclosed a list of the better hotels near the river. Be good to yourself and keep your receipts."

"No one gives a thousand dollars for no reason. What must I do for it?"

"You must leave town and not return before late Sunday evening, nothing more."

"And if I do not go?"

"We will take you. Drug dealers are not Mendez' enemies, Julia. We are, and we need you be far away from here."

"How can you be his enemy? You are an old woman."

Pearl chuckled. "Not that old, little one."

"I will get off the bus."

"No one intentionally gets off a bus to be a whore, although you are free to do so. Please bear in mind, however, that the person assigned to follow you will contact me, you will be anesthetised, tossed onto the back seat of a car and driven to Savannah for as long as it suits us. After that you will be free to spend your life as a puta, opening yourself to old men like Wilder, or becoming a famous actress. So please stop being a difficult child."

Julia looked inside the envelope. "What will happen to him?"

"That is of no consequence to anyone. What is important is what will not happen to you," Pearl reached into her handbag for another photograph, one taken of Julia during her examination, "or other girls your age. There will be more Wilders, Julia, more old men with sick appetites who get off beating young girls. You can count on this happening again."

Julia stood looking at the photograph until her lips began quivering and she burst into tears. She buried her face into cupped hands, shaking her head as Pearl stood stoically by her side.

"My brothers will not know?"

"Not unless you make that decision and I would strongly advise against telling them. Sometimes we are better off not knowing."

Julia looked around, her face glazed with tears, her shoulders sagging with exhaustion. "I will go to Savannah. I will do as you say. Thank you."

Twenty-Three

Montreal, Quebec
Friday, August 10

Kendall hadn't eaten all day. He wolfed his supper, forcing himself to save part of one sandwich for a late snack and the other half for an early breakfast in the park with a beer. He slept on the rear seat of his car and by 8:00 AM he was propped up against a back-to-school bay window of a department store in the centre of the downtown shopping district. The sky was bright blue. The air was stifling with a suffocating heat particular to overcrowded and dirty cities during the final few weeks of summer.

His clothes were wrinkled, his shoes were layered with city dust, his face flushed from the previous night and covered with dark stubble. He pulled up his pant leg and pushed down the sock. On the way from the park he practiced what he would say and how. He tried to sound humble, not pitiful or theatrical. He spoke to be heard over the din of car horns and pedestrians. He called out that he was a wounded war vet and needed money for antibiotics that would ward off infections.

By noon he earned thirty dollars, which he calculated would be fifty or sixty by day's end. The guys in jail were right. Why work? Fifteen minutes later the sidewalk was alive with people hurrying past him, jumbled together for as far as he could see. Men wearing suits and polished shoes passed him by, women in high heels and short dresses stopped to look into their purses and throw down a dollar. He never looked into their eyes, they would know, and he watched each one walk away hoping for the slightest glimpse.

By 12:55 he stopped counting at forty dollars and did the math. Thirty K a year, tax free, for stress-free living and always something nice to see. Now everyone was ignoring him. They were pushing against each other or squeezing between the less agile. Some were running; most were looking at their watches, not him, all of them wearing the same harried expression, save one woman who cared enough.

She knelt in front of him and examined his leg. She wore a red hat, a red cotton dress and sunglasses. She was brunette and good-looking from what he could see. She wore red gloves, which told him she was an arrogant bitch and he kept his head down wanting to see under her dress. Short skirts and long legs were his primary distraction. She placed one knee on the sidewalk, balancing herself as she reached into her handbag for something to give him, assuring him that he deserved so much more than how he'd been treated so far. He said thank you and kept his head low, waiting. He would never be good enough to do a woman like her, he thought. He didn't care. Her dress wasn't short but the bottom buttons were undone and she wasn't wearing nylons. Right then the anticipation of seeing what she was wearing under her dress was enough for him and he wondered what anyone would do if he reached under the dress and grabbed her to find out.

Her entire arm was hidden inside the handbag. Pearl looked at him with a smirk. She said "never again, Kendall" as she reached out with a gloved hand, pressing deceptively hard against his right shoulder and putting two muffled nine-millimetre cartridges into his chest as she stood and walked away in a single smooth movement. His body twitched once. No one would have noticed. The facilitation took a mere four seconds.

She had no need to look over her shoulder; no commotion had begun by the time Pearl glided into the revolving doors of the department store and into the ladies' room. Once inside the cubicle she removed her sunglasses, her wig, her dress and her underwear. She checked herself with a make-up mirror for possible blood splatter and slipped into a fashionable white-on-white slip dress. She kicked off her shoes and fastened the straps of her white sandals at her ankles. She ran her hands through her titanium hair, cleaned the compact 9000-S Berretta with lens cleaner and unscrewed the suppressor. She removed a white clutch from the handbag, put the gun in its place, rolled the red dress into a tight ball and packed it into the bag along with the underwear, wig, sunglasses and her shoes.

Claire Duval verified the cubicle. She checked herself again in the larger mirror over the row of sinks and left the building through a rear entrance. She sauntered six blocks to a movie theatre, disposing of the suppressor along the way, and dropped the contents of her bag into separate washroom garbage containers before the movie began. She left the empty bag by her seat when the early show finished and went home to shower and phone in her report before disposing of the gun with her second outfit and picking up her son at school.

Twenty-Four

Quebec City, Quebec
Friday, August 10

Driving to her hotel Miranda hated talking with the taxi driver. She wanted to think about her weekend and she wanted to cry. She needed to cry. When she did arrive at long last she went to the front desk and asked the night clerk what time the boutiques would open in the historic old town and his response made her cringe. She knew exactly where she must go and for what, despite knowing she would be late for the airport and her rendezvous with Green Eyes.

Locked in her room she put her shopping bags from earlier in the day on the bed, emptying them one by one. She took a single vodka from the mini bar and ran down the hall with her glass for ice. She had one suitcase and needed another, which was last on her unexpected list of priorities. First she would change her 6:00 PM Sunday departure from Montreal to 10:00 PM. She would be home in Toronto by midnight, a time and place she pushed from her mind. The second priority was the jeweller whom she had previously visited and she would put the clothes she didn't need for the weekend in a laundry bag and leave them in the car until Sunday.

She had gone into the lounge in the old town expecting or wanting to feel good about who she was and perhaps pretend for a little while that someone would want her for longer than one night or until they discovered she worked atrocious hours to sweep scum from the streets and was possibly a little jaded. Her careers were her life. One existed in a world thought by most to be real, the other, a parallel world, was the real world to a privileged few and she'd ended her evening by accepting a date with a woman who shared those worlds. She knew she wasn't going on a real date with the woman she would never know and to whom she had felt an immediate attraction. Green Eyes was straight and Miranda would have to hold herself in check, yet she knew the moment Green Eyes kissed her cheek that the meaning went beyond a simple "see you tomorrow." She didn't imagine the warmth and feeling, or the pressure against her cheek surpassing the French thing.

She dropped onto the bed, reached for the phone and called the desk for a 6:00 AM wake-up. Then she set her own alarm clock for 6:30, not trusting herself. She began packing her clothes at 2:00 AM and finished thirty later, putting what she didn't need into laundry bags, keeping aside what she would wear to the airport. The restaurant opened at 7:00 and she eventually fell asleep wondering how to look perfect for Green Eyes.

She nestled her head into her pillows, curled into herself and peered into Morgan's deep brown eyes the way she did most every night before sleeping. She'd been gone such a long time, Miranda murmured, so very long. She told Morgan about her day and her new clothes, about meeting Green Eyes who was a policewoman, how nothing would ever come of it and that Miranda would never stop missing her best friend and lover. She explained how alone she felt. The coming Christmas would be her eleventh one alone. She told her about the daring new bikini she would wear over the weekend because she wanted to. Her time alone had lasted so long and hurt in so many inexplicable ways.

The nightly tears had stopped years before, though not

the crushing heartache or the sick feeling that would invade her without warning. Miranda had never spoken to Morgan about Pearl and never would. Morgan would never understand.

Six AM came early. She awoke with a start and thanked the recorded voice on the phone. She stretched away her grogginess, pulled herself up and reached for the small brass picture frame resting on the night table. She kissed Morgan, telling her how sorry she was, and held Morgan over her heart as she climbed from the bed to place the frame into her suitcase between layers of delicate clothes.

Miranda checked out by 8:00. She was in le Vieux-Québec by 9:00 and late for the airport. She stood by the jeweller's door tapping one foot, then the other, growing more impatient. When the unsuspecting man finally did arrive he didn't understand the flurry of excited English words she threw at him, ecstatic when he discovered she would be his week's best client.

Dina arrived at the Jean Lesage Airport at 9:40, at 10:10 she assumed the usual bad traffic on the bridge or that Chérie had misunderstood her directions from the bridge to the airport. At 10:30 she assumed a bad hangover or second thoughts about being with a cop, or wasting her time with a straight, and at 10:40 she realized Chérie had gone back to Toronto. She yanked the handle from inside her suitcase and walked from the shuttle stop, not certain which emotion fit the occasion.

"Green Eyes," Miranda shouted. "Wait up. Come on. Wait for me."

Dina twirled on her heels and lost her breath. The woman running was something from a picture or book or a perfect dream, and whatever doubts Dina might have entertained vanished. Miranda let her suitcase fall behind her and was running towards Dina with her arms waving, her beautiful blonde hair dancing at her shoulders to an uncontrolled rhythm of its own. The moment would be indelible for Dina: completely bare legs topped in pure white high-rise satin shorts à la forties cinched with a black patent leather belt, a bare and tanned midriff, a loose-fitting off-the-shoulder sweater and three-inch sandals on a collision course with her. Worse, she thought, she liked what she was seeing. She liked watching Miranda run towards her. There was no logic in what she was doing, no reason, and she didn't care what was crazy, ridiculous or dangerous. She wanted to be with the woman for the weekend and opened her arms.

The impact was soft, Miranda hugging and kissing her new friend, leaving pouty red lips on each cheek.

"I know, I'm late, and you thought I wasn't coming. I'm sorry, but when you find out why you're going to give me a big straight kiss."

"I was going to the ladies' room."

"No, you weren't, and don't lie to me. We'll be deceitful enough over the weekend. You thought I wasn't coming. I wouldn't miss this for the world, but I do have to say you cops can sure put it back. Shit, my head hurts."

"Mine, too. I usually don't get a buzz on, though in my defence it's not every night a lesbian asks me out on a date, and I accept."

"We're on a date? Alright, Green Eyes!"

She hugged Dina again, pressing their cheeks together.

"Nooo, we are not on a date," she pried herself from Miranda's arms, "even if you are breathtaking. I feel like a frigging grandmother beside you."

"You don't believe that, maybe an older sister by a year or two. We're both hot and we both know it. Who are you wearing?"

Dina giggled. "This isn't the damn Oscars, Chérie."

The response wasn't good enough. Miranda spun Dina around and pulled her hip-hugger pants from her hips.

"Wow, great ass," she exclaimed, "and backless. Alright."

Dina regained control of her pants. "You will die if you don't let go of me."

"We could be sisters, Green Eyes, but," Miranda put her hands against Dina's bare hips, "you should show these strings or people will think you're not wearing panties. Get with it, girl. Don't you know these things?" She moved her hands to Dina's shoulders and adjusted her tank top to one side. "Good, no bra. You don't need one and your sandals are fantastic."

"Okay, that's it. I'm leaving, I'm going home. I can't take a whole weekend of this." Dina stepped back, waving the open palms of her hands. Miranda stayed as she was, speechless, the happy colour draining from her face. "Oh, come on, I was kidding. Listen, honestly, I'm a little nervous about all this."

"You're nervous because of me?"

"Yes because of you, because you're into girls. I never considered for a second my first weekend away since Christ was a teenager would be with a woman so much younger than me, and, okay, a lesbian. Hello. Let's not forget important little details."

"I'm thirty-two, and so what if I saw your bum? If guys can look at your ass and think it's to die for, why can't I? Anyway, now that I have we can relax."

"Okay, good point. I'm sorry. I'm thirty-nine, so I guess I could be an older sister."

"You could pass for ten years younger and you're not the only one who's scared. And, by the way, I was late because I was shopping for a little something to help you remember your weekend with the lesbian freak. Okay." Miranda stuck out her tongue.

"You're far from being a freak. Say anything like that again and I'll slap on the cuffs." Dina nodded towards the parking lot. "Anyway the bus is coming and I want a weekend with a crazy blonde as much as I need a weekend with a crazy blonde." She paused. "What did you get me?"

"You'll have to wait until tonight. Did you say handcuffs?" Miranda questioned.

"Yes, handcuffs, real ones, and I think I'm going to need them."

Miranda feigned a moment of deep thought. "Perhaps not, it's been so long since I've had any I forget what it's like. Maybe I'm one of you." She shivered. "Yuk."

Dina made a soft chortling sound. "Well, if that's how this all works, perhaps I am a lesbian. The last time I had some there wasn't a two on the calendar page."

She put out a hand, signalling the driver to stop before the actual pick-up spot, insisting her inherent cop-body language saved them a walk. Miranda countered that more likely their outfits and what was in them stopped the bus. The driver put one suitcase into the rear of the vehicle and ran happily into the parking lot for Miranda's as the women climbed onboard.

They were the only passengers and Miranda couldn't resist pressing the palms of her hands into the firm flesh of Dina's buttocks and squeezing. "Sorry, Green Eyes. I was testing to make sure I'm still into girls, so you must still be straight. It's good that we know." She looked up to see Dina shaking her head. "Okay, I promise, that was absolutely the very last time. And by the way, all I've brought with me is sweats and flannel, straight stuff so you won't get hot and bothered looking at me."

Dina turned, forcing away a smile. "Now I am going home. I mean it."

"Okay, maybe I brought some silk and satin, and other stuff."

"You're crazy. Do you know that?" Dina hugged her. "Are you sixteen, or what?"

"I haven't been this crazy for a long time and it's your fault. If I hadn't met you I'd already be going home and you'd be writing traffic tickets."

Dina shrieked, pushing Miranda onto the bench seat. "I

don't write tickets. I'm the frigging ..." she stopped herself, "I'm the one with the handcuffs."

"Like you said, Green Eyes, it'll be weird. So let's do the Vegas thing. What happens at the spa stays at the spa. Besides, she told me last night and this morning that she likes you."

"Who?" Dina questioned seriously. "Who knows about this?"

"No one, Green Eyes. She's someone special who will always be with me. Don't get me started."

When the shuttle pulled into the luxury spa centred in the pastoral setting of Sainte-Germaine-du-lac-Etchemin the women were comfortable with each other and Dina was wearing her hair swept up into a triple French braid. They were given gift packs at the desk, agendas for the forty-eight hours and keys to a luxurious suite.

Miranda left her suitcase in the hallway and scurried in, leaving Dina to struggle with both pieces of luggage and the door. "You are sixteen, aren't you?"

"This is so charming and romantic, Green Eyes. I am definitely learning French. As soon as I get back I'm quitting my job and moving here."

"No, you're not," Dina answered, straining.

"And why not?"

"Because I will personally shoot you in that cute ass of yours; Quebec isn't ready for you. Anyway, are you really a trial lawyer or have you escaped from somewhere?"

Miranda didn't answer. She was standing in the entrance to a bedroom with her arms folded, looking disappointed.

"You can have the big one. I'll take this one."

Dina peered into each room, shrugging to show her indifference when she saw the master suite had one king-size bed and the smaller room a much smaller double. She went into the bigger room with her luggage, dropped her suitcase onto the bed and unzipped the top. She pulled out an unopened bottle of Jean-Marc XO and sent Miranda for ice. When she returned both suitcases were in the larger room and two glasses were poured one-finger deep. Miranda beamed.

"Remember, Chérie," Dina warned, "I've got cuffs and I will use them."

"Won't you have to frisk me first and read me my rights?" Miranda ran over to Dina and squeezed her. "We're going to talk all night."

"Oh, God. What have I done?"

"For starters, you've made me super happy. So let's have these drinks, get into our cosies and get down there. I want to see what you look like all covered in chocolate." Miranda licked her lips and cooed: "I love chocolate."

Twenty-Five

La Montérégie, East of Montreal
Friday, August 10

The two-storey mansion with its lush gardens overlooking the blue-green and ribbon-like Richelieu River twenty miles east of Montreal was hidden from the private and winding road leading to its wrought iron gates by hundreds of mature trees and high manicured hedges. The home was expansive yet unpretentious, designed to visually please and blend with the pastoral setting, constructed for quite another purpose in mind.

Trees lining the winding road were equipped with concealed lenses every fifty feet for a mile, the fifteen-foot spiked fence encircling the hundred-acre property was similarly equipped every twenty feet with motion detectors in-between, and from dusk until dawn the riverside entrance and main gate shone as bright as day.

The interior was contemporary and decorated to reflect the owner's inclination towards simplicity in most matters, particularly in regard to purposefulness. The lower level was an office setting equipped with wooden filing cabinets, colour-coded phones, computers and monitors in constant contact with the exterior cameras and motion detectors. A dual fire prevention system was also in place: one would automatically extinguish an unexpected emergency; the other would initiate an incredibly violent and unmanageable inferno once ignited by the insertion of three keys which would simultaneously fortify the mansion's points of entry.

The housekeeping staff had been with her for years. They were more like family than employees and treated her with the deserved reverence of an aging parent. She was sitting on the veranda enjoying her traditional late afternoon Chardonnay when Beverly Price arrived.

"Good afternoon, Beverly. Thank you for coming on such short notice. Sometimes talking on the phone is so impersonal. Frankly, I don't like the things at all anymore." She looked out over the gardens to the river. "Isn't the day lovely? We must appreciate each and every one. One never knows, does one?"

"Good afternoon, Mother. Yes, the day is very lovely." Beverly followed the old woman's gaze. "Coming here is always so enjoyable. The grounds are so peaceful and serene."

"Please sit, Beverly. How is your Fred? Does he treat you well?"

"Yes Mother, he does, and you know very well he does. He's fine. When he heard where I would be this afternoon he wanted to drive me. He spent the morning thinking of every excuse. He was disappointed when I told him you wanted a few words with me in private and wants you over for dinner one evening very soon."

"He is a good man, I know. Tell him I have always enjoyed his invitations and, in particular, his culinary talent." Beverly nodded and smiled, understanding even the simplest request from Mother was a direct order. "Beverly, forgive me if I sounded out of the ordinary on the phone. I did not intend to alarm you."

"Are you well, Mother?"

"Very well, other than I seem to be distressing everyone lately. The people around me are fussing so much these days, constantly asking whether I need this or that and my daughter has become the worst offender by far. I believe she's a little miffed with me of late. She wants me to leave all this and move into her home. I told her no. Why she and her husband would want an old lady hanging around when they should be travelling and enjoying themselves, I have no idea. She's so headstrong."

"Could it possibly be a family trait?"

The old woman smiled widely. "I might possibly have had a small influence, I suppose."

"I wish I could have known her. I'm sure we would have been very good friends under very different circumstances."

"I find it peculiar you would think to say such a thing, Beverly. I have always considered you her best friend, despite never meeting her, which is one reason you are here today."

Another elegantly dressed woman in her late forties appeared through the doors carrying a tray with a decanter and a single crystal goblet. She greeted Beverly as Pearl and poured her glass half-full before leaving the decanter on the patio table and the two older women to talk.

"Beverly you have been with us for thirty-six years. Thank you for such exemplary dedication. Above all, thank you for a particular night so many years ago. You saved her life, Beverly. I don't believe I have ever adequately expressed my appreciation and I wish to correct that situation forthwith."

"As you were the one to save my life so many years ago, Mother. We both know he would have killed me. I see nothing to correct. We are, shall we say, even."

The old woman nodded and smiled weakly. "We lead double lives and we lie to our loved ones about whom and what we are. At times I deeply regret what I created so long ago, and then I think of all the good we have done and continue to do. Pearl can never be allowed to fail, Beverly. We must go on."

"How would one stop an avalanche of such huge proportions, Mother? We are an engine too finely tuned not to continue."

"Thanks to so many, Beverly, and the time has come for change which will ensure Pearl's continuance ad infinitum. As long as the need exists, so must we. You are that change, Beverly. I am stepping down. As of this moment you are Mother of Pearl." The old woman took up an envelope and passed it to her guest. "As you might expect a few perks do go along with the position, perks which you still have wonderful years ahead of you to enjoy." Her thin lips curved into a mischievous smirk. "And you might want to begin thinking of an answer when your Fred questions how you acquired a private jet out of the blue, so to speak."

Beverly was stunned. "Mother, I never once contemplated what you're suggesting."

"I'm not suggesting anything, Beverly. Please let me finish. As you so adequately expressed, Pearl is a finely tuned engine and you will soon learn that what I do is by and large titular, which is not to say perfunctory. Mother of Pearl is a crucial component of our success. Whether mythical, mystical or illusionary, these rings we wear do not come from five directors, nor are they gifts to thousands of women from caring Enablers. They come from me, and now they will come from you, the mythical and omnipotent Mother of Pearl. You will have to learn to deal with what is essentially a seat of power. What I am conferring on you is not a gift, Beverly, nor a kindness. Better said, I am transferring a burden which you are amply qualified to assume."

Beverly Price was openly shocked. "I don't know what to say. You have grown into the position over time, Mother. You have always been who you are. How can I possibly become in a moment what you spent decades to achieve and perfect?"

"You will, because you must, and you will make provisions for the moment when you must choose one of your five directors to replace you. We are no different than any organization where leaders come and go, yet structure and discipline remain. I entreat you to accept the position, Beverly, and to continue your devotion. I would not have selected you otherwise. To that end, I want you to convene a meeting of the Directorate for Monday. Letters were couriered this morning to the other four announcing my decision and I expect all four will be pleased with your appointment. I want the meeting in the morning, right here, and I want them to stay over. After lunch I want you to meet with Jasmine Leclerc, alone. Select an appropriate venue downtown. I want her to replace you as director of your zone. Should she accept the appointment, she will return here with you to join us for dinner and meet with the other directors. I have no reason to believe she will refuse. I also want you to meet separately with Dina Becker and Miranda Stevens Sunday at a suitable downtown location. You are to remove them at once from active facilitation. Neither girl is to participate in any such future assignment. They are both in their tenth year of service and I want them sent overseas as soon as possible to train as Enablers. According to her file Dina has only a few years remaining with the police and Miranda has a wonderful legal career ahead of her. Let us make certain both objectives are achieved. Meet with Dina first. An hour or so with each one should be adequate, with sufficient time allotted between meetings to avoid embarrassing complications. I would have enjoyed being with you to see them, without their knowledge of course. I do miss that little bit of cloak and dagger intrigue. Tell each one I am thinking of her and give each one my heartfelt appreciation with a bonus of fifty thousand dollars for their past service. The transfers to their offshore accounts should be made on the first Monday as usual."

"And in the event either one declines the position of Enabler?"

"It's well-deserved whatever their decisions."

"I agree."

"Neither woman is to know of your new position within the organization or of the possible change to the Directorate. Above all they are not to know of my departure or that their respective replacements are about to return from overseas."

"I will call them this afternoon. Considering the slump in their social obligations I would assume they will both be available. Miranda must have arrived home from Quebec City late Thursday. You might have forgotten, Mother, with everything else on your mind. Miranda was in Dina's sector this past week with special permission."

"Yes, the Preston case study."

Beverly acknowledged the old woman's acuity with a nod.

"Yes. She performed well, and while we're discussing case studies, Benoit Voisine, the man who murdered Dina's sister may be released from prison in the very near future. His parole review is slated for Monday the twentieth, which puts him on the street as early as the next day. We're hoping he chooses not to return home. Three facilitations within three weeks in a city the size of Quebec would be foolhardy in the extreme and we want to avoid anything as overt as a drive-by, which would be potentially dangerous for us and possibly for civilians. We intend to convince him to re-establish himself elsewhere."

"I concur. And are we certain of the board's decision?"

"Theoretically, yes, although we must regrettably act against one of its members to ensure a satisfactory outcome, a woman by the name of Heather Hancock."

"We don't have much time, Beverly. What actions have taken place thus far?"

"We have begun tracking Miss Hancock to establish a pattern of her habits. By all accounts she leads a quiet life."

"Any action must be of a temporary nature. No permanent harm must come to her, mental or physical."

"The operative has been instructed to use the least force

possible. Claire Duval is well-trained. She's been with us for five years and will go out of her way not to inconvenience the woman more than is absolutely necessary."

"Claire is an excellent choice. I feel an overwhelming sorrow to even contemplate the need to injure a woman, though we do so for the greater good. Be certain Claire understands my feelings and reward her beyond the usual facilitation fee for attending to the Hancock woman, whether or not she is the one to rid the world of Monsieur Voisine. This case is important to us, Beverly. We must not disappoint Dina. Now, what can you tell me of Ms. Hancock?"

"She's fifty-four, divorced, both children have moved out and she's been on the board throughout most of her career. She works hard and takes her job seriously. She lives on rue Fort in one of those converted condos that were old in the seventies and she attends Mary of the World for Sunday mass."

"Be certain she is able to continue doing so for many years to come. Are we able to compensate her in any way for what is about to happen?"

"No, Mother, unfortunately not."

"Who will be her stand-in?"

"Noelle Barton." Mother tilted her head, her surprise showing in her dark eyes. "She was moved to the top of the replacement list and any trace of the administrative adjustment was permanently eradicated."

"Please reward Noelle with a bonus equal to Claire's fee. Has either woman been told this facilitation is on behalf of a Pearl?"

"Yes. But, now, what of you, Mother?" Beverly sipped her wine, following the slow passage of a two sailboats crossing paths in the distance. "What will you do? Pearl is your life? Can you spend your days watching boats and sipping Chardonnay?"

"Pearl is my life, which has gone so very quickly. Can you believe you and my daughter have been retired for three years? I remember the first time I met you. You were such a pretty little thing and so frightened. And on a personal note, you have not changed very much at all. Your Fred has done very nicely for himself. He should be very proud of his conquest over you. I remember your moments of doubt when he was first smitten with you."

"Sometimes I giggle, when he asks me why I ever thought to possess such a collection of letter openers." The women chuckled. "How will I explain all this to Fred, Mother?"

"I'm fantastically wealthy, Beverly. Life has treated me well. The jet is my gift to you, from one friend to another. I know Fred believes your design firm was sold for somewhat more than the actual amount, however, still not sufficient to manage that particular mode of travel. This morning my attorneys deposited ten million into your offshore account, from me personally. The gift has nothing to do with Pearl."

"Mother."

"It's a mere drop in a very large bucket and, of course, certain other benefits will accompany your new status within Pearl beyond the jet and inconsequential pin money."

"A good deal more than pin money, mother. What of your daughter?"

"She has been well provided for throughout her life and will be to a much greater extent after I'm gone."

"Mother I can't believe any of this and please don't speak of being gone." Beverly paused, visibly upset. "My poor Fred, he was thinking of retiring, of travelling more."

"What is your point, Beverly? We work continent-wide and you know very well the directors make most of the important decisions. Go wherever you want. Your retirement will not be interrupted in the least. The position

257

does entail dealing with certain encumbrances, of course, but in great part your life will be quite enhanced by your new position. And now I must hear your acceptance. I must hear the words."

"I do accept, Mother."

"I knew you would. You are also to expect an anonymous contribution of eighty million into the Pearl account. Be certain the funds are distributed equitably throughout the zones."

"Eighty million, Mother, will change thousands of lives."

"We hope and pray. Perhaps I have waited longer than I should have for this moment. Who's to know what is truly in another's mind. I am confident in my decision. As for the money, I would never leave Pearl without proper funding. Now, do you also agree with Jasmine, Dina and Miranda? You now have the privilege of veto. Tell me your true feelings. Speak to me as Mother, not a member of the Directorate."

Beverly had no hesitation, no doubt in her voice. "Mother, Jasmine Leclerc should be my replacement and Dina Becker should replace her. I do agree. Dina has done excellent work and I agree the time has come for her to stop what she is doing. Though I do wish she had some balance in her life. She's convinced the real Dina can only exist by escaping to exotic locations and pretending to be someone she is not."

"Perhaps the one who escapes is the real Dina and the Captain of SVU who is not. Who's to say? Don't we all want to be someone else at some point: taller, shorter, thinner, fatter, richer or poorer. Who amongst us is happy with oneself all the time? What matters is Dina learning to define herself and that she continues to be protected by Pearl as much as we remain unthreatened by her."

"I have complete faith in her. I would trust her with my life."

"You do, Beverly, now particularly so," the old woman responded matter-of-factly, "as do we all. Frankly, she's one of our best and I harbour not a single doubt as to her ability to function effectively and detachedly. It's the young woman herself I worry about. What is the expression the young ones use, get a life?"

Beverly coughed a short laugh. "Yes, Mother, I believe so. She has one of the worst real-time careers of any Facilitator. I suppose she sees most men as potential offenders. Who can blame her? Perhaps that might change when she becomes an Enabler. I do hope so. She's wasting her life. A few weeks each year in Saint-Tropez or wherever don't make up for eleven months of sleeping alone."

"The key is balance, Beverly. When we facilitate we do so against one specific being, not a whole gender. Stay with her, keep her balanced, and now what of our little Miranda?"

Beverly laughed softly. "Each time I see Miranda I think of how I once was."

The old woman nodded. "Yes, I don't believe Fred ever knew how much he was taking on when he found you, the poor man. So, our Miranda gets a little naughty at times."

"She could be if she let herself go. She's so young, so delightful, yet she won't let go of the past. I feel so very sorry for her. She certainly knows how to distract a man, and I daresay she's given a good number of women cause to look twice, yet she's never found anyone special to replace her girlfriend."

"Which is an entirely unacceptable situation, dare I say wasteful."

"Mother?" was all Beverly could think to say.

"The girl's murder was so terrible. I remember the event clearly. I can't accept such a young and vital woman as Miranda spending all these years alone. Such an absolutely meaningless and inexcusable sacrifice, completely unnecessary. She should be severely scolded."

"We don't all heal with time."

"Truer words have never been spoken and I sit here as proof. You know the girls somewhat better than I do. Can we do anything to help them, short of playing Cupid and finding them suitable partners?"

Beverly pondered the question. "The time will come for each of them when the time is right. I waited a very long time, and I'm glad I did. One mistake in life of such magnitude is enough for any woman."

"Do tell." Mother sipped her wine. "Beverly, the appellation Mother of Pearl came into being very much by accident, the inspiration, if you will, of a very old and dear friend. However a mother is precisely what you will be. What you will ask of these women is unthinkable and extraordinary in the extreme, yet they will do as you ask without question. Incumbent upon you in return is to never let them down, to never let them exceed their limitations, never to let them suffer as a result of what they do. Until now your contact was limited to the operatives in your zone over many years. There are so many more like Claire, Noelle, Dina, and Miranda, to name a few. We are a bizarre anomaly, even unto ourselves, and so we must remain if we are to survive. Not even my staff here at the mansion is privy to that information. I alone know them all by their true names, Beverly, my daughters who are now yours to adopt and protect. You must come to know each one. They number one-hundred and sixty, from twenty-three years of age to sixty." The old woman frowned. "Of course, so many more have retired or passed on into oblivion because the encrypted files were destroyed, as mine will soon be." She paused, ringing a porcelain bell to alert her assistant. When both wine goblets were refilled she passed her guest a second envelope and continued. "Now, Beverly, to more serious business. Most executives are welcomed to a promotion with keys to fancy bathrooms, new cars, bonuses and gifts from the subordinate upwardly mobile. All you get is a private jet and ten million. It's not enough, not by far, because what you also inherit is a horrible story about a poor little girl in Miami called Julia Saunders who recently turned eighteen. She's a full-time student and a category one: urgent. Her parents live in Cuba. Julia lives with her brothers who are also students and work part time at the same hotel. Fortunately for them, or for us, their work schedules will coincide conveniently with what we intend. The brothers are currently being observed in case something should go wrong. We can't allow either one to become a possible suspect."

"So the brothers are not the case study."

"No, that would be her so-called boyfriend, one Eduardo Mendez. He's a Mexican, nineteen, a dropout and has made Julia believe he works as a bartender. He's a real piece of work. As the story goes, he got into some trouble with some local dealers several months ago. Subsequently, he was able to convince the poor girl of his undying love for her, that he wants to marry her, but that if she didn't sleep with strange men to help him pay off the debt they would kill him. Pity."

"Despicable. How often does this happen?"

"Her recurring nightmare has been taking place several times a week since April, at night after Julia finishes work as a restaurant hostess or days between her classes. She works from 4:00 until 10:00 and weekends. He meets her outside his supposed apartment. It's not. Data from the DMV puts him in one of those fancy glass buildings by the ocean." The old woman paused, taking a deep breath before sipping her wine to moisten her throat. "Beverly, according to what we have ascertained, there are no dealers out to kill Mendez for cheating them and there is no bartending job. In fact, he has no job at all. Information as recent as a few minutes ago tells us he apparently assured Julia the despicable encounters would come to an end after a few months, by which time the poor girl would be in much greater trouble. Based on photos taken of him this morning and inconsistencies between his bank account and his lifestyle, we reasonably presume other girls are involved, most likely young and impressionable students. He likes fancy cars and expensive jewellery, if not somewhat gaudy as you can see and, as you can also see, Julia was a pretty girl until a few hours before these photos were taken. He's using her and the others to support his lifestyle and we found her not a moment too soon."

"He's a pimp."

"Small time, which is how he gets away with it…or did. It's very clear his last customer wanted somewhat more from Julia than she was willing to give. The details are in the file. Sadly, the cruelty she endured is also her saving grace."

"What measures have taken place thus far?"

"She was enabled by a woman called Piedra Batista whom you don't yet know. She operates under Carmen Alondra whom you do know, and who was unreachable last night, as were you. Piedra then called Christine Lafleur, her secondary director, and Christine called me. As time was of the essence we concurred regarding the need for immediate facilitation before the eleventh hour. Otherwise, I certainly would have conferred with you and the other directors. Unfortunately the luxury of time is seldom ours to enjoy. My intention was not to snub you."

"I understand entirely, Mother."

"The case study was a difficult one. Julia wanted very much to believe Mendez is real and, despite her fear of them, that the dealers do exist. I suppose cerebrally she was seeking to justify what she was doing, which is impossible. These photos helped. Being away will also give her a few days before facing her brothers with a little more make-up than usual. Her worst physical injuries can easily be hidden from them. The emotional wounds are always the most severe. We assured her the brothers will not hear of her situation from us, at the same time advising her against such a confession which would certainly serve to injure her all the more."

"What is her current mindset?"

"Afraid. We had very little choice but to be direct with her in view of the inherent peculiarities of the case study. She refused to speak with the police, although she did mention Mendez' name several time during her examination, which is to say an unfortunate link between them. There was no medical reason for keeping her any longer in the hospital, which would have been a perfect alibi for our purposes and difficult in the extreme for Julia to explain to her family. We told her she had no choice, if for no other reason than to prevent her brothers from becoming involved with presumably dire consequences. We told her that, in fact, we are Mendez' true enemy, that he's a pimp, that steps have been set in motion to get him off the street and we won't tolerate her getting in the way."

"Difficult words for a young girl to hear."

"True. It's distasteful at best. She's also afraid of losing her job, which she cannot afford to lose. She's paid hourly and earns enough to scrape by after her share of the rent and tuition, with nothing left over for the slightest luxury. We have given her sufficient funds to get through the weekend, the usual sort of thing, as well as briefing her as to what not to do."

"It will be difficult for her. I assume she's pro bono."

"Indeed, and we will soon be discreetly arranging for a small outpatient corrective medical procedure when the time is right, one she will have no difficulty explaining."

"And what of the brothers?"

"They'll find a note telling them Julia had an opportunity to go away unexpectedly for the weekend, returning Sunday evening. Whatever she tells them upon her return will be the full extent of their knowledge."

"How did we learn of her?"

"Piedra Batista works as a social worker in Dade County. She's been with us for fifteen or sixteen years. By the time she was ready to see Julia, the girl had left the hospital, which is precisely what we wanted in order to avoid future complications. She called in to open the case study when Mercy Hospital called her to visit with Julia who refused to meet the police or press charges. She told the hospital Mendez was always curious about trying new ways to please her but this time they both got a little excited in the heat of passion"

Beverly shook her head. "And she thought they believed her."

"She's young and she's afraid."

"Being afraid is what will save her. Do we know the customer?"

The old woman smiled maliciously. "Yes we do. He's seventy. He's vacationing in Miami with his wife who, fortunately for her, will be going home alone."

"Thank you, Piedra," Beverly added.

"Yes, Piedra, meaning "stone" and the name fits. She's no one to toy with. She sits on various boards, she intimidates local and state officials with her eyes alone and she proudly wears our ring. She is a Pearl beyond all others."

"Is she aware Mendez is about to be facilitated?"

Mother nodded. "She knows to expect as much."

"Julia might lose her job."

"A minor setback, however she will have her body and her life. At the very worst she'll have a lifetime secret to guard. Not the worst thing in the world, is it?"

"No, it's not. We are an adaptable specie and we can do something about Julia's job situation later."

"Yes, we can, Mother," the old woman said in response. "We certainly can."

"And what is subsequently planned?"

"The boyfriend, the once-was boyfriend. By this time

264

tomorrow he'll be looking into the dark eyes of his Aztec ancestors who may, or may not, want to cut his throat a second time."

"May we certainly hope so."

"And I have spoken with Carmen about the old one, Wilder. What he did to the girl was unconscionable and atrocious. He'll be second and somewhat of a departure from our usual detached approach. Consuelo Moreno will facilitate both of them. She is also a reporter and will be making a point of showing the world the real Mr. Wilder. As an extra bonus, I would imagine his wife will return home despising the old pig."

Beverly was perusing the Saunders file. "Whatever way it's done will be too fast and too easy for what he's done to the poor girl."

"Indeed, Beverly, and on another note I will expect you here each day for the next week. You have much to learn...and hear me closely. Should I happen not to be here to receive you, my assistant and staff are instructed to allow you full access to the lower levels where you will discover the encoded history of Pearl. They are aware of your new status. As well, the other directors will acquaint you with their respective operatives on a more personal level throughout the coming weeks."

"Pearl's history is archived here?"

"Yes, though our operatives' files are stored separately and destroyed when their service is terminated."

"And your personal staff."

"Five in all, each from a different zone, women you have never met and I trust them implicitly. You will meet them this evening, after which they will report to you. I'm dying, Beverly, which does not come as a big surprise to someone who is eighty-two. More to the point, I have waited too long to appoint you as my successor." Beverly Price stared at the diminutive and charismatic woman who had never lost the youthful sparkle in her eyes once she regained it so many years earlier. "My final gift to you, Beverly, as Mother of Pearl, is this estate and my wish is for you to one day pass it on to another who will succeed you. This is all yours."

"Mother, I refuse to believe what you're saying. You look in fine health and you'll enjoy this marvellous river for years to come."

"It's my time, Beverly. Don't argue with fate."

"Does your daughter know?"

"She does not, nor will she for the time being. I have much to do in a very short time and I would not have a moment alone were she to know. As for the property, I never intended for her to inherit anything relating to Pearl and what would she do with a jet. She has her own home and lives well. You are so much like her, Beverly. I don't have months or weeks remaining. I have but a few days and I wish to establish you as Mother so I might spend those few remaining days with her. In my defence, years ago I prepared a confidential document to ensure your position as Mother of Pearl. The transition is a fait accompli. You are Mother of Pearl and my decision will not be contested."

"Mother, you will always be with us."

"Yes, in your hearts, and knowing that makes my heart glad. No one has ever known my true identity with the exception of very few directors. Mother of Pearl must continue to exist beyond the physical. Beyond the Directorate no one must ever know who you are and I mean to include Fred. I daresay the dear man would be quite shocked. I might suggest you tell him that your personal assistants here at the estate manage a non-profit organization which sees to the needs of disadvantaged women. I doubt whether one more little white lie will make a difference." Mary Bingham sipped her wine. "I have one last request beyond your requisite visits, Beverly, which is to call upon my daughter as a friend. Tell her my story which you are about to hear, and tell her the truth without telling her."

"Mother, I dislike the tone of this meeting immensely."

"We all have our time and I feel grateful to have sufficient notice in order to bid farewell to my friends... and to tell you my story." Mary sipped more wine, disregarding Beverly's pale expression. "Beverly, meeting with my daughter is my final instruction to you, and I realize a difficult request. You will take control of Pearl forthwith and you will take care of Julia Saunders. She will be your first charge and, when the time is right, you will take care of what my daughter must know of me. I leave the timing to you, Mother of Pearl. That is who you now are."

Twenty-Six

Miami, Florida
Friday, August 10

Piedra Batista bid farewell to a bewildered Julia Saunders at the bus station. She stopped waving as Julia climbed the steps, giving her attention to Carmen Alondra who would inconspicuously accompany Julia to Savannah. Moments later Carmen retrieved her phone from her purse and dialled another number. The voice that answered belonged to exotic and dark-haired Consuelo Moreno and within the hour her lethal alter ego knew most everything about Eduardo Mendez, including the established time of his death.

Whatever else Piedra Batista would learn of Mendez, she knew she would do so from the morning papers. She had no doubt Julia Saunders would transfer buses in Jacksonville and follow her instructions to the letter. Pearl never failed to complete a case study. Eduardo Mendez and Eric Wilder perhaps had a few hours left to live and Julia Saunders had regained her life.

*

Eduardo Mendez knew everything about Julia Saunders and he knew where to look for her, which made Consuelo Moreno's surveillance of him all the easier. He spent the first part of the morning with the girl who was photographed in his car, dropping her off at a gentleman's club moments before noon before going to the Ocean Drive apartment.

He went in cautiously. The doors were ajar and he needed all of a few seconds to scan the room. He called her name. Nothing. The only sound was running water. He saw the shattered vase and traces of blood on the couch. He saw her panties and the open patio doors.

He phoned her, furious at hearing her message and what he had seen. Doing his best to control his voice he told her to be there at ten o'clock, not half past the hour. They needed to talk. The night before had gone well. She would be pleased with what he had to say. He ran to where he parked the car, hurried through traffic to the School of Arts, then to the restaurant and her apartment where no one answered. He'd never seen the brothers in person or in photographs, and didn't want to see them, but the hotel was all that was left to him until 10:00 that evening. She wasn't at the hotel. He searched the lobby, the bars, the pool and the dining rooms. He phoned her again and left the same message, paying no attention to the woman wearing a long, white vented summer dress, wide-brimmed hat and sunglasses standing a few feet behind him.

As he exited the hotel, Consuelo Moreno followed with long strides as she opened Julia's cell phone to monitor the message. On the other side of the main doors she stopped and watched as Mendez climbed into the Z4, slammed the door and sped away with his tires screeching against oppressive heat of Miami asphalt.

Wilder was next. His car hadn't moved since Consuelo attached the transmitter to the undercarriage earlier that morning. Driving the seventeen hundred miles to Phoenix, or doing anything else with a bashed-in face, would be impossible for a man of his years. He would either be in bed, at the pool or the beach using his cell phone to snap candid shots of topless girls in thongs.

He wasn't in his room when she called from the lobby, so she sent a bellboy to walk the pool area calling his name for an important message. When he returned, unsuccessfully, she gave him a twenty and sent him to the beach. The young man returned moments later with Wilder's detailed description.

"Señor Wilder, how are you feeling? Better, I hope."

"Are you the one with some sort of message?"

"Sí, I am. My name is Pearl. What has happened to you is terrible. I come from Eddie Mendez." She stood into the wind, letting the breeze play against the hem and open front edges of her dress. "He is so sorry. How can I say? This bad thing is so bad for his reputation, no? He wants to return your three hundred dollars and offer you someone much better." She knelt in front of him, undoing one more button at her thighs. "You may have me for one hour or for the evening. Eddie wants you to be satisfied." She paused, tugging at one edge of the dress. "Mr. Wilder, you will be very satisfied. I promise you."

"That little bitch stole my wallet."

"I will make certain it is returned to you."

"How old are you?"

"Twenty-one," she lied, "but that does not matter. I am the best at what I do."

"When do we get together?"

"Right now, in your room, if you believe this is wise, or tonight at the apartment at 10:30, when we will have more time. Take a taxi. I will drive you back here whenever we are finished. It will be my pleasure to meet with you. It is what you deserve, no?"

"You're damn right it's what I deserve. I get my four hundred, plus the taxi?" Consuelo reached into her purse and counted five bills. "Five is better, yes? It is a little matter." She gave him the five hundred. "I will be waiting for you, and I will be ready to make everything right. You will see. I am very good."

"Ten-thirty and tell the Mexican kid we're even, once I get my wallet." Wilder smiled. "Guess I'll be at an unexpected all-night poker game," he held out a hand, "even got my winnings to show for it."

"Thank you for not disappointing me. Tell me, what do you like to drink? I think it must be whisky, no?"

"Yeah, and forget the damned ice."

Consuelo stood. "I am looking forward to the evening. We will enjoy ourselves."

Consuelo Moreno walked to the water and along the beach until Wilder was out of sight. She went to a novelty shop to fulfill a particular need, a liquor store, and home where she arrived by 5:00 to catch up on e-mails, speak with the editor of the newspaper where she worked and begin a rough draft of the next day's front page story. At seven o'clock she laid out the clothes she would wear for her evening, combed out her new wig and prepared a light meal. At 8:00 she showered, removed her jewellery, trimmed her nails, put in her contacts and went to the bedroom for her pearl-handled stiletto. She dressed, put the wig in her backpack, checked herself in the mirror and left her apartment.

Twenty-Seven

Sainte-Germaine-du-lac-Etchemin, Québec
Friday, August 10

Miranda and Dina were in their suite exhausted from being pampered all afternoon. They sat wrapped in thick towels, sweating together in a cloud of steam, they were massaged side by side, covered with smaller towels serving no purpose at all, and giggled while being plastered with hot mud, moaning and groaning as a gentle warm shower rained on them to wash the thick, herbal coating away. Wrapped in fleecy robes they were served green tea and left alone to drift into other worlds until roused for fifteen minutes in the flotation tank, the moment Dina would one day remember as having said: "what the hell."

The unit was obviously designed for two; their personal attendant made preparations for two, and wearing bikinis would have been ludicrous after what each of them had already seen of the other. The door was opened, the robes were tossed onto a chair and the two women stepped into the dark while being cautioned to talk in whispers.

"Thank you, Green Eyes. This weekend is the best ever."

"Yeah, it's pretty neat."

"I don't feel anything, or see anything. Wow."

"Do you think we're moving?"

"No, but don't you think we should hold hands in case

we float away from each other and get lost."

"Give me a break. Now you're afraid of the dark?"

"No, I want to hold your hand. It's not like anyone can see, including me."

Dina put out an arm, barely feeling the movement as they locked together.

"This is too weird. I'm floating in the dark, holding hands with a naked woman."

"I think you're beautiful. Whenever I find someone I want her to be like you."

Dina gulped and remained silent with no sense of time.

"Whenever I find someone I want him to be exactly like you, crazy, and he has to be gorgeous." She paused. "Do you think the others here think we're an item?"

"No. Maybe lovers, you know, dykes, certainly not an item. I don't think so."

Dina tried squeezing Miranda's hand in hers to scold her. The effort was too exhausting. "Let's be quiet, Chérie. Let's pretend we have everything we want. Let's pretend we're different women in a different place."

Not another word was whispered until the door opened and the outer lighting grew from dark to dim. Neither woman could walk faster than a snail's pace to the eucalyptus room where they were once again relieved of their robes and asked to lie on their fronts. By the time the attendant finished putting the warm stones along the women's spines from their necks to the small of their backs, they were asleep. Thirty minutes later they were roused once again by the attendant who held out their bikinis to them. Each woman looked at the other's small handful of strings, showing mutual appreciation and anyone who wouldn't like what they'd be seeing could look the other way.

The water in the outdoor pool was heated, yet when they held hands for balance and dipped in their toes, they decided mutually that basking in the late-day sun on chaises-lounges was the wiser choice. All eyes were on them as they laid out towels, lay on their fronts and undid their tops. The other dozen or so women were sitting in armoured one-piece suits with front panels or fleecy robes to conceal what a day at the spa could not. Chérie and Green Eyes wore barely-there thongs on toned bodies that had everything in the right place and proudly displayed. Even with their hair hanging in wet ponytails they were gorgeous, until evening encroached on their reverie and Chérie sat to tie Green Eye's top.

Dinner was being served at 8:00 and the spa did not want their guests missing the renowned chef's masterful work. While Miranda showered, Dina laid out her clothes. While Dina showered Miranda put on a new tap pants and bra and lay on the bed flipping through 120 different stations. Green Eyes came into the room dressed in a silk robe and asked Chérie whether she should wear black or red and rummaged through her suitcase for black. She tossed the bra onto the bed, then the matching panties and sat on the bed with her back to Miranda before dropping the robe from her shoulders and leaning forward to slip her feet into the satin thongs. She put on her bra, clasping the front and stood to pour herself a Jean-Marc neat before stretching out beside Chérie.

"Did you really buy me a gift?"

"Yes." Miranda rolled lazily onto her side. "Do you want it now?"

"I don't have anything for you, Chérie. I wasn't expecting this."

"You do have something for me and you've already given it to me. Thank you. Hold my drink." Miranda swung her legs around pushed herself from the bed. Dina couldn't help but stare, struggling with the mixed emotions of enjoying her day with Chérie yet being nervous about sharing even a large bed with a woman she was ogling. "Here. I hope you like it."

Dina sat on her knees and accepted the box. She held the gift to her ear, shook it and tore at the wrapping as she felt her body go cold. She shivered. "Chérie, what is this."

"Open it. Hurry up."

"No. I won't. I know this jeweller. He doesn't have anything under a few grand. What are you doing?" She paused, mesmerized by the box. "Listen... I can't give you what it is you're searching for. I can't fill that void. You should be giving whatever this is to a girlfriend, not me. Nothing is going to happen between us."

"Don't spoil my moment. I wanted to get you something to remember me by. It's been so long since I've had anyone special enough, like ten years." She snorted. "Don't worry. It's not an engagement ring and it's not a bribe. I'm not that hard up ... yet."

Dina's cheeks filled with air before she let it burst from between her lips. She closed her eyes and separated the distinctive bronze-coloured lid from its base. When she opened her eyes she blinked once, her eyes remained wide open with disbelief and her mouth sucked in air. "Chérie, no way, I can't. These must have cost you ..."

"Do you like them?" Miranda cut in. "They'll look great with your hair."

"Chérie, I can't. Listen, we haven't known each for twenty-four hours and on Sunday you and I are going to leave this place. We'll say goodbye at the airport and maybe we'll remember the weekend and maybe we won't. These cost more than our weekend combined. You need to return them."

"You're spoiling my moment, Green Eyes. Tell me you like them and put them on."

"They're gorgeous, like you, and they'd be perfect on you. You should be wearing them."

"Sure, if they belonged to me, but they don't. They belong to you, so you put them on. And I won't hold you to the big kiss you promised me." Dina expelled a long breath, closed her eyes and lowered her head. "Okay, so you didn't promise. We'll shake hands. Come on, put them on."

"Chérie we don't even know each other. These could pay for a vacation somewhere."

"I am on vacation, with you, and I'm not returning them. I'd be too embarrassed. I told the man they were for a friend. Now what's he going to think? Loser, loser and everyone in the store will think the same thing." Miranda persisted. "Hey, look at her. She's a loser."

"Okay, I suppose we can't let that happen. Can you help me?"

Miranda practically flew onto the bed and knelt behind her, reaching to take the ruby pendant from the box and drape the delicate silver chain around Dina's neck. When she finished Dina decorated her ears with the matching ruby studs and clambered from bed to the mirror. The rubies glittered and the chain sparked like nothing Dina had ever worn.

"Chérie, they're beautiful. I've never seen anything so beautiful."

Miranda was at the edge of the bed, still on her knees. "From my perspective the whole package is beautiful. Sorry, but you are, and that ass. Wow."

"Chérie, I don't know what to say. This is absolutely ridiculous, not to mention excessive."

"I don't think so. They're from me to you, to remember me."

"As though I'll ever forget you." Dina faced away from the mirror. "I've changed my mind about what I'm wearing to dinner. A shirt would spoil it. Don't you think?"

"No argument here."

"I suppose these are worth a kiss and a hug. I have to admit that much. Get up here."

Miranda raised herself from her knees, leaned forward, and the two women wrapped each other in their arms. Dina felt she was going to explode, confused and excited. She eased the younger woman away and felt Miranda's hands glide from her back to her hips. She looked at the pendant and into Miranda's blue eyes to see the mischievous glint Dina was beginning to realize was natural. She cupped the younger woman's head in her hands, pressed their lips together and closed her eyes to hide and lose track of time.

Caught completely off guard Miranda let the moment happen, thinking her heart would explode into a million heartbroken pieces. She pressed her hands ever so slightly into Dina's sides and gently pulled her closer. Moments later, when they parted, Dina breathed in deeply and threw back her head before releasing a controlled stream of warm air from between her lips. Miranda brought up her hands to rest them on Dina's shoulders.

"Wow, Green Eyes!"

Dina felt her face change colour and her stomach constrict. Her mouth was dry and her heart was racing. "Ooookay, that wasn't so hard, uh-huh, but…oh boy…oooh boy."

"Gee, what would I get for a bracelet?"

Suddenly she found looking at Miranda difficult. "A pair of handcuffs."

"Oooh, I like that." Their faces were inches apart. Miranda's breath was sweet; her body was warm to the touch, her natural scent intoxicating to Dina. "Hey, don't French girls always kiss twice? I think they do."

"Not like that." Dina's hands still framed Miranda's face. She didn't want to move for fear her legs would crumple.

Miranda eased a hand between their bodies, pressing against the centre of Dina's chest. "Gee, Green Eyes, was I that good? I think your heart's going to burst any second."

"Guilty on both counts." Dina tried to laugh. "How was I?"

"I could answer you a few ways. One would be very naughty of me, another would be to say you're a terrific kisser with great lips, or I can answer you this way."

Miranda's hands wrapped themselves around Dina's neck, pulling her closer. This time Dina let the inevitable happen. She let her hands drop to Miranda's waist, closed her eyes and forgot to be afraid.

Dina had intended to wear a deep blue silk blouse, unbuttoned to show her bra under a blue-on-black satin vest. Instead she opted for a centuries-old women's prerogative, left her shirt on the bed and wore the vest with straight-leg satin slacks and low-heeled shoes. Miranda wore stilettos, a mini wrap-around sarong and the lingering taste of raspberry on her lips.

Twenty-Eight

Miami, Florida
Friday, August 10

As she drove by at 9:40 PM she saw him on the doorstep, toying with a beer. She could have picked him out from a crowd without the photograph. He was 5'10" with slicked-back, black hair, black jeans, cowboy boots in August, a white tee-shirt, a dime-store Aztec god tattoo on his right arm and much of the Aztec god's gold around his neck, wrist and ears. Eduardo Mendez: Level One. Use Extreme Caution. Good. She liked challenges.

Consuelo Moreno spread a thin coat of suntan oil onto her arms and legs and rubbed what was left onto her face before spraying herself with a fine mist of water. She did a few jumping jacks while humming to a nearby Latin beat, adjusted the peak of her baseball cap, secured her stiletto into the left side of her micro-fibre gym shorts and jogged along Ocean Drive in the oppressive heat.

She stopped a block later to rest. She leaned forward, panting, her chest heaving erratically, bracing her arms against her slippery knees. Taking her time to straighten, she reached to the side of her backpack for the water bottle, swearing under her breath when she saw the container was empty. She saw him peripherally, studying her like a piece of meat. She was sweating profusely. She looked vulnerable and needed to sit down.

"Muchacho, ¿puedo sentarme aquí un momento?"

"Claro, ¿por qué no?" he answered, pointing to the steps.

"I pushed myself to the limit. I should have known better in this heat, but my trials are coming soon and I have no money to waste on expensive air-conditioned facilities. It is more important for me to eat, no?"

"Sí, but it is also important not to die on the street."

She climbed the few steps with effort, holding onto the handrail. "What I need is another job. My parents send me what they can, but times are difficult for them. I have applied this week to a few hotels. I have a good chance to be hired."

He noted the time. "To do what?"

"I asked for work in the restaurants or the pools. The truth is, I need the money and will do anything. Running on the street is not a good way to practice for the State Finals. Not to succeed will mean losing my partial scholarship." She took a few deep power breaths, replacing her water bottle.

Mendez held out his arm. "Take some of my beer."

"It will make me sick. Water is all I can drink without getting drunk." She glanced behind her and upward along the interior steps, assuming there were cameras, as she'd been trained, keeping the peak of her cap low over her forehead. "Do you live here, muchacho?"

"No. My friend lives here, up there. I live at the Vista." He pointed to the second-floor balcony to his right and towards the car parked at the curb. "That car is mine."

"You are fortunate to live in such a fine place. I have heard of it. You must be very successful." She looked around once more. "I was going to ask you to fill my bottle for me, if you lived here."

His eyes traced her body unabashedly. "I can do that. I have the key."

"Muchas gracias, muchacho." She handed him the bottle and stood in sync with Mendez.

"I will not be long."

Mendez skipped up the stairs. As soon as he disappeared to the left, she followed with measured steps, keeping her head down. She heard the door open without closing, and she listened intently for the slightest noise.

"Muchacho," she called out, walking through the open door, "muchacho."

"Come in. I am letting the water get cold."

"Ay, muchacho, what a nice place your friend has here. I sleep on the floor, on pillows, but not for long. One day I will have something like this, and train inside with the others." Consuelo scanned the room. There was a bed, a couch, small end tables, a walk-in kitchen, a television and stacks of VHS cassettes. "Can I use your friend's toilet, please?"

"Go ahead. It's behind the door."

Once inside she manoeuvred quickly to release the straps of her backpack. She released the slim blade of the stiletto from its handle and positioned it into of her shorts. She didn't need the knife, which was a quieter and more practical choice. Too bad, she thought. Anywhere else she would have enjoyed breaking every bone in his body before snapping his neck. She flushed the toilet, waited a moment longer and went out holding the knapsack by the dangling straps.

"That is better. Thank you."

"It is not right to sleep on the floor. I believe that you were meant to stop in front of me tonight, muchacha. I can help you, at least for this week. My friend has gone, I am looking after the place for him and I have the key. I can give it to you. You will be safe. There is a lock and I think I can help you find a good job. I work in a bar and my clients are always asking me if I know someone who is single, someone they can take to supper, just supper. It's like having a free meal each night and they pay. It's like tipping. Another girl, one who stopped a few months ago, when she graduated, she paid her last year with the money she earned and she worked only a couple of hours a day."

"Is it true?"

"Yes, it is true. You can have a place like this, or a better one, like mine, and nice clothes. I'm telling you. And you can train with the rich, white girls."

"I would like that very much, but my clothes are not very nice. They would not like me."

Mendez hesitated, seeming perplexed. "Okay, one thing I can do, because I have sisters like you. I can buy you one dress and one pair of shoes. You can repay me when you start to work. You will see. It will be better than cleaning toilets. These gringos, they talk big, they promise many things, but still we clean their toilets. You are better than that."

"I can stay here tonight?"

"Yes, tonight." He grinned, shrugging his shoulders. "How come you do not have a boyfriend? You are so good looking."

"I know no one and I am very busy studying and practicing. One day I will, when I am finished."

"If you were my girlfriend I would give you everything, you would never have to work and you would see the ocean every day. Who could not love someone such as you?"

Consuelo lowered her head. "One day it will happen. What is your name?"

"Eddie. What is yours?"

"Pearl," she replied.

"Pearl, drink your water. There is someone I am expecting downstairs. After they leave I will drive you to your place for your things and tomorrow we will go shopping."

She dropped her bag to the floor. "You are so kind to me, someone you do not even know."

"Would you not help someone who needs help?"

He came towards her, proffering the bottle. Consuelo ran her left hand down the front of her shorts where the thin material accentuated her most delicate contours. "Eddie, if you want I can," she hesitated, "I mean... I don't mind."

"Later, chica. I feel like you have been sent to me."

"I have been sent to you, Mendez. Adios." The slim blade tore through the soft flesh at the base of his sternum with a violent thrust. She twisted once and before he died she withdrew the blade and jabbed upward under his jaw to pierce his brain. She let the body collapse to the floor before extracting the blade.

She stripped the body of its jewellery, its watch, 10:10 was the hour, its wallet, the car keys and placed everything into a side pocket of her backpack which she placed by the bathroom door. She pushed her wig into the other side pocket, replaced her water bottle, dragged the 185 pounds of dead weight to the only closet and by 10:20 she was standing in the middle of the room in a full-length spandex jumpsuit that revealed every possible detail of her body. Wilder arrived like clockwork at 10:30.

"Come in, Señor Wilder. I have made a drink for you, whisky. It is what you said, no."

Wilder looked around. "Yeah, that's what I said." Consuelo went to him with the glass. "It's Pearl, right?"

"Yes, I am Pearl.

"You got anything on under that thing?"

"No, I do not. There is not enough space. And now I will make the shower for you while you enjoy your drink. When I come out you will be ready for me, no? And I will have one drink also while I undress for you."

"Where's the bottle?"

"It is by the bed, where I thought would be the best place, no?"

"Good thinking. Now get that shower ready and keep that thing on till I can watch you peel out of it."

Ten minutes later the waterline of the whisky bottle was down by an inch and Eric Wilder was slouched against the wall with his legs sprawled over the bed. He was naked from the waist up, his feet were bare and his zipper was open, for which she was thankful. She called out his name, hoping he hadn't taken more than a few sips of the medicated whisky. He was groggy, but his words weren't slurred, the way she intended him to be. She ordered him to lay flat, to push down his pants and remain still with his hands by his side, which he managed to accomplish with a series of clumsy and breathless contortions.

"Mr. Wilder, I'm ready. I want you to look at me."

Wilder strained to raise his head as Consuelo focused on the center of his chest. Taking a firm grip on the limp wrist closest to her, she raised the stiletto in an arc and swung the blade in a silver streak with enough force to bury the blade to its hilt. Wilder's head snapped into the pillow and his body twitched, held in place by its own weight.

"Mr. Wilder she was eighteen and you are on your way to hell for what you did." Consuelo pried the blade free while his eyes still bulged. She raised her closed fist slowly into the air for him to see and plunged the stained length into his right lung. "You're now in hell, Mr. Wilder, and you won't be alone. Vaya con el Diablo."

Consuelo Moreno yanked the dagger from its chest. She wiped the blade against the sheets, hauled the body onto its side to search for its money clip and removed its watch and its ring, which she carefully placed in her knapsack with what she'd removed from Mendez. She went for the glass and the bottle, cleaned both surfaces with the whisky and his shirt and tossed them by the body after pouring what was left over the stiletto. She retrieved her first outfit and put it into a plastic bag. She stripped off her jumpsuit that had minimal splatter and put it into another with her running shoes and socks. She used a third bag for the sundry articles excluding Wilder's eight hundred dollars,

Mendez' twelve hundred and his car keys. She wasn't wearing jewellery or underwear. She reached into the backpack for a fresh tube dress, panties and shoes, slipped into them and put on a more elegant cap. She checked to see all compartments of her backpack were empty and shoved the three plastic bags into the centre compartment along with her gloves. She counted out the five hundred she'd given Wilder and tucked the bills into the front of her panties with the stiletto. She scanned the apartment once and walked out leaving the door wide open.

At 10:55 when Consuelo tossed Mendez' car keys onto a front seat of his Z4, dropping fifties and hundreds as she strolled several blocks to where she'd parked her car. By the time she knelt to retrieve the key she'd wedged behind her front wheel, all that remained was the empty backpack which she discarded before arriving at her North Miami beachfront home.

She sanitized the stiletto while she showered. She changed into jeans and a sweater, left a cryptic message for a person she knew would not answer her call and prepared a rum and soda while she waited for her cell to chime. The call came at midnight as she finished putting the final touches to a column she knew would hit the newsstands early Saturday morning.

She listened to her managing editor tell her of a double homicide, asking if she was anywhere near the bottom of Ocean Drive. She lied eagerly, telling him she was a few blocks away and would be at the address within moments. All that remained for Consuelo Moreno was to finish her drink, gather up her article, her briefcase, her camera and a white plastic bag filled with new clothes for someone to find.

Twenty-Nine

Sainte-Germaine-du-lac-Etchemin, Québec
Saturday, August 11

Dina and Miranda sat up most of the night in teddies and camisoles, nursing a few nightcaps and listening to each other talk to exhaustion. They spoke about the day, the day to come, their likes and dislikes, fashion and travel, Dina regretting her earlier slip regarding Saint-Tropez and Miranda knowing better than to pursue Dina's dream. By the time they kissed each other's cheek goodnight and turned off the lights Dina knew everything about Miranda's early life with Morgan, the tragic ending of her love story, and Miranda knew all Dina could think to tell her about her sister Nancy and how she died.

Saturday morning Dina was enshrouded to her shoulders under a thick duvet with both hands buried under her pillow. Her eyes remained closed, her mind working to clear the heaviness of a deep sleep and she began to sense a warm weight resting on her hip. Then she remembered and her breathing changed

"Good morning, Green Eyes. Rise and shine. I know you're in there."

Dina opened her eye that wasn't nestled into the pillow. "We're not naked are we?"

"No. You wanted me naked, but I made you go to sleep."

"No way. That's not true," she moaned.

"Okay, I wanted to be naked and you made me go to sleep."

"How long have you been staring at me?"

"I think about an hour, maybe two. I think more like two. I was planning our day."

"Our day is already planned and, hey, weren't you over there when we crashed?"

"You were mumbling when I woke up. I wanted to be sure you were okay. I was worried about you."

"Thanks, and I don't mumble."

"Yes, you do. I love your voice, Green Eyes. It's so soothing. I could listen to you all day."

"Oh, please, give me a break." Miranda stayed quiet. "Okay, so tell me, what was I saying?"

"You were mumbling. How would I know? Hey, I can make something up."

"Thanks, this is weird enough."

"I know, sleeping with a hetero. What's next?"

Dina brought a hand from under the pillow and stroked Miranda's cheek.

"I hope something and someone very good happens for you very soon. I'll buy you a set of handcuffs for your ceremony."

"But you won't be there, will you? And where are those cuffs of yours anyway?"

"If you get any closer you're going to find out for assaulting an officer."

Dina realized too late she'd said the wrong thing. The glint in Miranda's eyes came to life in an instant. She clambered onto Dina's waist, straddling her, pinning her arms to her body and tousling her hair. She bounced up and down, reaching for her pillow which she raised high over her head without thinking of the strategic consequences, her enthusiasm and confidence tainting her judgement as Dina struggled to free her hands. She reached up, grabbed

Miranda under the arms, rocked sideways twice and rolled her over: the blonde lawyer on the bottom, the redheaded cop on top, straining against down-filled blows to reach for her pillow.

Miranda maintained advantage. She bounced and squirmed as she struck out with her pillow, wrapping her legs around Dina's waist, squeezing hard. Dina was losing, defeat was imminent. She had one free arm. The other was holding her away from Miranda. The impossible was happening. She had one angle of attack while Miranda had three and was freely assailing both sides of Dina's head and face as she giggled, bounced up and down and called her a loser.

Dina was beginning to tire, she struggled to extricate herself from Miranda's leggy grasp and the more she strained the blonde adversary squeezed all the harder. Weary of the battle, she slackened, showing her vulnerability and weakness, allowing Miranda to take full advantage. She swept back her pillow for the momentum that would bring her certain victory, feeling a surge of confidence at the very moment Dina fell upon her, closing the gap, muffling her frantic giggles. Victory went to Dina "Green Eyes" Becker.

Dina tossed away the pillow, reached out for Miranda's wrists, studied the squirming loser and began to laugh.

"What?" Miranda asked.

"The thought just occurred to me. I've never wondered how I look to a perp when they're being arrested."

Miranda thought for a moment, her chest heaving. "I would have to say pretty damn sexy, Officer Green Eyes. And, by the way, your arrest procedure is doing nothing at all to make me go straight, so to speak."

Dina was panting. "If all my arrests were like this," she exhaled a deep breath, "I think I would have to work twenty-four-seven."

"Do you ever grab them by the collar, Green Eyes? Do

you ever pull them in close to you and, you know, kiss them?"

"No. We throw them down, kick them in the balls and tell them it never happened."

"Then you frisk them, right, from their tops to their bottoms?"

"No, then we cuff them, drag them to their feet, kick them in the balls and throw them into the squad car."

"Hmmm." Miranda thought for a moment. "Okay, what about fingerprinting, officer? You must check all their pockets first, frisk them, pat them down or rip away their shirts to make sure they're not concealing anything dangerous."

"No. They empty their own pockets, they kick themselves in the balls for being so stupid and we throw them into a cell until the interrogation begins."

"And then, if they tell you lies, you must grab them, throw them around, loosen your tie and put your head right up against theirs, you know, to show them who the boss is?"

Dina pondered the question. "You know, Chérie, frisking someone, patting them down or ripping away their shirts can be scary."

"Why?"

"Because you never know what you'll find. It could be something totally unexpected, really good evidence, and then, bam, some trial lawyer comes along and the prisoner walks."

"But you have the right to hold them for twenty-four hours before counsel arrives. A lot can happen in twenty-four hours and, who knows, maybe she'll screw up during a vacation or a weekend and do something else to be arrested. Even better, some criminals are habitual."

Dina's heart was wildly pumping anew. She released her loose grip on Miranda's wrists and sank beside her.

"You're under house arrest for twenty-four hours and, if

you act half as badly as you did yesterday, or just now, we are going to bump heads. I'll frisk you, pat you down, and cuff you before I put you under a cold shower. Got it?"

Miranda frowned. "Yeah, I got it." They lay still, letting their breathing subside. "You know what, to hell with it, we both know the system's crooked. Screw the system." She threw herself on top of Dina, grabbing her head gently and pressing their mouths together between a tousled cloud of luxurious chestnut red and blonde.

They went to breakfast in silk robes and slippers, to the chagrin or envy of those in cotton sweat suits or fleecy dressing gowns. They sat in the eucalyptus room until 10:00, they suffered through a Swedish massage until 10:30, and lay side by side in aroma therapy until 11:00, talking endlessly through a pedicure and manicure until noon. Their lunch of grilled Mahi Mahi and black pepper over a green salad was accompanied with a Fumé Blanc imported from France and for dessert they savoured the bitter sweetness of sorbet sprinkled with field berries. They waded in the pool until 2:00, showered, were taken for their facials until 3:00, their make-up consultation lasted through till 4:00 and the hair salon had them reserved until 5:00. Dinner was at 8:00 and they needed each of the three remaining hours to regain their energy.

The outside temperature was in the high-seventies, the sky was bright and clear, and the wind had gone elsewhere. They'd seen only two other guests at the patio pool and Miranda wanted to spend some time lounging in the late day sun with a cocktail. Dina agreed. Green tea was out. She poured two-fingered vodkas to take with them, one with a single cube, the other with a trace of crushed ice and tossed her fleecy robe onto the bed to rummage through her luggage for the embroidered thong and bra set she had intended to wear under her red dress at dinner.

Miranda reclined, absorbing what she was seeing. "Green Eyes, are you forgetting I'm a frigging lesbian? You do realize I'm horny as hell for you, that you're more adorable and more delectable each minute, and that I'm trying my best right now not to jump you. Shit. Are you trying to tease me or just really piss me off?"

Dina ignored her. She sat on the bed, slipped one foot into the strings of her T-back thong, then the other, standing to pull them to her hips before reaching for the matching three-quarter bra. She slipped in one arm, the other, reached behind to clasp the hooks and cupped her breasts to adjust the fit while standing in front of the mirror. When she was satisfied she turned her back to the mirror, ran her hand over the bare curves of her cheeks and whistled.

"How do I look, Chérie?"

"Like a beautiful bitch. You can't wear that to the pool. It's underwear."

"We're in Quebec. Believe me. No one's going to mind."

"Okay, that's it. I'm killing a cop tonight. We're going to dinner, and then I'm going to kill you before you kill me."

"Get dressed for the pool, Chérie."

"No. I've worn it once already and I'm not wearing a frigging two-piece when you're prancing around practically naked in an eye patch. No way."

"I'm leaving." Dina smirked. "Did I ever tell you what Chérie means?"

"Okay, what's going on here?"

"Just put on a thong and let's go. I told you if you were bad I would frisk you and pat you down." She shrugged. "But, if you don't want me to ..."

Miranda dropped her robe, ran to her suitcase and knew exactly what she wanted to wear. She slipped the two tabbed ends of her panties between her legs, snapped them together, and reached down for the other side tabs. Snapping them together she pulled at the bottom of the small V, pulled at the side bands and reached for her strapless bra that she stepped into and yanked up to cover her breasts.

"So, cop?"

"You already know. You take the lotion, I've got the drinks."

"I've never gone public in my underwear. They're going to stare at us."

"We're even. I've never gone public with a lesbian and they'd stare anyway. Let's go blow some minds and be the best things on the patio, which won't be very hard."

Miranda followed, feeling as confused as Dina had felt until the pillow fight. When Dina dropped her robe at the corner of the patio where the sun would warm them the longest, and lay face-down on the towel she spread over the chaise-longue, Miranda thought she would lose her mind. Dina ignored her, sipping her drink as Mirada dragged over another lounge chair, spread a towel over it, dropped her robe and sat looking at her increasingly frustrating roommate.

"I could sink my teeth into that tight ass of yours right now, Green Eyes? What's going on here? This is too freaky."

Dina squirmed. "Chérie, would you lotion me, please. Not too much."

Miranda scanned the pool. The other couple who seemed somewhere between forty and sixty were looking their way, disgusted by what Miranda and Dina were wearing, chattering about the indecency. Miranda understood not one of the silent words, flinging her head into the air to dismiss them all the same. They understood the snub and searched for another focal point as Miranda unhooked Dina's bra. With long strokes spread lotion over her back and, when she went to re-hook the snaps, Dina asked her not to. She raised one calf, then the other, kicking at the air and moaning until she felt the first thin bead of lotion from her ankles to the tops of her thighs and the warm sensation of Miranda's hands gliding over them.

"Done, now me," Miranda said.

"You haven't done all of me. Some lesbian you are."

Miranda was about to faint. "Green Eyes, you're not playing with me, are you? That wouldn't be fair. Really, I'd rather go home."

"No, I'm not teasing, but could you finish what you're doing so I can switch sides to get my front done. Please."

"You're freaking me out."

Miranda squirted lotion onto her palms. She rubbed them together and pressed each one against Dina's warm flesh, massaging in the lotion with a gentle pressure. When she was done, she dug in her nails and left a trail of thin pink lines across Dina's buttocks as she pulled away.

"That was a nice touch. I think I liked it, Chérie. Let me flip over and then I'll do you." Dina clasped her bra to her breasts and flipped over to lay with her hands by her side and her legs slightly parted.

"I'm dying here. You're killing me. Is this a game, Green Eyes?"

"No, Chérie, not a game. I've never done anything like this. So it's a little overwhelming. I've never stared at a woman in her lingerie before and liked what I saw. I've never kissed anyone the way I kissed you last night or this morning, and my gift blew away a good part of my mind. You have to admit this is pretty weird, and I have to admit it's pretty good."

"This is too much for my head. I'm sitting here trying not to get horny and all I'm doing is prepping you for someone else. I should never have gone back to the bar Thursday night."

"Shut up and lotion me, or I'll get those cuffs. Remember, you're under house arrest."

Miranda did one leg, then the other, and moved her hand slowly past the tiny triangle to Dina's belly, spreading lotion in widening circles before bypassing her partially

293

bared breasts to rub what was left on her hands into Dina's shoulders. She put down the tube, hesitated, and finally put her fingertips to the lower ridge of Dina's bra. She pressed forward and let her hands linger, pressing into the soft flesh beneath before pulling them back and reaching for her drink.

Dina eased onto her side, glistening under the sun and sipped her drink. Miranda was lying on her front, facing away with her head resting on folded arms. Seeing her that way made Dina feel horrible for how she'd acted. She stood, straddling Miranda's chaise-longue, and drew a line of lotion from her left ankle to her shoulders to her right ankle. First she massaged the cream into Miranda's shoulders, kneading them, then her back, her buttocks, that she whispered were the best ever and her legs. She asked Miranda in the most exotic voice she could muster to flip over, she did, and Dina streaked her with lotion from her right foot to her bra to her left foot. She manipulated her fingers with expert smoothness, making her new friend groan, moan and cry out as she dug her fingertips into Miranda's firm flesh and under her top, letting the sensation of another woman's breasts absorb into her mind.

"I'm glad you came back to the bar Thursday night." She paused. "This weekend will be as difficult for each of us as it will be fantastic. Let's not do or say anything to spoil the time we have left."

"I won't let you say no to me tonight, Green Eyes. There's no way you're going to say no to me." Miranda sat, crossing her legs. "Sit down. We're freaking out the old ones."

Dina reached for her drink, placed the glass between them, and put her hands on Miranda's knees. "Remember, in the bar, when I said something about most women thinking about doing it or having experimented with it?"

"That it was like touching tomatoes."

"Yeah, well, I either forgot or I was wrong. Those aren't

294

tomatoes, and that kiss this morning. I thought I was going
to lose what's left of my mind. And while I was oiling you a
few moments ago my gut was twisted into knots. I swear if
I had leaned over another inch my heart would have jumped
out. I would never have done such a thing if I knew for sure
I didn't want to. I wasn't expecting any of this, Chérie.
Until I met you I was okay with being home alone."

"I wasn't expecting any of this either."

"Actually, I'm glad. There's definitely something going
on inside me. I just don't know what exactly."

"I hope it's me."

"So do I," Dina agreed, "because if it is me I won't
know how to handle myself."

"It's not worth ruining our weekend, Green Eyes. It'll be
easier for me to pretend I'm straight than you worrying that
you're not. I've been in a dream state for the last thirty
hours and I want thirty more. Isn't that what this is all about,
to forget our miserable lives, if only for a little while?"
Miranda sipped her drink. "At the airport I was teasing you
when we climbed onto the bus. I didn't mean for any of this
to happen." She looked at the tiny triangle between Dina's
open thighs. "But a girl can dream."

"You're incorrigible."

"Can you keep a secret, Green Eyes? If I tell you a
something very personal, can you deal with it?"

"I'm a cop," Dina squeezed Miranda's knees; neither
woman could ignore the ring, "amongst other things. Yes, I
can keep a secret."

"Green Eyes, my name is Miranda."

"Chérie that was stupid. Say one more word and you've
got new jewellery and a hotel suite to yourself."

"Say it, Green Eyes, say my name."

"Miranda, Miranda the trial lawyer from Toronto,
Miranda, the Crown prosecutor from Toronto. That is what
you are, or am I wrong, another dumb cop? There's no way
you could work to save the assholes we drive eight-inch

295

stilettos into. You're a provincial prosecutor."

"Very good, Detective Green Eyes of the Quebec City PD with beautiful red hair. Like I ever thought you were a street cop. Oh, like that'll be a tough one to figure out for a Crown attorney."

"You're changing me from a very screwed-up bi-curious to a very nervous and ranking Pearl operative."

"I would never do anything to endanger you, Green Eyes, never, and you should already know me well enough to feel secure with me. You think your gut's in knots? My mouth's so dry I can't swallow. This morning I wanted all of you, every inch, I still do, unless that means not being with you tomorrow. And, by the way, just to let you know, I've got four stilettos... four, including the coveted blacklip. So let's not talk about rank. You're looking at the best. How many do you have Detective Green Eyes?"

"Four, if it's any of your business. There is no fifth and I believe you must mean you're the best in your sector. Here you're second best."

Miranda sat silently staring, feeling a surge of inherent courtroom aggressiveness. "Try me."

Dina moved her hands away from Miranda's knees and took up her glass, afraid to bring a smile to her lips. "I'm sorry, Chérie, I didn't mean to sound or be so cruel."

"Apology accepted." She brought her hands to Dina's cheeks. "I was being a pouty bitch. I'm the one who should be sorry. Green Eyes, I'm very proud of what I do for Pearl and of my almost perfect conviction rate in court. One day I'll sit on the bench. Then I can make a significant difference."

"You already are. We both are."

"I would never do anything to hurt you or betray you. What happened here will remain here, like I said. You know, like in Vegas. And you know another thing? This wasn't a good idea. You were right." Miranda brought up her legs, swung them over the side and raised her wrist to see the time. . "There's a shuttle back to the city at 6:00. I want you to stay here and give me until then to check out. I couldn't deal with you watching me pack."

Miranda put an arm around Dina's neck and hugged her without words. She stood, reached for her robe and walked away, strutting slightly past the older women at the far side before dropping her robe and bending from her waist to retrieve it. She waited until she was at the doors to slide her arms into the silk sleeves. Dina watched the immodest show with a satisfied smirk, stretching out on her front to absorb the comforting warmth of the late-day sun when Miranda disappeared behind the doors.

Her mind was a whirlwind of confusion. Miranda was seven years younger. Being together was stupid. Miranda hadn't been the one to tease her, she had led on Miranda. She was virtually naked under the sun, wearing something she could conceal in one closed fist, and she had done that for Miranda. She would never have worn her underwear to the pool on her own and that morning, when Miranda climbed on top of her, she'd summoned all her will power not to grope and explore, to discover who she was or who she wasn't. She'd been alone for so many years since her sister's murder, turning down dates from men for no other reason than her own fear of what might be. Even before her sister's death she hadn't dated very often, preferring to be alone to study throughout her university years and at the academy. Then, when she heard the worst news she could ever have imagined, she metamorphosed into a single-minded socio-phobe. And why did she offer to buy a beautiful blonde stranger a drink in the bar when she'd never done such a thing before? And why had she gone to Le Discrèt the second time. Why had she lied to Miranda and why had she missed Miranda the Prosecutor when she walked out of the bar? Because she was lonely and she knew Miranda was not making her uneasy, rather she had come to face the reality of what she might have mistakenly excluded from her life over the previous ten years.

Dina saw the women at the far side talking, trying to appear as though they weren't staring. They were, and Miranda had been gone five minutes. She appraised the women, wondering whether they'd come to the spa to be together or escape what they'd left behind. She decided they'd come to get away. And why did she come? Miranda had suggested shopping, separate hotel rooms and a girls' day. She was the one to suggest the spa.

She had lied to Miranda, and not for the first time. Her stomach wasn't twisted into knots. The invasive and urgent feeling came from deeper within her, compelling, impossible to dispel as she coated Miranda's naked body with oil as slowly as she could manage. Dina pushed herself from the chaise-longue. She grabbed her robe and waked with urgent strides to where the women were sitting. She glared at them as she passed by, telling them in French to try it, they'd like it. Then she flung her robe over her shoulders.

She didn't knock. She opened the door, dropped her robe as she walked past Miranda without saying a word and went to her purse. She told Miranda to face the wall and assume the position, insisting she wouldn't repeat herself. Miranda obeyed, shocked by the commanding tone of Dina's voice which wasn't at all sensuous. Dina came to her from behind, lifting the hem of Miranda's dress, sliding the soft folds to her shoulders and over her head in one fluid motion. She nudged Miranda's feet apart with her own, stood in close, encircled Miranda with her arms and ripped apart the front clasps of her bra. She ran her open hands from Miranda's collar bone to her breasts to her belly to the front of her legs. She kissed her ass, stood, and tore apart first one side of her panties, then the other. She put her hands to Miranda's shoulders and pressed hard into the concave of her back. She squeezed her ass and trailed her hands along the outside of each leg and up the inside to the tops of her thighs, freeing one hand she let glide deliberately over Miranda's hips and belly to where her fingers came to delicate folds that were moist to the touch. She swirled Miranda around, ripped away her own thong and bra, grabbed Miranda's wrist that was opposite her own and slapped on the open cuff dangling from her wrist.

"You're not going anywhere and you can screw your rights. You'll get counsel when I say you do, not before. You're under arrest for messing with my brain." She tugged a stunned Miranda to the bed, threw back the covers and Miranda over her hip and into the centre of the bed with such speed and ease the young prisoner yelped with glee and utter surprise.

"Green Eyes!"

"Did I ask you to speak? No, I didn't. So shut your mouth until I tell you to speak, or is there something about what I'm saying that your beautiful blonde hair doesn't understand. Listen, we're not leaving here until we get a few things figured out. First of all, I need to figure out how this happened in the first place and how I feel about you. We have twenty-four hours left and I have to know. You should never have happened. So why did you? That's number one. You did happen. So what do I do about it? That's number two. Do you think I can let you go and forget you ever happened? No. That's number three. I shouldn't be excited being with you or seeing you naked, but I am. That's number four. And there's no way I should be sitting on top of you naked. So why am I? That's number five, and until we get all this figured out you're not even going for a pee."

"Not even under guard, Green Eyes? Oooh."

"I told you to shut up, and it's not Green Eyes. My name is Dina and I want to hear you say it."

"Dina. Dina and Miranda. I like it, Green Eyes. I like the sound. I've never been handcuffed." Miranda raised her head, straining to see. "You have to be the sexiest cop ever. You're a vision. I always thought lady cops had steel wool down there, or some sort of rubber male thing. Did you do that for me?"

"Shut up."

"I want to make a statement, Officer Dina. I decline representation. I want to defend myself."

"You've got one minute."

"Okay, let's back up. I do hope it's me making you crazy, because you're making me crazy and if it wasn't me you wouldn't have crashed in here like some sort of task force to arrest me. We might never know what we're doing here because we can never see each other again. I know you feel something for me and I know you didn't want me to leave the bar Thursday night. I could see in your eyes you wanted me to stay. Number one: I didn't happen. We happened. We happened because we're both tired of being alone. Number two: I have no idea what to do about any of this right now. Number three: We will leave each other because if we don't we'll lose focus and one of us might die or compromise what we believe in. But you're not letting me go until tomorrow, and I never want you to forget me, or us. Number four: What's wrong with seeing me naked or being turned on by me? Not a thing. It's not like I'm a frigging dog. Can you have any idea how long I've waited for someone to tell me I'm beautiful without wanting to get into my pants? And, number five, if you don't like riding me bare back, I do. So deal with it, detective, and let's start talking about a plea bargain because you're not the lightest cop in the world and I really do have to pee."

"Serious?"

"You can wait and see."

Dina rolled from Miranda, onto her side. "Promise not to escape."

"I promise. Where's the key?"

"I don't know."

300

Both women bounced from the bed to search Dina's luggage until Dina grabbed one side of the suitcase, Miranda the other, and together they emptied the contents onto the bed to search for the little key piece by piece. When Miranda was at last able to run free, Dina could only stand where she was and watch, hardly believing or caring what she was about to do.

When Miranda came back she was glowing. "We don't need those anymore, Dina. I'll be good, though having them on was sort of neat."

"Not so neat with a knee digging into your back and your face pushed into the pavement. And, Chérie, I think I'm too nervous to eat."

"I know. On second thought, look at us. We look fantastic and we've blown a few major bucks to be here. Besides, I want to show you off, not that we didn't at the pool. Ooooh, that was sexy. I think the old biddies hate us."

"I think they hate what they're not." Dina rolled onto her side. "You know, it's a long time until after dinner, Miranda. I don't want to change my mind. And I did do this for you, not that I don't other times."

"It would be a shame to waste such a well-executed police raid and we do have almost two hours, officer."

Eight o'clock came and dressing for dinner was anything but anticlimactic. Miranda wore satin stilettos with a naughty camisole dress which made anything but standing dangerous. Breathing would be risqué at best, climbing stairs an eye-catching event. Dina wore a simple red slip dress designed to show her legs to the lettuce tops of her nylons when she sat, low-heeled sandals and her new jewellery.

Each of the eight courses seemed be served with progressive slowness. They used each other's pet name, they sat beside one another, not across and when Miranda held her hand Dina turned a shade deeper than her rubies, yet she didn't pull away. They laughed and they giggled, lost in the moment, and as the last course was being served they feigned polite fullness. They requested room service for breakfast and left the table.

When the discreet knock sounded at the door the following morning Miranda leapt from the bed. She hadn't slept a wink and wanted Dina to sleep longer. When Dina fell into a deep slumber as the sun began to rise, Miranda was fully awake caressing Dina's body, stroking her hair, explaining to Morgan in tearful whispers. When the waitress left she straddled Dina's midriff with her robe loosely belted, leaned forward to gently kiss her lips and pinched her nose. "Wake up, Green Eyes. Wake up." She bounced up and down.

Dina kept her eyes closed and grimaced. "Tell me I'm not naked."

"Okay, you're not naked, but wow!"

"Are you?"

"This time, yeah, pretty much, except I had to put on my robe to answer the door. If you want, I can take it off."

"So that's your bare ass on my bare stomach?"

"Sort of."

Dina waited a moment. "Damnit, I knew I forgot something."

"What?"

"I left my backup weapon at home. Now I have to kill you with my bare hands."

"Yeah, right. Good luck with that dream. And by the way, I love you, Green Eyes."

Dina's eyes opened wide. "Didn't you say that enough last night and this morning?"

"No. So, what's the verdict? How do you like being a lesbo? Pretty cool, huh? Can I sign you up for a membership? It comes with free magazines and special Valentine's Day offers."

"I'm not a lesbian. I was experimenting." Dina brought her hands to Miranda's silk-lined hips. "I'm tingling everywhere and my frigging jaw feels like I've been sucker-punched."

Miranda giggled. "That's why I tingle everywhere. Yummy, yummy. You're way too good to waste on a penis."

"Let me up." Miranda stood on the bed, pulling Dina into a sitting position. "Shit. I look like I've been mauled by a monster lipstick."

Miranda opened her robe. "You paint a pretty mean abstract yourself, Green Eyes."

"I did that?" Miranda nodded and Dina grimaced. "You're right. I am a frigging lesbian." Dina buried her face in her hands. "Did I say anything stupid apart from telling you my name?"

"No, but you did say you love me. And don't talk to me about the heat of the moment. I want to believe you do for as long as I can."

"I guess it would have been ridiculous to say I hate you."

"Breakfast is here. Get a robe on. I've got plans."

Dina eased her body gingerly from the bed. "Miranda?"

"Yes."

"I meant it."

"What?"

"You are easy to love. I wouldn't have gone as far if I didn't feel something. Guess it's my Catholic upbringing, something for the priest to write in his Dirty Book during confession."

"I know you do, Dina. So here's what we're going to do. Breakfast first, then I'll scrub my lipstick off you and you'll do me so we don't freak anyone out, we'll soak in a steam, we'll have a massage, get out of here by 12:00 to go shopping in the old town and have a very late lunch. I'm going to buy a camera and ask someone to take our picture together. We'll take my car from the airport and if you want to run a trace on the plate, go ahead."

"Chérie…"

"I want someone to take our picture, dozens of them. So just shut up and after lunch I'm leaving the restaurant before you, Green Eyes. I won't live through a long goodbye."

"Okay, a couple of pictures. I kind of wish I had a camera now. You're a pain in the ass. Do you know that? And aren't you leaving something out between breakfast and scrubbing me clean?"

"Like what?"

"Like me. I know I won't sleep for the next year because of this, but don't you think it seems kind of silly to scrub me twice?"

"Ooooh, you're so right. To hell with breakfast," and Miranda collapsed on top of her.

That thought was apparently intended to include the steam and the massage as well. By noon, when their luggage was packed and left at the door, both women might have been walking out from a glamour photo shoot.

At the airport they hugged, Miranda went one way and Dina went the other, until moments later when Miranda drove up to the bus stop with the convertible top down, excited. Dina was making the bright sunlight seem dull. Though, despite her radiant glow she appeared completely distraught.

"What's wrong, Green Eyes?"

"Chérie, Miranda, I'm so sorry."

"What Dina, what's wrong? What happened?"

"I have to leave you, right here, right now. I'm sorry. It's police business. I have no choice."

"Dina, I'll stay downtown. I can wait for you. I can stay over one more night. Please, Dina."

Dina grabbed Miranda harder than she could ever have imagined and held her close. "Chérie, I'm sorry. I am so sorry." She pressed a heated kiss onto Miranda's lips with ardent passion, looked deep into her eyes and kissed her again. "You know how I feel, Miranda. I know you do. Don't forget me and try not to hate me."

She walked away.

"Just like that? Not a chance." Miranda shouted, "You get back here. You can't leave me standing here like this. We haven't had enough time together."

When Dina disappeared Miranda screamed as loud as she could over the car tops, "go to hell! I hate you!" And no sooner did she speak those words than her shoulders drooped and she whispered, "I love you."

Thirty

Montreal, Quebec
Sunday, August 12

The downtown heat was sweltering and suffocating. Crumbling and littered streets were dotted with orange cones, congested with confused traffic and broken sidewalks were alive with bewildered tourists and frustrated residents who should have known better than to be downtown in the first place. The Ritz was the most majestic hotel in the increasingly dilapidated city, a jewel whose setting had tarnished badly beyond repair, and Dina had told Beverly Price she would arrive by 5:00 PM, latest.

She had hurried to her home to change from the open-knit sweater and tights into an elegant beige coat dress, red sunglasses and a wide-brimmed beige hat accented with a deep red kerchief. She hated herself more than Miranda ever could. She despised herself for what she did and throughout the two-hundred mile drive she didn't stop thinking about how coldly she acted.

Cops didn't give ranking cops tickets for speeding or any other infraction, and knowing the streets of the city's core she arrived ahead of schedule. Stepping from the XKR she was the personification of femininity, nothing less was acceptable or proper for a meeting with her director. The maître d' escorted her to Mother's garden table and pulled out her chair.

"Good afternoon, Dina."

"Good afternoon, Pearl."

"Dina, I am very pleased to be with you today. I would have preferred Friday or Saturday, at worst this morning, so we might have had more time together. In any event, here we are with certain important issues to discuss. Unfortunately, I find myself constrained by the clock and this meeting will be brief."

"I called as soon as I heard your message."

"I understand. You need not explain, dear. We all have separate lives. I meant no criticism. I must say, you are looking extremely lovely." Beverly admired Dina's pendant. "May I be so bold as to enquire whether your jewellery was a special gift?"

"Thank you for noticing, Pearl. Yes, it is from someone special, a special friend."

Beverly smiled. "I'm happy for you, Dina. I met with Mother two days ago to talk about you, amongst other topics of current interest. She wants you to know she's thinking of you. She will be very pleased to hear you have found someone." Dina nodded. "Was I correct in ordering white wine?"

"Yes, thank you. Pearl, why am I here? I was expecting a phone call, not a meeting. It must be a year since we last met in person. Is there a problem?"

"No dear. Your work is beyond reproach and it's been nine months. However, Dina, please understand, as of this meeting, you are removed from your role as Facilitator. You will no longer be required to assume the role."

Dina paled. "That can't be. For what reason? I've done nothing wrong and my work is exemplary. So what reason can you possibly have? The de Beaufort case study closed without incident. So what's the problem? It's already been filed as a random killing. The file's as dead as he is."

"It's not you, dear, or de Beaufort. It's one of Pearl's most essential covenants. No operative is permitted to serve as Facilitator for a term exceeding ten years and you are a few weeks from your tenth anniversary."

"I don't believe this."

"Do you remember, not far from ten years ago, when we first met a few weeks after your sister's murder? I told you then, in no uncertain terms, and again before we sent you overseas, that you would serve Pearl in that capacity for a period not exceeding ten years or until we recognized the need to terminate your active involvement. I also explained what would follow, were you to accept."

Dina nodded. "Yes. I remember."

"Good. I am not here to disassociate you from Pearl, Dina, quite the opposite. Mother and I want you to assume the role of Enabler, albeit in a sector outside your current boundaries due to your position with SVU, which will require a little bit of personnel shuffling on our part, so to speak. The woman who fills that very important position in your sector at this time is being asked to fulfill another mandate. In addition to becoming an Enabler, and in gratitude for your participation over the past ten years, fifty thousand dollars will be transferred to your account. Needless to say, quite apart from the usual fee pertaining to the de Beaufort file."

"Pearl, I'm a cop. It's all I know. I throw people to the ground and against walls. I intimidate them, I feel nothing when they cry or wet their pants, and right now I have a Beretta in my purse alongside an eight-inch stiletto. My official profile shows two shootings, one kill and thousands of arrests in nineteen years. My record at Pearl is equally flawless. What is it, thirty-five, thirty-six? And now you expect me to sit beside grieving widows or tell battered women we intend to kill their husbands for a ten percent fee?"

"Thirty-seven, dear, and yes, we do expect you to accept the new mandate. You're a valuable asset."

"No." Dina pinched the stem of her glass, swirling the

wine before tasting the Chablis. "I won't do it."

"Dina, each year your psychological report shows you to be stable and healthy. We don't want that to change. Frankly, I believe ten years is excessively demanding. The reason we do so is to limit the possibility of compromise, beyond that our primary concern is your safety."

"I'm still fit."

"And we intend for you to stay that way," Beverly's eyes dropped to Dina's pendant, "for that person as well. As an Enabler your fee structure will be reduced in accordance with the Covenants of Pearl, and you will be sent overseas for additional training. You are quite right to presume a certain adaptation will be required of you."

"What will happen if I refuse?"

"Including your fee for de Beaufort you will be seventy-five thousand dollars richer, you will have four pearl daggers to display in a curio cabinet and remember your service as dedicated and irreproachable since day one. I presume you will retire from the police force in six or so years and, I hope, find what you want if you haven't already." Beverly grinned. "I would, of course, expect an invitation to the ceremony. Your necklace, my dear, is exquisite." Dina swept her hair to show her ruby studs. "Mother will be as happy for you as I am. You must be ecstatic."

"I'm not sure about any of this."

"Well, dear, you don't have many choices. One is to become an Enabler, the other is to retire. We do retire, you know. It's for that very reason operatives must never know one another's true identity."

"My weekend is turning out to be one big surprise, Pearl. How long do I have, before I give you an answer?"

"I believe the day of your return would be appropriate, which brings us to our second topic." Beverly sipped her wine, ignoring Dina's quizzical expression. "I need you to leave the country. Be gone by Saturday and don't return before the thirty-first."

"Nancy?"

"Yes. You must be gone by this Saturday. Don't disappoint us. His review might well happen as early as the twentieth, his possible release as early as the following day. However, in view of our close association with this particular case study we want you at your usual escape destination in Europe. We want to avoid the slightest suspicion. Let's not forget the IA detective from so many years ago who sought to undo you."

"I remember. And what if they happen to review him on the second Friday? What then?"

"They won't."

"You know the date."

"Yes, I do. The specific date will remain privileged information and we expect you not to use your position as a police officer to investigate this matter on your own. It suffices to say you will be quite safe to return on or after the thirty-first unless contacted. Be certain you are gone by the eighteenth, irrespective of your decision to remain with Pearl. Do you understand me?"

"Yes."

"We will not tolerate disobedience, Dina. Is that also understood?"

"Where will it happen?"

"We have no idea at this point. Suffice it to say we will not disappoint you. Now, please answer my question, young lady."

"I understand, Pearl. All I need to know is when and where the facilitation happened. I can arrange for crime scene photos when I return and get the lab to enlarge them." Dina snickered. "They'll make great practice targets for my squad."

"You will know. You have my word."

Dina undid the snaps on her purse and placed a linen napkin on her lap. "Pearl, I have one favour to ask."

"I will do whatever is within my authority."

"I want whoever is chosen to carry out the facilitation to use this. Mother sent it to me for my twenty-first facilitation. I've only used it once. They guy was pure trash and I want it back. It's on loan, for a special occasion." She reached across the table to pass Beverly the dagger inlaid with the iridescent and multi-coloured mother of pearl harvested from red abalone. "It would mean a lot to me and my sister."

Beverly unfolded the edge of the napkin discreetly. "I will attend to the matter personally. You have my word on that as well. I will return it to you as soon as possible, in pristine condition. Enough said."

"Not quite, Pearl. I want to pay the fee. What I inherited from Nancy is now worth about twelve million."

"Thank you, dear. I accept your graciousness on behalf of Pearl and refuse your generosity on behalf of Mother. You're family, enough said. The subject is not open for discussion."

Dina sipped her wine. "Thank you, from both of us. It's been a long time in coming."

"Indeed, and closure is one of the rewards enjoyed by those of us who enable, being able to see the joy of relief first-hand, and many more that Facilitators are not privileged to see. Might I suggest, dear, you use your time away for retraining? It would be timely apropos your new position and we can arrange for valid proof of your time away, should your passport not suffice. We don't want to lose you, Dina." Beverly placed the napkin into her handbag. "Now, we still have a few moments. Why not tell me about your special person whose heart you have obviously captured?"

Dina cupped her ruby pendant in an open hand. "I'm afraid it was a goodbye gift, Pearl. Like I said, my weekend's been one big surprise."

"I am sorry."

"Yeah, so am I. Thank you, for my sister, and for what's in the napkin. I'll think about our talk and call you when I get back."
*

Miranda sat for close to an hour in her parked car, wondering what happened to her, wondering how her weekend ended in an instant and now was a perfect dream she could never relive. She wanted to erase the last words Dina would have heard. She did hate Dina, she told herself. She was the one who was supposed to walk away, not Dina. She was supposed to have pictures to remember her, another day to remember, and now all she had was too much time on her hands before going home from a memory she knew would fade with time. She did hate Dina; she told herself reaching into the glove compartment for her phone, and knowing the reason made her feel worse.

When she heard the message she swore aloud and took a moment to think before pressing send to connect with her director. She explained how she hadn't heard the message until a few moments earlier, that, in fact she was already in Montreal attending a garden party hosted by an old friend and that she would have to come as she was. They agreed to meet at 6:30 and, closing the phone, Miranda cursed. Her afternoon of shopping and fitting rooms had evaporated. Instead she'd be driving into a city she didn't know.

Meeting Pearl in a bustier top and mini skirt would not do at all and the only other outfit she hadn't worn, or hadn't squeezed into her suitcase, was a black satin mini evening gown with an empire waist that would look completely out of place in an airport. She had no hat to wear. Her crystal-studded black plastic head band would have to do and she had no intention of making a spectacle of herself by parading through an airport to change in a public washroom when everyone else would be wearing sneakers and polyester sweat suits.

At the rear of the car she raised the lid of the trunk and

leaned in to prepare her dress and shoes. When she was done she stood by the left rear panel where she unfolded a map while scanning the immediate vicinity. She knew the security cameras might catch her, she didn't care about that either. So what if she made someone's day. No one would report a beautiful woman for undressing.

She stepped behind the car, kicked off her sandals, stripped off her skirt, reached in for the dress, stepped into the waist and tugged it to her hips. She unzipped and stripped away her bustier, hurled it into the trunk, pulled up the front of her gown and zippered the back before stepping into her evening slippers. She was on the A-20 heading to Montreal by 2:30 with nothing on her mind but getting home. She had no idea why the director wanted to see her. Pearl said nothing on the phone, and she truly didn't care. All she cared about was an afternoon she could never remember and how Dina deprived her of their last few hours together.

She arrived at the hotel at 6:15. She had met her director on several previous occasions and knew her by no other name than Pearl. She gave her keys to the parking valet, went to the ladies' room to freshen her make-up and walked out through the main entrance onto Montreal's once-glamorous rue Sherbrooke to count down the remaining five minutes. Beverly Price had specified 6:30 and Miranda knew that meant not a moment earlier.
*

Across the wide boulevard Dina Becker sipped her wine, waiting for her salad and didn't know whether to be shocked or captivated. When her meal was served she waved the waiter away and refilled her own glass. Her entire focus was on the blonde dressed in black whom she knew was waiting for the exact moment to meet the director. Seeing Miranda's face marred with grief tore at Dina's heart. She knew she should have stayed longer. She should have given Miranda one last kiss, one last hug, one last tender caress. She didn't, and would never. Her last memory of her time with Chérie would be the hurtful words. Miranda was so beautiful, Dina thought, invaded by a rush of sensations they shared, words they spoke and endless images of Mirada's nude body. She wanted to scream across the street, she wanted to stand, to wave her arms, to shout out Miranda's name.

She didn't. She watched the doorman tip his hat as Miranda passed through the door. Dina had enough on her mind. She loved being a cop, a career which indisputably helped to damage her personal life, and being a Facilitator had given her a deeper purpose. Now she was asked to give up what was most important to her. She could never be an Enabler and had no reason to wait until month's end to give Pearl an answer.

She spent the entire weekend with a beautiful and vibrant woman who was silly, annoying, loving, frustrating and fun to be with. She should never have gone to the spa. She hated herself for not resisting Miranda's coquettishness, for succumbing so willingly to what she convinced herself was a fanciful curiosity and not wanting the weekend to end. Adding a lesbian lover to the equation was unthinkable. Miranda was better off without her and in time they would both get over it. She had been a Facilitator and now she wasn't. She'd been straight all her life, and now she doubted her sexuality. And what was so good about being a cop if all she could do to make a difference was play catch up with scum? She had too much to consider and the last thing she needed in her life was a female lover who would complicate and upset her life in the extreme.

Dina paid the bill, left the table and crossed the street to where the parking valet was arranging his collection of keys for something to do. She identified herself as a police detective and was escorted to Miranda's vehicle with the keys in her hand. She went through the glove compartment, found nothing, and through both suitcases until she discovered what she wanted to know about Miranda Stevens. She copied the information, closed the suitcases, slammed the trunk closed and walked away.

*

"Good evening, Miranda."

"Good evening, Pearl."

Beverly Price shook her head, grinning.

"I truly wish I could see you more often, Miranda. You are a breath of fresh air in an otherwise drab and changing world which has forgotten the exquisite feeling which accompanies glamour and style, not to mention my first operative to ever meet with me in formal evening wear. You look fabulous, dear, and I suspect our meeting has interrupted more than a formal dinner party? I trust I have not caused your day to end badly."

"No, Pearl. The day was ending badly before I heard your message. I kind of got stuck between wearing this or something better suited to a different occasion. I'm sorry about the hat thing."

"I should be cross with you, it's quite against the rules," Beverly subtly shook her head, doing her best to appear put off, "but your band is delightful, dear. I would expect nothing less from you and I believe we can make an exception this one time." Beverly admired the gown. "Was anyone special fortunate enough to see you in this charming outfit?"

"No. It didn't work out."

"That's certainly her loss. Now, do a little pirouette for me."

"Director?"

"You heard me." Beverly stirred the air with a forefinger. "Do a little swirl for me, do one for everyone here. You are completely ravishing. Be proud of yourself."

Miranda held out her arms and twirled. "Like this."

"Yes, thank you. You've made all the men very happy and all the women very jealous. They deserve to be. I believe the cost of what many of them are eating will exceed what they are wearing. Imagine…running shoes and shorts in such an elegant patio as this." A young waiter hurried over to pull out Miranda's seat. They exchanged different smiles and he poured her wine. "It seems like mere months since I was exactly like you, dear. Now I see dresses and hate the hemlines I would love to wear, and wear bathing suits instead of bikinis which would make me feel more conspicuous at the beach than daring." Beverly sighed. "We all have our time, Miranda. Don't waste it. We grow older on the outside much more rapidly than we do on the inside, but we do grow older. Now, tell me why such a pretty young woman looks so sad. I allowed myself the liberty of ordering you a red wine."

"Thank you, Pearl. It's not that I'm sad, I'm tired."

"Take a vacation. Go somewhere, take a cruise." Beverly sipped her wine. "Was the relationship serious between the two of you, interrupted by a little spat soon to be surmounted with a dozen roses or a romantic dinner?"

"No, Pearl. What happened was impossible, and incredibly stupid of me."

"Love is seldom stupid for someone as selective and self-effacing as you, dear. It's often frustrating, often disappointing, though seldom stupid."

"Director, with all due respect, my flight is at ten o'clock and I'm not very familiar with this city."

"I understand. I'll get right to the reason for this meeting. First, congratulations on your most recent case study. And now, Miranda, I am here to remove you from active facilitation. Effective immediately we will no longer contract you to perform in that capacity. Mother and I want you to assume the role of Enabler in your sector." Beverly let the meaning of her words sink in. "We want you to one day become the magistrate you have dreamt of becoming. We want to see you on the bench. More importantly, we want to see you enjoying a more balanced life. On the third you will be seventy-five thousand dollars more comfortable and it's well-deserved. Take a long vacation. As Mother said, "get a life."

"I don't believe this. You're demoting me. There's no one better than me, no one. I'm the best."

"That is true, you are, and there was no one better than me at one time. Then one day I saw myself in the mirror." Beverly leaned in closer to Miranda. "I saw someone who knew how to kill more than love. I will not allow you the same dubious introspection, so deal with the news young lady and remember that being an Enabler is very important work, not a demotion. To say so demeans those who work tirelessly to help others. Your stilettos have been retired. Keep them as precious mementos or use them for peeling potatoes. They are no longer required by Pearl. What we need is you, what we want is you." "It's not fair. I've never failed you."

"That's not the point, young lady. The point is we are doing this so we are not the ones to let you down."

"I don't understand."

"We don't require that you do, dear, merely that you answer yes or no."

"And if I say no I remain status quo, right? I remain as Facilitator in my sector."

"Wrong, dear. Should you not accept the new position, we would understand your need to retire from Pearl forthwith. Need I say, with great regret?"

"Pearl is my life."

"That's not a good thing to admit to me or to yourself. You're thirty-two, you're so very pretty and somewhere a special lady is waiting for you. Let it happen, Miranda. It's been our experience that working as an Enabler will be a good thing for you, therapy if you will. You have done excellent work for us, but you must realize being a Facilitator is, in and of itself, self-destructive. Ten years is far beyond what we should expect, yet we do, and we are never disappointed. Take a week or two to consider your decision, take a vacation. If anyone deserves time away, you do."

"To do what, feel alone again?"

"No, rather to have time alone in order to make a decision without external influences."

Miranda rubbed her hands over her face. "I am so fucked up. My life is the envy of absolutely no one, my first weekend away in years, which was supposed to be so much fun went to crap, and now this. Fuck." Miranda's eyes suddenly lit with awareness. "Pearl, I'm sorry."

"No you're not, and don't think for a moment you're shocking me or that I haven't used that particular nuance upon occasion over the years. I remember when Mother removed me from active service. I said similar. I felt everything you are now feeling, and I got over it." Beverly lowered her voice. "I learned to transfer my energies from one expertise to another, the other being compassion. Finally, I understood Mother was right."

"Will I ever meet her?"

"That's very unlikely unless you become a director, which, as you know, requires you to first serve as an Enabler."

"Catch twenty-two."

"Possibly, in your eyes. However, let us not forget we have existed for fifty years, the idea being not to be caught."

"Do you have a husband, a family?"

"I have a husband, no family."

"Does he know?"

"He does not." Beverly waited a few moments before continuing. "Miranda, if I had ever had the daughter I always wanted so much, she would have been like you. I would like very much right now to ask what is in your heart, but I doubt I would hear the truth. Our meeting is over. We want you to serve Pearl as an Enabler, your time has come. However, if you know for certain at this very moment you

318

cannot perform the requisite duties you must walk away from us."

"I can't walk away, not now. I wasn't expecting this. I need time to think."

"Was she very special to you, the one for whom you bought this beautiful gown?"

"Yeah, she was. I didn't buy it for her, but I hoped she would have seen me in it. I think she would have liked the way I look."

"I know she would, judging by the somewhat less than candid reaction of those seated around us when you joined me."

Miranda shrugged. "So what. It's all bullshit."

"No, dear, it is not. What appears to us as bullshit in our youth becomes a lesson learned in our later years. Learn from it, seize the moment. We all learn more from our disappointments than we do from our happiness."

"Philosophy 101, Pearl?"

"No, dear, life: the graduating class, I regret to say. Are you sure it's too late for the two of you?"

"Yes."

"I hate to sound trite, dear. You're so young and so beautiful. You must believe someone is waiting for you. How could there not be?"

"No, there isn't. Until very recently I might have believed you. Thank you, but some dreams are meant not to come true."

Beverly sighed, pushing back her chair to stand.

"Miranda our meeting is over, after I hold you and tell you things will work out, despite what you may believe at the moment. Stand up, child." She stepped to Miranda's corner of the table. "Looking at you is like looking at my own image from so many years ago. Pearl sends many messages, dear, the most important is the most final for the inhumane who merit our interest. However, one that goes unspoken is unequivocally the most fundamental element of

Pearl: Pearl itself, you and hundreds of others. Get back to me soon with your answer and look into your heart for what is missing, not the space you occupy. Feel sorry for those who do not know you, never yourself. Goodbye, my dear. And if this must be our last meeting, I will always remember you as having found happiness."

Beverly embraced Miranda and let her walk away. When she was seated once again she looked up, surprised to see Miranda standing by her side.

"Do you feel old, Pearl? I don't know your age, and you don't look old, but do you feel old?"

"No, Miranda. I do not. I feel as young as you are."

"Then you should buy those short dresses and bikinis, for the person inside you. Perhaps your time hasn't come; perhaps you should consider how your husband would enjoy seeing you wearing them."

"Thank you, dear. I've never quite considered my dilemma in that particular light. Thank you for the insight and caring. Now we both have certain aspects of our lives to assess."

Miranda nodded. Her face showed no expression as she walked to the portico to leave Beverly with a notion to ponder.
*

Miranda left the garden dining room moments before 7:00. She was curt with the valet, apologized to him with a fifty and drove through the city streets to the expressway as thoughtlessly as any resident of the city. She arrived at the airport at 7:30, checked her bags and searched for a quiet corner to be alone. She had no book to read, she thought she looked like a whore dressed all in black and what she wanted above all was to rip off her dress and put on her jeans. She hadn't slept for thirty-six hours and very soon she drifted off to another place and time, oblivious to the ratchet sound of warm steel closing onto her wrist.

Dina sat by her side flipping the pages of an in-flight

magazine, her gold detective's shield hanging from her neck on an 18kt gold chain. Fifteen minutes later Miranda stirred, she looked towards the Departures monitor, to one side then the other, and closed her eyes before jolting herself awake.

"Green Eyes," she murmured, exhausted.

"I thought you would sleep right through our last night together."

"What?"

"I had your bags redirected." she dangled her shield. "Call it a professional courtesy."

"That's illegal seizure."

"My actions were necessary to an ongoing investigation. Unfortunately, unless you come up with a good defence, you may be required to remove your fantastic dress and anything else you're wearing that might be introduced as evidence, not that you're leaving much to the imagination as it is."

"You know who I am."

"Yes, I do."

"Why? What's the point? And how did you get here so fast?"

"I got here before you, Chérie, for my meeting with Pearl. I saw you at the hotel, from across the street. If you hadn't come out onto the sidewalk I would never have known."

"How did you find out my name?"

"It wasn't difficult, a simple police procedure." Dina grinned. "I used my badge to get the keys to your car, happened to see your rental agreement and airline agenda in your suitcase and…voilà."

"That's illegal entry."

"Find a judge who cares."

"You lied to me."

"Yeah, and if you had checked for your messages first, you would have lied to me. Anyway, you hate me."

"No, I could never. I hated myself as soon as I said the

words. I knew I would never see you again. All morning I made myself believe I could leave you my way. Then you left." Miranda stared at the handcuffs. "So what do we do now, not that I shouldn't be angry with you for what you did?"

"I know. I acted on impulse. Our whole weekend was one big impulse, except this. Your bags are being held for you at security and we're booked into the Hilton for the night. You've got a flight at 7:00 AM, Executive Class."

"I'm already booked. I leave at 10:00."

"If that's what you want, otherwise you leave at 7:00, which gives us nine hours."

"I thought I would never see you again."

"And after tomorrow you won't. Don't think leaving tomorrow will be any easier on us. If anything, it's going to be harder. As good as this feels at the moment, it's wrong. I should have gone straight back to Quebec to get on with my miserable life and let you hate me and forget me. This will make our next goodbye worse. I just can't help myself. So, it's your call."

"Did you really hold my luggage?"

Dina nodded, raising her arm and taking Miranda's wrist with it. "I saw her, Chérie. I saw Morgan. She was so pretty."

Miranda frowned. "No. You had no right to see her. Morgan belongs to me."

"But you no longer belong to her. She's gone beyond girlish jealousies, Miranda. She would want you to move on. She would be happy for you, so will I be happy for you."

"Dina, she's all I had. You've taken her from me and now you're going to leave me."

"I didn't take her from you, Miranda. She will always be with you. What I feel for you is what she would care about. What anyone will feel for you is what she cares about, not me seeing her picture. It's what you feel that matters, to you and to Morgan. That's what she would care about. She would understand you have to let her go, which doesn't mean you have to forget." A long pause seemed timeless, Dina stroking Miranda's hair and cheek. "So, Miss Stevens, do I release you on your own recognisance or do I take you in?"

Miranda looked at the gold shield centred on its small leather background and into Dina's eyes. "You are a detective. I knew it."

"You can read it if you want, Chérie. I won't stop you. You'll know who I am and what I am. You also know I will never be a cop in your city and you will never be prosecutor in mine. Even if such an impossible scenario did happen, Pearl would ask us to resign. Such is my life and yours. I think it's better not to know. If I hadn't needed to know your name for all of this I still wouldn't know who you are. Truthfully, I should have walked across the street and invited you to dinner. It would have been so much simpler."

"We could happen one day, Dina, if we want each other badly enough."

"We won't. We happened too fast for each other and we have no time to take it slow or think about why Thursday night happened at all, not to mention what's happened since then. What we have is right now. That's it. It's all we've got. I can walk Miranda. You should hate me for leaving. I should be walking away right now and hope I never forget you."

"I won't let you forget me. Take these things off me, Green Eyes. And how come they always make me want to pee?"

"Are you coming back?"

"Yes, I'm coming back. Are you kidding? I'm staying and you're paying for dinner." Dina removed the restraint from her wrist and let it hang free from Miranda's. "That's not fair."

"You're wasting time, and I wouldn't suggest any metal detectors."

Dina leaned into her seat, laughing at the stares her blonde in the short black dress and handcuffs was attracting as she walked away. Twenty minutes later Miranda came bouncing into the gate area, her face hidden behind a new digital camera, blinding Dina with a rapid sequence of blue-white flashes. A second camera swung from her shoulder.

Thirty-One

Miami, Florida
Sunday, August 12

Julia Saunders climbed from the taxi in front of her apartment building; Piedra Batista pulled in several feet behind her, aware Julia's brothers weren't home. Before driving to the bus terminus she left a sealed package for Julia with the building's superintendent, offering a twenty-dollar tip to ensure he would deliver the envelope to the young woman as she arrived home.

He was a man Piedra presumed to be in his twenties. He was Latino, good-looking, well-spoken and polite. She believed him when he said he would personally hand-deliver the package, surprised when he refused the twenty, saying that, for Julia, he would stay up all night to wait for her. Being an Enabler meant being invisible, being detached, but she had to ask: He was a student from Puerto Rico, in his third year of Latin American Studies and he would do anything for Julia. Piedra asked him if he had ever asked her out. He said no, and she asked why not. Because he wasn't in her league and one day she would be a famous actress with no interest in a lowly musician or a much poorer student.

Piedra told him how she suspected Julia would need a good friend in the coming weeks, how she had been through a rough time with her job and her studies and deserved a night out with someone who had no expectations. She repeated "with someone who had no expectations" and the young man looked puzzled. Piedra dipped her fingers into her purse, counted out three hundred dollars in crisp bills and gave them to the man, telling him she thought Julia would prefer a few inexpensive meals to one fancy dinner.

He refused the money, until he saw the shadowed glare behind Piedra's fake glasses and contact lens. He must have thanked her a dozen times before she reached the outer doors of the building. Now she saw he was sitting on his first floor balcony wearing a different shirt with his hair combed as Julia crossed the street.

"Julia, hola, I have package for you. Wait one moment." He bounded over a second chair, nearly tripping and probably cursing himself, Piedra thought, watching him through long-range Bausch and Lomb. Moments later he stood beside Julia on the sidewalk. "It is from a woman. She came this evening looking for you. She said the package is important, that you must have it right away."

"What lady, Luis?"

"I do not know."

"She did not say her name?"

"No, she did not. She was a real lady, and very kind."

"What did she look like?"

"She wore a hat and glasses. She was older, about my mother's age." He gave Julia the package. "She said it was important that you have this package, Julia. I waited for you."

"Thank you, Luis. You are very thoughtful. Good night."

"Good night, Julia.

Julia walked up the steps and through the doors, leaving Luis with slumped shoulders and his hands buried in his pockets. Piedra Batista counted to three, stepped from her car and pressed the palm of her hand into the centre of her steering wheel. The horn blared. Luis jumped, twisting his torso to see the woman who had come to his door straightening her back in an exaggerated way and shooing him into action. He waved to her and ran through the doors.

"Julia, Julia. ¡Un momento! Wait!"

"What is it, Luis?"

"Julia. I know you are very busy with your school and your work, but tomorrow, after your work, maybe we can have a glass of wine, or maybe a coffee."

The surprise on Julia's face was real. She had spent the entire weekend reliving her summer and what she had done so many times believing she was helping to save Mendez' life. She had thought often of what Pearl had said, of the well-dressed woman she'd seen stepping from the bus and again at the hotel once Julia had checked-in. The woman had smiled at her and nodded her head as though telling Julia she was pleased. In her room she thought of Mendez and threw up. She thought of her brothers and her parents and cried.

The woman called Pearl told her not to worry, that she should not be afraid to make new friends. Her life would be better very soon, the woman promised. There were no drug dealers and she would never see or hear from Mendez again. Her brothers would never be the wiser, she was not to worry about her job and a special gift in plain wrapping would be waiting for her upon her return. But the woman's voice was gentle and seemed so harmless. What could she do against Mendez and the dealers, Julia thought throughout the weekend, and why did she want to believe a perfect stranger? She had not thought of the gift once, afraid the woman had lied to her.

Julia looked at the package.

"I cannot, Luis. I do not know if I have my job. I did not have time to call them before I left the city. I think they have fired me because of it."

"Then we can have a small dinner and maybe go to the park to talk."

She smiled. "Thank you, Luis. I cannot, but you are very kind to ask me. Good night."

Julia continued up the stairs, leaving a dejected Luis behind. Walking into her apartment the phone was flashing red and her first thought was of Mendez. She went into the kitchen for scissors to open the package and emptied the contents onto the table. There were several envelopes, a folded square of newspaper and a tiny box wrapped in dark blue foil and pale blue ribbon. She unfolded the newspaper first and shrieked. Consuelo Moreno's front page piece showed graphic black and white photos of Eduardo Mendez' body crumpled on the floor of a closet and Eric Wilder's half-naked body sprawled for the entire world to see on a bed she knew all too well. The sheets were stained with dark grey blood and a black square had been added to the photograph for reasons of social propriety.

Pearl had told her the truth. There were no drug dealers. Pearl was Mendez' enemy, but what could he have done to make her so angry and how could a middle-aged woman kill two men? Julia went to the phone and listened to the message her boss had left, bewildered. He'd heard from Julia's aunt Pearl how an urgent family matter required Julia to leave town unexpectedly. He understood and hoped she was well. She was his best hostess and not having her would be difficult. He would manage without her until Wednesday when they would talk about a new five-day workweek and better hours. He didn't realize the strain her job was putting on her studies. He apologized, yet was unwilling to do without her. The customers loved her and he needed her.

At the table she opened the thinnest envelope first. Inside was an unsigned note explaining how she should place the money into a safety deposit box and that she wasn't to worry. The money was legal with no strings attached, to be used for her education and to reduce the financial burden on her brothers. Their fondest wish was for

Julia to be happy and the gift was an important symbol of a new beginning. Pearl's sole request was that, as a symbol of great significance, the ring never be bequeathed to another.

Julia opened each of the five remaining envelopes one by one until she counted fifty thousand dollars and sank into her chair, wondering who Pearl was and why she had come to Julia as a guardian angel from a fairy tale. Lastly she opened the black velvet box lined with silver trim, excited. Inside, set in white velvet, was a perfect black pearl gleaming in a Florentine shell.

Julia cried for an hour, mesmerized by the ring on her finger. What had happened to her, what was happening, was too much to grasp. When her tears subsided she looked to the phone. Pearl had spoken with her boss who wasn't angry with her, and then her eyes went to the article, which she tore into tiny pieces and threw into the toilet. Mendez was dead. She would never think of him again. She would conceal the money under her mattress until she could go to the bank and she would find a way to share the windfall with her brothers without telling them. She tied the note into a scroll with the ribbon and placed it in her dresser drawer with the gift box. She would keep them forever and never forget her guardian angel.

At eleven o'clock the night air was thick, her skin was moist and her eyes were red. She showered in cold water to revitalize herself, brushed out her hair, put on her prettiest skirt and blouse and walked out the door before she could change her mind. He was always on the balcony playing his guitar and no one ever complained. His music came from the heart and his voice was sweet. Yet she heard no music, no tender lyrics as she stepped beyond the open doors.

"Luis, why are you not singing? You sing for us every night. You know we enjoy it."

Luis stood and leaned against the railing. "Julia, hola. You look so pretty, like an angel." He leaned closer. "Why were you crying? What is the matter?"

"There is an angel beside me, Luis, a real one, and a beautiful one. I know it is true, I do. I was crying because I am happy. But why are you not singing?"

"It is because I am worried. I have something belonging to another and I have no way to return it."

"Keep it for them until they come back. Luis, I have my job. He did not fire me. He wants me to work only his busiest nights. Now I will not be so tired."

"My heart is happy for you, Julia."

Julia gulped and moistened her lips. "What you said about taking me out, Luis, did you mean it?"

"¡Sí! ¡Claro! I did."

"Then maybe, if you are not tired, I can make some coffee for us and we can sit here on the steps while you sing for me."

"I will get my guitar and sing you the most wonderful ballads until I can sing no more."

"And maybe tomorrow we can have a glass of wine and you can sing for me in the park."

"¡Ay! Your angel is now looking out for me, Julia."

Julia pranced from sight, acting more revived than she felt, knowing the true feeling wasn't far behind her. Luis pushed himself from the rail and disappeared inside his apartment as Piedra Batista did a thumbs-up and drove away feeling content. She understood every word silent word Julia had spoken.

Thirty-Two

Montreal, Quebec
Monday, August 13

From the time Miranda and Dina left the airport Sunday evening they lived for the moment and when the time came to leave Monday morning Dina used her badge once more to get through security with privileged attention. They said their goodbyes at the hotel and strolled through the concourse arm in arm, appearing to everyone as elite socialites, Miranda stepping up to the gate agent with her ticket and photo ID. When she twirled around to wave goodbye, Dina wasn't there.

Dina Becker strode to her car in the airport parking lot feeling good. She did the right thing. She spent the night with Miranda and after dinner neither woman wanted to sleep. There was too much to say and to discover of one another. She was a cop again. The weekend came and went. What remained was a bizarre, quixotic memory. She would be in Quebec City by 9:00 and report for duty by 10:00. What else mattered, other than seeing her ex-brother-in-law laying in a street or alley with a bullet hole in his head or on a gurney in some forensic lab with a deep stab wound under his sternum, put there by her personal dagger? Contacting Pearl to advise her director she would no longer be part of the family would come first, prior to her departure.

When she arrived home she called in sick and cried for

the first time in ten years. When she awoke early Monday evening she cried again and went back to bed.

Thirty-Three

Peggy's Cove, Nova Scotia
Monday, August 13

Brianna was so happy. She had never smiled as much and had never seen as much water. She spent the week playing in the sand by the shoreline, splashing in the tranquil water of the cove with her mother who tried her hardest to explain why the all water went away every day when they were having the most fun. From Brianna's perspective the answer was too complicated to be important, as long as water stayed in the pool and the ocean came back each morning, glittering with leftover stardust that fell each night as she slept. And if she didn't sleep, Alicia told her the first evening, the angels wouldn't shake the stars and all the beautiful mermaids who lived in the sea would have nothing to eat the next day.

Alicia Stone didn't know about ebb or flood tides. She remembered her days at the beach as a child and nothing more. But at night, while Brianna helped the mermaids to survive, Alicia borrowed books from the motel lobby and returned to the quiet of their room to read about them so her daughters would know the truth.

Monday afternoon she sat watching Brianna play. She had never felt so alive or so afraid Rick Kendall would find her. She lived for her daughters and would die for them. She thought of the woman who came to visit her in

Montreal. She never did believe in her heart she would ever be safe. The nice woman in the beautiful clothes didn't tell Alicia how she would be safe from Kendall. It was easy for the woman to say not to worry about money, she was rich and elegant. None of Alicia's twelve hundred dollars was left and she'd taken a cash advance on her credit card the day before. She had no job, and was in debt with no idea when to return home. The woman said she would know, but she didn't know and tried to force the burden of haunting doubt from her mind.

Tired of feeling desperate she stared across the glittering sea, telling herself she would search for work the next day and all would be well, startled by the sound of her name from close behind her. Someone was calling Alicia Stone and she lurched from her seat on the trunk of an old tree which had drifted to shore too many years in the past for anyone to remember. She saw the uniform before she saw the man. He was an older gentleman, large, in shape that belied his years, she thought, and his complexion was ruddy and slightly weathered as though he might once have been to sea. His face wore a kind and strangely sad expression and she was instantly afraid.

The sergeant from the local RCMP detachment was at the seaside motel to speak with her and asked for a few moments alone. She hadn't thought to expect the police, she didn't know what to expect. Hearing his words, which were neither harsh nor intimidating, she stood frozen.

"Miss Stone, I'm here to speak with you about Richard Kendall. Please don't be alarmed. You have no reason to be afraid of me or worried. However, we should talk privately."

"We're getting divorced. I had a legal right to bring my daughter here. We're taking a vacation."

"And from what I see she's enjoying herself. Let's not spoil her day, shall we? I know you're on vacation and I'm glad for you and your daughter, although you may want to

334

return home sooner than expected, Miss Stone. Whether you do will be your choice after you hear what I have to say."

Alicia's mind flashed back to the woman. Go home? Why? The woman promised she would know when to return home. "Why do I have to go home?"

The officer directed Alicia's gaze to a secluded picnic table where they wouldn't lose sight of Brianna. "Please, Alicia, you really must hear what I have to say. I know about your husband, the hospital and your reason for being here. Please, for the girl's sake."

Alicia crossed her arms defensively, instinctively rounding her shoulders. They left Brianna by her sandcastle to speak in sombre tones as he explained how Alicia's husband was gunned down by a random killer in broad daylight while panhandling on a street corner in downtown Montreal the previous Friday. There was no witness, despite heavy noontime traffic, and not a single clue. The authorities had done their best to locate her, waiting for her first credit card transaction which alerted the system the day before.

Alicia sobbed, letting her head fall into her lap, not wanting Brianna to see, uncertain what to say. He put a very large hand against her back, telling her to take her time.

"I wanted my Brianna and her sister to be safe. I'm pregnant. She's going to be a girl."

"I was told. Congratulations."

"I never wanted him to die. I wanted him to leave us alone, to be nice again, like he was before he was wounded."

"I reviewed his file this morning, Alicia. I also spoke personally with the detectives who were with you at the hospital and with him at the house. I know you came here to hide. You're free, Alicia. No more running. He wasn't allowed in your home by himself. The police closed your home for you. You're safe to return home."

"I will go home... to sell the place and leave. That's what I want. My daughter likes being here and I think I can find work here and go to night school. The people here are so nice. Can I take the next flight out?"

"Yes, and I know people in these parts would welcome such a fine family."

"I'm not being arrested?"

"Of course not, which doesn't mean I can't arrange for Brianna to arrive at the airport with a siren and flashing lights, if you think she would like being the centre of attention."

Alicia smiled for the first time. "Are you serious? You can do that for her?"

"You bet." He gave Alicia a card. "You give me a call at this number, tell me what flight you're on and we'll give her a ride to remember. It's pretty cool, as long as you're going to the airport and not somewhere else." He winked.

"She would like that a lot. Thank you."

The sergeant stood. "Be sure to call me, Alicia, or I'll be disappointed for little Brianna."

"She won't understand why she has to leave the water."

"Just promise to bring her back...in time for school."

"Thank you."

The next morning Alicia flew home with Brianna. They arrived at the airport with flashing lights and the ear-piercing shrill of the police siren, Brianna locked into the caged rear seat with her teddy bear, listening to each official word the sergeant spoke into the mike, confirming he was escorting a top secret passenger and her mother to the airport. She saw the riot gun, the computer and her mother. She told him "thank you" when they arrived and he reached inside to sweep her out. He gave them official police caps and walked them to the gate where the ticket agents did their part with First Class seats on a half-empty flight.

Alicia felt like Alicia: insignificant. She had no way to thank the officer and he knew what was running through her mind. Alicia felt as though engulfed by a mountain as he wished them good luck and, before letting them go, he told each one he expected to see them soon. They arrived home Tuesday afternoon, by which time Brianna had forgotten the beach. She was anxious to shop with her mommy for new school clothes and didn't care that her father was in another place she didn't know.

Alicia's birthday cake was on the floor. She knew what caused the damage to the wall and Brianna called her mother into her bedroom to see the broken beer bottle and shattered picture frame hanging tilted on the wall. Then she realized: She'd been told when to come home.

No one attended Kendall's funeral on the Wednesday. He was buried by indifferent men in black suits sometime after Alicia left the funeral home without asking to see him and he went to hell as she had hoped. What mattered was shopping with Brianna. She had his insurance, or soon would, enough to start over with her daughters who would never know violence again and by late afternoon her house was put on the market. The home was fully insured against his life, for which she was thankful, and when she asked Brianna where she would like to live the little girl answered "by the ocean" and her mother nodded in agreement. They would live by the ocean.

She checked her mailbox Wednesday, as instructed. There was nothing. She did the same Thursday. Nothing. Friday morning, trying not to wonder why the beautiful lady had insisted on the curious ritual, she found a single brown envelope which she hesitated to open. Inside she found one hundred thousand dollars and a note wishing her a good life, cautioning her to rent a safety deposit box for the money until her house was sold and she was re-established with Brianna and her new sister. The amount was excessive, however none of the directors voted against the decision. The girls would need help as much as their single mother.

Alicia sank to her knees and kissed her ring. She cried a

torrent of tears for how she'd begun to doubt the woman until the RCMP officer arrived at the motel, then again.

When Brianna walked into the room to see her mother crying, Alicia swept her into her arms and promised her a perfect life.

Thirty-Four

Toronto, Ontario
Monday, August 13

At the airport Miranda knew Dina wouldn't be standing behind her. She'd asked Dina not to leave right away, yet she knew, experiencing an instant pang of regret. She boarded the plane doing her best to imagine the weekend as something other than what they shared and fell asleep before the A-321 rolled from the gate.

She hadn't slept for two days and was oblivious to the jolt of the landing gears coming down and the ensuing screech of dormant rubber tires colliding onto warm concrete. She stirred when the attendant pressed a hand against her shoulder and, for a moment, she thought the red-haired crew member was Dina.

At home she dragged herself into her condo, showered, changed into more appropriate attire for an officer of the court and left her luggage unopened on her bed. At the office she was quickly the focus of attention. Everyone in the prosecutor's office recognized the stainless steel jewellery on her wrist. She explained to a room filled with smirks and playful innuendo that, as usual, she was introducing the latest in European and Quebec fashion and no one knew whether to believe a woman who'd worn chic designer fashions and accessories for as long as they had known her.

Dina did give her the key, which she refused, and Dina hadn't argued. She spent much of the day in a fog and arrived home early after speaking with the Chief Prosecutor who was as much a father-figure and friend as her boss. He agreed wholeheartedly: a real vacation was long overdue.

Watching the sun rise in the east from the nineteenth floor was a morning tradition for Miranda, witnessing the sun set from her patio was a rarity she'd never thought to miss and she sat absorbing the late-day warmth until the glittering amber of the setting sun transitioned into the silvery sparkle of a full moon.

She was happy, content. The director was right. She had no reason to be sad. She closed a hand over the handcuffs on her wrist. For ten years she'd locked herself in the past, held there by gradually waning memories she struggled each day to cherish, and one inexplicable weekend had set her free. Dina set her free. Dina was never the cause of her sense of betrayal. She didn't walk away from Dina at the pool for that reason, or scream at her in Quebec for walking away. She had betrayed herself. She was afraid her dream weekend had failed, that she failed to finally say goodbye to Morgan and would always love only Morgan. Now she knew otherwise. She had felt no guilt Sunday morning, seeing her body smeared with Dina's lipstick, and she experienced none as they said their goodbyes before leaving the hotel. Dina did that for her.

Miranda padded to the bedroom to arrange the clothes she'd worn over the weekend and found the key Dina secreted into the ruffled pocketing of her suitcase. She would keep the steel bracelets and the key. She was Miranda Stevens; she always had been and would be from then on.

She would wear the key on a stainless steel chain and wear the ensemble at her next court appearance. She went to bed without supper and put the key by Morgan's photograph. She cried, this time her tears trickling over a smile as she told one woman how much she would forever be missed and the other how much she would always be loved.

Tuesday night Miranda loaded her computer with countless images of Dina. She dimmed the lights and ate her dinner, one image fading into another. She was a detective. Miranda had confirmed that much by Dina's gold shield hanging from her neck. She had taken hundreds of photographs, using the multiple frames feature to capture the perfect pose. She stopped eating after increasing the speed of the slide show, bringing Dina to life. Each set of images was so similar the effect was as though Dina was actually moving.

Seeing her dressed to kill in the hotel restaurant, posing in her lingerie and lying on the bed the way she did, Miranda couldn't imagine her with a gun on her hip and another strapped to her ankle. She thought of the shots she might have taken at the spa's pool or at the airport Friday morning as they waited for the shuttle. Her mother would have said "spilt milk" or "water under the bridge." Her time with Dina raised the bar, yet she had much to think about, not the least of which was Pearl.

She hadn't expected Beverly to demote her. Despite Pearl's firm rhetoric, she'd been demoted, prevented from doing what she did best. She thought of Pearl as an essential and natural extension to her legal career. What she could not do in court she did after hours. The least important aspect of her life was her life, since the gang rape and Morgan's murder. She lost herself in her work. She averaged four facilitations a year, never letting herself enjoy a vacation. She didn't know what a vacation was and when she did leave the country ostensibly on vacation; she had no idea where she was. She was met each time at a different airport from Britain to Bulgaria, taken to a private jet where she was blindfolded and flown to a private airfield that could be in any of a dozen countries.

Pearl's annual week-long training was mandatory and rigorous, commencing each day at 5:00 AM and continuing until 5:00 PM with fifteen minutes for breakfast and lunch. She was tested and graded. Nothing less than one hundred percent was acceptable. They weighed her, measured her and examined her the first day. Each subsequent day she went through a barrage of physical and psychological endurance tests. She was tested in weapons use, tae kwon do, lip-reading, being invisible and given a scenario for a mock facilitation which would take place the following day. Nothing was taken for granted. At 5:00 she was allowed time alone in her private suite that was walled and boasted a private patio and pool. Several other Facilitators and Enablers were at the compound at any given time, although she would never see them, their individual schedules never coincided. There were no cameras in the suites or at the patios and Miranda always left her bikinis at home.

At 7:00 she would either be escorted to the dining room to enjoy a six-course gourmet meal alone or dine privately in her suite. She'd never gone to the dining room. She preferred her suite and the luxury of not dressing for a dinner prepared by a talented team of French and Italian chefs who had no idea about Pearl. They were well-paid for the work they did at an exclusive compound for the rich and famous and knew not to pry.

There was no radio, nor television, her purse and luggage were scanned for a cell phone and cameras were forbidden. No link to the outside world existed and after dinner she was expected to meditate until 10:00 when lights across the compound extinguished. Miranda never meditated. She spent the time remembering Morgan and swimming, not causing the slightest ripple. She was never tempted to call out over her walls, never certain who would answer. Being caught by an instructor would mean immediate expulsion from Pearl. Contact between operatives was verboten, considered the most perilous and

342

careless conduct and would not be tolerated

The sixth and seventh days at the compound were the worst, the most crucial to continued service. Day six was all about evasion, not being identified or captured. Day seven was arrest and interrogation, subsequent to a failed facilitation. The relentless and hostile interrogation began at 5:00 AM, lasted twelve hours, and each hour on the hour another intent inquisitor came into the windowless room to take over from her colleague.

Miranda's first experience was the most terrifying and real, meticulously designed to be real. She was twenty-two, alone in a cruel world she was trained to withstand and escape. She was taught how to act, eat, stand and sit in all social situations, she learned how to kill, how to defend herself, how to dress to be seen or not to be seen, how to lie with perfection and how to consistently work alone without the slightest proof Pearl even existed.

The training was exhaustive, not allowing for the faintest glimmer of a smile, but, by far, the worst were the last five days of the seven months. Once apprehended, they assured her, she would have no reason to fear comparatively innocuous police procedures and when the last woman completed her hour-long inquisition on Miranda's second to last day she walked out without saying a word. Miranda waited until she could no longer hear the woman's footfalls, trembling, before hurrying to her suite unattended to jump into pool and scream as loud as she could under the water. Not even her first facilitation was as terrifying as those five days; such was her new life. The day of her departure they presented her with an eight-inch stiletto inlaid with white mother-of-pearl and each subsequent interrogation session over the years would become more demanding of her mental and physical endurance.

Beyond her director, and the woman long ago in the supermarket, Dina was her only proof that Pearl did exist. Dina was the best thing in her life since Morgan, captivating her instantly with the husky, sultry quality of her voice and her coolly refined manner. Yet she was inherently sensual and warm and something definitely did happen between them. Another place another time, that's what she said. Miranda had no regrets, although she would never know the real Dina behind those beautiful green eyes. She zoomed into one of a dozen shots she'd taken of Dina's face, remembering her scent and her smooth skin. Beautiful green eyes she would never see again, emerald eyes that would never look upon her again.

Miranda touched the screen and brought it down over the keyboard. Seeing Dina was difficult, the memories were too recent and wonderful. She had her law career and she had Pearl. What more did she need? The time had come to stop feeling sorry for herself. The healing she'd denied herself for so long had begun. Dina had been alone since her sister's death and lived her life without self-pity. She could do the same. If she was meant to be with someone, she would be. She had lived with self-imposed misery for too long. Being with Dina had changed her. Her time had come to be happy, to feel fulfilled and to be with someone special.

Assuming the role of Enabler would one day bring her closer to sitting on the Directorate. She would call Pearl first thing the next day. She would accept the position and establish a schedule for her training at the private compound somewhere in the world. Then she would plan the Caribbean cruise she had always wanted to take with Morgan and she would enjoy by herself.

She raised the screen. Dina was smiling at her with full crimson lips. Miranda took a deep breath and exhaled. "Thanks, Green Eyes. You helped me to work things out."

She kissed her fingertips, putting them to Dina's lips before closing the screen and putting herself to bed to dream of sunny beaches and beautiful girls.

Thirty-Five

Quebec City, Quebec
Tuesday, August 14

Dina Becker lost herself in her work throughout the five days following her spur-of-the-moment weekend tryst with a woman she would never see again. Yet something indefinable happened to her. The men and women of her squad recognized something had changed in her, yet they knew not to invade her private world. They knew Dina's personal life was off limits. Case files were overflowing and for everyone other than Dina the tragedy of Nancy Becker's brutal murder ten years earlier had diminished with time.

Her first night alone Dina loaded images of Miranda into her computer. Tuesday night she printed two dozen large format photos of Chérie and scattered them around her home, reliving the sensations of Chérie's exotic caresses, teasing and gentle, probing kisses. At first her responses had been timid, her own caresses hesitant and deliberate until the heat and texture of their melding bodies combined to implode her inner misgivings and she abandoned herself to the moments and hours to come. Sunday night there was no such worry and Monday morning, she told herself, no regret.

She missed Miranda, she thought, she hoped. She didn't know. She had no idea what exactly she missed: a friend, a cautious confidante, Miranda's soft touch, the feel of her body or all the years Dina let pass her by. She poured herself a generous Jean-Marc and flipped open the disposable phone she received by courier the day after her most recent facilitation. What she did know as she dialled the number she'd committed to memory was that Dina the Facilitator no longer existed.

"Yes."

"Who is this?"

"This is Pearl, and who would you be?"

"No, you're not Pearl. Thanks. Goodbye."

"Yes I am." The accented voice hurried to add, "from what sector are you calling, Pearl?"

The long pause was tense.

"Zone one, sector two," Dina answered.

"I know who you are, Pearl. Your code is Z-1, S-2, 457. I was told to expect your call. I'm your new director. Your previous director has retired. I believe you have something to tell me. Have you made a decision regarding your continued service?"

"You know?"

"Yes, as does Mother. She's very concerned about you, as was your previous director."

"I can no longer be a part of Pearl. I cannot operate as an Enabler. I can't do it. It's not who I am. I doubt whether I can even continue with my real life."

"I take your implication to mean professionally, not dramatically."

"Yes, of course, and now I need to know what happens next."

"What would you expect to happen? Future contact between us will simply cease and at some point in the years to come we will seem less real to you if, in fact, you won't deny whether we exist at all. Your funds will be deposited into your account on the first Monday of the coming month and what happens after is up to you. You're retired. I have reviewed your record. You will be sorely missed.

Personally, I will regret not working with you."

"Tell Mother this is her doing, not mine. I can't function as an Enabler. I wear guns seven days a week. How can she expect me to do that and wipe teary eyes? It's not who I am."

"We believe otherwise. Please reconsider. Take a vacation, time away? Pearl will gladly cover your expenses, wherever you wish to go. Your decision is not final until we end this call. Please reconsider."

"Thank you. My decision is final. I can't enable and there's no reason to pretend I can."

"Thank you for your candour."

Dina exhaled a slow breath. "So what do I do with my back-up MOP? Do I throw it out or return it."

"Has it been used?"

"No."

"Then destroy or dispose of it in an appropriate manner. It's legal, but we don't need unnecessary concerns."

"Understood. On another note, I was previously told my decision to leave would not affect my sister's situation."

"You were told correctly. I believe you have already arranged your departure date. We will not disappoint you or your sister, should the board approve his release. I was asked to inform you that certain newspaper articles of interest will be forwarded to you along with the primary MOP you left at the restaurant. Goodbye, Pearl."

"Wait." Dina held her breath, searching her mind for words. "Tell Mother that Pearl will always be a part of me. I will always look to help someone in trouble."

"She knows of your feelings and dedication already. However, as much as we regret your decision, we recognize the need to let you go. You will have no way to contact us in the future. Goodbye, Pearl."

Dina dropped onto her sofa, drained, completely depleted, staring at the disposable cellular in her hands. She was no longer Pearl. She was no longer Z-1, S-2, 457. She thought of Miranda. She had met with the director as well on the Sunday and she possessed a blacklip dagger, Pearl's coveted honour in recognition of thirty-one facilitations. The fifth service reward came to them as a cash bonus of fifty-thousand dollars. Miranda had accomplished as much by the age of thirty-two, which would boggle a reasonable mind, and she'd been asked to become an Enabler. Dina was certain. Miranda was too young to become a director, an appointment never awarded before age forty-five, and being an Enabler was a mandatory prerequisite to the exalted position.

Dina pushed herself to her feet. She redialled the director's number, the line was dead, but the director was wrong. She did have a link to Pearl. She went into the kitchen to wash and destroy the phone; she threw the pieces into the garbage and carried it to the garage. The pristine nine-millimetre 9000-S and silencer sent to her by Pearl to replace the weapon she'd discarded following the facilitation of a man she shot in the front seat of his car after he'd taken her to dinner would be sanitized, made unusable and taken by Wednesday's garbage collectors.

She had been on her way to a hotel with the man when she asked him to pull to the curb for a moment, explaining she felt ill. Seeing no one in the immediate vicinity, she leaned into the open door, shot him twice in the temple, took his wallet and watch, checked her dress and arms for splatter and walked several blocks to a restaurant for a dessert of cheese and wine. Before leaving she visited the ladies' room, paid the bill with cash and gave what remained of the man's few hundred dollars to a homeless woman as she strolled to her car.

Arriving home she undressed in her garage, showered thoroughly and went out to discard every piece of costume jewellery and clothing she'd worn to facilitate the man whose wife, days earlier, had taken her first vacation without him, a vacation paid for with his card as a birthday gift. The real gift was to never again be the victim of his rage. The police report was written up as a failed car-jacking and she heard a few days later how the woman had cried happy tears.

The last thing Dina wanted was a third gun, beyond that she didn't know what she wanted. That revelation wouldn't come to her until the following week. Her kitchen clock chimed 8:00. She was on her second vodka, retracing her steps from room to room, studying the dozens of photos she'd taken of Chérie posing in every possible position. Her lips curved into a smile. Going to the airport was the right thing to do and she was right to stay the night. Miranda's expression told her so in every photo.

She scooped up the glossies one by one and put them by her bed. Saturday she would buy an album, print more and file them by silly, seductive, naughty and nude. Nude. She snorted. She had a stack of nude pictures of a beautiful woman she met in a sophisticated bar and took to an exclusive spa for the weekend, a woman who bought her jewellery worth thousands of dollars, a woman who made her feel afraid, curious, uncertain, and now, more alone than ever. She would get over it, so would Miranda. They should never have happened and never would again. Dina would never be a cop in Toronto, Miranda would never be a trial lawyer in Quebec and they lived five hundred miles apart. They should have known better. What they did was ludicrous, stupid, and what the hell had she been doing in Le Discrèt of all places.

No sooner had Dina taken up the receiver of her bedside phone and punched in the number of her travel agent than she pressed a fingertip onto the nodule of its cradle cancelling the call. She had become a Pearl operative because of her sister, believing she would make a difference. Miranda had come to Quebec to facilitate Preston on behalf of Pearl and had gone to Le Discrèt because she was lonely. She had known what to expect, so had Dina. Le Discrèt wasn't frequented by straights. The club's theme was discretion, a step above and sophisticated. Not everyone got in. So why had she gone and why hadn't she left the moment Chérie walked out the door? Why did she stay and why did she so quickly suggest a weekend retreat.

Pearl had brought them together and would keep them apart, all for the best, she knew. What closeness they shared was ephemeral, dreamlike, as though Miranda had crept one night into her lonely dreams. There was no love between them. She'd spoken the words tenderly, caught up in the moment, so had Chérie. Not to play the part would have been absurd and, in someone else's real world, they might have become long-distance friends, eventually putting the silliness of the weekend behind them. What they shared was borne of loneliness, one woman's need and the other's curiosity. What they shared wasn't passion or romance, simply the need to escape desolate and parallel worlds. The weekend was a short-lived adventure that had gone too far. So what? She had a one-night stand with a woman that lasted three days and soon they would get on with their lives. Miranda would find someone she would genuinely love, not pretend to love while saying the words because they fit the heated mood, and so would she.

Dina redialled the number and left at a message at the sound of the tone.

"Sandy, hi, it's Dina Becker. Book me a First Class seat to Saint-Tropez this Saturday, the 18th, returning on the first. Book me into the usual place, the top corner suite and I'll need three or four theatre tickets for one. Some things never change. And don't forget a convertible, one I can fit into, something like an SL Class. Thanks, Sandy. You're a doll. Confirm ASAP."

She undressed and climbed into bed. Leaving the message for Sandy made her realize there would be no album the following day. That Miranda had awakened unfamiliar or suppressed emotions in her was sufficient.

She would put the photos in an envelope and store them in the bottom drawer of her dresser until one day she would come across them, laugh at what she had done and discard them. No one would ever see them. In four days she would be stretched out on the French Riviera and by the first there would be no Miranda lingering in her mind.

One day she would find someone special, so would Miranda. Pearl no longer existed; neither did the need to spend hours at the dojo or to sit in front of her muted television to practice reading the lips of someone she would soon kill. She was free, liberated. She had time. From now on she would join her squad for drinks on Fridays and become the old Dina they once knew and missed. Wednesday she would wear a short pleated skirt with a camisole under a sheer blouse to headquarters. On her hip she would wear her Berretta in the hand-made holster crafted from Italian leather with her name written in crystal sequins: a gift from Nancy she hadn't worn in years. The old Dina would walk in looking good. She would put her hair in a triple French braid, the way Miranda had taught her en route to the spa and call the commissioner from her office to advise him of her vacation.

Dina glanced over to the scattered pile of photos. Miranda had awakened long-forgotten feelings and all she had to do was determine whether those feelings were old or old mixed with new. She pulled the covers to her shoulders and waited for sleep.

Thirty-Six

Toronto, Ontario
Wednesday, August 15

The only girl who came to Miranda in her dreams that night was tall and sensuous with chestnut red hair and deep green eyes. Together they began each day aboard the party ship gazing beyond the railing of their luxury cabin toward the sun creeping above the horizon. In port they ran up and down white sandy beaches in the tiniest bikinis or strolled hand in hand, planning a future together. Each evening they danced until depleted of energy or consumed with passion when they returned to their elegant cabin to share a chaise-longue and stare at the moon.

The last morning of their Caribbean voyage Miranda awoke early and jumped from their down-filled bed to see and feel the golden sun, calling out for Dina. There was no response and what she saw from her bed was a heavy grey rain falling over Lake Ontario that blurred the more she blinked. Her head drooped. The dream was so real: the caressing, the kissing and laughing. Miranda let herself slump sideways onto the mattress and yanked the sheets over her head.

When the alarm sounded she shouted at the clock-radio, telling it to shut up and go away. There would be no morning balcony ritual. Rain was cascading down her windows in thick rivulets, the sky was black and for once in his career the weatherman was either right or lucky. She dragged herself from the bed and into the shower. Stepping into the glass stall she stubbed her toes hard and cursed, absently swinging the lever from off to full as she leaned forward to examine the scraped skin. Harsh pellets of frigid water instantly assailed her warm body, producing a high-pitched scream and more expressive vocabulary. She tried to escape the onslaught by pressing herself against a glass wall, which was no better at 6:00 in the morning. As the water warmed to tepid she reached for the empty shampoo bottle, stomping her feet, and when she reached to the top edge of the stall where she neglected to put her towel she knew the general direction her day would take.

She screamed inwardly, a deep frustrated groan. She wanted to call in sick, but she promised Troy Torrington she would bring her files up to-date and brief her co-workers on pending cases before leaving on vacation, a vacation she hadn't yet planned.

Breakfast was out of the question. She would either burn something or the milk would be sour, so why bother? She would grab something on her way to the office, she thought, and die of food poisoning. Dressing, she put runs in two pairs of thirty-dollar pantyhose, she put her blouse on inside out and when she tried again she mismatched the buttons.

Seven AM was too early to make the call. She hesitated. She thought Pearl might be too old to have a full-time job, unless being a director at Pearl was her full-time job. She didn't know. She wondered whether anyone knew besides Mother. She dialled and the call was answered on the first ring.

"Yes."

A worried Miranda Stevens pressed end. Whoever answered the phone was not Pearl. Before she could punch in a secondary number which would connect her with the west coast director her cell chimed.

"Hello."

"Good morning, Pearl. Thank you for your caution. I am the newly appointed director for Zone One. My code is Z-1, S1-189. The previous director is no longer available to you, though I am familiar with your dossier. If you wish you may verify with your secondary director before we continue."

"When did I last meet her?"

"Last Sunday. You spoke about continuing on with a change in responsibilities. She sends her regards."

"Where is she?"

"You know better than to ask, perhaps buying a new bikini or short dress."

Miranda relaxed. "I hope so. If you see her, tell her I liked her. She was always kind to me."

"I will, and have you given your future further consideration, though you need not tell me at this very moment?"

"The answer is affirmative at this point. I can't speak to the future. Who knows?"

"Good. Mother will be very pleased, as I am."

"I'm leaving on a vacation this Friday, no phones, nothing. I'll be back sometime on the twenty-sixth."

"Which is your first vacation in a long time, I believe."

"Yeah, something like that."

"Enjoy yourself. Goodbye, Pearl."

"Goodbye, director."

Miranda slipped the phone into her purse, rubbed a wide circle of fog from her front window, deciding against taking the Aston Martin to avoid an inevitable side-swipe, fender-bender or having to report it stolen at the end of the day. Anyway, she could walk to work as quickly as driving in stalled traffic.

Dressed in a bright pink rain cape, a sou'wester and matching rubber boots, she set out for a day of hell trudging along with one hand securing her hat, the other trying to control her purse, briefcase and shoe bag.

Mother of Pearl

By the end of the first half-mile, bent into a cutting wind and cold, biting rain, she was assaulted by Styrofoam coffee cups, soggy sheets of airborne newspapers and her cape was littered with bits and pieces of street dirt that wouldn't wash away with four more blocks to go. At last, the building was in sight, less than half a block. The boulevard was a virtual river and she stopped dead with her eyes opened wide as the drab yellow cab and brown wall of dirty city water rushed at her like an urban tsunami. She turned her back to the onslaught and braced herself against the impact that jolted her in real time and continued on in slow motion, washing away her hat, flooding under her raised collar which acted as a conduit, filling her calf-high boots with icy, gritty water.

A passer-by who was soaked through returned her hat, grimacing sympathetically, asking whether she was hurt. He was good-looking, thoughtful to have run after her hat. She was fine, she replied, seething, making a great effort to be kind in return. She thanked him, and continued on her way before she thought to strangle him.

At the doors to the Justice Building she emptied one boot, then the other to the amusement of many, though when she practically tumbled through the double doors of the Prosecutor's Offices in stocking feet her day reached its peak. She dropped her rubber boots and three bags onto the floor, added her hat to the pile and wrestled from her cape. Her co-workers looked on in awe, one of them reaching discreetly for a phone and seconds later a curious Troy Torrington nonchalantly exited his private office ostensibly to discuss an urgent matter with the caller. No one spoke a word.

She glared at them, a dishevelled mess, silently daring them. Her dripping hair hung in thick, tangled braids, her eyes were ice blue centres set in small black wells and her cheeks were streaked with dark, blue-black veins. He blouse was soaked through, pulled partly out of her wet skirt that had ridden to the tops of her thighs and her push-up bra showed through perfectly as she stood panting in her stocking feet.

Troy broke the ice. "Mir, what's with the party costume? Hell, if you need extra money that bad, you can dance for us. Isn't that so, men?"

The men cheered, each one reaching into his pocket for a ten to wave. The women wanted to smile; Miranda was quite the spectacle despite their compassion for one of their own. Miranda failed to see the humour and stooped over to gather her belongings in one sweep of her hands. Some of the men leaned this way or that or craned their necks, booing in unison as one of the women hurried to tug down the back of Miranda's skirt.

When she stood she held her head high and sauntered past them with as much dignity as she could muster, leaving wet footprints and a narrow trail of water across to her office where she closed the door quietly, slumped against it and covered her mouth to laugh. She was drenched with nothing to wear save the black robe strictly reserved for court appearances.

Pushing off her wet pantyhose was like peeling a skin not quite ready to shed. Her skirt was next, which she kicked to the far side of her office before shedding her clammy blouse and bra. That done, she opened her door and curtsied to loud applause with one hand holding the lower edges of her robe together as a single, bright flash filled the room. Then she snubbed them and went to work. Her first priority was leaving town on Friday. By the end of the workday her clothes were returned to her in original condition by her intern and tickets had been delivered for the air and sea portions of a one-week cruise through the islands sailing from Miami on Saturday.

She spent thirty minutes on the phone with the travel agent explaining she didn't care what ports of call the ship would sail into, all she wanted was to get away and bask in the sun for a week. The cabin was secondary. She would spend her time at the pool and on the beaches. Besides, at the prices he was quoting the accommodations would be superior. She understood two days wasn't much time, she repeated a dozen times, assuring the agent before disconnecting that she would be satisfied with whatever cruise was available.

She leaned into her executive chair and stretched. Suddenly the forecast seemed promising.

Thirty-Seven

Quebec City, Quebec
Thursday, August 16

Dina had more on her mind than Miranda, though Miranda was at the root of each thought which went far beyond self-doubt. She had to get away, not strictly to avoid being a primary person of interest in an upcoming murder investigation, but to find herself, discover the true Dina Becker, and perhaps make a dream come true. The recurring daydream had been with her for years: a fanciful whim, something to hold onto.

Wednesday at the precinct there wasn't a person she passed who didn't stop what they were doing to appreciate the view. In the squad room her team of detectives was initially taken aback. The men recovered first. One took her by the hand and twirled her in a tight circle, others came over to stare at her legs and a handful of others swore they were simply admiring the gold pendant hanging from her neck. The women in the squad checked the waistband of her skirt and the collars of her blouse and fitted jacket looking for labels they should have known wouldn't be there. When they saw the chrome Beretta in the special red holster they knew the old Dina was back.

One man, a senior detective whom Dina called to task for his shenanigans on a weekly basis, yelled out "camera" as he effortlessly swept his captain into his arms and planted her on his desktop before proceeding to help Dina cross one leg over the other. No one else would have dared. He had special privilege whether she would ever admit as much or not. He was the one to physically remove Dina from her sister's murder scene and the one to keep her focused and sane throughout the several weeks of mourning and the trial of Nancy's killer. He was a good friend.

He eased onto the desk beside her, draped an arm around her shoulders and beamed. The other men wanted in, complaining their aging mothers would show more leg, and the photo session lasted five minutes with Dina constantly slapping away teasing hands. They all found a need visit her office several times on Wednesday, if only to ask the time. She loved the attention and ignored them.

Thursday was no different, other than a different coloured skirt and blouse, until the same mischievous cop asked aloud where Dina was concealing her backup weapon. Her face flushed in concert with the guffaws of the men and curious expressions from the women and she walked out shaking her head to meet with the commissioner who had gone to SVU himself the previous day to witness the rebirth of his favourite cop and godchild: a fact known to them alone.

"You've made my week, Di. When we lost your sister ten years ago, we lost you as well, and then my Camille was taken from me. I wish she was here with me to see your renaissance.
Losing the three of you in such short a time was difficult."

"I'm not sure I am all the way back, Claude. Let's say I've cleared the first hurtle. I'm trying very hard."

"Whatever you need, Di. Quite apart from the gold shield on your hip, captain, you're still my girl. I haven't forgotten my promise or responsibility to your father and mother."

"I know, Claude. You've always been there for me and I'm afraid I've taken a lot for granted too often, and again today. I need a vacation. I've booked a flight to France for this Saturday. I'll be gone a couple of weeks. There's something I have to do, or not, something to help me come to terms with myself one way or the other. Either way, that's where I'll find the answer."

"Are we talking about your dream villa, Di?" Claude Jordan sounded concerned.

"Yeah, we are. Something happened this week, Claude, something completely off the wall. It's behind me and not a topic for conversation, but what happened forced me to look inside myself to see who I am. I've missed out for ten years, my own doing. I know. It's time lost, time I'll never recoup and I don't want to lose anymore."

"Then don't. Go. Do what you have to do. Build the damn thing once and for all."

Dina nodded. "Yeah, I might just do that to know whether I've been escaping all these years or coming home for no reason. Thanks boss."

"I believe you already know the answer and the blame is undeniably your father's. He should never have made me promise to send you and Nancy away to that bedevilled school. Bless his and your mother's souls. You've been smitten with the cursed Côte d'Azur ever since. Home is where the heart is, Di. What you've neglected these past years is your heart. Find that and you'll know where your home is." He leaned forward onto his desk. "I'm not so old that I can't visit occasionally and treat my favourite godchild to a superb glass of wine."

"I'm your only godchild, Claude, and a woman in case you haven't noticed."

"Apparently everyone's noticed lately, young lady. Now get out of here."

Dina leaned over the desk to kiss her godfather's cheek. "Thanks, Claude. I'll bring you a bottle of Bordeaux and when I get home we'll go to dinner so you can hear all about it."

"I would prefer a home-cooked meal. It's been quite some time since you've invited me to enjoy an exquisite dinner. So bring me a suitably fine bottle."

"I will."

He watched her walk to the door. "Di... one more thing before you leave."

"Yes, Claude."

He grinned. "You're looking very hot, if I may be so bold, from the perspective of a fellow cop and godfather."

Dina's face lit and her mouth opened into a wide, silent laugh. "Camille would call you a dirty old man for saying that."

"Camille would be right. Now get out of here and, in future, please do not disrupt the entire building with anything shorter unless you intend to captain a squad of cheerleaders." He cleared his throat. "I'll ignore the Beretta."

"Thank you, sir."

Thursday night Dina left the squad room at 8:00 PM and sat waiting in her XKR. The weekend was a tease, a game, which began one week earlier because she wanted a quiet place to think without being bothered by lonely men with expense accounts or loud music. She went to Le Discrèt once on a whim, with no understanding why she had gone the second time or why she wrapped her arms so tightly around Miranda twelve hours later at the shuttle stop en route to a spa weekend. They came together so unexpectedly, so naturally. She spent the weekend at a spa the way another woman might have spent a weekend at a ski resort with an absolute stranger, a man, no strings attached and no commitment. But she didn't do that. Or did she ...with a woman?

She pulled out from the driveway. What began as a girls' weekend seemed so natural, as though she'd known Miranda her entire life, she thought repeatedly as she drove along the crowded Grande-Allée and through the historic gates of Vieux-Québec, or was the weekend inevitable and Miranda merely a catalyst? The valet recognized her. He greeted her with a smile, the doorman bowed slightly and she walked past him into the quiet ambiance of muted lighting and soft music. She sat not facing the bar, intent on leaving after one drink.

The bargirl greeted her with a wide smile, asking if the other lady, the one who was with Dina the week before, would be joining her. Dina smiled weakly and shook her head, explaining how the lady had been in town on business and had come to Le Discrèt by mistake, believing the lounge offered a more conventional ambiance. The girl frowned sympathetically, her disappointment real, telling Dina how she thought the lady was so friendly, so genuine and how they seemed to enjoy each other's company.

Dina agreed, unable to resist a smile. If anything, Miranda was genuine and friendly. Oh, yeah, very friendly. Dina ordered a Jean-Marc XO with a single cube of ice and when the vodka came she leaned into the plush sofa to contemplate her vacation and wonder why she said Miranda came to the lounge in error when neither one had. What had she really meant to say? And why was she sitting in Le Discrèt dressed to kill when she knew very well no guy would pick her up.

Thirty-Eight

La Montérégie, East of Montreal
Friday, August 17

Pearl Bingham arrived at Mary's estate a few minutes after a dark and ominous dawn to spend the day with her mother, surprised to see Mary awake in her private rooms and speaking with one of her staff. Pearl had spent the previous day at the estate until Mary insisted she go home to spend the evening with her husband, promising an agitated Pearl with feigned annoyance she would not be so selfish as to pass away in the meantime.

Pearl had been death's courier for thirty-two years, telling loved ones of patients their nearest or dearest had passed on. This was different. This was Mary dying and Pearl found any reason not to sleep until she could be by her mother's side and the day could not have portended the worst of all outcomes any more ferociously. The sky was black with rumbling clouds streaked with lightning and heavy rain swirled in wild, cyclonic gusts. Trees along the road swayed violently in all directions and the river splashed up erratic curtains of dark grey water along its narrow bank. Even the wrought iron gates seemed portentous as she activated her remote and passed through them to drive a quarter-mile to the understated façade of the mansion she had never thought of as sinister or unfriendly until then.

Peering into her rear-view mirror from inside the lighted garage she saw the raging tempest as a morbid canvas splashed with the silver of swirling rain. A deep sense of gloom and foreboding swept over her and she stayed as she was, afraid she had arrived too late. She hadn't. Despite her failing heart and strict instructions from her doctor, Mary had been up for an hour. She had spent much of the past week with Beverly Price, transferring responsibilities and meeting with the Directorate who accepted Beverly's appointment without the slightest resentment. Jasmine had Leclerc accepted the position of director and had met privately with Beverly to discuss the recent meetings with Dina Becker and Miranda Stevens as well as the histories of the other women who operated in her new zone.

Before their departure Tuesday evening, Mary met with each woman to say goodbye and gave each one a personal gift which they weren't to open until after her passing. The already well-to-do women were soon to become much wealthier and Mary would spend her remaining days with her daughter Pearl.

"Darling, the day is much too frightful to be driving around. You know perfectly well I would have sent the car for you, you silly girl."

"I know, mother. However, there's no one on the road out here this time of day and I'm perfectly capable."

"You were always so determined."

"I learned from you."

Mary gazed beyond her window. "I'm very proud of you, darling, and of my ring. I have so much to say and so little time."

"I have known doctors to be wrong in the past, mother. I'm not letting you leave."

"She's not wrong, darling, and you have no choice. Now you must listen to me, very attentively."

"Feldman Cosmetics will change owners officially on September 06, as you requested, and your staff will be remembered by you per your instruction."

Mary raised a hand to stop Pearl from talking. She had no doubt of her daughter's ability to act as temporary CEO until the sale of Feldman was completed.

"Pearl, I asked you to listen. Please do so. What I have to say is important, darling."

"Yes, mother, of course. I'm listening."

"It was on a night like this that I first gave myself to him. I was a virgin. I was so excited to have a man in my room, which was very scandalous in those days. The very thought of entertaining a gentleman privately was outrageous. He went to sleep on the floor right away, without so much as a word, so did I, in my bed. The next thing I remembered was waking to a horrible pain. You were born nine months later and I took you home to thirteen years of deprivation and misery."

Pearl knew not to mention his name. "No, mother, you took me home to years of love, your love. I enjoyed growing up with you. I remember our times at the lake when we swam and spoke about everything."

"You were too young to know. Our two brightest days were the day we left that horrible place and the day I met Marge Feldman."

"I remember how you looked when you came home. You were so pretty. I would never have believed when I used to walk from school to the mill that one day I would wear French imports and fly in my mother's personal jet, not to mention becoming a surgeon."

"Not a surgeon, darling, the best surgeon. I'm so happy you decided not to spend your career writing prescriptions for the flu." Mary looked at her ring. "There are so many pearls, darling, so much work still to be done, work we will never finish. Everyday there's another pearl somewhere, another velvet box held in trembling hands." She hesitated. "Do you remember the day of Averly's funeral, darling?"

"Yes, I do remember."

"It was the day I gave you your ring."

"Mother..."

"Please listen, Pearl. On August 31st I would like you to be home by yourself. You might send Robert off golfing or fishing. Please find an excuse for him not to be at home. You will receive a visitor, darling. Her name is Beverly. She is a very good friend of mine and you have a good deal in common. I have asked her to tell you a story." Mary held up a hand. "If I wished for you to know now, darling, I would tell you and you must believe every word Beverly tells you and take time to understand the full meaning of her words before making a judgement. Promise me you will take the time."

"Is she a lawyer, an employee at Feldman?"

"I do hope it's a lovely day when she visits. She's not far from your age, darling, a very nice woman as well as a very long-standing and good friend."

"I've never heard you mention a Beverly."

"Had things been different you might have been friends. She is a very nice lady and I want you to be kind to her."

"Why would I not be kind to her, mother, and why must I send Robert away?"

"Because, darling, I have asked that he be away. If I did not consider his absence necessary, I would not have asked."

Pearl rested her hand over her mother's. "Mary, Mary, quite contrary."

Her mother brought a thin smile to her lips. "I used to pretend I was quite miffed with you when you would sing that as I was trying to be stern with you. I never could be angry with you. I have always loved you so very much."

"I know, mother. You always were more like my older sister...you always will be."

"Tell Robert goodbye for me. He is a very good man."

"I'll do no such thing. He'll be here later this morning to cheer you up."

Mary chortled weakly. "In that case, darling, I trust he has a heavy foot." Mary inhaled a shallow breath and paused. "All I have to leave you are a few simple photo albums of our trips abroad together and a little something for your nest egg. I could have been more generous, darling, but so many others share a greater need."

"You made me very wealthy before I was thirty-five, mother. Robert was very uneasy when he first discovered exactly how wealthy. He still tells me he would have preferred a poor woman, not that he doesn't enjoy occasional trips on the jet. He constantly complains about being a kept man."

"I've always liked him. I've never doubted him, not like the other."

"Mother, I don't ..."

A lucid Mary ignored her daughter and pressed a fingertip against her ring. "I will leave this to my dearest friend, darling. It's all I have to give her from my failing heart. She will know whenever she wears it how much her friendship has meant to me since we first came to know one another, as one day very soon someone will wear yours."

"But, mother, you once asked me never to part with my ring."

"And you won't." Mary's voice was becoming weaker. She asked Pearl to fluff her pillows and to hold her hand. "My lawyers will act on my behalf and according to my wishes. There is no need for you to bother with anything so mundane. They have negotiated the sale of the jet and I'm afraid Robert will have to suffer with public transport in future or buy his own. This place has also been sold. Nothing from the estate is bequeathed to you, darling. It's not quite your taste and will go to a charity in accordance with my wishes."

"Mother, I don't like this. It's time to rest. Close your eyes, for me, and I'll see to a light breakfast for us."

"Darling, the time will come one day when you will not want to close your eyes." She squeezed Pearl's hands with feeble fingers and exerted a tender smile. "I want to see you for as long as I have left. Closing my eyes will hasten what I most loathe in the little time which is left to me: not seeing you."

"Such talk is making me angry with you."

"No, darling. What you are is sad, and you should not be. We have been like sisters since you were a little girl and you will miss me, for a time darling. Remember, you have Robert and, one day, I hope a very long time from now, we will be sisters again in a much better place."

"Mother, please rest. You're exerting yourself for no reason and upsetting me."

"You're quite right, darling. The time has come for me to rest, after I tell you one last time how I love you so much. I will always love you, if I cannot be with you. Promise me, darling, to take the time and remember there is good in everything we do... in everything we do."

"I love you, mother. Now rest while I see to your breakfast."

"Promise me you will remember my words, Pearl. Very soon they will become important to you and eventually you will understand them."

"I promise, mother, and I insist that you rest. You are much too weak to be argumentative."

"You're quite right. I should rest. Goodbye, my darling."

Mary held out her cheek for a kiss and turned her head into her pillow as Pearl tiptoed to the door which she left slightly ajar, leaving Mary to speak her daughter's name in a whisper and close her eyes for the last time.

Thirty-Nine

Miami, Florida
Friday, August 17

When Miranda walked into the Prosecutor's Offices Thursday morning no one acknowledged her, until she passed them and stopped at her door. The blow-up of the bedraggled and dark-eyed sorceress from the previous day swirling in her black robe was framed and mounted on her door. Below the frame was the brass caption: Knock First! At her feet was a 12-inch square box wrapped in pink foil.

She reached for the gift, her scowl widening into a bright smile, saying they certainly had better knock first, particularly on rainy days. She tore at the packaging and the wrapping of the little boxes inside, oohing and wowing over the sun screens, après sun creams, lipsticks and eye shadows from the girls. The men had chipped in as well, Troy Torrington giving a willing intern extra lunch time to drive into the suburbs in Wednesday's torrential downpour in search of the quintessential thong set which he found in an exclusive boutique well-known to the young man.

She hugged each of the girls and disappointed the men. She wouldn't model the bikini for them, adding they had seen quite enough of her the day before. However, she did give them each a peck on the cheek, bringing them hope. She might have her picture taken in it, she taunted, holding the thong to her hips with a sensuous "oooh" escaping her

369

lips, if she could find someone to hold the camera. They went wild, causing the women to shake their heads with feigned disgust. Miranda was impossible not to love.

Friday she was at Person International four hours ahead of time, the one woman not draped in pastel polyester or looking like a hooker with straw-blonde hair, low-rise jeans with thong handles, tank tops and artificially dark skin. Miranda was Miranda in a linen suit with a short skirt, a silk hair band and a Gucci handbag. She looked fabulous, so fabulous, in fact, that no one spoke to her at the gate or in the First Class cabin. She didn't care. She was on vacation and the first ten minutes soaring through a low, buffeting ceiling streaked with jagged white light was a small price to pay, irrespective of the nervous young girl sitting beside her who held her hand and was crushing her fingers to pulp.

Above the clouds was not much better, her sole distraction the talkative little creature who wasn't letting go of Miranda's hand and who thought Miranda should be brought up to date on her school work and her vacation with her grandparents. The mainly one-sided conversation lasted through to the announcement that all trays and seatbacks should be brought to their upright positions as the jet circled for its final approach.

The taxi was a Jeep Cherokee, which she thought was somewhat unusual. Crossing the yacht-filled inter-coastal waterway the taxi slowed for no apparent reason. There was no traffic, nor was there anything of particular interest to see. The waterway was dismal, abandoned, and more ominous-looking than impressive. The tall, exotic rows of high-rise condos and hotels lining the A1A appeared dull, the black ocean was dotted with drab white caps and what she found the most peculiar were the few people who were out were walking, seemingly unbothered by the torrential rain.

The hotel was chic. In her room the bellboy placed her luggage inside the door, drawing the drapes and explaining she might have to wait until morning to see the Atlantic Ocean. He slipped the twenty into his pocket and promised to be at her door at 6:00 AM. Alone, she opened the bag she'd carried onboard the plane as a precaution, although, much to her surprise her other suitcase arrived safely. She showered, changed into linen slacks and a sweater and went to dinner. She never ate airline food, believing those meals consisted mostly of leftover food donated to the failing airlines by hospitals. She was starving and stood staring in awe at the hectic display of hungry humans vying to be the first to fill their plates from the communal troughs.

The maître d' noticed the undisguised grimace and approached her, concerned the young woman might be daunted by the clamour of dishes and the general melee of bodies narrowly avoiding collision, more intent on balancing overloaded plates or wine goblets defying the basic principal of cohesion. The hotel was noted for its buffet selection and the wine list was second to none, he explained. She asked whether room service was taken from the buffet. He replied definitely not and politely wrote her order, accepting the responsibility of selecting an appropriate wine.

Miranda went to her room with no intention of eating food previously examined or prodded under something called a Sneeze Shield by men with hairy, bare arms or children whose social etiquette wasn't yet perfected. She fell asleep on a full stomach by 8:00, in a superior suite lit solely by the kaleidoscope of colours emanating from the plasma screen in the armoire. The wine bottle was half-full, and the first day of her exotic vacation was behind her.

Dina Becker was nursing her second vodka in a bar appropriately named Le Flic for its primary customer base: the cops of the First Precinct. She felt good. She felt right being with her squad once more and they felt good having her there.

Forty

Miami, Florida
Saturday, August 18

The young bellboy was at Miranda's door at 6:00, thanking God and his Aztec ancestors for deeming he should be a man as he gazed upon the golden-haired angel in hip-hugging Capri pants, sandals and a loose-fitting open-knit three-quarter sweater draped over one shoulder. She was perfection and he screamed at himself to focus on her deep blue eyes, remembering the creed of the hotel bellboy: see a little and remember a lot, see a lot and get fired. He needed his job, almost as much as he wanted to see more of Miranda as she sauntered in front of him to the elevators and through the lobby.

The cruise liner was white and enormous and the port authority looked more like New York's Fifth Avenue on Easter Sunday lined with high-rise buildings and thousands of coloured streamers floating to the street. She was one of the last passengers to board.

The purser greeted her with effusive attention, insisting he personally escort Miranda to her cabin, discovering nothing more than her name by the time she closed the door on him. She knew everything about him and didn't care. What she cared about was what had become of the luxury cabin she had imagined for the past few days. The entire suite could fit into her bathroom at home. The king-size bed she dreamt about was a berth, a lower bunk bed, her closet was a phone booth with hangers and the bathroom would force her to hold in her already tight stomach and arch her already slim back to avoid touching the sink, toilet or sides of the shower stall.

She called the purser's office. He was apologetic in the extreme, suggesting all he could do to make her first day more pleasant would be to arrange for her to dine with the captain that evening. Unfortunately, the ship's passenger roster was full. She groaned, telling him she couldn't care less about the captain and demanded to be transferred to Cabin Service who assured her the bottle of Ulimat would be delivered within the quarter-hour.

She was locked in her room staring out from the single twelve-inch diametre porthole with nothing to see other than the port side wall of a neighbouring ship. The moonlit balcony she had dreamt of, had looked so forward to, was a dream long gone as she counted the portholes of the first neighbouring ship, followed in quick succession by the second and third as the one she was on manoeuvred into open water. She was on her second vodka when, at five past five, the purser knocked on her door to remind her of the mandatory procedure being performed on deck.

The sky was furious, the air was surprisingly chilled, and Miranda dropped her lifejacket onto a deck chair when the mundane routine was over. She wanted to scream. Instead she went to her cabin, poured a stiff drink and looked out over the raging sea. By the time she forced herself into a strapless cocktail dress for the 9:00 PM sitting she had thrown up three times, looked the way she felt and hated the world. She wanted off and didn't care at what cost. She wanted off. Six of the seven passengers joining her for dinner were attached, the seventh was the purser. Go figure, she thought, as though he would ever have a chance in a freezing hell. He'd have a better chance of screwing the captain.

She went to bed and lay atop the covers in twelve-foot seas, staring at the toilet. She already regretted the small portions she had managed to ingest of the six-course dinner. Her throat burned, her mouth tasted of gastric acid and tiny bits of regurgitated matter she hadn't washed out still clung to her palate and tongue. Her body was shivering, yet she was sweating. She moaned, curling into a ball, making herself feel worse. She sat on her knees, looked into the mirror and smiled with her arms outstretched, thinking that would make her feel better, seeing her eyes grow wide as her mouth instinctively snapped shut in response to the mounting gastric surge about to explode from between her lips.

She half leapt, half scrambled from the berth, barely reaching the ceramic bowl in time. She rinsed her mouth with bottled water, repeated the process with expensive vodka and stuck her finger into her throat, waiting. Nothing. Then she poured two-fingers deep into a glass, took a few sips and went to bed where she sat with a pillow between her knees and her chest.

When she woke, nothing but blackness existed beyond the cabin's single porthole and she cursed. The ship was still being pounded by waves, though not as severely. The rollercoaster ride replaced by a gentle rocking motion broken by occasional jolts. She had no television and she hadn't thought to bring magazines or a book. She knew she wouldn't fall back to sleep and sunrise was hours away, although she did feel better. She looked at her drink and grimaced. Booze never looked as good after a nap as before one. She cupped her hands over her face and inhaled a puff of air she expelled from her mouth, making her cough.

She tossed aside the pillow and threw her legs over the side of the narrow bed. She was miserable, although intellectually she knew the emotion was moot, like someone yelling or swearing when they're alone: wasted energy. She was beautiful, young, and had a great career happening for herself: the dream of every modern girl next door. That's what people like Troy repeatedly told her. So what?

Miranda pinned her hair, showered, changed into a warm fleecy top and shorts, slipped under the covers and buried her head under the pillow to wait out the night. She breathed deeply, telling herself to grow up and to stop being pitiful. By noon the next day the sun would be out, she would be sunning on the beaches of Grand Cayman, shopping at beachside markets in her new bikini and making some woman crazy. Out of all those women, someone had to look twice.

Miranda had no sooner begun feeling better about the day ahead than she bolted upright at the deafening blasts of the ship's horn. She threw aside the covers and bolted to the porthole, expecting to see an iceberg or another ship on a collision course. What she saw was another ship passing in the night. She turned on the cabin light and went to her purse to check her watch. The time was 11:30 AM, Sunday, and black as night.

In Saint Tropez Dina Becker was sitting at a café-terrasse, sipping Pernod. The late-day sun was pleasant against her bare arms and face and a gentle sea breeze teased her long, flowing hair. To her left was the blue Mediterranean; to her right on a hillside cliff was a villa whose every detail could be seen by her alone. Directly in front of Dina was the architect who would design and build the villa for her.

Forty-One

Montreal, Quebec
Sunday, August 19

Claire Duval loathed the idea of what she would do in the coming hours as she sat in a pew directly behind the congenial Heather Hancock, watching the woman pray and sing so joyously. No matter how gently she wanted to treat her case study the older woman would suffer terribly over the coming days and likely not feel safe in her own home for a very long time.

Claire tracked her at the end of seven work days and throughout the previous two weekends. Each night Ms. Hancock stopped at the local market to pick up fresh ingredients for dinner. The market's staff knew her. They called her by name, smiled at her as she paid at the cash and told her of the next day's specials. Once at home behind the locked door of her first-floor apartment she stayed in. She had no friends, her phone bill was basic and her credit card reflected a life that was as modest as her wardrobe. Her big day was Sunday when, after the market, she would rent DVDs of Hollywood's golden era.

Mother of Pearl had one consistent and unalterable directive: The operatives of Pearl were to pay meticulous attention to matters of dress. Their wardrobes were their camouflage, their ultimate defence after skill and planning.

Claire Duval was twenty-eight and a svelte 5'7" with

white titanium hair. She loved life, now that she had one, she loved dancing and she loved each new day. She'd begun dating several months earlier after the report came back from Pearl that everything the man said of himself was accurate. She'd been to hell and wasn't going back. She loved her son; she was beginning to love her man, suffering a pang of regret that Heather Hancock would go home alone after a brunch given by the Women's Club at Saint George's United and stops at the market and video store.

The Benoit Voisine parole hearing was being held the following day and her director agreed the action should take place Sunday afternoon. Each of the previous nights Claire wore different ten-dollar sweaters, shorts she had bought at a bazaar, running shoes, baseball caps and drugstore sunglasses. By the nineteenth the inexpensive wardrobe was given to the mission. The outfits were camouflage suitable to the month of August in a low-rent part of a city fast becoming known for litter-strewn streets and a decaying infrastructure, its European charm and flavour diluted into non-existence by the same immigration that had spawned fifty different street gangs.

La rue Fort was no exception. The alleyways were dark and dank any time of year, parked cars substituted as available seating for those whose steps and doorways were too unclean or too uneven to spend idle afternoons and evenings sitting on while drinking beer or toking. Heather lived in a place she could not afford to leave and Claire would fit in perfectly. She even called the building's super enquiring as to which apartments might be available to buy or rent. Then she rented a van.

At church on the second Sunday Claire was ravishing from her chapeau to her shoes. The elders greeted her at the door with smiles, unabashedly letting their eyes follow her as she sat behind Heather in the same pew as the previous week. She refused the offer to stay for brunch, claiming she was a tourist on a timetable to meet her husband who believed more in plastic chips than God. She left promising to worship with them sometime soon, and she would. Claire would return the following week. Beverly Price and Mother hadn't devised a way to compensate Heather Hancock for the experience she was about to endure. The ideal reparation came from Claire. She would return to Saint George's United the following week, the final weekend of her ostensible vacation, when she would place an envelope containing seventy-five crisp thousand-dollar bills into the collection plate. Twenty-five of which would be Claire's fee she told the director she could not accept.

Moments after the priest's benediction, Heather stood in line to perform the weekly post-service ritual expected of all good church-goers. She shook hands with her minister and the elders; she complimented the choir leader on his selection of hymns and praised his wife's buffet. Then she grabbed onto the handrail, guided herself down the granite steps and walked away singing a hymn that was as unfamiliar to Claire as any other.

This time Claire waited outside the market as Heather went in to plan her dinner. Seeing her enter the video store Claire climbed into the rented van she parked at the strip mall before walking to church. When Heather came out Claire had changed into dirty sweats, a faded and shapeless tee-shirt, black running shoes, huge sunglasses, a wool cap drawn down over her forehead with purple hair spraying outward in all directions, tattered gloves and had gone to the apartment. Claire didn't believe in God. She believed in what she was doing and that any kind and benevolent God would understand.

Heather Hancock stopped at the bottom of the stairs and looked up at the young woman who was cursing at not being able to open the door.

"The lock hasn't worked properly in a long time, miss.

The girl turned, sounding exasperated and annoyed. "What?"

"Here, let me help you. There's a trick."

"Never mind, I got it." Claire tried again, raising her voice. "Why don't they fix the damn thing?"

Heather moved in closer, holding her own key. "Let me try. You must be the new tenant."

"Duh, I think so. I'm in like 211." The door opened on the first try. "No shit."

"Welcome. I'm sure you'll enjoy being here. The people are very nice."

"Whatever."

Claire couldn't believe the mild-mannered woman beside her was the key component to a team of three whose sole function was to define a man's or woman's future with a simple yes or no. She could have been a grandmother or a nun. Claire squeezed through the half-open door first, leaving Heather to manage the door and her bags. Once inside Claire stood at the bottom of the staircase, waiting for Heather to pass.

"My name is Heather, Heather Hancock in 109. I hope you have a nice day."

Claire looked over her shoulder. "What?"

"I said have a nice day. I'm in 109, if you ever need anything."

"Yeah, whatever."

Heather continued on, stopping at her door. Claire waited for the sound of the deadbolt she'd seen on door 109 the previous day.

"Hey, lady, hold on."

"Yes?" Heather asked.

"I do need something. Can I like use your phone or something?"

"Of course you may. Come in."

Heather stepped in to hold the door open for the young woman whom she thought would look so pretty in a dress after a good wash and a haircut. Claire stepped in behind her and counted to three as Heather's bags fell to the floor and her body toppled against the door, closing it. Heather Hancock would remain unconscious for twenty-four hours, by which time the puncture wound would disappear and she would awaken to a violent headache and extreme nausea that would cloud her memory of the girl she'd invited into her apartment.

Claire remained half an hour to complete her assignment, leaving with a full suitcase. Before she left she knelt by Heather's side and apologized, explaining how a young woman was once shot in the back of the head as she returned home from what her jealous ex-boyfriend believed was a date with someone new. She had gone to a museum, alone, and met a neighbour on the way home. The murder was senseless, cold and cowardly, Claire explained matter-of-factly, and they couldn't take the chance he would live a day longer than required to eliminate him, whether in prison or on the street.

Claire walked the half-mile to the van, inconspicuously tossing the wig, cap, gloves and glasses into separate garbage bins as she went. Closer to the van she pulled off her top, a block later her sweatpants and shoes and arrived wearing flat sandals with shorts and a halter top she would dispose of later in the evening along with her church outfit, the syringe and what she'd taken from Heather's apartment.

When she stepped from the van across town she was once again fashionable Claire Duval, feeling no pride when calling her director to confirm a successful assignment. Moments later Jasmine Leclerc placed a call to Noelle Barton, telling her to expect a call from a member of the parole board the following day.

Forty-Two

Sainte-Anne-des-Plaines, North of Montreal
Monday, August 20

The Montreal police responded to a call from Heather Hancock's worried supervisor when she failed to report for a pre-assessment meeting at her office or the Sainte-Anne-des-Plaines medium security correctional institution as scheduled at 11:00 AM, nor was there a response from her home phone or cellular. They discovered her lying unconscious on the living room floor, covered with a comforter someone had taken from her bed and her head was resting on a pillow.

An ambulance was called to the scene immediately and, due to her status as a senior government employee, a physician was also requested. The police were mystified. Nothing appeared out of order; though they wouldn't be certain until they could question Heather. Her jewellery box was untouched, her wallet hadn't been taken from her purse, nor the seventy-five dollars, her credit cards hadn't been taken nor her DVD player or any other possession. By all appearances, someone attacked Heather Hancock for some groceries and shoes.

Heather was rushed to Saint Mary's. The doctor on call who arrived on the scene shortly after the ambulance had no idea what chemical was used to sedate her. There was no sign of forcible entry and Heather Hancock would have known better in that neighbourhood to open the door to anyone she wasn't expecting. She'd been drugged by someone she knew.

Her supervisor arrived at the hospital within minutes of the ambulance, wasting no time in contacting Noelle Barton, the two other members of the parole committee and the Sainte-Anne-des-Plaines penitentiary. Heather Hancock would be on sick leave for several days.

Monday afternoon Heather had never felt worse in her life. The most whispered word screamed in her head, resounding, pounding, and the stainless steel pan at her bedside had been replaced four times since she regained consciousness. When they asked whether they could do anything for her, she asked to see her minister and the police were more visibly put off when she began to answer their questions.

The young girl was somewhere between twenty and twenty-five, with purple hair and was dressed like a boy, like a street-wise kid. Heather remembered the girl being very rude, though somehow she believed the girl had not meant to be rude or hurt her. Her voice belied her speech. She was educated, as though pretending to be someone she wasn't. Enough people were sitting in jail and prison, she told the police. If all the girl took was food and a few pairs of old shoes, where was the crime?

Noelle Barton went by the hospital on her way to the prison to wish Heather well. She knew Heather by reputation and merely wanted to express her concern and ask Heather's opinion of the Voisine case file. Her heart broke when she saw Heather lying propped up in the sterile bed with intravenous tubes leading to mercurochrome-stained bandages on both arms.

Noelle had been put in charge of the case file, being she was a senior government official and several ranks higher than Heather. They spoke about Voisine. Heather had intended to grant his release with strict conditions, pending her interpretation of his body language and attitude. Noelle concurred. Voisine's crime was one of passion, his temporary insanity plea had been accepted by the court and Heather believed his nightmares would be penalty enough throughout the rest of his life. Noelle held herself in check, smiling compassionately as she held Heather's hand, really wanting to smack her. Instead, she concurred with Heather's thinking and left the hospital believing Heather Hancock needed a reality check as much as she did intravenous or perhaps to work in a centre for abused women. Had she not seen the photos of Nancy, the horrific images of a young, vital woman with her half her head blown away and lying in a puddle of her own thick blood?

The parole meeting was delayed until 4:00 PM. When Noelle Barton arrived at the front gates of the prison she and was led to the warden's office to meet with her two co-committee members. No one doubted she was in charge. Ten minutes later a shackled Benoit Voisine was led in.

"Sit down, Voisine, and keep your mouth shut until you're spoken to."

Voisine obeyed the warden's curt instruction.

"Mesdames, monsieur, he's all yours."

"Voisine, tell us why you should be released." Noelle Barton began in her maternal French. "And make it good unless you want free food and anal sex for the rest of your life."

"Madame, what I did to my girlfriend was a terrible thing. I did it because I was insanely in love with her and could not deal with someone else knowing her that way. When I saw her lying at my feet I wanted to shoot myself but I was too much of a coward. Instead, I fell to my knees and waited for my comrades, the same cops I worked with day after day. They arrested me as though I was dirt."

"You were never intimate with her."

"No. I wanted to be and in my mind I was. I was sick, was sick. Now I am not."

"What you are is dirt. You butchered her."

"Yes, I did. And I have relived the scene each day since."

They weren't impressed. The man on the committee proceeded as planned. "What are your plans? What do you intend to do if released from here?"

"I've thought about that since the warden told me my parole hearing was accepted. I don't know. I want to go home. I want to start over, begin a new life. After ten years I'm old news. I'll get a job as a security guard or a bouncer at first, and I'll go for retraining."

"Meaning?" the parole officer asked, perusing the pages of Voisine's file.

"I don't know. Maybe the law or teaching. I'm still young. I'm thirty-six. I have time to start over and I know both sides of the system. It's a natural for me, I suppose. I could make a difference."

"And you think a law firm or school would hire a killer?" Noelle asked.

"Yes. I believe so, if what I did can help others in some way."

The woman sitting between the man and Noelle cut in. "You blew off the back of a young woman's head. Tell me what you felt when you saw her head fly away."

"It was a fleeting moment, ephemeral, may I say. I heard an explosion and saw her body twist into the air. When I saw her at my feet, lying in her blood, nothing was real to me. I was in a dream, a nightmare. Only when I touched her did I realize and I was too afraid to do the same to myself. I will always love her and always live with my nightmares. I loved her, I will always love her."

Noelle cut in. "So you kill women you love. That's not a big plus in a meeting like this."

"I killed a woman I loved because I believed she was leaving me. I was crazy...then, not anymore. No one had ever loved me before her and I needed that not to change."

384

"She never loved you."

"I know, and I should have known then."

"So if you love someone who doesn't love you, you'll kill them. Do I have that about right?"

"No. In fact, who would love me knowing what I am, what I've done? That part of my life is over. I will die alone and deserve nothing more."

"What have you done in prison that has made you a better person?" the man asked.

"I have not become a worse person. In here, what more can anyone expect? I stay to myself, I keep my back to the wall and I keep my nose clean. I work in the library and laundry and save my money. I don't spend it on drugs or cigarettes. I have saved enough to get by until I find work."

"In ten years you could have earned a degree."

"I have one already. What good would another do me when I was never certain this day would come?"

"Who said the day has come?" Noelle flipped a page without looking at the file. "You never went to counselling."

"I don't need counselling to tell me that killing my girlfriend was wrong."

Voisine sat straight, peering into the eyes of each committee member who addressed him. His mouth wasn't dry, his hands were steady and his voice was calm.

"I don't believe you're old news back home as you call it. Good cops never forget bad cops and you were a bad cop," the man said.

"No. If anything I was young and insanely jealous, but I was a good cop with a perfect record. I made a terrible mistake and have paid dearly for ten years. Prison is not a good place for people like me. There is never an end to settling of scores, never a day to feel safe or a night to sleep without fearing the worst. Outside people do forget, cops forget, in here they do not."

"At best you were an average cop with nothing

385

outstanding in your file. You might as well have been a meter maid."

Noelle Barton addressed the warden, asking that Voisine be removed from the office. He was a model prisoner with nothing of a negative nature in his file beyond a few clashes with other inmates when he first arrived and a week in solitary. The warden had nothing to add in Voisine's defence or against him. She didn't care either way. For each convict leaving her prison another was coming in.

The man and woman with Noelle were aware of Heather Hancock's viewpoint. They knew if Voisine wasn't paroled by them he would reapply each year and eventually parole would be granted. He wouldn't likely kill again, the system was overcrowded and their real mandate was to make room for career criminals who would not rehabilitate. What wasn't in his record was how he treated Nancy prior to killing her. Noelle asked the warden to order Voisine into the office.

"I'll make this very easy for you, Voisine. Do the rest of your time or relocate. We don't believe you can return to where you're not wanted."

"I don't understand."

"Yes, you do. You go east or you go west. We don't care, as long as you go. We don't want you here. Those are your options. Choose one, or you stay here. You can apply as often as you want, you'll be denied. Do you understand that?"

Voisine looked to the warden who remained silent.

"There is no choice. I will go to Toronto. What would I do in a smaller town?" He shrugged. "And Montreal, what is there here for me? I read the papers and hear the news. There is nothing here for me."

"Your release would be conditional on your leaving. Stay longer than it takes to buy a bus ticket and I'll have you arrested on the spot for parole violation. When I say as long as it takes to buy a ticket, I mean not a second more."

"I understand."

"Make sure you do." Noelle addressed the warden. "Warden our office will process the paperwork. When he leaves, arrange for a police escort to the station." She looked to Voisine. "You'll be told where to report and when. Not reporting lands you back here. Your case officer will tell you how to live and breathe for the balance of your term. Warden, we're done with him. Bring in the next applicant."

Forty-Three

Roatán Island, Honduras
Tuesday, August 21

Sunday was a real disappointment to Miranda. The Fun Day at Sea was no fun at all. The seas were high, she spent most of the day in her cabin throwing up and when she went to explore the ship from the bow to the stern she thought seriously several times of screaming "man overboard" and jumping into the sea to save herself from a slower death. She thought to soak in the hot tub to seek relief, quickly deciding a movie would be the better choice. None of the boisterous men who invited her to bathe with them was under seventy. The theatre was full and the main features of the game rooms were the dozens of spoiled brats.

She ate a late lunch à la carte, booked a late afternoon appointment at the hair salon and went for a one-hour massage before dinner. After dinner she refused an invitation from the purser to join him at the nightclub for the show and went to bed. Monday she awoke in the dreary port of Georgetown, Grand Cayman to continuing bad weather, though she did stop throwing up and began feeling more human.

She had no desire to walk in the rain, or meet pirates, or learn to scuba dive in thirty minutes or snorkel with fish. The old men once again commandeered the hot tub and she spent most of the day in the gym to compensate for the

388

meals. In the evening she let down the purser who invited her to join him for an evening of dancing and went to bed instead.

Tuesday was day four, on Roatán Island. The slow-moving weather system was stalled over the Caribbean although the rain had let up and she was determined to walk on the beach. She put on the thong the men at the office had given her and her choice was made. She looked great, she told herself while packing a bag for the day and slipping into a strapless sundress and sandals.

At the bottom of the companionway she hailed a cab and instructed the driver to drop her off at the island's best beach. She wasn't disappointed. The white sand of Coral Cay was damp and the sky was dark, yet the air was warm with a gentle breeze. More people were walking the beach than she imagined and from what she could see most were a generation younger than the mean age onboard the ship.

She ordered a tall vodka and soda from the beach bar and strolled along the shore. Most of the women wore thongs, many were topless and Miranda left her top in the bag to the delight of a few passers-by when she stopped to unbutton her dress and brush sand from her shoes. She walked the entire length in both directions, put on her top to return to the bar and tugged at the strings once at the shore.

The men with women who wore similar thong bottoms looked to appreciate, so did the women and Miranda reciprocated each new smile. The others stared, the ones she assumed were from Idaho or Kansas or contest winners who hobbled along with their overweight women dressed in one-piece armoured bathing suits. One man raised his cell phone as though making a call as he came closer to Miranda who stopped to spread SPF 30 over her body. She went directly to him, explaining with a straight face that if she so much as saw his phone before leaving the beach she would kick off his balls and stuff them into his wife's mouth. The couple was shocked into silence and the man stumbled backward when Miranda's right foot caused a whirring sound by his left ear. Those close enough to hear and see the confrontation applauded.

She spent the entire day at the beach alternating between walking alone, wading in shoulder-deep turquoise water alone and going to the bar alone. Everyone was attached or uninterested. She was topless, her thong had no back, she could cover the front triangle with the palm of her hand and not even the conceited-looking European types approached her.

She was a loser. Stretched out on a chaise-longue she absently ran her hands across her breasts and down to her belly. She had a great body and if her breasts weren't the biggest at least they would never be affected by gravity. Her belly was sculpted, firm, and she waved a scolding finger and smiled at more than one man she caught in the act of admiring her other outstanding feature once they passed her by. So what was wrong with her?

The one woman she had ever wanted after Morgan had left her and would never come back. "Green Eyes," she murmured, reaching into her bag for her top and her camera. It was time for another drink and a photograph for the office, for the few men she really did like. The barman gladly accepted the responsibility, nodding his agreement that her co-workers did not need to see her bum, as long as he could, she saw in his eyes. He reclined her against the palm tree, enthusiastically directed a dozen different poses as Miranda rolled her eyes and shook her head, and finally he convinced her that not to include at least a few side poses would be a crime against all men. She reluctantly acquiesced, making clear that she trusted his good judgement and was placing her virtue in his hands.

When he left her after a rewarding smile she pulled away her top and reclined with her drink. She saw the plump couple twice more before leaving and each time they avoided her, quickening their pace and all too quickly the time came to leave. At the ship, a card had been slipped under the door to her cabin inviting her to dine with the captain.

She wore a cocktail dress consisting of a mid-thigh, chiffon skirt and two narrow chiffon strips from her waist to where they tied at the nape of her neck, three-inch sandals, stainless steel handcuffs and her hair in a single French braid. She was the centre of attention, not the captain who received her graciously and clearly understood he'd been upstaged.

She danced with each of the men, the captain invoking special privilege to be the first and everyone at the table was intrigued by the woman they'd all seen at different times who turned out to be a trial lawyer. The captain chanced to mention how his young purser was quite smitten with her and she answered with a question: "What was there about her being a lesbian he didn't understand?" Conversation at the table stopped instantly, all eyes turning to the captain who saved the day with casual charm. His daughter had a tendency towards similar sentiments and she was onboard trying to get over a failed relationship.

The captain was tall and slim. He had a full head of hair, clear skin and didn't look a day over forty-five, though Miranda judged him to be fifty. The daughter would certainly have inherited a few of his genes, she thought, and asked with a sly smile whether the daughter was big boned. The answer was a definite no. She was slender, beautiful, temporarily lost and trying to find herself.

Miranda responded without looking at him that being a dyke was a bitch. He coughed and replied that he didn't believe her. No one as beautiful could ever be alone for long and she would be unwise to settle for second best for the sake of a few lonely weeks or months. He knew enough about the subject to realize the father should supplant the captain for a few moments. He pushed out his chair and stood, leaning slightly forward to ask her for the pleasure of the next dance. She accepted graciously, placing her hand on his arm. His daughter's name was Seabring. She wasn't ready for a relationship, yet she did need a friend who could understand and empathize with her better than an aging father.

Tuesday evening ended for Miranda in the Moonbeam Lounge with Seabring and the purser was called to the captain's quarters for a cognac and gentlemanly conversation. Across the Atlantic Dina Becker awoke to a new day, thrilled about her villa and new life, while on the West Side of Chicago a battered Anastasia Denelle sat wrapped and shuddering under a woollen police blanket, huddled in the doorway of her humble home, waiting in agony for paramedics to come and take her away.

Forty-Four

Chicago's West Side, Illinois
Tuesday, August 21

Several neighbours called 9-1-1. They admired and respected the kind-hearted Anastasia as much as they despised the ne'er-do-well Ambrose Leroy, though her first scream came too late. She peered through swollen slits at the surreal light show of flashing electric blues and reds as six police officers dressed in raingear pinned her common-law husband against the wet asphalt.

One cop dropped heavily onto Ambrose Leroy's back with his knee, forcing hard with gloved hands against his head while another held his ten-millimetre weapon inches away. Two other cops each held a forearm as the fifth cop wrapped eighteen-inch tie-wraps around wrists too thick for standard handcuffs, locking them together with a third tie. The sixth cop stood alone with his weapon drawn, talking into the mike under his coat. They knew Ambrose Leroy. He was bad news. He had been since the age of twelve when he happily ran errands for the twenty-one- year-old drug dealer who owned the block at the time. That was thirty-three years ago and now Leroy owned the block, or so he believed.

The man Leroy admired in the day had been gunned down a few years later in a drive-by shooting and Leroy went out on his own, taking advantage of his mentor's reputation to intimidate and dominate the weaker neighbourhood kids with his stature and unpredictable outbursts of violence. His career blossomed. By age twenty Leroy had been sentenced on four separate occasions to terms not exceeding a few months and by thirty had been incarcerated a total of seven times, the longest term lasting six months. He was a small time aggravation to the system, and at forty-five, boasting a rap sheet detailing a history of vandalism, dealing, possession, B & Es, DUI, driving without a licence and spousal abuse, Ambrose Leroy's six-foot-three frame lay spread-eagle in the middle of the wet street.

The men who were once those impressionable street kids stood in the rain, looking on with obvious satisfaction, exchanging nods as the cops ordered Leroy to his feet. He saw them all staring as he struggled onto his side, into a sitting position, pushing his 300 pounds from the ground and up the side of a police cruiser. He screamed invectives at them, and the cops who had dragged him from his home and into the deluge to humiliate him.

He knew the cops were laughing at him. Their faces were expressionless, they were speaking in monotones, but their eyes were mocking him. He knew not to struggle against the tie-wraps. The cop had fixed them to the point Leroy could barely feel his hands and his head ached to where he was oblivious to the cold rain washing over his face and drenching his tee-shirt and jeans. They wouldn't need much reason to shoot him. Being black was irrelevant. They were black. White cop, black cop, colour didn't matter. They were West Side cops. One officer noted the time of arrest at 12:10 AM when they closed him into the backseat of a squad car.

Anastasia and Leroy lived together on West Side amidst rail yards and acrid smoke billowing from the stacks of heavy industry. Every day was a struggle to avoid moving to the deteriorating tenements of the lower South Side, a struggle which came to a brutal end on the twenty-first when Leroy arrived home early to tell Anastasia he'd been called to his manager's office and told his job as janitor at one of those smoking mills had been outsourced, effective immediately, though his salary and benefits would continue until August 31.

He arrived home at 5:15 with a quart of cheap bourbon and, by the time Anastasia was ready to leave for her second part-time job as a late-night waitress at a twenty-four hour roadside diner, he was ignoring his glass and drinking from the bottle. Anastasia's first mistake was staying. Her second was telling him all would soon be well again. There were worse things in life than living on the South Side, she told him, and she knew. Anastasia was born and raised on the South Side.

Anastasia Denelle was fifty-two, 5'5" and weighed in at one-ninety. She had spent her first forty years of her life without him and had never travelled beyond Chicago's city limits. She had never had a lover, although she had been with a few dozen men over the years who had all promised to be faithful to her. She had six children whom she hadn't seen in years. The youngest was twenty-two and resided in a state prison, her eldest would have been thirty-eight, had he not been gunned down in an ally at the not too tender age of eighteen.

She knew the South Side intimately. Until Leroy, the South Side was all she had known and he was the first one not to move on after being intimate with her. He didn't love her, she didn't love him. They simply knew neither one could do any better. The first few years together were no different from the day-to-day lives of their neighbours. They lived from pay to pay and worked long hours, Anastasia at two jobs. He spent his weekends watching television or sitting in the doorway drinking bourbon while she did charity work for her church and the local Y, working with young girls who might one day have a real chance to escape the inner city.

Men beat their women, though maybe they didn't mean to. And what did that matter to a battered woman? Men always had and always would. What did the courts know? Such was human nature, history, a human quirk. Men beat their women and today's beatings would be tomorrow's history. Her father had abused her mother and boys abused their sisters or girlfriends, whom they would later console in the backseats of cars or behind bushes. Such was life, the way it would always be, and why saving even one girl's life had become Anastasia's raison d'être.

The paramedics wasted no time and when she felt the compassion of one man's arms she burst into tears. Anastasia could have passed for seventy. Her once black hair was an unkempt and lifeless shade of grey, her once deep, black skin was a chalky-grey hue and she'd long since forgotten when her once bright eyes turned to a dull yellow streaked with red. Her face was covered with purple bruises, red gashes high-lighted her thick, pink lips and under her waitress' uniform each breath was agony.

The ambulance sped off leaving the cops to close up the modest home and canvass the neighbours who had nothing good to say about Leroy. Anastasia was fortunate. Her inventory of injuries hadn't gone beyond severe contusions, a broken tooth and two broken ribs. She would spend the next several days recovering in the hospital, paid for by Leroy's workplace insurance that would expire on the thirty-first. She would survive. Leroy was arrested and would spend the next three days in custody pending his bail hearing on Friday.

Anastasia remained conscious throughout her transport to Chicago General's ER. The female paramedic held her hands and wouldn't let her go. She asked Anastasia questions that were answered between laboured gasps for air by a victim who wanted only to feel the warmth of the woman's hands and to hear her comforting words. Within minutes of Anastasia's priority arrival at the doors of the ER the paramedic stirred her director from a deep sleep.

Gwyneth Flynn padded away from her sleeping husband. She listened intently to what her Enabler was saying, noting the information in cryptic style and unhesitatingly approving the case study. Ambrose Leroy had nowhere to hide.

Forty-Five

La Montérégie, East of Montreal
Wednesday, August 22

Wednesday was the second time in as many weeks Gwyneth Flynn left Chicago to visit the pastoral setting of la Montérégie. The raging storm that had lasted through the weekend had abated, leaving the rolling hills a lush green and the sky a brilliant blue. She stood with Beverly Price, Jasmine Leclerc and three other women who flew in the day before from Miami, Las Angeles and Vancouver.

Pearl Bingham stood by her husband's side, taken aback by the list of notable names attending Mary's funeral. The meandering lane encircling the cemetery grounds was lined bumper-to-bumper with limousines of every description. Captains of industry, the upper echelons of banking, high-ranking police officers and politicians had filled the church to express their condolences and admiration for Mary. Now they stood quietly by as her mother and best friend was about to be laid to rest.

Feldman Cosmetics closed for the day and none of the few hundred employees failed to bid farewell to the woman who had done so much to improve their lives. Yet Pearl was most intrigued by six women she had never met. She hadn't seen them at the parlour; they weren't at the church and were the last to arrive at the cemetery.

They were elegant and poised. They were dressed in

dark blue suits and dresses, wide-brimmed hats and each one wore sunglasses, dressed no less tastefully than Mary had required of her senior staff at Feldman Cosmetics and Pearl noticed that when they spoke each woman discreetly raised a gloved hand to her mouth.

Mary was the only woman Pearl had ever known to wear gloves in the summer. Who were they, she wondered? They certainly weren't related to one another. One woman was black, two others had the naturally attractive hue of Latinas and they appeared incrementally years apart in age. Yet they were all physically fit. Many of the other women in the crowd looked their age or older, these women did not. Seeing six attractive women similarly dressed and unaffected by age was uncanny, almost theatrical.

"Robert, who do you think those women are?" she whispered.

"I have no idea. However, I have to imagine there are some lucky men somewhere. Not exactly a motley gaggle by any standard."

"You're a pig."

"A proud pig, get it right."

"When was the last time you saw six such women at one time?"

"Indeed, their outfits are quite appealing to the eye. They clearly enjoy womanhood, as do I at the moment, and it's not difficult to imagine Mary standing amongst them." Robert cleared his throat. "You do realize, Pearlie, they are aware of our interest in them. Each one has stared you down behind their glasses."

"They cover their mouths when they talk, Robert. What's up with that?"

"Ask them when you meet with them, or I dare say I am likely not to hear the end of it."

The minister stepped in front of them. He clasped Pearl's hands in his, telling her how much he would miss Mary, the most unpredictable member of his flock. Then he shook Robert's hand and walked to the head of the grave.

The metal casket had been treated to Mary's favourite dark shade of blue, the handles were pale blue enamel and the lid was decorated with a pearl-handled stiletto with the slim blade extended. When Pearl discovered her mother had special-ordered the casket weeks earlier she cried through the night, not understanding whether she was angry or sad. When she saw the macabre crest, she looked questioningly to her husband for answers that were lost to him.

Pearl found comfort in seeing so many teary eyes, so many faces showing sincere grief. The six women raised their hands at once, their attention focused on the disappearing casket. Mary's strict request, which she imposed with an impish grin, was that she not be left hanging while others looked on. She was to be buried, period. Mary was never a woman to leave hanging.

Mary Bingham had gone from their lives, not their memories. She had grown Feldman Cosmetics from a successful firm into the best known cosmetic firm on the continent. She had sent hundreds of girls to university, sponsored hospital wings and gave away millions anonymously. She favoured charity, giving to help others and despised vanity. Giving for the sole reason of being thanked was not allowed by anyone who acted on her behalf.

There would be no wake. Mary didn't see the need to have a party in her honour which she could not attend. She deplored waste. Instead, requesting that individuals and corporations make donations they judged appropriate to her scholarship fund. Pearl leaned against a stoic Robert. Her best friend had been taken from her and he knew he could do nothing to make her feel better. The healing would take a lifetime.

The six women in blue were the first to amble towards their limousine. Pearl decided she didn't like them. They hadn't acknowledged her, they hadn't come to the parlour to pay their respects and they were leaving with no more sentiment than someone having come to witness a ground breaking event. The snub was inexcusably rude and she noticed something else different about them as she called her husband's name and squeezed his hand, telling him to look. The limousine driver was a woman dressed in a blue pant suit, sunglasses and a visor Pearl knew had all come from a select boutique.

The woman might have been a mannequin in an haute couture window, or a model on a catwalk, yet she was chauffeuring a limousine and, as Robert correctly pointed out, she also looked as though she could deal effectively with any man. They all did and, at that moment, each woman made unmistakeable eye contact with Pearl before climbing into the car.

That night Pearl and Robert remembered Mary. They would always remember Mary who came from such humble beginnings to influence so many lives. As Robert was pouring a glass of his favourite scotch and a glass of wine for Pearl he said something that would stay with her the rest of her life.

"Pearlie, the thought occurs to me that Mary Bingham possessed qualities we were never privy to."

Forty-Six

Chicago's West Side, Illinois
Thursday, August 23

Anastasia awoke at 2:00 PM Wednesday, unaware her personal angels were already working at delivering her to a better life that would one day change the lives of so many other unfortunate women. Anastasia asked to be released from the hospital Thursday against the advice of the attending physician and head nurse who wanted her to stay over the weekend. Her bed in the ward and her care was covered by Leroy's insurance, but she was paid hourly by both restaurants and relied heavily on tips. She needed the money.

The police had come to her hospital room Wednesday evening, encouraging her to press charges. She refused. Leroy would have enough trouble finding another job without the complication of another jail term, she told them. His final judgement day would come when he would be faced with atonement everlasting, not another three-month jail term. Leroy could be a good man, she knew, given the chance to prove himself.

One of the detectives answered by asking Anastasia what Leroy had proven by breaking her ribs and tooth, almost blinding her, and what would his atonement everlasting mean to her if it came to him during his final hour on death row for having killed her. She was adamant.

The officer walked out shaking his head, the other remained behind making sure Anastasia understood Leroy would be out by 5:00 PM Friday and would certainly blame her for his arrest. He was small time and the system was too overburdened to care what might happen to one woman who refused to cooperate. The detective gave Anastasia a card, advising her to enter the personal phone number into the speed dial of her cellular and not waste time calling 9-1-1. The police would not respond in time.

Anastasia had precious little money for extras, let alone a taxi. She took the bus home. When she arrived she dropped her thin, vinyl purse by the door and eased herself into a threadbare recliner, exhausted, thinking to phone the restaurants to ask for one more day. Instead she fell asleep. When she awoke a woman was sitting by her side in a wooden kitchen chair.

"Good evening, Anastasia. The door was unlocked. I knocked several times. I think the doorbell must be broken. Don't be afraid. I'm a friend."

Anastasia examined the woman from her hat to her shoes. She was black, though her skin was lighter than Anastasia's and the similarity ended there. She was dressed in fine clothes like those fancy women on TV and in magazines and she spoke like one of those university-educated women. Anastasia hadn't completed eighth grade, dropping out to help her mother feed a growing family and to raise her first baby.

"Miss …?"

"You belong in the hospital. You left too soon."

"I need my jobs. Ambrose, he's lost his job again."

"He was caught drinking."

Pearl knew Anastasia was aware of the actual cause for dismissal.

"It helps him get through the day."

"Perhaps so, though it's not the first time. I've researched his past very thoroughly, Anastasia. There may be a slight possibility you know many of the details, though I doubt you do. More importantly, he will be released tomorrow and will need a cooling off period. It would be best if you weren't here."

"Who are you? You're not from the mill or the church, no one at church has fine clothes like those and you're not from the centre. Miss, this is the West Side. You don't belong here."

"My name is Pearl. I'm a social worker of sorts and I'm here to help you. All I ask is that you believe me."
"I have nowhere to go, and no money. This is my home. It's all I've got and where I belong."

Anastasia raised her wrist to see the time. She would have to wait until morning to speak with her managers. She wriggled in her seat, wincing, trying to make herself comfortable and sighed deeply.

"I'm so tired. Sometimes I try to imagine what it would be like not to be tired. I can't. I've never known anything else. I can't ever remember not being tired. I want to sleep so badly forever and ever. I wish it would end."

"That's not the end you want. You want the pain to end and the weariness to go away. It's not the same thing. The pain will end when you leave here Anastasia, and soon so will the weariness. You will see that I'm right. Three or four days will be enough time for him to understand what he's done to you and to find redemption and peace."

"It's all I've ever wanted. I know he can be saved, but how can you help him. He won't listen to you. He'd take one look at you in those fancy clothes and I can't imagine what he'd do."

"Yes, he will listen. You have about twenty hours before he's released. All you need is a weekend away."

"I have nowhere to go."

"Take what money you have in the bank, we'll get you a plane ticket to Detroit, and stay with your brother."

Anastasia's shock showed in her face and eyes. "How

do you know my brother?"

"I don't know him. I know of him."

Pearl stood. Anastasia followed with her eyes taking in the woman's total appearance. She had never seen a real lady wearing gloves and looking so fine.

"Anastasia, I don't have much time before I must go. Let me help you. Phone your brother. Tell him to expect you. Tell him you were in a car accident. Do not tell him the truth. Doing so would serve no purpose. The last thing you want is your brother in Chicago looking for trouble."

"Tell a lie to my brother."

"To stop him from doing what any brother would do knowing the truth, yes." She smiled. "Besides, you would be telling a little white lie. They don't count."

"I haven't ever been on a plane, Miss Pearl, not even to the airport. I wouldn't know how to do any of that and me not being here would make Ambrose worse... and the money in the bank will hardly pay next month's food and rent."

"I asked you to believe me. Next month is not important. Don't worry about the rent, just believe me and do as I ask."

"Believe a fine lady who doesn't belong here. What do you know, Miss Pearl, such a fine lady as yourself? Look at me. This is all I've got."

"You have the girls at the centre on Saturday and Sunday. Are you forgetting them? I grew up on the South Side and wished each night for someone like you to come along and save me. Twenty-five years ago there was an Ambrose in my life, until someone finally cared enough to step in and help me. I'm not a fine lady, Anastasia. What you see on the outside is a very small part of who I am, like what I'm seeing is a very small part of you. Let me help you." Pearl reached into her purse. "This is one thousand dollars. Use the ATM at the airport to withdraw from your account and keep all your receipts, all of them including the taxi. With what is left in your account you will have enough for the flight and various other expenses. Don't worry about next month and I would prefer that you tell no one about this money. Do you understand me?"

Anastasia accepted the thin bundle as though it were sacred.

"Who are you, Miss Pearl?"

"I'm someone who was helped many years ago by others, when I most needed help. Now I'm returning the favour." Pearl looked into her notebook. She dialled the number and passed the receiver to Anastasia. "Say hello to your brother."

Pearl stayed thirty minutes longer, coaching Anastasia on what to expect at the airport and helping her to pack. With the suitcase by the door she took Anastasia's hands in her own. The taxi would arrive promptly at 7:00 AM and would take her to O'Hare International.

"Goodbye, Anastasia. We won't see each other again." Pearl reached into her bag. "Before I go I want to leave you with a special gift. Whenever you remember this day, and me, think of all the days ahead of you."

Anastasia took the box wrapped in blue foil and ribbon with trembling hands.

"Open it when I go and, when you do, make one promise to me: Promise me no one other than you will ever wear it. It's very important and all I ask of you, Anastasia.

"I promise, Miss Pearl."

She moved in closer to the stranger who had come into her life so unexpectedly, wincing with pain as she went to move her arms upward.

Pearl embraced her instead and walked out, closing the door behind her. The next morning Anastasia's phone rang on the half-hour between 5:30 and 7:00. At one minute past seven the taxi's horn blared once. Anastasia never answered the phone. She had no caller ID and knew not to expect a response. She had made herself ready for the day ahead shortly after Pearl left and spent most of the night staring at the thousand dollars and beautiful black pearl in a silver shell.

Pearl had explained to her about porters and airport services and she felt special when the airline supervisor wheeled her through security and to the gate. She was the first to board and knew to accept the complimentary orange juice and breakfast tray. When the aircraft rolled from the gate she was nervous, wondering how the pilot could possibly see anything if she could not. When the jet soared from the runway she praised the Lord aloud and clasped her hands together against her chin. When the engines cut back at altitude, and the plane seemed to drop, she asked for His forgiveness and everlasting mercy.

Soon after, the gentleman beside her suggested Anastasia might want to open her eyes if she had never seen an endless field of clouds. She wondered what he was saying, until finally she did open her eyes and gasped. She'd never seen anything as wonderful and told the man so, asking how anyone could see such a sight and not believe. He shrugged with a noncommittal grin and returned to his laptop.

Anastasia brought her right hand to her chest, placing her left hand over the black pearl. She hadn't been dreaming after all. Everything would be alright.

Forty-Seven

Montreal, Quebec
Friday, August 24

Voisine had been segregated from the prison mainstream since his hearing. Thursday evening he ate alone in his cell for the last time and stayed awake all night wondering whether he would ever forget the smells, tastes, sounds and textures of prison. He hoped so. He needed to forget the smell of fear oozing from most first-timers, the flavourless food, his own blood, doors slamming, inmates muttering messages, muffled screams from behind closed doors of whatever workshop the desired victim happened to be in, the feel of his hands pressing against iron doors, institutional bedding and coarse clothing.

Days before his parole hearing he began dreaming of soft beds, new clothes, roast beef and gravy that didn't taste like chalk. Now, with his release a couple of hours away, he was auditing the accounting system he'd copied from the walls of his long-time cell. With what he earned in the prison workshops, and the reintegration cheque he authorized the warden to cash, he would walk away with over eight grand. Now he was dreaming of women. He was calculating the time he would arrive in Toronto and how much he would spend on real clothes that didn't smell of harsh detergents. His primary quandary whether he would blow a few hundred on a private dance or call some rent-a-date from the yellow pages who would share his first real bed in over ten years, favouring the latter. He could spare a few hundred to enjoy his first night of freedom and he would eat breakfast at the bus station. Detectives from la Surétè would arrive at the prison. He would arrive at the bus station at 10:00 AM, in Toronto by 4:00.

Along with the breakfast tray he pushed to the side he was issued basic street clothing, which included a windbreaker and a pair of laced shoes. An hour later, when the same guards came to escort him to the warden's office, he stood from his cot and walked from the cell without a single memento to remember his time. The warden had him sign a number of documents. She gave the stone-faced Voisine an address in Toronto, instructed him when to be there, handed him eighty-two hundred dollars in hundreds and told him to get out.

Outside the officers of la Sûreté handcuffed him and ordered him into an unmarked car, advising him with smirks not to inadvertently injure himself. He understood the implication. He had enemies. He was an ex-cop with a record. He was big, they were bigger. Nancy Becker might just as well have been a cop as a cop's sister.

He hadn't thought of Nancy Becker in years. Eventually his memory of her had faded and he had stopped ruing the day they met. She was the reason he'd lost a quarter of his life. She was the one who betrayed him, never taking his love seriously. So many times he'd asked her to move in with him, to marry him and become a family. He knew there would never be anyone else for him. They were meant to be, yet all she had done was to smile and tell him she hadn't spent her first twenty-two years in school preparing for marriage. What came first was her new career, a dream come true. She was a criminologist working with her sister, and wanted to see a little bit of the world before settling down with someone. With someone, that's what she had said.

She would meet her damned sister after work every Friday night at Le Flic and dance with other cops, flirting right in front of his eyes. And whenever he suggested they should leave, she would tell him to get real, telling him she was having too much fun and if he wanted to leave he could call her on the weekend. He never did leave and, the times he did phone her, she seldom called back the same day. She was always with her sister, her favourite excuse, the sister who often told him to "back off" in front of others. Until the night he discovered the lie, the night she was supposed to be with her sister, when he saw her with the other man, the man who was taking his place, acting as though he could love her as much.

Over the previous few weeks he rehearsed silently in the dark for his parole meeting, making certain they would see his profound sorrow, feel his deep regret and understand the heavy burden he would always carry. Had he been able to put the gun in his mouth that fateful night he would not have fallen to the ground to wait for his fellow officers, he would have located Dina Becker and killed her before killing himself. She was the root cause of his genuine regret, a festering thought that never left him.

The officers pulled up to the main doors of the bus station, ordered him from car and paraded him through the narrow and crowded concourse. At the ticket counter they freed his hands, made a discreet yet obvious show of the handcuffs and stood aside as Voisine purchased his one-way ticket, which they confirmed. In the restaurant they drank coffees by the doors, watching him eat his breakfast hunched over in typical prison form. When the departure was announced over the intercom they went to him, one on each side. One officer pushed the half-full plate aside without speaking a word; the other snapped his finger for the bill. Voisine paid the nine-fifty charge with a hundred, seemingly indifferent when they hauled him from the chair. They had no time to wait for change.

At the doors of the bus they pulled him aside to advise him with few words that he would not survive any attempt to disembark before his arrival in Toronto. One cop knelt by Voisine's side and jerked up his pant leg, pretending to verify the electronic leg monitor which would be removed by the PO in Toronto. They watched him board, stood stoically as the bus backed away from its space onto the street, and walked to their illegally parked vehicle.

The other passengers who saw him restrained at the counter or witnessed the leg monitor were afraid to stare and no one sat beside him. When he arrived in Toronto he called the parole officer to set a time and place for the first of what he knew would soon seem to be interminable meetings, though a damn sight better than prison, he thought. They would meet Monday morning to arrange employment, the removal of the monitor and his future plans. The PO had arranged for housing in North York, eleven miles north of the bus station and sounded disinterested when Voisine responded that he would like to spend his first free night in a hotel, maybe the Holiday Inn down by the airport.

The PO knew why, instructing Voisine to call from his new home by noon the next day. The time was 5:15. Voisine grinned, hailing a cab. He would be well-fed and well-dressed by 10:00. By 11:00 he would be in bed with someone who was twenty-two with long, red hair. She would be tall and slim. Nancy Becker had kept him waiting long enough. He hadn't thought of her in prison, he had no reason. Now he couldn't stop thinking of her and what she had done.

*

Claire Duval had no difficulty trailing the bus through the city and within minutes of Vosine's arrival at the terminal she was standing at arm's length as he spoke with his PO; when the ex-con hailed a cab she was in the one behind him. While he was checking the cab's meter, Claire gave her driver a hundred and told him not to disappoint her. When she stepped out at the Eaton Centre she was footsteps away, half hoping her unknown counterpart responsible for Toronto would be unavailable to complete the Voisine facilitation.

It would be her pleasure. From her position she could easily put two silent rounds into his head or a slide a blade between his ribs before returning home to her son. No one would notice or care until they might see his distorted body leaking blood onto the sidewalk. To any one of them Voisine's corpse would be a tragic murder, a mother's son lost, fuel for excited talk around the office water fountain, their chance at fifteen minutes of fame, making a simple event seem more like a horrific tragedy from a surreal play.

They didn't know. Claire Duval had seen the photos of his work. She knew. She waited for him outside a jean store, a shoe store where he bought dress boots and a mid-range men's store where she watched him purchase socks, underwear and a leather jacket. When he left the mall he had no bags and Claire Duval had several digital close-ups.

She trailed him to the Holiday Inn on Airport Road where she watched from across the lobby as he checked in and paid cash for one night. She sat behind him in the restaurant as he gorged himself and watched from her table as he paid the bill and went to the bar where he stayed for his second, third and fourth whiskies in over ten years.

At 9:45 he went to his room, Claire Duval went to the bar to wait. At 10:30 a young woman in a halter top and flip skirt walked through the main doors directly to the elevator with a purse dangling from her shoulder. She wore platform shoes, making her appear as though both her legs had cramped, she was chewing gum, her spiked hair was purple streaked with red and didn't look real. Her lip gloss was deep maroon, her tired eyes accentuated heavily with black liner. She slumped against the elevator's mirror and blew the gum from her mouth as the doors closed.

Claire wondered as she sipped her wine whether the girl would ever work the streets, or whether she would be fortunate enough to survive that one violent or sadistic customer who might ironically change her life for the best. She wasn't escort material and never would be. The elevator stopped at the fourth floor. Claire Duval paid her bar bill with cash and left.

There was nothing she could do to help the girl who likely believed she didn't need help. Pearl's mandate was to assist those in dire need, not interfere with those who had chosen the wrong path and operatives were trained to never dwell on what was beyond the current case study. She took a taxi to where she parked her car at the bus station and returned to Airport Road and the room she reserved at the Hilton. She left a cryptic message for Jasmine Leclerc who had already authorized Claire to facilitate Voisine in the event Pearl was unable to contact the zone's resident Facilitator by Sunday. When she ended the call she phoned her son to say goodnight and told the man in her life she loved him.

Saturday morning she would have breakfast at the Holiday Inn and wait in her car for Voisine to leave.

Forty-Eight

Chicago's West side, Illinois
Saturday, August 25

Seeing Leroy leave jail on Friday, the cops had no reaction. They would see him again. The Leroys of Chicago were what kept their frustration levels high and job satisfaction low. They never caught up. He was a waste of their resources, never doing anything severe enough to warrant serious time, yet antisocial enough in his behaviour to require their constant attention. And his common-law wife was no better. She should have pressed charges. People like her, the so-called victims, were equally at fault, their actions or inactions preventing the system from doing its job. Yet, the next time, and the time after that, she would expect them to respond, expect them to save her life when she would do nothing herself but watch.

Ambrose Leroy arrived at his ramshackle home furious and hungry for supper. He had no key. He tried the handle, expecting the door to open and when it didn't he crashed through easily, hardly feeling the contact with his shoulder. He bellowed Anastasia's name as he slammed the door behind him, demanding she come to him. When she didn't respond he screamed her name a second time, giving her the count of three if she knew what was good for her. Then he saw the note telling him she'd left for a few days to give him the time he needed to calm down and find his way.

She'd also taken money from the bank to last her through to Tuesday or Wednesday, she wrote, and he wasn't to worry. His severance cheque would be deposited by the time the rent was due. She might even try to find a job outside of the city, possibly in Wisconsin or Indiana. She didn't know. She wasn't sure.

A slur of common invectives flew from his mouth. He called the bank asking for the balance of his account and looked for something to throw or kick when he heard. Leroy had gone through dozens of girlfriends since taking over the block in his prime, the lucky ones escaping unharmed. Others became unhappy mothers, a few had permanent scars and one was thought by most in the neighbourhood to have left town to become something or someone impossible. No one knew. Then Anastasia happened by at a time when Leroy was working as a bouncer at a club that charged the going rate for lap dances and considerably less than the usual hundred per hour for the use of the club's private salons which were either the men's or dancers' washrooms.

He lost his job the night he broke one customer's jaw and another's arm. One of the women was in the men's room with her customer, undressed as usual, which meant her spandex skirt was pushed up and her spandex top was pushed down, just beginning to earn her twenty dollars on the edge of the sink when another man walked in. The washroom was never off limits and neither the women nor the customers seemed to mind. She thought he'd come in to use the communal urinal which was a long stainless steel trough along the wall with a mirror at shoulder height. He did, watching them intently as he faced away, and when the man between the woman's legs was done the man at the trough moved in to take his place.

Not giving him time to begin the woman cried out, bringing Leroy inside the tight space within seconds. He pulled the second man away from the woman, grabbing his hair and smashing his face into the side of the sink. The first man tried to escape through the door, though took too much time to adjust himself and felt his arm snap as he reached for the handle. Leroy threw him out first, and then his friend after taking another twenty dollars owed to the woman.

She was already there, she hadn't moved, and Leroy mistook her fright for gratitude. By the time he extricated himself from his pants and picked her up by her buttocks the woman realized Black Goliath was about to impale her. She began screaming hysterically at the very moment the manager barged through the door to see Leroy with his pants to his knees, white feet flailing against his bare black legs and white fists smacking the sides of his head. Somewhere in between was the woman he couldn't see. He yelled at Leroy to put her down, but he came in too late and stood by watching as the woman screamed until Leroy finished. Leroy went home that night to Anastasia to explain the club had been raided and shut down.

A series of minimum wage jobs ensued, until the janitorial position at the mill. The mill had not outsourced his job, nor had they sent him home strictly for drinking. He was unmanageable, the final straw being when he pulled a female co-worker onto his lap and groped her, claiming she had been coming on to him, taunting him, and asking for it. They didn't want him. He would be paid to month's end and his benefits would continue until then on the condition he would not return to the mill.

Saturday morning his bourbon was finished and there wasn't enough food in the house for one day, let alone three or four. He had a credit limit of five-hundred on his credit card, four-thirty-five of which was interest on past purchases and sixty-five dollars remaining, enough for four bottles of bourbon and frozen dinners.

The first bottle was half-full by three o'clock and he was growing all the more infuriated with Anastasia. She was a waitress, too stupid to hold down one good job. Instead, she needed two jobs that paid her practically nothing. The liquor would last until Tuesday. He would ration himself to a bottle each day. Wednesday she would have to ask her bosses for an advance, tell them she would work extra hours or the weekends until he could find another job.

He was not moving to the South Side. Her idea was stupid. On the West Side he was someone, on the South Side he'd be nobody. He hated looking at her. He hadn't seen her naked in a year or more and when he did feel the urge to have her he did so in the dark and it was never worth the trouble. His life was shit since the day she moved in. She needed a place to stay and he needed money to pay the rent in a place he couldn't afford without losing his car. Then he lost his job at the bar and went months before finding another short-lived job as a labourer in a construction firm. Since then he went from one nothing job to another, until the mill, and now she'd taken all their money. She might as well have thrown what little there was into a sewer. No one would ever hire her for anything but the most menial work. She was obese. She had trouble walking, and had been refused work by every hotel in town. She looked old enough to be in a home, pitiful enough to be on welfare and had taken all their money.

He put the bottle to his mouth and swallowed. When he woke with a start the room was dark and he stumbled from the couch, knocking over the empty bottle as he went for his baseball bat.

Forty-Nine

Chicago's West Side, Illinois
Saturday, August 25

Leandra Courtney belonged anywhere but the West Side. She was white and wealthy. She was college-educated and volunteered most of her week to a free clinic where she counselled and tutored inner city kids. At thirty-five she was a widow of some seven years, she wasn't anxious to remarry, she had no family and lived in comfort off the proceeds of her husband's estate.

She was fit, attractive, accomplished in tae kwon do and limited her travels to two weeks each calendar quarter in order to keep her sanity. She had been a Facilitator for a little over six years and was very aware the time might come when the best martial art would be the art of running faster than the one chasing her. Leandra was 5'8" and weighed 125, most of which was muscle disguised by very feminine contours and she hoped the Ambrose Leroy case study would not require such an uncharacteristic tactic. He would tower over her, probably not flinch at any of her strikes and she wasn't convinced the eight-inch blade of her stiletto would reach his heart.

She had spoken with Gwyneth Flynn on Wednesday evening following Mother's funeral. Leroy was to be facilitated ASAP and he wasn't to be toyed with. He was Level One, extremely volatile and dangerous and Gwyneth had minced no words in her instructions: Leroy would be dealt with instantly, preferably from a distance. There would be no counting, no last-breath reality check. He did not have to know why he was being facilitated. He would get the idea soon enough. His life insurance expired on the thirty-first and Anastasia Denelle was the sole beneficiary. She would need the hundred and fifty thousand. She would never comprehend the nature of Pearl, the need to be saved from her own lack of self-esteem, her belief in the goodness of others or except anonymous financial assistance.

Expediency was of utmost importance, however not at the cost of Pearl or any one operative. Leandra Courtney's safety was the first priority. She was not to jeopardize her well-being or compromise Pearl for any reason. She understood the concern. She wasn't being chided or lectured. She was being told someone, many people, cared about her.

Leandra chose her wardrobe and make-up with great care. Her skin was too smooth, which would have to change. Her hands were delicate, despite the fact she could shear a one-inch plank in half. Her ash blonde hair was full and voluptuous, framing bright hazel eyes set in a chiselled face, thin lips and an aquiline nose. She turned men's heads and infused women with a sense of envy.

She chose penny loafers, slacks and a pullover for ease of movement. She opted to cut her hair short and change the colour to black with a rinse. The last thing she needed was Leroy pulling away a wig and swinging her around by her hair. Her eyes became brown, the lenses of her glasses were plain glass and her gloves were the thinnest kid skin she could find. She decided on four weapons. She would employ two stilettos, not one, and the easy-to-handle backup MOP with a fixed suppressor. The pepper spray was a last resort if, for whatever reason, he made contact with her.

She drove by Leroy's home a half-dozen times. The lights were on and she was pleased the windows at the front of the house were small and covered over with sun drapes. They would prevent any passer-by from witnessing what was about to take place.

Hidden by the open car door a few blocks away she concealed the gun under her waistband, activated the stilettos and inverted the custom sheaths against her abdomen. The small canister of pepper spray went into her back pocket and she reached in for a paper lunch bag before closing the door and guiding the key under the front wheel with her foot.

She walked the first block smudging her mascara and streaking her cheeks with glycerine. Discarding the applicator, she jogged along the second block and ran most of the third. At the door she placed the lunch bag out of sight and pounded as hard as she dared, waiting to cry out a desperate "please" until the door swung open and a fierce Ambrose Leroy stood with his legs apart, ready to smash in her face. His eyes were wide and white, his nostrils flaring as he drew in much needed air and raised the bat.

He had been sleeping. Leandra saw the bewilderment in his eyes and jumped back, her eyes glistening with tears, her chest heaving, her hands raised to protect herself against the blow.

"Whatever you're selling, lady. I ain't buyin'."

"Please," she whimpered again, "I need help. They're chasing me, three men." She gulped. "My car broke down and I was looking for a garage. They stole my purse and my phone. Please!" She implored him, drawing out the word with practiced pitifulness. "I saw your lights. I didn't know where else to go."

Leroy leaned out from the doorway, searching the street. "You're crazy. There ain't no one out there."

"They are, I swear." She was sobbing, quietly, choking on her words. "Please, just let me call for a taxi or a tow truck. Please. I can wait outside after I call. Please. I know they're hiding, waiting for me." She reached into her pocket, holding out the two twenty-dollar bills with a trembling hand. "It's all I have. Please, let me use your phone."

Leroy snatched the bills, scanned the street once more and stepped aside, signalling Leandra inside with an exaggerated nod.

"Then you go. I don't need no trouble."

"Thank you, thank you so much."

She hurried in, cowering. He was huge, she thought. Leroy tossed the bat onto the floor and turned for an instant to close the door, repeating he wanted her gone after the call. He didn't finish the sentence. In a split second Leandra drew both daggers from under her sweater and, commanding all her strength, she plunged them into his sides with a loud groan, leaping away with nimble speed to avoid the power of his arms that struck out uncontrollably.

He turned and looked dumbly at the pearl handles protruding from under his ribs, looking across to Leandra who was taking aim and pulling back on the trigger of the compact 9000-S. Six silent and precise nine-millimetre rounds tore through his abdomen forming a deathly circle, slamming him against door. His face was pained with horror, grabbing at the sickly patch of dark blood and over to the petite woman standing impassively with her legs apart, her arms raised and pointing in his direction.

He pushed himself from the door, staggering towards her as two more rounds ripped through his undershirt and into the left and right sides of his chest. He stopped, and stared at the two holes, his breathing laboured, his nostrils flaring in the centre of a ghoulish mask. Leandra could see the question forming in his mind.

She answered in a quiet, level voice: "On behalf of Anastasia," she said clearly, seconds before two more rounds shattered his forehead and flung him to the floor. She wasn't taking a chance. She put one more into his head before using both hands to retrieve each dagger. Then she collected the eleven casings, turned off the lights and went to the windows to observe the deserted street.

She stepped onto the broken porch, reached for the bag and hurried back in. She went into the bedroom, to what looked like Leroy's bureau, burying the plain, grease-stained bag under the clothes in the bottom drawer. Ten thousand was a believable amount, she and her director agreed. Anastasia wouldn't suspect charity. Rather she would believe Leroy had kept the money hidden from her. Leandra also took the note Anastasia put by the phone and left the door ajar when she left.

She drove a circuitous route to her suburban home, first disposing separately of the gun, the silencer and a handful of casings in the canal. Her gloves went into a public trash can along with the pepper spray, the letter into another. At home she left her shoes outside and drove into the garage to completely undress and place her street clothes and underwear into three separate bags. Her sheaths went into a fourth, which she left open for her shoes. Her stilettos would soak in a jar of medical disinfectant for a few hours.

Showered, her shorter hair once again a lustrous shade of ash blonde, she dressed and went out. When she returned she called her director to confirm success, returned her daggers to their respective cases and went to bed as Miranda Stevens was sitting cross-legged on another hotel bed in Miami.

Fifty

Miami, Florida
Saturday, August 25

Miranda spent the rest of the week with Seabring. The weather never completely cleared, yet Wednesday, Thursday and Friday the young women strolled along beaches when they could or found quaint bistros to sit in and talk girl-talk. They became good friends, two lost and lonely souls searching for the same elusive happiness.

Thursday night the ship's second officer presented himself at their table. The captain was asking whether they would care to grace the bridge with their charm and beauty. Seabring practically yanked Miranda from her seat and moments later more uniformed men were bowing or removing their hats.

The bow of the ship was dull white and seemed indomitable under the dim light of a moon partly eclipsed by thin clouds and Miranda let a long "oooh" escape her lips. The captain explained the instrumentation in detail that was interesting, not overwhelming, explaining currents, tides, datum and standing by her side as a junior officer helped her plot a course to Cozumel. She sat in the pilot's seat, crunching her brow and pinching her lips together when they chuckled at her concern that there was no steering wheel. The second-in-command put his hat on her head and pointed to the chrome lever directly in front of her, centred to the helm, and when the time came to alter course according to the ship's heading she plotted, as though touching a magic wand, she couldn't refrain from a spontaneous giggle.

Her five-minute command seemed more like an hour. Helped from her seat by the second officer, she saluted and returned his hat which he tucked under his arm. She shook each officer's hand and thanked the captain for her once-in-a-lifetime experience and a cruise she would never forget. She spent the rest of the evening dancing with Seabring.

Friday evening a bottle of champagne was delivered to their table with the captain's compliments and regrets. He would be unable to join them. After dinner they stood wrapped in warm shawls at the stern of the ship, staring across a black sea streaked with white foam.

They had been good friends for three days, never lovers. They decided against exchanging numbers, content with having enjoyed their time together. Seabring lived in Fort Lauderdale. She worked as a pier manager at the port and detested snow. Miranda didn't like snow, though she thought she might miss the bitter cold, snarled winter traffic and the four months of long, dark days. They laughed, each one wrapping an arm around the other's waist. There was nothing between them, no spark. They had simply enjoyed being with each other, thankful they were girls and could walk arm in arm, neither one seeing the need to say goodbye twice. Seabring wouldn't be disembarking with the other passengers in the morning and had decided to have breakfast in her cabin. Miranda agreed and went to her cabin to pack.

Saturday morning the purser greeted her at the companionway. He extended his hand, she did the same and he apologized for being an idiot. Miranda hugged him and giggled. He wasn't an idiot, she rebuked, adding that even lesbians liked to believe they were attractive to men.

Saturday night she sat on her hotel bed listening to the

ocean through the open patio doors, scanning the dozens of photographs she taken those final three days on her camera's screen. Being with Seabring had been good for her, talking with someone who could actually understand was good therapy.

She hadn't thought about work for a week. She hadn't thought about Pearl. She stood and went to the small mirror in the bathroom. Her breasts were a few shades paler than the rest of her and the bottoms of her two-piece had left a similar influence. She had decided against wearing a thong when she went to the beaches of Belize and Cozumel with Seabring who preferred one-pieces, albeit in micro-fibre and not very concealing. One day on her condo patio would correct the imperfections. More importantly, she saw a younger Miranda looking back at her, a Miranda who was no longer sad.

Sunday the same bellhop from the week before was at her hotel door at 7:00. Her flight was at 9:00 and she would be home in her condo by 2:00.

Fifty-One

Saint-Tropez, France
Sunday, August 26

Dina Becker stood on the balcony of her top-floor suite, leaning against the white stucco wall, absorbing the early sun as she gazed out over the intricate iron railing to the Mediterranean. Local time was twelve noon. All the café-terrasses lining the street below were crowded with patrons doing lunch or meandering into their favourite bistros for a glass of wine, which was good enough for her. She reached for the small glass of a fine Bordeaux she had left breathing for the last hour.

She'd been gone one week. The weather was ideal and the forecast promised equally good weather for the duration of her trip. Each day she met with the architect, twice aboard his yacht and each night she studied and made changes to the drawings of her new villa, save the nights she went to the theatre unescorted.

She was happy. She had made the right decision. She would change her flight to Friday. Pearl assured her Voisine would not be facilitated on the second Friday, in fact she had even suggested Dina could return on the thirty-first, and she would. She would tell Claude Jordan in person, in the privacy of her home Saturday evening, friend to friend on September 01st. She was no longer a Pearl operative and by dinnertime the following Saturday her home would be put

426

up for sale and she would no longer be Captain of the Special Victims Unit.

Monday, and throughout the coming week, she would meet with the architect and the builder together, ensuring the villa would look onto the Mediterranean precisely as she envisioned. Then she would leave France Friday morning to return home for as few weeks as possible.

She emptied her glass and refilled it. An entire week had gone by in a blink. Pearl almost always facilitated a deserving target midway through the absence of a person enabled. This was the midway point of her absence. She wondered where he was, what he was doing and who was tracking him. The director had been adamant and Dina kept her word. She hadn't initiated a privileged inquiry regarding Voisine's release from prison.

She wondered whether he was already dead, by her own dagger, or a gun, face to face or from behind. She wondered whether he wet his pants, or would, whether he cried again like a baby, or would. She was certain he didn't or wouldn't die like the man he never was. She wondered when she would know, when she would get the call, when she would see the proof, when she could kneel by her sister's grave and cry for her one last time. Voisine had to be dead. She tilted her head, focusing on a solitary and fluffy cloud. She wanted him dead so badly.

He would be a fool to return home, she mused, sipping her wine, not that any location was better than another. No one escaped Pearl. Pearl was omnipotent, omniscient and as compassionate and benevolent as she was unforgiving and deadly. Voisine had to be dead and the call could not be long in coming.

Dina filled her third glass. She let her robe cascade from her shoulders to the floor and stretched out on the chaise-longue. The Thursday night at Le Discrèt prior to her departure was disappointing. She had met someone, much to her surprise. She even left with the woman and went to dinner with her, but when the woman suggested another evening together Dina told her the truth. She was uncertain. Instead she suggested another rendezvous at Le Discrèt following her return, without any obligation, and when the woman asked for her number she declined once more. Dina was experienced in reading facial language and knew the woman understood the polite rejection.

In France she had been too busy, though there were dozens, if not hundreds of admiring glances from men and a few women. She didn't care. Her immediate focus was her villa in her adopted country. She was closing in on forty and had no reason to pretend anything was left for her in Quebec. She would go home to close one chapter of her life and begin another, see Voisine dead and hold the stiletto that killed him.

Of course she would miss her squad, for a while, though she would miss not finding herself more. She was happy. She was doing what was right. Her parents' estate and Nancy's insurance policies had made her wealthy, not to mention anyone serving a full term with Pearl would have no need of a full pension from the force. She had come to understand she needed a new life, a new beginning. She hadn't been missing something in her life, she'd been living the wrong existence and had carelessly let the new reality she had lived for so short a time slip away when she should have reached out to never let her go.

Dina laid her glass on the ceramic floor of the balcony and drifted into a deep sleep under the blanket of a warming sun to relive for the briefest time what would never again be hers. She would call Claude Jordan later in the day to invite him to dinner.

Fifty-Two

Toronto, Ontario
Sunday, August 26

The doorman of the exclusive condominium opened the door of the taxi and greeted Miranda with a polite bow. He retrieved her luggage from the trunk, opened the doors to the building and waited for Miranda at the elevator while she went to her mailbox. None of his residents was as generous as Miss Stevens at Christmas and often she would bring him a boutonnière for his lapel.

Once in her apartment the vacation seemed never to have happened. She rolled her luggage into her bedroom, emptied the contents onto the floor in separate piles for laundering and dry cleaning, added what she was wearing to the bundles and went to the kitchen to pour a glass of wine.

The table phone wasn't flashing. Good, she thought, resisting the temptation to check her cell phones. Despite being home she was still on vacation and she intended to repair her flawed tan by dinner time.

Sailboats dotted the lake and from where she lay the vast lake was more like an ocean. For the first time she was lying on her chaise-longue enjoying a glass of wine and reading a book instead of legal briefs. Her resolve was firm. From then on her home would no longer be an extension of her office. She had not read a single book in a year and that would change. She would also begin having lunch, going out and having a life.

During the first few days onboard, held captive by the weather, she imagined selling her condo and moving to a faraway place where sun and warmth prevailed year round. During the last few days with Seabring she thought a lot about starting a new life. She was rich, and didn't have to work another day, night or weekend in her miserable lifetime. She could do it. She could go somewhere to find real balance, perhaps Europe, not just a fanciful one-week cruise that had done nothing for her.

The entire patio would be bathed in sun for another five hours. The heat felt good on her body. She forced herself to stand. The end of August had arrived with its usual indifferent speed, although the sun was strong. She coated her body with lotion, looked out over the lake and thought to go in for her telescope to see whether any of the boaters would see her seeing them.

She hadn't looked through it all summer and couldn't remember whether she had the previous summer. She must have zoomed in on forty boats, wondering why most of the women were wearing nylon jackets and baseball caps on such a beautiful day instead of bikini bottoms and nothing else. She had been standing at the telescope for an hour, enjoying every moment, until at last a man filling her field of vision lowered his marine binoculars and waved. She shrugged her shoulders and waved back from behind the four-foot smoke-glass panels of her patio, wondering what the man thought of her breasts before she eased onto the lounge chair and wiggled deeper into the towel-draped cushion, unaware her director was once again transferred to her cell phone's message centre.

An hour later she went to refill her glass and saw her cell phones on the counter. She hadn't thought of Pearl for a week, or that she was to become an Enabler. Nor had she checked for possible messages, which should have been instinctive to her. There was no particular reason. She was no longer a Facilitator, she wasn't trained to enable and Pearl knew any supplemental training would have to wait until her next scheduled vacation. Until then she was essentially in limbo. She slid the off button to on, left the phone on the counter with the wine and went to shower. Ten minutes later, with her damp hair hanging over the headrest of the chaise-longue, she sipped her wine and fell asleep. At moments before 6:00 her eyes blinked open. The sun was low in the sky, her skin had begun to cool from an early evening chill and she grabbed for the phone on the third ring.

"Yes."

"Good evening, Pearl."

"Good evening."

"Pearl, I'm glad you picked-up. This was to be my last attempt to reach you. We have a problem with two possible solutions and you are being given the option of first refusal, which you may do with respect to our previous discussion."

"Give me one moment." Miranda stood to wrap herself in the towel. Speaking with her director while in the nude somehow made her feel vulnerable. "I'm back. What's up?"

"We have a pending facilitation in your sector, one whose location we could not establish until very recently. However, your successor is not yet in place."

"And you want me to volunteer?"

"Due to the fact the case study is in your sector, yes. However we do have an alternate operative in place as we speak, should you decide not to participate?"

"Another Pearl in my sector, I don't think so."

"Good. This is a very unique case study, Pearl. You will be participating on behalf of one of our own, with a special request. The operative has asked that we carry out the facilitation with her personal MOP, which we will deliver this evening by special courier. The case study is thirty-six with ten years of prison savvy. He knows how to take care of himself and is not about to fall for the pretty girl routine.

431

He must be facilitated with the utmost caution, expediency and your backup MOP first, if need be. Revenge is secondary, even for one of our own."

"Ten years is a long time to carry a grudge, not to mention a long prison term for abuse. How badly did he beat her?"

"He killed her, shot her from behind. The situation is much like your own of several years ago. She was the operative's sister and for that reason they will both remain anonymous."

"How old was she? Will I see the usual photographs?"

"Not the victim's photograph. She was young, early twenties. Before she was killed she was pretty with bright green eyes and beautiful red hair. One bullet in the back of her head changed all that. Seeing the results would serve no purpose other than keeping you from sleeping and we feel pre-event photos in this case would serve no purpose. You will be given the address where he's been living since yesterday, a photograph taken Friday after his parole and the MOP which must be returned clean and by courier."

Miranda clutched her towel, feeling her entire body succumb to a surge of cold. What she was hearing, what she was thinking wasn't possible.

"What's the time frame?" she asked, scarcely able to concentrate.

"Maximum two days, no longer."

"I understand. Tell the operative I will do my best to be creative."

"Pearl, I don't know you as well as I hope to one day. Mother tells me you are a very special woman in very many ways. I don't want any theatrics. I want you walking away."

"You're not the only one. Get me the information."

"Be home at 8:00. Goodbye."

The line went dead.

"Goodbye."

Calls from directors were always so warm-hearted, she

thought.

Miranda undid her towel to cover her shoulders. She straddled the lounge chair and stared at the phone, certain she was about to facilitate the bastard who gunned down Dina's sister.

At 8:00 PM she was dressed when her phone rang. The doorman was asking whether he should deliver a package to her door or wait until morning. She opened the door to him and a few minutes later held the stiletto in her hands, Dina's stiletto. She activated the spring-loaded mechanism and stared at the slender blade. She was actually holding Dina's stiletto.

She went to her computer and opened her photo album, gently touching the screen as the slide show made Dina seem real once more. She hadn't seen Green Eyes in two weeks and had tried not to think about her. She cupped her chin into the palm of her hand and leaned in closer, freezing the slide, zooming into Dina's lips, touching them, scrolling to her green eyes.

Nancy had green eyes and red hair. Miranda touched the screen once more, closed the laptop and reached for her car keys. Forty minutes later she was in North York, Claire Duval was heading east on the 401 and Dina Becker was gazing at the stars, asking Nancy if she had done the right thing, wondering whether Nancy was looking down.

Fifty-Three

Toronto, Ontario
Monday, August 27

Monday was a day like any other in the Prosecutor's Office, apart from the welcoming banner, the cake and a line of desperate men begging to upload her digital thong. She rolled her eyes in disgust, promising them one peek and no more. They pleaded their case as best they could and by 9:30 she was the screen saver du jour for everyone except Troy. The last thing he needed was seeing his senior prosecutor undressed and smiling at him, though throughout the day various matters did require his attention at some of the men's desks; the women were equally transparent.

Miranda loved the attention. At noon she opened her office door to cat calls, howling and proposals of marriage, one woman calling out that if her boyfriend didn't start treating her better, she would ask Miranda to marry her. Miranda replied with the most sensual "oooh" she could manage, encouraging more howling.

Troy asked where she was going. She answered for lunch and walked out. She went home at 6:30, not 10:00 or 11:00 and went shopping before stopping into a French-style bistro for dinner. In twenty-four hours she would kill the one she believed to be Nancy's killer. How could he not be? And how could she have fallen in love with Green Eyes before she had even stepped onto the shuttle bus at the airport. Green Eyes, and very shortly she was going to kill the man Dina had waited ten years to send to hell, prevented from doing so herself by the strict Covenants of Pearl.

At ten she drove to North York, this time to reconnoitre the area and the building which was a low-rise with eight dwellings in a rundown neighbourhood populated with poor people and bad. No one wanted to live in North York. They wanted better lives in Oakville or Burlington by the lake many in North York had never seen. The closest most of them would ever come to water was a garden hose and, then, in their jeans. Girls in North York got pregnant at thirteen. Boys joined gangs at twelve and went to jail when they were too old for juvenile court. North York was not a nice place.

Miranda remained in her car. She could take care of any unsolicited business that might come her way, however she wasn't there to test her skills or be noticed. She knew how good she was and didn't need validation from a street punk.

Her mind was crammed with so many thoughts she would have to dispel by the following evening. She whispered a promise to Green Eyes. He would die badly for what he had done to Nancy.

"I'm going to make you proud of me, Green Eyes, even though they'll never tell you. And I will never stop loving you."

A single tear splashed onto Miranda's hand and she hated herself. She went away to forget, and she did. Now Pearl had brought them together again and Dina would never know.

At home she tried on her new outfit and coughed a laugh. She would have to lose the tan. She tested the unfamiliar stiletto a dozen or more times and made certain the gun she would later discard was well-oiled and would not let her down.

Making herself ready for bed she decided she had no reason to force Dina from her past. Dina happened. She never would again, but she did and Miranda curled into soft pillows to watch Dina smiling, laughing, being sexy, being Dina and pretending to be angry.

Miranda slid under the covers for comfort, not warmth, with tears in her eyes, missing Green Eyes and remembering what Dina told her about a beautiful girl with a love for people and life who could never be replaced:
*

Nancy Becker came of age at twenty-one, the year of her graduation with honours and a cheque from Claude Jordan for six million dollars. Like her older sister and idol she graduated at the top of her class, albeit in behavioural psychology and criminology and, like her sister, wasn't foolish enough to dismiss Claude Jordan's influence as Police Commissioner. Her dream had come true. She was assigned to her sister's precinct: Police Headquarters. And, like her Dina, she was dedicated to a fault.

She dated very seldom while attending university. Boys didn't interest her. She decided to wait, not to give herself to a man on a whim, to make her first time special. She never had the chance. Benoit Voisine was tall, which was a prerequisite because Nancy stood a very erect six feet. He was charming, handsome, twenty-five and he sent her a single rose each day until she gave in to his invitation to dinner, after which they became each other's platonic significant other. She made that particular facet of her life very clear to him: She was in no hurry.

He, however, was in a hurry. He wanted her. They had been together four months when she told him one Thursday night at dinner. She didn't like his constant attempts at groping her, nor did she like his comments that no other man in the world would wait so long to love his woman. She didn't like the innuendos and rumours at the precinct that she was his woman. She wasn't his woman, she was her own woman and he had to understand the distinction. He stormed from the restaurant, infuriated, leaving her to pay the bill.

Friday morning they avoided each other at work. Dina noticed the difference in her sister and invited her to dinner that evening. She didn't like Voisine and never cared to disguise the fact. The time had come for Nancy to move on, to plan the vacation they'd been talking about for months and for Dina to convince her sister to join her at the beach party.

Nancy wasn't in the mood for frolicking with co-workers. All she ever talked about with Voisine was work and began to find his company depressing. She wanted someone who knew more about art than guns, whose world went beyond a few city blocks and she certainly wanted to hear about the striptease Dina had planned with a few of the cops' wives.

They spent the rest of the evening drooling over exotic destinations, both agreeing on Saint-Tropez. Nancy would meet with Voisine for a drink Saturday afternoon, terminate a dead-end relationship and the sisters would do lunch on Sunday before booking their trip with an agent and shopping for a requisite new wardrobe.

They were best friends, more so since their parents' tragic deaths. They had each other and Claude Jordan who raised them through their formative years and into womanhood. They were each other's family and Claude wasn't pleased when they each told him of their career choices.

Saturday Dina did her striptease much to the delight of everyone while Nancy met with Benoit Voisine at a café-terrasse on Grande-Allée and this time she left him with the bill. She went home and called her sister, leaving a message, giving Dina the details of the break-up during which she saw another side of Voisine. Listening to Nancy say they could only ever be casual friends, he said nothing, not a word, his face contorted and clouded over. He lowered his head and put his hands under the table. When she asked him to say something, he said nothing, looking dejected, slowly shaking his head as though not believing her.

She didn't ask twice. She stood and walked away, leaving him looking pathetic. She could have accepted an argument, denial, anything, she told Dina, but not a grown man sulking. She ended the call telling Dina she loved her and she would pass by Sunday morning. She hoped Dina was enjoying herself at the lake and she would be going to the museum for distraction.

The museum was within walking distance. Art was Nancy's escape, her way to lose herself in time and space. Not far from her apartment she crossed paths with a neighbour and they walked home together. He was married. Unfortunate, Dina often commented, and one day she actually asked whether he might have a brother for her sister. He didn't.

Nancy said something to make him laugh as they neared the walkway leading to the entrance to the building. He told the jury he remembered touching her shoulder and how bright her smile was, how she was thrown into air, how he was splattered with her blood, and how his ears ached from the explosion. He told them how her body lay sprawled at odd angles across the cement walkway, most of her head blown away, and how he stood, helpless, staring at Nancy, waiting to die with her.

The gunman never looked at him. He told the ten women and two men of the jury how Voisine crumpled to his knees, how he put the gun's barrel into his mouth, and how he sobbed. When the gun fell from Voisine's shaking hands the man kicked the weapon away and began screaming for help. Another neighbour called 9-1-1. He told the jury how the police cars converged with flashing lights, how they were ready to shoot him, and how they ordered him to the ground. He remembered lying beside Nancy, staring into her puzzled eyes, her face completely coated with blood. He remembered crying. What he remembered most was the horrible sound of one cop screaming for someone to get Dina Becker.

Dina was at home an hour after returning from the lake. They weren't her men, but she knew them. She knew they wouldn't fabricate such a horrible lie. The men assigned to bring her to the morgue wasted no time. Nancy was one of their own and every cop at headquarters knew Dina Becker. They warned her, one man sitting with her in the back of the cruiser, holding her hand, pleading with her not to see the body. There was no need for her to see Nancy that way. But Dina was adamant. She would.

When they arrived and Dina pulled back the sheet, six men struggled to restrain her until one senior member of Homicide arrived to literally drag her away by the wrist. She swore at him and slapped him, stinging her hand as though she had slapped a brick wall. Some years later he transferred to SVU at her request.

Voisine was transported to another jurisdiction on the commissioner's orders and those who knew of the location were ordered not to tell Lieutenant Becker who the commissioner placed on compassionate leave, pending his decision to return her to active duty.

Weeks later, during the week-long trial, Dina was searched by another female officer each time she entered the courtroom. When called to testify she answered each question without expression, without looking at the defence lawyer or the prosecutor. She looked directly at Voisine. When the jury deliberated and the judge passed down a sentence of sixteen years, Dina Becker calmly asked the judge to speak for her sister.

The judge allowed the request. She had no choice and Dina continued, staring directly at Voisine. The court had denied her justice, yet she sincerely wished him an early parole because without it he would have too long to live. She would count each day of the sixteen years. Dina returned to work in the afternoon and a week later she opened the door of her home to a woman whose name was Pearl.

Fifty-Four

Chicago's West Side, Illinois
Monday, August 27

No one left doors unlocked on the West Side. Leaving them open was plain stupid and the mailman assumed either Anastasia Denelle or Ambrose Leroy was at home. He stepped in closer to the door jamb and called out both names. There was no response.

He pushed open the door and stumbled back over his cart. He called 9-1-1 on his hands and knees. The stench of decay flowing through the open door was worse than seeing Leroy's body lying in a puddle of blood with his arms and legs spread wide.

The police arrived the way police do: sirens blaring, lights flashing, and big men wearing shirts one size too small rushing towards the house with weapons drawn. The mailman stayed as he was, standing away from the door with his hands by his side and very happy he was wearing his uniform of shorts and knee socks. Two cops positioned themselves at either side of the door, two ran along the left side of the house and a second duo disappeared down the right side.

No one on the West Side had money to splurge on movies or the theatre, this was their theatre. The cops ignored the mailman. One went into the house waving his weapon with outstretched arms, covered by his partner who looked this way and that, which the mailman thought was strange since he was the only other person around apart from the growing crowd encircling the patrol cars.

Soon the four other cops were in the front, running into the house with their weapons at the ready. The mailman remained as he was and within a few minutes an unmarked car screeched to a stop. One detective went inside. The other pressed the mailman with a barrage of questions which had no answers.

Ambrose Leroy was wheeled to the ambulance at noon, by which time the crowd had grown by the number of people who answered their cell phones. No one frowned or cried, grins and wide smiles prevailed. No one would miss Leroy and all were glad the day had come.

The cops didn't take long to find the vinyl address book Pearl had asked Anastasia to leave on the kitchen table. The one who called the Denelle home in Detroit spoke to Anastasia's brother first, trying to interpret the shriek and agitated conversation in the background. He noted the flight numbers, the times and the reason he believed Anastasia left Chicago. The questions were a formality. He'd already been told by one of the uniforms what Leroy had done to her the previous Tuesday. She was not a suspect. What's more, they didn't care.

Anastasia arrived home on Tuesday, arguing with her brother she had to be in her own home and promising Leroy would be buried with the least possible expense. When she arrived home she was shocked by the invasion of privacy and shambles. The police were into every nook and cranny of her home, each closest and drawer. By the phone was a number to call, left by the detective she'd spoken with the day before. When she called he picked up right away, telling her he would be at her home within the hour.

When the cop arrived he gave her the bag matter-of-factly and watched her closely. Her gasp and disbelief were real, leaving him with not much else to say or do without clues, casings, the smallest detail and the neighbours claimed to have seen nothing unusual. Somebody wanted him dead and did a good job. He was shot eleven times and stabbed twice by someone who knew what they were doing. Whether the hit had anything to do with the money the person didn't want to waste time finding was pure speculation.

He told her where Leroy had been taken, that he was ready for a funeral director and left without expressing sympathy he knew she didn't want. He had no leads to pursue, although he would keep her apprised of any development. She asked him not to bother. Leroy was dead. That was enough for both of them.

When she saw him drive away she phoned the mill. They told her of the events leading to his dismissal and confirmed she would be receiving a cheque from the insurer. She gave them her brother's address and ended the call by thanking them and apologizing for Leroy's disgraceful behaviour towards the young woman. She fanned through the yellow pages to locate a local funeral parlour and called for a taxi. At the parlour she paid cash for Leroy to be cremated as soon as possible. What they did with his remains she didn't care. A few hours later she packed a suitcase and called for another taxi to take her to the airport.

She would never tell anyone about Miss Pearl.

Fifty-Five

Toronto, Ontario
Tuesday, August 28

Miranda thought nothing of Voisine during her day as she sat in court listening to pre-trial testimony. She left the courtroom at 4:00, drove to the downtown Delta where she left her car and went home to prepare a light supper. After eating she showered, removed her jewellery, applied her make-up and dressed for the evening ahead. Her test would be the ever vigilant doorman who never failed to compliment her outfits, her hair, or whatever else he thought would brighten her day.

The middle-aged, stern-faced woman stepped from the elevator wearing a sombre woollen suit, sensible black footwear with thick heels and laces, gloves, a man's fedora, an ordinary black vinyl purse and woven satchel. She was pale, her dull black hair streaked with grey was pulled into a severe bun, her thick-rimmed glasses were tinted dark amber and she wore no jewellery he could see. She was all his teachers from the nineteen-forties rolled into one caustic-looking woman who, he assumed, hated life.

He smiled as she came towards him hunched slightly forward, forcing himself to continue the pretence as she walked through the set of doors as though they had opened by themselves. Two blocks down the road Miranda hailed a cab, telling the driver to take the most direct routing to

North York.

The street was dark. North York was no different from other suburbs that showed signs of neglect during the day and appeared only marginally better at night when street lights were never bright enough to illuminate the disrepair and the obvious poverty. North York was a dark and dangerous place at night. The staggered trail of streetlights did nothing to alter that fact in Miranda's mind. When she paid her fare and stepped from the cab her hand was firmly attached to her compact 9000-S.

She went into the building as though she had done so hundreds of times before and climbed the flight of stairs clearly focused on her case study. She knocked once on 201 with a gloved hand, reaching out and knocking again. The third time she heard footsteps, then nothing as the peephole went black and shadows appeared at the foot of the door.

She held up a badge she had bought at a costume store. "Parole check. Open the door."

"My PO was here this morning."

"And I'm here now. Open the door or the police will, which won't be a good thing unless you miss slippery bars of soap and big, wet men."

"Wait a minute. I'm not dressed."

"Don't waste my time. I can smell you from here and couldn't care less if you're drinking. Open the damn door."

The door opened and Voisine took a step backward.

"Do your thing, lady. You won't find drugs. The booze was here when I rented the place. The guy who was here before me forgot the bottle when he moved out."

She ignored him and walked in, telling him to close the door. He did. She scanned the living room and kitchen, peered into the bathroom and bedroom and came to within a few feet of where he was standing. She put her satchel on the coffee table, undoing the snap and reaching in.

"There's one small matter to take care of and I'll leave. You cheated yourself. You could have had six more years."

445

He stepped away from the door, sounding annoyed. "What?"

"You heard me. Shit happens, asshole." She laughed. "In your next life be more careful what you ask for."

Voisine stopped and stood straight, seeing the suppressor equipped weapon in her hand. "What the fuck."

"Good choice of words. That's exactly what you are: fucked. But don't worry. I'm not killing you with this." She reached into the satchel again for the stiletto and pressed down on the spring-loaded release. "I'm killing you with this."

He looked at her, tilting his head and snorting derisively. "Bullshit, lady."

"No, it's not. You're up shit creek, but first tell me the name of the girl whose head you blew to shit for no reason. What was her name?"

"You knew how to find me. You should know that."

Voisine relaxed, knowing she was studying his body language. He had time.

"Tell me and I'll do you by the count of one. Don't, and I'll blow off your balls and your joints before I ram the barrel up your ass. What was her name?"

"Nancy. Her name was Nancy."

"What was her last name?" She remained focused.

"Becker. Her name was Nancy Becker. Happy? She was a cheating bitch."

"She was coming home from an evening alone. The man she was with was a coincidence."

"I didn't see it that way."

"No one cares. What's your name?"

Voisine's genuine shock was genuine. "What?"

"Your name, what is it?"

"Voisine." He hesitated. "Who the fuck are you?" he demanded, clearly agitated.

She didn't answer. "Face sideways."

446

"No."

Miranda aimed the gun at his groin.

"And the second one goes up your ass. Turn sideways."

He did, and she blew out the front part of his mouth to prevent him from yelling or screaming. The impact snapped his head sideways, spraying blood, bone and cartilage into the air. The nine-millimetre slug lodged into the wall beside him. He glared at her, horrified, clutching the shattered mass in blood-stained hands. She took precise aim, shooting out his right elbow. His scream was a ghastly gurgle, more blood spraying the air, his face a hideous mask as he raised his left arm in futile defence and she took aim to blow apart the left elbow. The arm was flung backward, spinning him around and she moved with him. He teetered on unsteady legs, the forearms of his white shirt dangling and drenched in red, and before he collapsed she obliterated his kneecaps with unerring precision.

She went to the table and dropped the gun into the satchel. Standing over him once again she tapped the tip of the dagger with a covered fingertip.

"Okay, so I lied about your ass. Not about this." She knelt by his side. "This is Dina Becker's dagger. You remember Dina, don't you? She made you a promise in court. She regrets not being able to join us. She and Nancy have waited ten years for this moment and, believe me, asshole, you're getting off easy. Bon voyage."

He made a feeble attempt to avoid the blade, inadvertently helping her. She grabbed a fistful of matted hair from behind, pinning the side of his head to the floor to help prevent him from choking to death. She put the stainless steel tip to the side of his neck, avoiding the jugular and pressed until she broke the skin. She maintained the downward pressure.

His body was convulsing, his mouth coughing erratic spurts of blood. She had no need to see his eyes. She had seen the final flicker of fear so many times before and this

447

one was no different. She let the blade penetrate half its length, twisting once to the left and once to the right before standing to let him take his time with the dagger in place.

In the bedroom she found his jacket and more than six thousand dollars which she put into her otherwise empty purse. In the living room Benoit Voisine lay dead. She pulled the dagger from his neck, wiped the blade against his shoulder, collected the shell casings, dropped them into the satchel and left without closing the door.

She was thankful no one on the street paid attention to her. Three blocks away she hailed a cab, dropping the vinyl purse and the money onto the street as she climbed in. At the downtown Delta she threw her stained gloves into a trash can and visited the ladies' room where she disposed of the wig and glasses. When she came out she was a beautiful blonde with a tan, sauntering to the elevators in a décolleté sweater, a belted miniskirt and low-heeled pumps.

In the garage she retrieved her purse from the trunk and put the satchel on the passenger seat. By the time she arrived home not a single item remained and the gun had become a Lake Ontario artefact. What remained to be done was confirm the successful completion of another case study.

The man whose name she was never to have known was her last facilitation. She told Jasmine Leclerc the process was swift, efficient, and she'd kept her word to the Pearl operative. The man died badly. She was on the scene three minutes at most and, throughout those three minutes the case study saw hell up close and personal. She asked the director to make certain the victim's sister knew that she sent him to hell, one step at a time.

As she spoke to Jasmine Leclerc she looked over to the kitchen counter and the jar of translucent blue disinfectant. Mother-of-Pearl taken from the red abalone was much sought after for its bull's eye pattern formed by the flowing contours of its many colours. The dagger seemed unreal, slightly distorted in the liquid. The primary MOP would be sent to the courier's Montreal distribution centre for pick-up, addressed to someone who hadn't existed for years for furtherance to its supposedly unknown owner.

She showered, dropped her temporary clothes into a laundry bag she would dispose of in the morning and walked out onto the balcony to comb out her hair. When she was done she slipped into silk tap pants and a short robe. She enjoyed being a woman and being seen as one. She poured a generous amount of Ultimat over crushed ice to enjoy one of the few warm nights left to her before cooler autumn breezes would herald the coming of another long winter.

She knew Dina's name: Dina Becker, beautiful Detective Dina Becker. So what? Big deal. Memories faded over time and that's what frightened her the most. She struggled increasingly each day to remember Morgan and soon her memories of Dina would fade. They hadn't seen each other for two weeks and Dina hadn't called. She never would.

Miranda refreshed her drink with a second generous vodka and less ice. She turned on the television, remembering the spa and her vacation. She had been alone for ten years with only the occasional dinner with women who could never take Morgan's place. Then she had walked into Charles Preston's life. Without Preston there would have been no Dina, without Dina there would have been no cruise and no Seabring. She would have facilitated Voisine all the same, most likely, and with equal professional detachment. Professionally, facilitating him was tantamount to destroying a mannequin during target practice. Subconsciously, in the deepest recesses of her heart, and in the comfort of her home, killing the man who murdered Dina's sister was like killing the four who had taken Morgan from her.

Wednesday morning Miranda woke to the sun rising

lazily in the east and promising a sunny, unseasonably warm day. She went to the patio, dropped her robe and swept the comb through her golden hair. She was greedy for the warmth and wanted summer never to end. She had been trained by Pearl year after year to examine negatives before positives, to put always-present danger and preparation before confidence and pride, to know when not to act as much as when to act.

She had been an excellent Pearl operative, a prosecuting attorney with an unequalled conviction rate and a complete failure at life. So what was the point? Or would she end up like the stern-faced and grey-haired hag her doorman hadn't recognized the night before. She was rich, she could live anywhere in the world she wished to go and do anything she fancied. She had never touched Pearl's regular facilitation fees, the bonuses or Morgan's million-dollar insurance policy and she no longer had a mortgage on her condo which had tripled in value. All told, she was worth not far from four million.

She had given the legal system and its parallel, darker justice system ten years of her life. When she wasn't at the office working late into the night, she was working at home, breaking boards with her hands and feet, performing kata or killing paper targets at the city range with a nine-millimetre Berretta.

What would her life be like in ten more years and would she ever be a director or sit on the bench. Did she want to, or were those seemingly real visions of the future merely her way of trapping herself in the present? Could she deal with abused woman and open case studies in lieu of closing them... and could she leave her career behind. She didn't know, and the one path to discovery would cause significant damage to her career.

She straddled her chaise-longue and took up her coffee cup. Apart from her team at the office, whom she invited to the occasional cocktail party she hosted alone, no one had ever been to her condo. No one had ever stayed over to eat pizza on the floor, to see the sunrise, to see her face in the morning, to tell her they loved her or to see her expensive and beautiful lingerie.

She sipped her coffee. Green Eyes told her she loved her; Green Eyes saw her in beautiful lingerie and kissed her. Miranda remembered closing her eyes to pretend she was lying with Dina in her own bed. Dina would never see her special sunrise, would never see her combing out her hair or see her lounging seductively on the chaise-longue wanting to be coated with lotion. Dina would never meet Troy or the people she worked with, they would never go to Christmas parties or dance clubs, and Dina would always remember her as a pushy lesbian or the Pearl who assassinated her sister's killer: a no-brainer. Dina would figure that one out in a split second.

Miranda would be late for work and she didn't care. So why didn't she care? She loved working with Troy and the others, but now she knew she could move on. Someone else would take her place and she would soon be forgotten. As for Pearl, she was a cog in vast wheel which would never stop spinning. No one or nothing would ever prevent Pearl's powerful momentum. Pearl was unstoppable and Miranda was unimportant in the greater scheme of things.

She was a lawyer and a professional killer, though she never thought of herself in those terms. What mattered more was that, without those elements in her life, she was reduced to nothing. How sad and pathetic, she thought. She chuckled, thinking of Green Eyes kicking perps in the balls and throwing them to the ground. What Miranda did know was that taking her lunch each day and not working on the weekends would never be enough. She needed more. She just didn't know what.

She was tired. She hadn't slept and wanted to stay home. She didn't. She pushed herself from the chaise-longue, left her coffee cup on the table with her comb and went to the kitchen where she stayed for an hour of silent debate. She lost, or did she win the argument? She didn't know. She didn't know what she knew other than she would never look back, she would never forget Morgan and moving forward with her life would mean leaving Pearl.

She would call her director at day's end to resign, giving her enough time to change her mind. She arrived at her office shortly after 9:30. The plainly wrapped package was delivered to the courier for twenty-four hour delivery to Montreal and her costume from the night before was discarded over several blocks, miles from the crime scene.

At noon she went to lunch and returned with an armful of travel brochures.

Fifty-Six

Saint-Tropez, France
Wednesday, August 29

Dina Becker's phone chimed at 6:00 PM, local time.

"Oui."

"C'est un fait accompli. It's done. The case study has been completed satisfactorily."

"When did it happen?"

"Twelve to fourteen hours ago. Your primary MOP was implemented as you requested and is being returned as we speak. The operative wants you to know the transition was painful. Apparently hell's doors opened very slowly."

"Where did it happen?"

"Zone One, sector three."

Dina stood abruptly. "Director, the operative, was she good? Was she experienced?"

"Yes, very experienced. She was one of our best."

"What do you mean, she was? Was she injured?"

"No, she's fine. I meant to imply the case study was her last. She's moving on to other responsibilities and your MOP will be delivered to you by the weekend." The pause ended in a heartbeat. "This is goodbye, Pearl. Good luck. Be assured your file will be completely destroyed within the coming hour. Thank you for all you have done and enjoy your new home."

"Thank you, and tell her thank you, Pearl. Tell Z-1, S-3

I'll never forget her, or what she did for me. Will you do that for me?"

"I will do so personally. Au revoir."

"Goodbye, Pearl."

Dina left her hotel room. She needed open space, she needed people. No sector had more than one Facilitator, no more than one Enabler and the operative was experienced. Miranda Stevens was Z-1, S-3. She was the one to execute Benoit Voisine. There was no doubt and no other explanation. Dina fought the overwhelming temptation all afternoon. Why did she even put Chérie's phone number into her speed dial? She had no idea, she just did.

At 5:00 her cell chimed once more.

"Oui." Dina answered abruptly.

"Di, it's Claude. Can we talk?"

"Claude, yes. I'm sorry. I was expecting another caller."

"Di, I have news. Wherever you are, sit down. Do as I say, young lady."

Dina remained standing.

"Claude I am sitting and the sand's a little damp so hurry up. Please."

"Di, he's dead. Someone did him last night."

"Voisine?"

"Yes. He was found dead in his apartment. Somebody did a very good and thorough job on him. He looks as though he was thrown from the Eiffel Tower and landed in a meat grinder. Each of his elbows and knees were shot out, there's not much left of his face and his neck appears to have been excavated, if I may say so. His last few moments were disagreeable to say the least. You can read the report."

"Screw the report. I want the crime lab photos. Claude, have them sent to me."

"They're not pleasant, Di. I caution you in the strongest terms not to see them. Be satisfied with the result."

"Seeing Nancy missing half her head wasn't pleasant either. Send me the photos, Claude. I need to see the bastard dead."

She heard his deep sigh.

"Your point is well taken. You'll have them in a few hours and don't say I didn't warn you."

"Thanks. Do we know who did it?"

"The crime scene was sterile, obviously a professional hit, though not officially. Unofficially, someone knew what they were doing and enjoyed Voisine's final moments a good deal more than he did."

"That's pretty much a moot point. Are we still on for dinner Saturday?"

"Are you still resigning?"

"Yes."

"I understand, Di, as much as I disapprove of your decision, although I remember a time when I didn't approve of your becoming a cop either. You know you could have my job one day."

"Not a chance. I wouldn't last a day with all the politicking you deal with. By the way, my guest room will look out onto the Med, with a private balcony. I'm calling it the Claude Suite."

"I'm honoured." Claude Jordan had more to say. "Di, I'm very happy you were out of country. IA would have had a field day with you. They know you wanted him dead. I doubt whether anyone's forgotten your persuasive declaration at the time of his sentencing. In fact, they've already asked for proof of your absence. You're clear, of course, and free to give them the finger," he chuckled, "in your inimitable fashion."

"Screw IA. After Saturday I won't be a cop. I expect you to take my badge and gun home with you, Claude. Being here feels right. I belong here. I always have."

"I'm aware of your need to have the last word, young lady, not to mention your affection for front and centre stage at the worst times. I'm sixty-five, not a hundred and five, and if I do appear to be older in years you're unquestionably the reason." He chuckled. "Anyway, he was a dirty cop in prison for ten years. He had enemies. Case closed. Now you can get on with your new life, find a good man to settle down with and raise a family." Claude Jordan interrupted the long, uncomfortable pause. "Di?"

"Claude, about the family thing, you should know something about me before our dinner on Saturday, and before you look forward to vacationing here with me."

Dina swallowed hard, feeling as much as hearing her heart pounding against her chest. If she couldn't tell Claude Jordan, who could she tell?
*

At ten o'clock the icon on Dina's computer screen advised her of the e-mail. The text in the body of the e-mail was from Claude Jordan and warned her once again of the contents. Dina was ready. She opened the attachment and pasted the images into her photo suite. She poured straight vodka into a tumbler and opened the slide show, setting the speed to manual.

The multiple images were gruesome. They showed a mutilated corpse mangled by five calculated and precise shots. Miranda took no chances. She disabled him immediately. Blood splatter was everywhere in the room, his body lying in a virtual lake of opaque red. The stab wound to his neck appeared like a puckered and bruised orifice and at his shoulder were twin half-inch red stripes. His face was a contorted mask, undisguised fear etched into his wide-open eyes. His mouth and jaw were gone and what was left of his nose was tattered. Claude was right. Voisine's killer did a good job.

Dina tipped her glass towards the screen. "From us to you, Voisine. I couldn't have done better myself. To Chérie, to the best of the best."

Dina studied each of the images several times before deleting them entirely, as she had promised Claude. She went to bed drunk and woke up to the worst headache of her life. She felt miserable. The sun was too bright, the sounds coming from the street six floors below her corner apartment were too loud, couples on the beach were too happy and she found flaws on each of the mega yachts in the marina.

Her final meeting with the architect and builder was at 2:00 PM. Her head ached, she had two hours to appear human and in twenty hours she would fly to Quebec through Paris and Montreal. Friday night was already planned. She would arrive home by mid-afternoon, contact a real-estate agent to get rid of her home and get herself over to Le Flic for her last few drinks with her squad. She would spend Saturday preparing for dinner with Claude.

God! Claude. Not once in her entire life did she dream she would ever tell anyone, Claude of all people, that she loved a woman, had loved a woman, and didn't feel badly about what she had done. In fact, as fleeting as the relationship was, she couldn't get the woman or the feeling out of her mind.

Her name was Miranda. She was a lawyer, smart and beautiful. Her last name didn't matter because they would never see each other again. It was all very complicated. They lived hundreds of miles apart, but the experience was a pivotal point in her life and with Nancy's killer no longer a constant dark cloud she could finally live life, whatever that meant. She didn't know. What was very clear was that her life would never be the same and Claude agreed.

She might as well have told Claude Jordan she was baking a cake. He was happy for her and scolded her for believing he would think less of her. He asked about Miranda and they spoke for an hour. Dina told him Miranda might have been her way of dealing with a mid-life crisis. He reminded her of her age and laughed, suggesting that buying a red Ferrari or a few dozen shoes might be so, certainly not feeling so deeply about another woman.

What was more important was Dina finding closure at

long last and, if closure was meant to open the way to a new and unexpected life, amen. And then he enquired as to what she would serve for dinner, what she would wear, casual or whether he was expected to arrive in a suit. Lastly, and of far greater importance, had she forgotten his wine? No, she hadn't forgotten.

Thinking back to her conversation with Claude she wanted to die. Talking on the phone was one thing, seeing him in person and spending the evening with him would be quite another. Dina left her suite at 1:45, moments later she strode back in and phoned the men she was about to meet. She was apologetic, explaining how something had come up. When they readily agreed to meet her at three, she stood looking at the phone.

Fifty-Seven

Toronto, Ontario
Thursday, August 30

No one paid attention to the early morning headlines reporting the Tuesday evening murder. Voisine's killing was the late news lead-in the night before and no one cared then. To everyone in the prosecutor's office Benoit Voisine was another piece of trash they didn't have to waste public money dealing with. He was old news and would be forgotten by noon, unlike the cheap vinyl purse persons or person unknown had likely found by the curb.

Miranda didn't call her director and didn't resign from the Prosecutor's Office. Her life was a mess, albeit a familiar mess. She could deal with it. How would she possibly deal with time and emptiness was another matter. She wouldn't.

Troy asked if she wanted to talk, lunch was on him. No, she didn't want to talk. She didn't have time. She thanked him and he knew not to press when he saw the travel brochures in the wastepaper basket. Thursday night she went to dinner alone, again, and walked home feeling as despondent as those around her appeared.

The doorman wasn't there to greet her and she ignored the flashing light on her table phone. She couldn't be bothered. She was exhausted and irritated. She'd be working until midnight. The late evening air was too chilly to stand outside and would be again on Friday. A cold front was moving in and early morning winds off the lake promised to be stronger than usual, dramatically lowering normal seasonal values. Friday was the last day of August and she would go to work in a pantsuit. She hated pantsuits. She wanted to yell or kick something. Instead she showered and went to bed muttering.

Unable to sleep, unable to close out the faint glow of the flashing red LED on her phone, she buried her head under her pillow and screamed. At 3:00 AM the light was still flashing, and at 4:00. At 5:00 she scurried from her bed, ran to the phone, grabbed at the receiver and misdialled her own code. She tried a second and third time before punching in the proper four digits. Hearing the message she sank to her knees in disbelief. The voice on the other end was throaty, calm and unfaltering.

"Thank you. I had to call to thank you. How could I not say thank you, Chérie? I know you were the one. I saw the photos."

Miranda listened to the long pause and quiet sipping, covering her other ear, trying to discern the subtle background sounds.

"Hey, guess what? I'm in Saint-Tropez, the special place I could never tell you about. That's where I am, somewhere I always thought was an escape. I've come to realize I was never running away from what I had or what I was. I was running towards what I wanted and who I wanted to be. It's time for a new life. I'm sipping Pernod and looking out over the Med. Is that neat, or what? I guess you can tell I'm a little pissed. I've sort of been drunk all morning. I'm quitting the force and moving here. I've also spoken with Pearl and she understands I can no longer be part of the family. So I guess that makes me some sort of orphan."

Dina had wanted to giggle. What Miranda heard was a sob.

"I think I've got the "who I am part" pretty much under

control and I hope I find someone like you. I'm leaving tomorrow for what used to be my home to hand in my badge, have dinner with an old friend and sell my home. I guess it'll take a few weeks. Anyway, who cares, right? Maybe one day I'll look into a mirror and see a beautiful blonde looking back at me. By the way, a big part of me hopes you never did find the key for those cuffs. Oh… one more thing: I love you."

The line went dead.

"You love me! You bitch! You love me! Aaaagh!"

Miranda scrambled to her feet and ran around her condo in circles, from room to room, punching cushions and ranting that morning couldn't come soon enough so she could throw herself from the balcony.

"You love me, you love me! We were in bed freaking naked and you have to call me from freaking France to tell me you love me."

She ran to her dresser for the handcuffs and tried frantically to pull them apart, hurling them at her bed, exasperated, collapsing beside them and whispering "Green Eyes" until she thought to jump up and run to her computer.

When Troy Torrington walked into his office Friday morning Miranda was sitting in his chair with her feet on his desk, sleeping. He cleared his throat once, twice, and three times.

"You look like the loser in a cat fight, Mir. What's going on?"

She did look un-Miranda. Her still damp hair was windblown, she hadn't put on make-up and she had dark shadows around red-streaked eyes.

"And why is the Chief Prosecutor looking at the bottom of your shoes on his desk?"

"I'm sorry, Troy, rough night." She dropped her feet to the carpet. "Troy, I need a really big favour, a Chief Prosecutor and really, really good friend kind of favour."

"Ah, Mir, don't tell me another parking ticket."

461

"No, Troy, I mean a really big favour. I'll owe you for a very long time."

"Okay, what is it?" He sat on the edge of his desk and listened. When she finished he smiled and shook his head. "Mir, you know what I love most about my wife?"

"No."

"I love that she never gave me a daughter. Now get your little rump out of my seat until you're able to fill it properly."

Miranda stood.

"Troy, did I tell you she's a detective, and tall with red hair, really sexy red hair, Troy, and a voice to melt butter."

"Yes, you did, and it was too much information the first time."

"Can you help me, Troy? I'll never ask you for anything again."

"And if I do, I'm going to lose you, right?"

"No. You'll lose your best prosecutor. You'll never lose me."

"Mir, this is way beyond the norm and I'm not making any promises. Give me some time and please don't do anything counterproductive in the meantime. Let me make a few calls. I may know someone who can help."

"Like who?"

"Like none of your business. Just get out of here and don't come through my door until I call you. Understood?"

Miranda threw her arms around him and patted his cheek. You're the best."

"Get out."

Troy waited to hear the click of the bolt on his door before opening his computer to refresh his memory. A year had gone by since he attended the week-long National Crime Study, convening Police Chiefs, Commissioners and Chief Prosecutors from across the country. Claude Jordan had thrashed him severely on the golf course and Troy promised he would one day demand a rematch. He enjoyed

Jordan's company. The man was well-travelled, erudite and gentlemanly, a rarity in the modern world. He shook his head, not at all certain how to proceed as he dialled.

Half an hour later the conversation between the two men ended and Miranda was called into his office. His expression was sombre.

"Sit down, Mir."

She did and Troy sat on the corner of his desk, silently lacing his fingers into a large fist. She looked like a worried schoolgirl waiting to hear she failed the year.

"Did you call me in here to stare at me or are you actually going to say something?"

"I'm impressed, Mir, very impressed indeed."

"With what, Troy? What did you find out? "

"Mir, your Dina is Captain Dina Becker of SVU in Quebec City. Apparently your good taste in fashion and fast cars extends to senior cops."

Miranda's eyes opened wide, filling with tears. "Wow," she answered weakly, "a captain."

"Well, she was in any event. She resigned, Mir. She's moving to France. And what's with the tears? You're one of the top prosecutors in the country. It's not becoming."

He passed her a linen handkerchief he didn't expect to get back.

"That's why I couldn't find her, Troy. I tried everything, the internet, 411, everything. It's like she doesn't exist and if I can't find her here, how do I find her in France?"

"She exists, Mir."

"Did you get her address?"

"I asked, but he declined and rightfully so. Giving out any officer's personal information is strictly against the rules. I'm sorry, Mir. However I do have some good news. Claude and I have planned a weekend of golfing next month. He needs time away from his office as much as I do from this place. I met him last year. He's a nice guy, classy, very old-school. I'm looking forward to seeing him again."

Miranda slouched into a high-back leather chair and crossed her arms.

"Great. I'm very happy for you."

"You don't look very happy for me."

Miranda gave him a look of disgust mixed with woeful disappointment. "So who is this guy, like I care?"

"He's the Commissioner of Police in Quebec City, Mir, and one hell of a good golfer."

Troy Torrington ignored her, quietly reaching into his drawer for two clean snifters and the bottle of cognac.

"Mir," he added with a self-satisfied grin, "Claude is also Dina's godfather."

Fifty-Eight

Laurentian Mountains, North of Montreal
Friday, August 31

Pearl Bingham sat on her veranda overlooking her private lake and remembered her mother. Mary had never seemed like a mother to her, they were friends eighteen years apart and now those days were gone forever. Mary always made certain her daughter would lack nothing and appreciate everything. Pearl had lived a privileged life, becoming a much sought after surgeon and she married well. Now she had no idea what she would do with the additional twenty million Mary's lawyers deposited into what Mary had called her daughter's nest egg.

Pearl would receive nothing from the sale of Feldman beyond a reasonable salary as temporary CEO and none of the few hundred women employees at the cosmetics firm yet knew to expect a personal tax-free cheque from the Bingham estate in the amount of one hundred thousand dollars. The remaining eighty million would be donated to Mary's favourite charity which the lawyers were not prepared to discuss.

Pearl was told by Mary to expect a visitor on the thirty-first and she spent the latter part of the morning and early afternoon waiting expectantly on her veranda after watching her husband nurse his favourite carbon clubs into the cargo compartment of his SUV and wave goodbye. Her home was surrounded by a lush forest; her closest neighbour lived a mile away and the loudest sounds she heard most days were the chirping of birds and the rustling of leaves already turning red and gold. When she heard the low rumble of a car grinding pebbles under its tires grow louder she stood and looked out toward the tree-lined perimeter of her property.

She walked to the steps as the car slowed to a stop behind a cluster of trees. She saw the deep-blue colour of the limousine, not the sleek contours and moments later a woman appeared at the entrance to the driveway. She studied the woman as she came closer without hurrying, almost strolling, and not at all what Pearl had expected. She was wearing tweed Bermudas with tights, walking shoes and a cashmere sweater with matching beret and gloves. Mary had made reference to her age, yet the woman looked several years younger.

"Good afternoon, Pearl. My name is Beverly. I believe you were expecting me. I was a very good friend of your mother. I do realize this is a terrible inconvenience and I apologize for not calling first."

"Good afternoon, Beverly. Don't apologize. I've been looking forward to meeting you. You could have driven your car onto the property and saved yourself a walk."

"Thank you. I enjoy walking and the view is breathtaking. I won't stay long. I'll take as little of your time as possible to tell you about your mother, which is my purpose for being here: to honour her last request of me, to tell you of her life. May I join you on the veranda?"

"Yes, please. I'll make us some coffee."

Beverly climbed the steps as she spoke. "Thank you, Pearl. You're very kind. However, if I may, I would prefer to begin a true story which Mary, a few days before her death, asked me recount to you this very day at this very moment. I believe somehow she must have known the day would be perfect." She eyed the lounge chairs and took a moment to appreciate the view. "Absolutely breathtaking. Might I suggest we sit here on the porch? The day is so lovely and I fear my story is as long and unbelievable as it is remarkable and true."

Pearl Bingham waved an open hand indicating the chairs at the far end of the veranda.

"Anything about my mother interests me very much, though I don't recall my mother ever mentioning you, Beverly, until my last few minutes with her when she told me to expect your visit."

Beverly smiled. "No, she never would have mentioned me and the reason why is part of my story."

"I doubt whether you have anything to tell me about my mother I don't already know. We were very close. As you drove up I was sitting here reminiscing about our times together."

"I know how close you were. In fact, I know everything about you, Pearl, and your mother's final wish to me was that you know everything about her... and you."

"This is all sounding very mysterious. My mother and I had no secrets. I can't imagine what you can possibly tell me."

A slight grin spread across Beverly's lips. "Truer words have never been spoken."

The two women took their seats, Pearl taking the opportunity to examine the woman. She was slightly shorter in stature, dressed in unpretentious haute couture, she looked in her late-forties, which Pearl thought was remarkable given her age, and her speech was refined. She was precisely the type of woman Mary would have known.

"Are you sure I can't offer you something, perhaps a tea or sherry?"

"Thank you, no." Beverly sat in the closest seat, crossed her legs at the ankles and placed one gloved hand over the other before she began. "Pearl, what you are about to hear will require you to have complete faith in your mother and to believe me unconditionally. The story contains no fiction, nor delirium, which you may be inclined to suspect. Your mother was fully lucid when we spoke, which was some days prior to her death. You will understand completely when I have finished."

Pearl's warm expression drained from her face. "What is this all about, Beverly? Does this have anything to do with Feldman Cosmetics?"

"No. The firm is one of the largest and best of its kind anywhere. The firm is fine and I am aware you were appointed interim CEO until the current negotiations for its sale are completed on the sixth."

Pearl Bingham tilted her head. "You seem well-informed."

"Indeed I am. Pearl, the story begins in 1957, fifty years ago this very day, this very hour, down by Deep Lake in upstate New York, the story of a pretty and young girl and a young Native American boy who spied on her from the woods as she bathed. You were the young girl... Billy Stream was the boy."

Pearl chortled softly, taking a moment to remember. "I haven't thought of Billy in years, yet now it seems only a short time ago. He was very bold. He wouldn't go until I kissed him, though I'm sure he wasn't spying on me. He'd just jumped in for a swim and we pretty much collided. I made him promise to close his eyes when I ran to shore, but he didn't." Pearl gazed out over her lake, taking a moment to summon ancient memories. "He called out that I was beautiful, like a naked angel."

"He didn't just jump in for a swim. He was peeking at you from the woods. He was being a boy."

"If that's true he got quite a show because I was being a girl. I was thirteen and beginning to discover a new me." Pearl covered her mouth. "My goodness, I wish you hadn't told me. For the rest of my life I'll be thinking about what he saw me doing."

"As I said, you will understand very soon and I must be completely candid. Mother would expect nothing less from me."

Pearl relaxed. "So was my mother very candid. She was as tough a lady in business as she was fair. She was the same way with me. She didn't let me get away with very much as I was growing up. I already miss her so much and she's only been gone a few weeks."

"Yes, as do we all. Mother was very special."

Pearl leaned forward. "Excuse me? I don't understand. You said we. You're talking as though my mother had other children."

"In a very real sense she did. There are hundreds of people who will miss her, whom you are not aware of, and literally thousands of people who will never think to miss her."

"I'm sorry. You're losing me." Pearl shook her head. "My mother worked each day until the last few weeks of her life and I realize she had several dozen contacts, but thousands. We're talking cosmetics here, not formulae for eternal youth. Is that how you came to know her? Did you work for her?"

"Yes, and I did indeed mean to say thousands of people. Though, we're getting ahead of ourselves. Please let me continue. Yes, I worked for your mother, for thirty-six years helping her make the world a better place. Actually, I thought I would be retired by now, though Mother had other ideas. Time goes so quickly. It doesn't seem at all like thirty-seven years since my first husband was killed."

"Was he killed in an accident?"

"No. There was no accident. His demise was well thought out. He died because he was a bad man, beyond help. Either he would be the one killed, or me, and I thought he was the better choice." Beverly smirked. "That's another story. He hit me on one too many occasions and paid for his temper with his life, enough said."

469

"You killed him."

"I wanted to very much, believe me. Sadly, I never got the chance. After the last time he beat me I spent a week in the hospital. We're talking the end of the sixties. People were getting more into dope and the cops had more important cases than a woman being slapped around. Then a doctor came to me and told me not to go home, that she would get me help. She told me everything would be alright, that I wasn't to worry. Of course, I didn't believe her. How could I? Anyway, long story short, she did help me. The day I was released another woman came so see me. I had no idea who she was. She sat with me and made me feel good. I remember she made me feel safe. I saw her on two occasions and knew her as Pearl. She was an Enabler. She gave me money and told me to leave the city, to go on a vacation and enjoy myself for at least two weeks. She assured me everything would work out." Beverly paused. "I was not to return until I knew I could, and that somehow I would know. I had no real family, so I took a bus ride to nowhere, or so I told everyone. The lady called Pearl knew where I would be and I collected a suitcase full of receipts to substantiate my whereabouts, just in case.

"In case of what?"

"In case the police wanted to charge me with my husband's murder, his facilitation which happened while I was gone. He was shot twice in the head and they never found the killer.

When I arrived home I found a message asking that I contact the police. My husband had already been buried by his family and his murder was never solved. The insurance was fifty thousand, not a fortune by today's standards. However then it was quite a lot. I donated five thousand to Pearl, the amount agreed upon and worth every penny."

"Pearl who, and to do what."

"Not who, what, and the five thousand was a ten percent retroactive fee for facilitating my husband. I paid willingly and gladly."

"I don't understand where you're going with this."

"You will, very soon. Several weeks later I was visited by another woman, whose true identity I would not be privy to for another twenty-three years." Beverly paused. "She was Rita Brennan, your mother's best friend and confidante. She asked me to work with her and we spent hours together discussing in great detail what would be expected of me. Of course, I accepted, albeit somewhat frightened, and she sent me overseas for several months to study and train, to become one of the best, and I did. I never once let Rita down, or your mother. None of us ever has. When I came home they put me through university to study architecture and never asked for more than the best grades in return, not a dime. They got the grades. I graduated first in my class."

"So you studied here and in Europe, lucky."

"I didn't say Europe, Pearl, I said overseas and to answer your question Pearl has two fundamental imperatives. Without them Pearl does not exist. One is to enable the abused; the other is to facilitate the abuser. My overseas training was in facilitation techniques. I served in that role for twelve years, somewhat longer than the current term. My subsequent term as an Enabler came later and fourteen years ago I became a director."

"I don't understand the language you're using. What does architecture have to do with Feldman?"

"Forget Feldman. None of this involves Feldman and has everything to do with Jack Fletcher and Billy Stream so let me get back to them. Also, let me be very blunt and remember what I am about to say comes directly from your mother and will shock you. Remember there is neither fabrication nor the slightest embellishment, purely the facts. That night in 1957, when your father brutally murdered Billy Stream..."

"What?" Pearl exclaimed, interrupting her. "Sorry. This is fantasy, pure fantasy. Billy was never killed. He swam away after my father tried hitting him. He went home." She looked out over the lake. "He would be about sixty-seven or eight today. I wonder whether he would even remember the day, what he saw, or how he squeezed me in his arms and kissed me."

"So you were a naughty little girl. Mary suspected as much and I suppose he would remember the day, had he lived. The fact is he didn't. He quite literally died to see a naked girl. Your father bludgeoned him on the side of the head with a crowbar. He died instantly, after which your father began beating you. Your mother was frantic. She knew she would never be able to fight him off, she knew she would have to kill him. The question was, with what. She was delirious hearing your screams as she searched for something to use against him, anything to stop him. The gun was in the house and would have taken too much time. There was a hammer and she ran down the hill from the old shed as quickly as she could to save you, not stopping as she reached up and lodged the hammer's head into his skull fifty years ago today. He died standing where he was, before he hit the ground, and she's regretted these many years that she could not have killed him twice."

Pearl was horrified. "You want me to believe my little mother killed a big man like him. He was twice her size."

Beverly Price continued, barely acknowledging Pearl with an indifferent nod.

"She got rid of the bodies after she put you to sleep with some brandy and returned the lake. She rowed them to the deepest part, one at a time, and let them go. She prayed for the boy, not Fletcher. By morning not a trace remained of either one, nothing at all, including the gun. Everything was thrown into the lake or burned. It took your mother most of the night. She left the country with you in the morning. Weeks or months later, anyone seeing the house would have assumed the occupants simply abandoned their home... possibly Billy's mother."

"I don't believe any of this. It's too incredulous. The bodies would have surfaced the following summer."

"Your mother was always a stickler for details and very determined. She made certain the bodies would remain interred. She always harboured a sense of remorse that Billy's mother never had closure, but she couldn't go to the police and risk being separated from you. Remember, we're talking 1957. Social attitudes were different then."

"None of this is remotely possible. What I'm hearing is ludicrous."

"On the contrary, Pearl. Why would Mary fabricate such an unbelievable tale? What you are hearing is real."

"You're saying my father and Billy have been at the bottom of the lake all this time."

"At least in spirit, so to speak. Yes."

Pearl brought her open palms to her face. "They were never found?"

"That's correct, to the best of our knowledge."

"What our, and what is this Pearl you keep mentioning? Now you must excuse my bluntness. You're telling me my mother murdered my father."

"No, I'm not. I'm saying she killed him protecting you. As for Pearl, and conveying your mother's wishes, it is sufficient for you know we do exist. We are known as Pearl, individually and collectively. We are many and your mother was Mother, Mother of Pearl. She is known to all of us, though a very privileged few have ever met her, more precisely the relative few who have been appointed to the Directorate. The Feldman cosmetic firm was a small part of her life. Cosmetics made her very wealthy; Pearl made her complete," Beverly smiled, "although you were always her most precious gem."

"I'm afraid you'll have to start making sense very soon. Please stop these riddles and get to the point. Mother could have told me years ago about my father and Billy."

"And she might have, were it not for Pearl and her

friend Rita Brennan. The women met by chance in 1960, days after you and Mary moved uptown. They became very close. Rita was a year older than your mother and married to a vicious, mean-spirited and domineering man, as though Jack Fletcher had reincarnated. He abused her in every way. Sadly, the sixties were in many ways a blind era and Rita was a dutiful wife. She stayed. She knew nothing else. It had been going on for years. Late one night while he was in a drunken stupor she was able to flee. She feared for her life and ran out. She went to your mother's home after you were asleep. She had nowhere else to go. Mary was her sole refuge."

Pearl searched her memory. "I don't remember Rita being abused."

"How would you? You were seventeen. She was severely beaten and she could barely walk. Your mother was the one person she could call a friend and she stayed the night. The next afternoon, when they were certain he'd gone to work, the two women hurried to Rita's house for her personal belongings. She never saw him again. He had refused to talk about divorce the one time she did call him and screamed through the phone that when he found her, promising he would, she would know the meaning of being a bad wife, that so far he'd been too easy on her. He was sober that particular time. Your mother insisted that Rita call him before he began drinking. The next week, while Rita was at a Vermont spa recuperating, her husband was killed. He worked as a taxi driver. He was found with his throat cut. The murderess was never found."

"That's horrific."

"Indeed it was, for Rita. Her husband's death was a godsend for her. She eventually became a successful manager at the cosmetics firm alongside your mother and when Mary bought the company she promoted Rita to VP. Their close relationship worked out wonderfully and they remained best friends until Rita's death."

"Knowing his throat was cut must have haunted Rita for years."

"Not for a week, not for a day. That's how severe her pain was."

Pearl tried to absorb all Beverly was saying. Suddenly she jolted.

"Your husband was killed while you were away." Beverly nodded, saying nothing. "And you said murderess."

Beverly nodded again.

Fifty-Nine

Montreal, Quebec
Saturday July 08, 1960

Mary Bingham celebrated her birthday the night before with her daughter because she had to work on the Saturday. She was thirty-five. Pearl was sixteen, starting to think about boys and she already had the best collection of rock 'n roll 45s in her class. Her idol was Billy Holly and she danced in her room each night after her homework to Peggy Sue while her mother attended night school.

Mary came home each day at 5:15 for supper with her daughter before leaving for her classes. She was in her third year at the cosmetic company and she had earned the Sales-of-the-Year award two consecutive years. She was adored by everyone. No one could refuse her, including the woman who would never have thought to hire such an improbable specimen as a saleslady. At the time she was gaunt, she had a different look, she wore an out-of-fashion dress to the interview, her shoes had thick unstylish heels, her purse was cracked, she wore no hat, her hair was ragged, she wore no make-up and her face and hands were sun baked and calloused.

The woman's name was Marge Feldman, though there was no name plate on the door Mary was ushered through for the meeting which Mrs. Feldman wasn't expecting. Mary walked in off the street and had never seen anyone so elegant or anything as elegant as the office. When Marge Feldman extended her hand Mary's skin was dry and rough to the touch, nevertheless she had such hope in her big, dark eyes. They sparkled with optimism, not tears.

The woman studied the work application as they sat talking. Mary's only family was a lovely daughter, her husband had recently drowned and she needed to take control of her life. She had no education, but would go to school at night. She couldn't drive a car, but she would learn. She couldn't speak French, but one day she would better than anyone. She had no experience, but she was quick to learn and if she could learn to kill and dress a chicken she could learn to put on make-up. And if she could do all those things she could learn to sell. All she needed was a chance.

She could work inside for the first week, Mary suggested, until her first pay envelope when she could buy clothes and start selling, and by then she would know how to drive. The woman in front of her held up a hand, begging her to stop. Mary did stop and Mrs. Feldman reclined into her seat. She told Mary the meeting was concluded, that she enjoyed meeting with her and wished her good luck in her future endeavours. Mary stood. She looked at the older woman and told her she would reapply when she could drive and look exactly like all the women she'd seen on her way into the building. She said one day she would be beautiful again. She might need a little time, but one day she would be the company's best saleslady. Marge Feldman smiled and said goodbye, certain she wasn't making a mistake.

When Mary walked out, closing the door behind her as quietly as she could, Mrs. Feldman's private secretary signalled her to wait. When the girl replaced the receiver she went to a cabinet and reached in for several little bottles, proceeding to explain each one to Mary as she applied various layers of make-up to the confused young woman and painted her nails. For the first time in seventeen years Mary felt the creamy richness of lipstick on her lips. She was flustered. The secretary wasn't giving her time to speak. Her hair was being brushed out and sprayed and her hands were being massaged with luxurious creams. The girl was saying so much, she didn't stop talking, and then without so much as the slightest warning she asked Mary whether she had understood everything, if she had any questions. Mary nodded. Then she shook her head, creasing her brow. She had no idea whether she had had understood everything or why she had to understand, too overwhelmed by what was happening to ask. She was disappointed in not getting a job and couldn't understand why the girl was making her look so pretty, though her answer was good enough for the girl.

She handed Mary an unopened box of each item she had explained and applied, arranged them into a little bag and told her to go into the office and sell everything in the bag to Mrs. Feldman, the owner of the company. Mary did. She marched into the office with the greatest confidence and enthusiasm. Within a week she could drive a car, though the permit came later. Mrs. Feldman advanced her first pay and arranged for a few of the younger salesladies to go shopping with her for the proper outfits and made certain Mary understood that her daughter was also to be well-dressed for her first days in a new school. Then, on the proud day Mary received her driver's permit, Mrs. Feldman gave her keys to a brand new company car.

Towards the end of the second year Mary came to notice a trend in who was and who was not buying her make-up. One Saturday she was doing an in-store demonstration for her largest retail account and noticed a woman standing in the background watching the other women having their make-up applied and walking away with small gift bags of various sample products. Mary motioned eagerly for her to come over and the woman refused with a timid smile. Mary motioned again, still the woman refused.

She was modestly dressed, about Mary's age, about her size, and Mary knew the look all too well. She motioned again and when the woman turned to walk away Mary took a gift bag from the counter and hurried after her. She touched the woman's shoulder and both women stopped. The difference being the other woman winced.

"They're free samples. I want you to have one," Mary said.

"No, thank you. I don't wear make-up."

"It's free. It's a gift from me to you. Please take it," Mary insisted.

"It's not the money. I've got the money."

Mary searched the woman's eyes, eyes that once were hers. "You're so pretty. This stuff doesn't make us pretty, it makes us feel pretty. There's a difference."

"Feel pretty for whom?" she asked.

"For ourselves, we are the most important. Come on. Let me put some on for you."

"No, I can't. He won't like it. He doesn't like make-up, not on me anyway. He probably would on you, not on me." She looked around. "Thank you for being so kind. It's nice to know there are kind people."

"My name is Mary." She held out the bag. "I can apply it so he won't notice. I promise, he won't notice and there's no smell. You will notice, that's what most important. I need ten minutes."

The woman was afraid, seeing Mary standing in her beautiful dress and shoes, the very way Mary once admired the well-to-do women who never noticed her.

"Ten minutes, that's all."

"Okay, I'll do it, but you can't let it show or I'll need even more in the morning."

"Do you mean he'll beat you?"

"Yes, he will. I don't care... those other women were so beautiful when you finished with them."

"I meant what I said. He won't know. Come on. Let's

do it."

And thirty minutes later Rita Brennan and Mary Bingham were talking as though they had known each other their entire lives. They went for coffee when Mary finished her day and hugged each other when the time came to leave. They exchanged phone numbers and Rita promised to call. It would be better for her peace of mind, she explained, in case her husband happened to be at home.

Over the coming weeks Mary thought Rita had forgotten her, until one night the phone rang. Rita hadn't forgotten. Her husband was driving the four-to-midnight shift and she thought Mary might like to meet for a coffee since they worked a few miles apart and with winter coming who could tell when the next time would be.

The evening ended too soon for both of them. Rita worked as a telex operator for a textile firm, typing orders and her husband drove a taxi six days a week. The reason she hadn't called before was timing. She was working overtime for extra Christmas money and Saturdays were always busy with housework.

Mary answered with kindness in her voice. "You're not telling me the truth. I can see in your eyes something is wrong."

"I am Mary, truly. I've just been so busy. I made time to call you because I didn't want you to think I didn't enjoy the Saturday when you did my make-up." She smiled. "By the way, he never noticed. Thank you."

Mary frowned and put down her coffee. "He did notice. Didn't he? And he hit you."

Rita inhaled deeply and sighed. "A few times, but not for the make-up. A few days later he saw the gift bag in my dresser. He accused me of having an affair, of seeing men from the office, as though they would be interested in me." She wrung her hands nervously. "I wanted to call you, really Mary. I didn't because I didn't want you to feel bad. I didn't want you to feel responsible."

"I do feel responsible." Mary printed her address on a business card as she spoke. "Next time you leave. You walk right out and this is where you come. Does this happen often?"

Rita took the card. "Thank you, Mary, but this isn't necessary. I'll be fine."

"Does he beat you often?"

"No, not very often, perhaps a few times a year. He doesn't like me working in an office and wearing dresses while he's driving a taxi. That's why he doesn't like me wearing make-up. He thinks women who do are asking for it, trying to arouse the men around them. Each time he has a woman in his car who might be wearing a little too much he tells me later how they looked and smelled like whores."

Mary chortled. "The last time I heard that word I'm pretty sure the guy regretted it. Leave him, walk out."

"I can't. I've been with him since high school. I'm thirty-five. I'm damaged goods and the packaging is a little bruised. No, I'll stay. We have a big mortgage on the house, I'd have to find somewhere furnished to live and then what would I do. I'd have nothing left and he would never tolerate a divorce. I can't tell you how many times he's told me."

"I left my husband. I simply walked away from everything with my daughter and a suitcase and never looked back."

"He never came after you?"

"No, and I'm sure he's doing fine where he is."

"Mine would come after me. I'm pretty sure he would kill me if he could, you know what I mean, if I had a friend."

The evening ended with the season's first snowfall and for the next several months Rita and Mary met regularly for coffee, Rita was at Mary's home for the occasional supper with Pearl and often they would go shopping together on Saturdays. Mary was never invited to Rita's home and never expected to be. She knew there were many more occasions of physical abuse which Rita didn't admit to. The agony showed in her eyes each time.

Friday, July 08, 1961 was a special day for Mary. She was celebrating her thirty-sixth birthday and the first day in her new two-bedroom home with Pearl. The furniture was new and she planned a big house warming for the Saturday. Rita called on the Friday, confirming she would attend, boasting of her new position. She arrived late, when all the other guests had gone and she was certain Pearl was in bed.

She rang the doorbell and stooped to call Mary's name through the brass rimmed slot for the mail, not wanting to frighten her friend. It's where she collapsed. She could walk no further, her eyes were discoloured, her glasses were broken, and her lips were cut. Blood had dried around her mouth and her arms showed where he slapped her and grabbed her by the wrists to bounce her repeatedly against the wall.

She'd waited for him to arrive home from having a few beers with the boys before leaving to see Mary's new home. His supper was ready and she spoke excitedly as she served him. She waited all week to tell him about her promotion, to show him her new dress, her shoes and matching handbag. She was the new head operator for the switchboard and telex rooms. The promotion meant an extra six dollars each week and now they could afford the little extras like a new dress for her and a new suit for him. She never told her husband about Mary, about her friend who recently moved into a new house and invited her to visit. She explained the house warming and promised she would not be staying very long.

Rita could never have imagined his rage. When the violent tirade subsided she stood shaking in the hallway. She was sorry, she pleaded. She loved him and would never do anything to hurt him. She told him she would stay home and serve him a drink in the living room while she reheated his dinner. She poured him a double and served him another with his meal in front of the television. She willed her trembling legs not to buckle. When she cleared the tray she brought him a third drink and sat on the chesterfield across from him.

Moments later his glass was empty. He told her to pour a decent one and went down to the bathroom. Rita ignored the glass and reached for her purse. She crossed to the front door with as much speed as she could muster and hurried out. She didn't look back, running was difficult enough. She would know when he caught up with her. She would feel his fist.

When Mary stooped to help her friend, Rita cried out in pain, and when a curious Pearl came from her room to see what was the matter she was summarily ordered to bed. Mary poured a tepid bath for her friend and tenderly coated her with ointments. She stayed awake, holding her close, whispering calming lullabies as Rita cried herself to sleep. When Rita opened her eyes the next morning, Mary was still holding her while Pearl was in the kitchen making them breakfast.

"Rita, have you told him about me?" Mary asked. "Does he know where we live, where you are?"

"No, Mary. I never told him. He knows I have a friend and I was going to see her new house. That's all. He doesn't know your name."

"Then you're safe and you'll stay here as long as you want or need. You will also call your work on Monday to tell them you're sick. They're the least of your concerns right now."

"I thought I would die, Mary. I truly thought he would kill me."

"He would have, I'm sure. You did the right thing and after breakfast I'll send Pearl on an errand so we can talk."

When Pearl returned from the store the two women left. The street was quiet and Mary went to the Brennan door as casually as though she was selling cosmetics. She wore a wide hat so none of the neighbours would see her face and left her car parked at the corner with Rita inside. She rang the doorbell twice and knocked twice. She waited five minutes to be certain and went to the curb to signal Rita. They filled two suitcases in ten minutes, removed her personal effects and left a postcard where he would see it. She wrote how she loved him, how she missed him and that she would be home in a week. Mary slipped the card into her purse when Rita went into another room.

That night Rita phoned her husband. He was outraged that she had sneaked into the house when he was gone and ordered her to come home. He would teach her a lesson. Then his tone changed and he promised he would not touch her, insisting over and over again he didn't want to touch her. She refused, telling him she would take a trip first, call him in a week or two and not go home until she could feel safe. He was furious. He began arguing, yelling, using expletives she'd heard so many times before. Nothing had changed and nothing would change.

Sunday morning both women hugged Pearl, Mary telling her she would be gone six hours and warning that boys were off-limits. She returned home by six o'clock, without Rita who was being pampered, and spent the evening helping Pearl decorate her new room. She loved her daughter; they were best friends and promised Pearl a special vacation before her first year at university. She loved her daughter, she told Pearl over and over again, making certain Pearl understood that measures were taken to ensure nothing would impede her plans of becoming a doctor.

Pearl had already decided to remain at home to take care of her mother rather than staying in a dorm during her upcoming years at university, convinced her mother was being difficult about finding a friend. They were modern women living in the sixties and about time her mother got a life. Her mother needed her, even though Mary pooh-poohed each occasion Pearl took to point out a possible love interest.

Mary worked the following week and attended classes at night. She also kept a constant surveillance on the Brennan home and Brennan himself. She was at a loss with no one to call upon. She was on her own. She knew where he worked, when he worked and when he left home.

On Friday the fourteenth Mary drove to within a few miles of Rita's spa in Vermont. She mailed the postcard to Brennan, ate lunch and drove home. On Monday the seventeenth she woke early to spend extra time with her daughter before leaving for work. She was ready for what the day would bring to her, for what she would give the day. She didn't want to let her daughter go and held her tight.

She had no choice. If not an epiphany she knew beyond any self-doubt what she must do. She had killed a man before, so what would be different. Brennan would be working the night shift. He would leave home at 3:30, leave the dispatch centre at 4:05 and end his shift at thirty minutes past midnight. All she required of herself was not to lose sight of him. Rita would never again feel fear. She had promised her friend, and if she failed Pearl would one day understand.

Mary prayed for the strength to succeed as she followed Brennan through traffic. She stopped behind him each time he dropped off a fare or picked up another. She was neither exhilarated nor afraid. She was intent. She knew more or less when and where the event would happen and at 10:45 another passenger was let out and Brennan pulled alongside the curb to wait out the red light. She saw him stretching and slouch into his seat. There was no better time.

Mary stepped from her car and hurried to the cab. She tapped on the driver's side door panel. "Excuse me, sir. Excuse me, are you free?"

Brennan sat up without looking at her. "Yeah, I'm free.

Climb in."

She did and he cranked the meter's handle before she had opened the door. She noted the street corner and slid in behind him.

"Where we going lady?" he asked, not caring.

"I'm going to the airport hotel."

"You got bags?"

"No, no bags, and please drive slowly."

The ride from downtown took twenty minutes to where Mary told him to stop one block from the hotel.

"This will be fine, right here. I would prefer walking the rest of the way for some fresh air."

She looked at the meter that read eighty-five cents and made noises consistent with rummaging through her purse. She saw him looking at her through the mirror as she had thought he might and asked him for a receipt, the momentary distraction she needed. He was a big man face to face, not so big from her perspective. Mary weighed 110, he was 170 and she was certain the sixty-pound differential would not be problematic. She had the element of surprise and leverage on her side. Face to face her small frame would have no chance against him, behind him her small body would be an aggressive killing tool. She had practiced each night since driving Rita into the Green Mountains. She was confident. Brennan was breathing his last few breaths.

As they drove through the streets of the city Mary uncoiled the single strand of wire she had threaded into a stocking days before and verified the knot. A garrotte wasn't her first weapon of choice, however she was unsure whether sticking a knife into a man's neck would kill him or how she would even do it. She had thought of a straight edge razor and then of the consequent blood and the possible noise she thought might make her sick. She had no idea how to go about buying a gun and a hammer was out of the question. Whatever she used would have to be compact, disposable, fast and effective. She wouldn't have a

486

lot of time.

She was ready. The homemade garrotte went over his head in a flash, before Brennan's mind could distinguish between a threat and the woman leaning forward to pay him. She jerked backward with all her strength and will power as she brought up her feet and braced herself between the front and rear seats, instantly inflicting the greatest damage as the wire sliced through his epidermis and tissue to his larynx. Her entire body exerted incredible force against his most vulnerable point. His hands were useless. His fingertips were stained with blood, tearing at his own throat. She saw him in the mirror. His eyes were bulging, his face purple in the dark, and then she saw his hands flailing in a futile attempt to grab her. He was straining, groaning, trying in vain to twist away from her. She yelled out Rita's name countless times from deep in her throat, each time feeling the rush of adrenalin and her determination rise. She began rocking from side to side, his head following her movements, then back and forth without jeopardizing her advantage.

It could have been two minutes or twenty when she felt his body slacken. The hammer in Fletcher's head left no question about his instant expiration, but how could she be certain Brennan was dead. Her arms ached. She looked through the windshield and saw people far in the distance standing under the hotel's canopy while she was killing someone in the backseat of a car.

She loosened her grip to judge the reaction, maintaining the tension. There was none. She jerked back violently, and still there was no reaction. She dropped her feet to the floor one by one, not letting go of the garrotte. Brennan was motionless. He was dead. She sat quietly for a moment, tense, ready to react. There was no reason. The body twitched and coughed once, expelling foul air and spraying the windshield and dashboard with an abstract pattern of blood and tissue. She succeeded. Rita Brennan would never be afraid again.

She reached forward and extricated the garrotte with a single swift movement, not quite certain how deeply lodged into his throat the wire might have been. There was a loud and eerie hissing sound, a heavier, suffocating stench making her want to vomit and a trail of red along the side windows. The garrotte was blood-stained and coated with flecks of torn skin. Her gloves were bloodied as was the edge of one sleeve and the front of her coat.

She wrapped the garrotte into a tight coil, buried it in her purse and hurried from the car onto the sidewalk where she put her gloves into her pockets and turned her reversible coat inside-out as she walked to the hotel taking deep breaths and nonchalantly climbed into a waiting cab. The destination was a chic downtown hotel where she walked through the lobby to one of the ladies' rooms. She went into a stall where she wrapped her coat into a ball and tossed it into the garbage bin before disposing of the garrotte and her empty purse on the mezzanine. Then she left the hotel, walked another few blocks and hailed a cab that dropped her off at a corner a block from her car.

The keys were under the front wheel where she left them and on the way home she stopped to dispose of the hat in a trash can. The following morning the front pages of the city's Montreal Star displayed the gruesome scene. Wednesday morning, while bathing in a eucalyptus sauna, Rita Brennan learned of her husband's tragic death from local police who were able to confirm the deceased's wife had been at the spa throughout the week. She was not a suspect.

Rita called her friend to come for her and Saturday, following a simple funeral, Rita and Mary went for dinner and drank champagne.

Sixty

Laurentian Mountains, North of Montreal
Friday, August 31

"After that Rita's life changed diametrically, Pearl. She remarried and lived happily until her death three years ago. You went with your mother to the wedding."

"You're saying my tiny mother killed Rita's husband, and after she cut his throat she drank champagne."

"Yes, "Beverly's face brightened," and I must say the theatrical manner in which your mother described the scene made us both giggle. Thinking back, the whole event must have been quite comical indeed. Remember, at the time, Côte-de-Liesse was a virtual horse trail dotted with a few minor hotels and a fairground on the way to the airport with very little traffic any time of day, particularly at night, and your mother was an untrained novice. Today it's a six-lane highway and a much more sophisticated technique would be implemented to ensure success. All our people are very well trained. Dare I say elite?"

Pearl lurched forward, clutching her chest. "Elite, really, and my mother thought a man's murder was a comedy sketch. That's absurd! I really do need to see your driver's licence or something. If you know all this and were so close to her, why weren't you at her funeral or the parlour?"

"I was at the funeral, Pearl. Don't you remember? I was with five other women. We were all wearing navy blue outfits and gloves and navy blue hats with pale blue ribbons. They were your mother's favourite colours. We came in a blue limousine, the one waiting for me at the edge of your property. We stood together and you noticed us while standing alongside your husband Robert, whispering to him that you wondered who we could possibly be. He suggested that you approach us after the ceremony, to speak with us, however we returned to our limousine before you had the opportunity. As we prepared to drive away you told him you thought us very rude and that you would probably never know us." Beverly chuckled. "We had to explain the meaning of 'motley' and 'gaggle' to the Latina ladies."

"How do you know that? I thought you were managers from Feldman Cosmetics."

"No, you did not. You had already met them."

"Who were they, the other women?"

"They were the five women who make up the Directorate of Pearl, a position they can hold until the age of seventy. They came from different cities across the North America to bid your mother farewell."

"There are six of you."

"No. There are five. I resigned a few days before Mary's death."

"But, you said earlier …"

"I am afraid you will never know the ladies' identities, or mine. Be satisfied knowing Mary and I became good friends over the last few years of her life, fourteen to be precise. I wish I had known her longer. She was a lady and will be sadly missed. She leaves behind an incredible legacy." Beverly let her eyes travel the expansive vista of rolling hills beyond them. "There is more, Pearl. It's the real reason I came here. You might want to go inside and pour one of your husband's favourite forty-year-old scotches. I might even join you, the way you did with your mother one night in Paris in 1972."

Pearl brought a clenched fist to her mouth, biting into

the soft flesh. "I want to scream. I really want to scream. I wish my husband was here."

"I understand. However, if he were here, I would not be." She smiled. "Let's go inside and you can pour us a drink. Believe me, you won't be sorry."

Pearl pushed herself from the chair. She walked past Beverly in a daze and into her home. Beverly glanced over her shoulder before stepping through the portal and a few moments later Pearl reappeared with two crystal glasses, putting one in front of her guest.

"My mother was a murderer."

"No, dear, she was not. She was a saviour of those who could not defend themselves."

"That's why we have police, not five-foot-three vigilantes with wire rope."

"It goes very far beyond that, Pearl. Your mother was not a vigilante, nor are we, the ones who she leaves behind to continue her work."

"And by that you mean continuing to kill more men."

"Yes. We facilitate their transition from a life they clearly are dissatisfied with into a place better suited to their draconian personalities. Hell, to be more precise. We send them to perdition to be amongst their own kind."

Pearl was lost for words. The woman was talking about her mother and none of what she was hearing was making sense.

"And the women, what happens to them?"

"We take care of them, although we don't nurse them. Those who have nothing receive more than they ever dreamed possible. Those who do have means are asked to share. In fact many of the donations exceed the ten percent and very often they bequeath very large sums of money."

"How many men have you killed?" Pearl finished her first drink. "How many men are dead because of you?"

"Me personally," Beverly asked, "including pimps, pedophiles and rapists?"

"Yes, you personally."

"Forty-eight."

"You've killed forty-eight men. You want me to believe I'm sitting here talking to a woman trained to kill, a woman who's killed forty-eight men?"

"Yes, to save many more than forty-eight women. Understand something very important. Your mother, we, did not and will not kill indiscriminately because a man slaps his wife once in the heat of an argument. We understand occasional frustration goes both ways, despite the issue of weight and strength differential and the fact that occasionally the preservation of Pearl takes precedence over individual and less critical dilemmas. We are more interested in men who have or will disfigure, break bones, throw women down stairs or potentially kill them. The most recent stats show three-quarters of people, most of them men accused of spousal abuse had no previous record and, of those, four percent are chronic abusers. Those are the ones we want. Forty percent of women are sexually abused, ten to fifteen percent are physically abused in a relationship and fifty percent of all murdered women are killed by their husbands or intimate friends. Close to a million cases of violence between significant others are reported in the US each year, here the number's closer to a hundred thousand. Sexual offences are on the rise, particularly here, by fourteen percent, and each year not far from a half-million cases of aggravated assault, sexual assault and murder are committed."

"And how many are yours? How many has this so-called Pearl killed?"

"We average about three percent. The problem is our figures are always four years ahead of the official figures."

"Which is?" Pearl asked, walking towards the decanter.

"It's somewhere between three-fifty and four hundred each year across North America."

Pearl dropped her glass. "I can't hear any more of this.

My husband will be home soon. You have to leave."

"Unless he is a terrible golfer he won't be home for another few hours. Your mother's suggestion, I believe. In any event, a vehicle is stationed at the turn-off to the highway to alert my chauffeuse and we didn't come here until we saw him arrive at the club. He's very handsome. Please, Pearl, sit with me and listen. Respect your mother's final wish. I have a close and personal affiliation with death. I'm sure she's watching over us. Please do not disappoint her."

"Don't disappoint her," Pearl cried, "my God. You're telling me my mother killed two men."

"Three of any particular significance to you. She killed the man who murdered Billy Stream, she killed the man who possibly would have killed you and she killed the man who would have killed the one woman she could call a friend after you." Beverly patted the cushion beside her. "Pour another and come sit beside me. Your mother was an angel on earth, Pearl, and today she is one in a better place. We all believe that...as you must. Come, sit down."

"She's been doing this for forty-six years since Rita? Are you insane?"

Pearl screamed, wanting to throw something. She stomped into the kitchen, her mind was racing. Her world was being destroyed and she had no defence. She tried to make her mind work, to understand who the woman was and who her mother had been. She stood in a daze against the counter until she remembered the woman in her living room.

"We're talking about thousands of men."

"To date we have recorded sixteen-thousand, two hundred and fourteen to be precise, over many years of course. The oldest facilitation, a short while ago, was seventy. He was a very nasty piece of work. The youngest was seventeen."

Pearl grabbed at her hair and pulled. "He was a boy."

"Yes, he was a boy. What's your point? The courts sent him to counselling which failed miserably, so we got involved. His girlfriend lost an eye, which to us was more important. The facilitation happened in Louisiana and was pro bono. The girl had no insurance and, with the rarest of exceptions, we never involve family."

"So, that's what you do, you kill people like some sort of vigilante. Was that your overseas training? You went to some sort of camp for killers?"

"In a word, yes, although I haven't facilitated anyone in years. Facilitation is forbidden once we become Enablers as is enabling once we become directors. Doing so would be quite unseemly and potentially detrimental."

"And my mother?"

"She wanted Pearl to succeed and survive. As much as a clear need exists to protect women in general, we must also protect our Facilitators and Enablers, hence the compound. Mary played a prominent role in the development of the training and was herself well-trained. However our training goes far beyond the successful conclusion of a case study. We are also trained how not to be seen, either by those around us or by cameras despite being very visible. And, apropos your previous question, have you ever wondered how Mary always knew your every thought, words you were about to speak before you did."

"How did you know that?"

"It's part of our training which is ongoing. We lip read. Your mother was extremely cautious and caring of her flock. There are none better than the operatives of Pearl."

"It was her camp." Pearl let the information absorb into an already confused and defensive mind. "Jesus... and it was named after me."

"Not quite. And the facility would be better described as a luxury compound, the location of which is known to a select few. Any such breach would be quite worrisome. As for our name, Pearl is derived, as was yours, from the ring."

494

"My mother created a secret facility recruiting and training assassins. I don't believe you."

"Trained facilitators who adhere to very stringent guidelines, the very strict Covenants of Pearl, and who are very closely monitored. We don't facilitate indiscriminately. Those we deal with must meet those specific guidelines. They must be repeat offenders, those who have sworn never to let the women go, or to hunt them down, or to have used the word kill in reference to the women. Those who don't fall within those parameters, though there are exceptions, are spared facilitation, not to say we don't keep an eye on them and those victims are given the opportunity to re-establish themselves with new identities and new jobs in new cities, that type of thing. It does take time, however, up to a year to change a name during which time we protect them. So you see we are quite diverse and not merely a bunch of crazed killers."

"Forty-six years. You're telling me you've been doing this for forty-six years."

"Yes, without incident."

"That's impossible. The police would know somehow. They would recognize the MOs, the histories of family violence, the women always being sent away."

"In theory, yes, you're quite correct. Remember, we are talking North America divided into five zones and dozens of sectors. A few hundred men each year in various circumstances are inconsequential when one considers the consequences of not taking action. Some are documented as suicides, possibly carbon monoxide in a garage, others are shot, might possibly be crime related, possibly random. Most are stabbed, which is very quiet and effective, and a few fall from bridges or have boating accidents." Beverly shrugged. "Many have never been found, period. So, you see, we are very skilled and very diverse. Consider also that most police forces are ineffective with relatively low clearance rates. They either lack proper funding, modern technology or lack interest. Of greater importance: there's never any evidence, never a single trace. We take great pride in what we do."

"You're assassins. My mother was an assassin." Pearl rubbed her face, hard. "So, how exactly do you do this? Or is it a trade secret. How the hell did my mother kill men? She was barely five-three for God sake. Did she carry daggers and guns as well, or did she always have a penchant for garrottes?"

"For the most part daggers, as do we all when our services are called upon, although occasionally a gun is more practical. Other times we are very capable without them, as was your mother. She was a fifth Dan. Be proud of her, though a few years have passed since either of us has thought of kicking anything or anyone."

"Mother was a frigging ninja? No way. I would have known. She would have told me."

"She was very proficient, I might add. Our training never stops. The facility is twenty-four-seven, irrespective of holidays. Though, as a doctor and a woman, you might be interested in knowing our most effective weapon, which allows us to use the preferred stiletto, is our bodies. We deal with men of a lower echelon, shall I say. They have no regard for women, yet, conversely, they are easily led to their facilitations by a bare thigh or the anticipation of denigrating us. Unfortunately they don't live long enough to appreciate the irony. We work quickly. We must. Though, many times, when we are able, we do deliver a final message." Beverly saw the look of disgust. "No, Pearl. We don't go that far. We titillate and lure them into a well-choreographed trap, nothing more. No Facilitator has ever done what you're imagining, including your mother. Perhaps you weren't listening when I mentioned the statistics." Beverly paused. "I personally saved one woman and I am fortunate enough to have seen her survive and to live happily with her husband. He was one of my first assignments. Had I not intervened, had your mother not intervened, she might have been killed."

"My mother approved all these killings, she wanted them to happen?"

"She never wanted them, not one, a critical fact you must believe and remember. What she wanted was to save the women, one in particular. She was directly involved for a relatively few number of years before creating the Directorate, a panel of five culturally diverse women from different backgrounds whose mandate is to assist her and support her judgments. She did so to prevent possible fanaticism, or perhaps single-mindedness would be a better word. Your mother never said yes without detailed information or consultation, nor does the Directorate and saying no was always more difficult for her. Many of those case studies are currently living new lives with new names in new cities."

"All these years she was deciding who would live and who would die."

"She was deciding who would live, in either case. New identities for the women mean no facilitation for the men."

"She killed men, Beverly, or whoever you are. She killed men. Use whatever name you want."

Beverly sipped the last few drops of scotch. "Pearl, do you remember your last day at Deep Lake?"

"Yes, of course, I was swimming and Billy surprised me."

"We know. Billy came up behind you and you played kissy-kissy together. How nice for you, but do you remember your father killing him? No, you don't, nor do you remember your father grabbing you between your young legs and yelling that you would not be the town whore. Do you remember him grabbing your throat and screaming that he would rather see you dead? Do you remember that? No. You were too young to comprehend such extreme violence and you blocked out the terror...

497

until Braxton Averly." Beverly paused. "Think back, recall the terror. Do you remember what Mother did to save your life?"

Pearl put down her glass. She was trembling, she was on the verge of convulsion and the woman beside her simply sipped her scotch.

"She was my mother, not yours."

"No, you're wrong. She was a mother to all of us. She was Mother of Pearl, but that will come. My story is not finished. I have a good bit more to recount, Pearl. You might not like what remains to be said, though it has been thirty-five years."

"So what's next? Who's next?"

"Think back, think 1972."

Pearl drained what was left in her glass. When she realized what Beverly was saying she jerked upward.

"Braxton, Braxton Averly."

"Yes, Braxton Averly, your first lover." Beverly took a moment, placing her glass on the tea table. "Do you remember him? Do you remember the way he beat you? He was a very bad man, quite lewd and quite despicable." Beverly paused, smiling warmly. "Take another sip, a big one. You see, Mr. Averly was the reason you were in Paris. You weren't in the City of Lights to get over him or to heal. You did that at the spa in Vermont where Rita went. You were in Paris because he beat you so badly, you were there because he was being facilitated, he was being killed and your mother needed for you to have a secure alibi. After his death your mother discovered he failed at most everything he ever attempted. He never would have become a surgeon, Pearl. He must have known. He cheated his way through every exam he ever wrote." Pearl sat awestruck, keeping the glass at her lips. "You were wrong not to run to your mother when the beatings began. When you did, and Mary saw how he abused you, she contacted the Directorate immediately, which at the time consisted of two women.

They then contacted me."

"You're the one who murdered him. That's impossible. How old were you?"

"I was twenty-three."

"You were a mere child."

"I was anything but a child." Beverly smiled. "Some of us are forced by circumstances to grow old faster. At the time I was necessarily older than my years. Happily, I regained my youth and quite recently was quite pleasantly surprised when a very special young lady prompted me to do something I never thought I would do again."

"What was that?"

Beverly's smile widened. "I bought a few skimpy string bikinis and new wardrobe that have made me feel years younger. So you see, we are quite human, not merely a bunch of disgruntled women."

"And you killed a man when you were twenty-three. You lured him into a trap and killed him in cold blood."

"I lured him into a trap and saved you or someone else who was lucky enough to never have known him. So let's not be so condescending or self-righteous, and think of this: fighter pilots begin their careers in their early twenties and you probably don't give a moment's thought to someone selecting a target and wiping out hundreds if not thousands of people with a thumb, many of them innocent. Conversely, Pearl operatives do not kill innocents, we facilitate potential killers and what makes the job easier is seeing images of the victims. We see the damage and we receive information about them. Our case studies are remarkably complete and knowing what we are doing is, in a small way, making the world a better place is rewarding beyond words. I saw the damage he inflicted on you and if you forget how you looked at the time, I don't. As a director I have seen thousands of faces, everything from contusions to acid burns to a lost eye. I believed at the time I was contributing to a better world and I believe so now. I was told where he would be, at what time, and the window of opportunity was very narrow, a few minutes as I recall. However I planned to lure him, so to speak, would have to be immediate and effective. I remember as though I met him yesterday. I wore a very short dress to make certain he would notice me. Suffice it to say he did. I was quite shameless and very brazen, I'll have to admit. We knew he had a penchant for that sort of thing and each move I made was choreographed to succeed. Today would be a different matter, what with digital and phone cameras. We spoke for a while and he left. I met him the next morning, wearing another short dress. We went to the park and I sat as provocatively as I could without appearing anxious and that evening we went out. He brought me flowers, red roses, and after dinner we went for a walk on the mountain and drank champagne. I put a hallucinogen into his wine. We spoke for a while and I asked him to turn over. He thought I was giving him a massage when, in fact, I was killing him. I was sent by Mother to facilitate Braxton Averly, the very reason I am here with you today. Your mother wanted you to know he wasn't killed by chance. He was facilitated, executed, for being what he was. The orders came from the Mother of Pearl, Mary Bingham, your mother."

Beverly removed her right glove.

"My mother had him killed?"

"Yes, she did."

"All the time we were in Paris, she knew?"

"Of course she did. Your absence was imperative. You would have been the primary suspect, your mother the second."

Pearl was about to faint. "That's her ring. She told me she bequeathed it to a friend."

"And so she has. This one is mine, given to me by Rita Brennan the day I left to spend a short time in the country. Back then there were no trips across the ocean, our budget was more modest. The ring is a symbol that bonds us together, Pearl. There is but one way to come by this ring and we keep our jeweller quite busy."

Pearl looked at her in disbelief.

"I know what you're thinking. Your ideological sense of right and wrong is getting the better of you. The authorities would never believe you, not for a moment. In fact, you are the one who would be discredited. In a word, they would think you quite frail of mind. Past and present Pearl operatives number in the hundreds across the North America, yet we are invisible. We are police officers, lawyers, judges, doctors and nurses, not to mention architects, dentists and social workers. Above all we are clandestine. None of the operatives knows the others and each of the five Directors is restricted to knowing the identities of the Facilitators and Enablers in her respective zone and one other, a structure designed to protect us all. Any breach would potentially undo us and bring about a catastrophic end to Pearl. The operatives know only those with whom they come into contact. I knew Averly, you, and so on. In your case, your mother was your Enabler. That's rare and you were never aware, as you will never know me. So, you see there's no evidence, no trail." Beverly ran a finger lightly over her ring. "The widow's black pearl is the one way for you to know us, the one way to recognize those whom we have saved. Of the thousands of women wearing these rings, each one has been involved in the process, either as an Enabler, a Facilitator, or someone who has knowingly donated as high as a million plus for being saved. Do you remember the day at the church, the day of his funeral, when your mother gave you your ring?"

Pearl stared at her own ring, her face twisted into a distraught mask. She wanted to throw up. "I never paid. There was never any insurance. The money went to his family."

"Your mother paid one million dollars cash because she could and because she did not want to exercise privilege of rank."

"I can't believe any of this." Pearl's face was flushed. "Is my husband safe or is he going to be killed also?"

"He's fine. You're mother liked him. That doesn't mean if the Directorate were ever to hear of mistreatment we wouldn't intervene. We do have a very large presence. Did I mention doctors?" She smiled. "Your husband's fine. He's one of the good ones, like mine."

"You're married?"

"Don't look so astonished. Yes, I'm married, for twenty wonderful years."

"Does he know?"

"No, he doesn't, though I can imagine his face if he ever discovered the truth. As I said, we're invisible. He believes the ring is an heirloom passed down by a dead aunt." Beverly noted the time. "I realize all this will take time for you to absorb, possibly a lifetime. I believe the most difficult part will be deciding how to remember your mother and believing you might have lived a lie. You have done no such thing. Your mother never lied to you. She was a good person, a kind and generous person. She did charity work and made people feel good. Remember her that way. When plagued by doubt think of your father at the lake, remember Billy Stream and your last moments with Averly. Think of the thousands of men like them who are out there. As we speak some woman's head is being pounded into a wall, or her face is being battered by a clenched fist or tool or slashed with a knife."

"Rita worked with mother at Feldman. You said they were separate entities."

"Indeed they are. Rita was the exception. Your mother's fortune and her final generous bequest to you have no connection whatsoever with Pearl. Your twenty million come from your mother's personal fortune, not Pearl. Those funds are in the hundreds of millions and are meticulously managed off-shore. She was an astute business woman. She knew who to trust and who not to. She was pragmatic. She also knew how to ensure success, how to implicate or, better said, how to protect Pearl, which you already know does not exist other than in your own mind."

Pearl shook her head and sank back exhausted.

"I need another drink. My mother headed a group of assassins and she gave everyone black pearls to celebrate murder."

"Perhaps now you can appreciate why your mother never told you, quite apart from your being her daughter. As much as she loved you, she would never have been able to hide from you. She could never have trusted you not to have a weak moment of conscience. Such a lapse might well have destroyed Pearl and the consequences would have been disastrous, if not fatal to thousands of women. Pearl is the epitome of all for one, and one for all. You would have been the weak link, the single constant threat. Your mother's passing obviates that fear. Imagine telling anyone what you know of us." Beverly breathed deeply, her expression compassionate. "I don't mean to sound contemptuous, Pearl, however I see your mother was wise to keep you in the dark. You were a doctor, after all. Prior to your retirement your career was one of saving lives, in that we are no different. We save lives. Our surgical procedures may differ," she paused, "but don't be fooled. It's surgery all the same. Perhaps after your drink, and a few more, what I am saying will make sense. That night at the lake, after your father bashed in Billy's head, he went after you. Had he gone after Mary would you have sat by and watched? I think not. You would have done your best to kill him, enough said." Beverly straightened the cuffs of her Bermudas. "It's time for me to go. Don't bother looking for a licence plate. It's been temporarily covered until we get to the main road and if you follow us the other car will be waiting to follow you. Your dear mother ensured Pearl would never be compromised. I intend to continue ensuring that never happens. Do not defy me, Pearl. Do we understand each other?"

Pearl nodded, dumbly. "Her last words to me were: "I will always love you, if I cannot be with you. Promise me, darling, to take the time and remember there is good in everything we do". Those were her final words. She made me promise that one day soon someone would wear my ring. I thought she was rambling. She died while I went for her breakfast."

"Mother never rambled and I suggest you do as she asked. She didn't tell you herself because she didn't want to tarnish your final and precious few moments together. She did love you."

"You're the new Mother of Pearl. You said you were supposed to retire, except my mother had other ideas." Beverly nodded imperceptibly. "So what now, what happens to Pearl? What happens to you?"

"There are so many Pearls out there. The number grows daily. We will continue with our stringent covenants and rules which serve to protect us as we do our work and each year we will grow and become more aggressive. One of those covenants is that the rings must never be bequeathed. They must remain with us beyond our passing." Beverly reached into her purse for a small gift box wrapped in shades of blue. "During your last visit with Mary she told you she would leave her ring to a wonderful friend. You are that friend, Pearl. This is her ring. Please open the box and take it. She also told you that one day yours would be given to someone who would treat it as something very special, as you always have. Unfortunately, I have no idea who the person will be, though I do know she will wear it one day soon." She handed Pearl the box. "Please take your mother's ring as an heirloom and return yours. You no longer need it. We do."

"I'm glad I retired from medicine. I could never practice knowing what I now do."

"Perhaps not." Beverly stood. "I am pleased your mother asked me to meet with you, Pearl."

Pearl stood. "One last question, Beverly, please."

Beverly's face turned sombre. "How did I feel killing him? What was it like killing Averly?"

"Yes.

"Many of us have the habit of counting in half-seconds. Doing so gives us focus, a beginning and an end. He was dead before two. Three's a definite problem." She chortled. "Then I forgot him before I went to bed. We're not in the business of self-doubt or self-recrimination, Pearl. The next morning I went to work to help design a shopping centre. I was good. He didn't suffer. I used to wish I wasn't so good. Sometimes it was all just too fast to be anything but over with," she sighed, "our catch-22."

"What you just said is so heartless, so cold."

"Corpses never have the chance to admit they were wrong, to admit they should have run when they had the chance. What's heartless is a young girl without an eye or another who must soon undergo delicate surgery because of an old man's vicious probing. Those young women will have that chance. This week we facilitated or, to you use your words, killed a man who years ago shot a young girl in the head because he couldn't have her. The case study was close to our hearts and carried out with particular effectiveness. The young woman didn't end her life by falling into an eternal sleep aided by morphine. She was in her early twenties, and her once beautiful green eyes never closed, filled instead with unimaginable terror, a snapshot of her final moments. Her last scream was frozen on her lips and her face was a ghoulish red mask. You have lived all but thirteen years and a few unfortunate months in a wonderful world and now you believe we have thrown you into another which is vile and contemptible. We have not. There is only one world, yours. What we have shown you is the primary dimension of that world, one which is cruel and increasingly devoid of kindness. In short, Pearl, more bad than good exists in your happy world and we work to maintain a balance. I enjoyed meeting you. Please, do as your mother advised. Let what you have heard sink in. She will always love you, and keep your promise to her. Take the time to remember there is so much good in everything we do. Otherwise we would have failed long ago."

"What do I tell my husband, Beverly?"

"What did you tell him about Averly?"

"Nothing at all."

"We all have secrets. Goodbye, Pearl."

Pearl escorted Beverly to the door in a daze, watching as Beverly strolled across the front lawn to the waiting limousine and disappeared into the forest. When she closed the door she went to the decanter and poured three-fingers of her husband's favourite imported scotch. Her head was spinning as she poured another and left the almost empty decanter on the server. When Robert came home from the club she was lying on the sofa, drunk and feeling nauseous. She pointed to the crystal carafe and told him she was sorry for wasting his precious scotch. She explained how she entertained an old friend of Mary's who dropped by, that her stories were so intriguing she didn't realize how much she was drinking.

He grimaced with a furrowed brow and pressed lips as he realized how little was left for him to savour. Her actions were a breach of wifely conduct of the highest order, he scolded, waving a firm forefinger at her, telling her she would be sorry in the extreme. Forty-year scotch was a man's drink, not meant to be frivolously wasted on gabby women whose palates were better suited to the ordinary, he continued. She would be very sorry and deserve all that would soon befall her.

She muttered something about hundreds of invisible assassins who were out there, waiting to kill bad husbands at a moment's notice. They were lurking everywhere, ready to strike with guns and daggers. She knew about them, she wore one of their most coveted and secret rings: the widow's black pearl. She knew them, she knew their secret leader. They were watching out for her. Robert chuckled compassionately through his nose as he poured the one or two remaining drops and reclined into his easy chair to watch Pearl drift into a deep slumber mumbling that they were everywhere, they contacted her, yet he was safe because Mary liked him.

The next morning Pearl awoke to her name being called by a firm and unsympathetic voice. She was still on the sofa, her eyes were blurred slits and her head throbbed mercilessly. She rubbed her eyes open to see her husband appraising her, shaking his head with a derisive smirk, but he was never good at teasing her and traded the smirk for a smile. He urged her to sit and waited patiently as she did. All he could do to help her feel more human was to bring her a simple breakfast and a freshly cut rose from his garden.

Sixty-One

Quebec City, Quebec
Saturday, September 01

Troy Torrington sent Miranda home in a taxi after her second cognac and before picking up the phone to invite a close friend and senior airline executive to an upcoming golf weekend. Before disconnecting the call Miranda had Executive Class seating on a direct flight later that afternoon. Then Troy poured another dram of his favourite amber elixir and leaned into his seat with his feet on his desk. He would miss her, everyone would. The fact she would be with them for a day or two to transfer briefs was no consolation.

Miranda arrived home in a fluster, worrying the poor doorman who wasn't certain how to react to his favourite tenant who was half crying and half laughing, although he did nothing to push her away when she grabbed him, wrapped her arms around him and jumped up and down. He hadn't understood a word.

She was too excited for lunch; anyway she had precious little time to prepare. Her phone chimed. She listened to Troy's message before kissing and patting the phone. Then she looked in the mirror and shrank back. She was ugly. She looked like a cheap tramp on dollar day and had no time to make an appointment for a facial or with her hair stylist. She was on her own. She sat in the bath for half an hour talking to herself, talking to Dina and practicing what she would say.

In tap pants and a fleecy turban she laid out lingerie and outfits for each evening, morning and afternoon through to Monday. She would stay the weekend and be home Monday night. What was she thinking, she didn't know. Neither did Green Eyes. That was the problem: Dina didn't know, but Dina loved her. She pulled out more clothes, enough for ten days, rationalizing that if Dina didn't want her she would still have enough for the weekend. For the flight she decided on a ponytail held in place with a ceramic barrette, and a pale blue sheath dress-jacket ensemble with deep blue shoes and purse.

Friday evening Claude Jordan left early to drive to the airport in his personal car. He stood waiting anxiously in the concourse with a dozen red roses, which he suggested to his conspiratorial Toronto colleague would be more discreet than his printed name and certainly more in keeping with the city's joie de vivre ambiance. No one apart from the press ever recognized the city's debonair police commissioner and to Claude his lack of celebrity was a perk beyond all others. All the same, what lay ahead was utter deception, more intrigue than he had seen in a decade from behind his desk and he would enjoy himself to the fullest.

He knew the young woman immediately and blew a narrow stream of air from between his lips. She would be his charge for the next twenty-four hours and had promised Troy Torrington not to lose her or put her in harm's way. Troy had understated her looks to say the least. She was absolutely stunning and Claude was completely taken aback when she came to him, hugged him, and unabashedly left red lipstick on his cheeks.

He handled her luggage and they drove to fashionable boutique hotel where he waited in the lounge while she went to her room to change, touch up her make-up and join him looking even more fabulous and a little miffed. She discovered by way of the bellhop who escorted her to her room that her bill was settled in full, including gratuities. She insisted she would pay the hotel bill. Claude insisted she would not and would not hear another word.

They walked to the restaurant arm in arm, talking in unhurried and quiet tones, Claude understanding immediately he was acquiring another godchild. She had no idea what he was saying to the maître d' as they were led to a secluded corner table. Claude allowed the man to pull her chair away from the table and remained standing until she was seated. He didn't ask. He already knew Ultimat on crushed ice was her preferred apéro and within moments of sitting he was touching his glass to hers and complimenting one of the two loveliest ladies in the city.

They spoke endlessly and listened intently without the slightest pause. Later they strolled arm in arm along la Terasse-Dufferin as he explained local history and assured her for the umpteenth time that being her humble servant and protector until Saturday evening would be his greatest pleasure. The honour was his and he would not be deprived. Nor would he hear arguments to the contrary.

He would meet her for an early lunch the following day at 11:00 and, yes, he promised, she would have sufficient time to shop for a special gift and acquire a new outfit for Saturday evening. He was not unfamiliar with women's fashion, or their charming idiosyncrasies, and when they were done shopping she would have the calèche ride she casually hinted would be such an enchanting way to see the city.

Claude arrived at the hotel at 10:55 Saturday morning. They dined at an open terrasse and Miranda's endless questions were none that he heard the evening before. After shopping she dropped off her purchases at the hotel while Claude waited outside on the cobblestone lane and when Miranda walked out onto the street she gasped a loud "wow" at seeing the black and red lacquered calèche. The horse was whinnying, shaking the length of its coarse black mane. The driver looked straight ahead and her gallant cavalier stood ready to assist her into her carriage.

One spot in particular was known for its spectacular view of the city and river and that's where they went. At the gate to the private road Claude Jordan discreetly showed his credentials to the guard, explaining the presence of the foreign dignitary he was entertaining. Miranda giggled when he explained what he'd said to the guard. Not only was she in heaven, she told him, she was a dignitary. Wow.

The view was breathtaking, magnificent, she told him. Claude nodded, passing her a fluted glass. The view was indeed magnificent, he agreed, toasting her health and future happiness. They stayed for an hour, talking. She completely captivated him and he was as anxious for the evening as Miranda. And, on that note, he added, the time had come for them to leave and Miranda showed her disappointment for the first time since her arrival.

At the doors to the hotel he helped her from the carriage and noted the hour. He would return for her promptly at 8:00. He kissed her hand and escorted her through the doors. Once inside he told her that she was to go directly to the hotel's spa where she was expected. He apologized in advance, claiming he had relied on the hotel's personnel to select the appropriate therapies. He was not to be held responsible, nor was Troy Torrington who was complicit and whom he was anxious to once again triumph over on the green within the coming weeks. The men had agreed Miranda's evening should be as special as possible.

Claude drove up to the hotel doors with moments to spare, parking his car under a No Parking sign with his badge on the dashboard. He felt like the man of the hour, dressed in a black suit, a brilliant white shirt with French cuffs, a silver tie, silver pocket hanky and an aura of sophistication most men would never know. He didn't expect Miranda would be waiting in the lobby, certainly not, nor would he expect any less from Dina. The hotel owner called her room as Claude waited at the foot of the staircase.

Miranda was striking in her new knee-length bubble dress of silver and gold, matching evening purse, low pumps, stainless steel handcuffs and a delicate chain and key hanging from her neck: a jewellery ensemble Claude resisted the urge to question. She was divine, an absolute angel and quintessential woman. He could scarcely imagine the shock that was moments away from impacting a woman who was now one of his two most favourite.

He took Miranda's hand and walked her into the centre of the quaint lobby where he clasped a corsage onto her wrist and twirled her in a tight circle for everyone to admire. She was the centre of attention, a rare vision and he told her so as he joined the quiet applause. He offered to carry her two silver and gold gift boxes, Miranda politely declined. She needed something to hold onto, she told him, and she didn't want to wrinkle his suit or crush his hands. She had never been as nervous. Dina wasn't expecting her and perhaps she'd been overly quick to interpret what she heard in Troy's office or since meeting Claude at the airport. Something was going to go wrong. She knew it. Something always went wrong.

At the car Claude opened her door, shaking his head. He ambled around to the other side, eased in behind the wheel and faced her with something resembling a compassionate grin she couldn't quite define. He knew Dina better than any other woman, he told her. If Miranda harboured the slightest doubt, he did not. He hadn't misconstrued what Dina confided in him a few days earlier.

Dina's great grandfather built the magnificent carriage-style home, her childhood home, over a century earlier. Claude no sooner said those words than Miranda asked him not to stop, to take her to the hotel. He ignored her, pulling up in front of the three-story mansion. What she was seeing was an old house, a museum, he answered, his voice sounding sad, an old house whose memories would never fade with its painted walls or one day crumple with its aging masonry.

He stepped from the car with a dozen roses. He opened Miranda's door, extended his hand to help her and embraced her. Claude Jordan was never late for dinner. He gave her gentle encouragement with an open palm to the small of her back, suggesting the For Sale sign she was staring at wasn't a witch's curse. She took his hand and squeezed all the tighter as they climbed the granite stairs.

Dina was glamorous with her hair swept up, her ruby earrings glistening against slender earlobes and her dazzling necklace highlighting a black chiffon drop-waist dress, although not everyone would have noticed her embarrassment, her uncertainty. Claude did immediately.

"Good evening, Claude."

"You are my vision of heaven, Di. Surely you did not dress so extravagantly for me. If I were not so old and obligated to your father and mother, I would feel tempted to make indecent advances."

"So we're okay, Claude. We're good with each other."

"Stop this nonsense this very moment. Can you not see these magnificent roses that pale beside you? You have always been your own woman, Di, without the slightest self-doubt, which makes your concern for my opinion in this recent revelation terribly uncharacteristic. I love you unconditionally, as do your parents and sister as they look upon us from a better place." He leaned forward in a bow, proffering the aromatic bouquet. "For you, Di, insignificant petals for a beautiful and charming princess who is forthwith instructed to stop being silly."

"Thanks, Claude. Now get in here, old man. I was beginning to think you weren't coming."

"Di, I cannot. I lament I am unable to spend the evening with you and delight in your company. Something quite unexpected has come up, a matter I was not privy to at the time of our last conversation. I am indeed sorry, and equally delighted."

"Delighted? That's not such a good thing to tell a woman who spent the entire afternoon cooking and dressing, Commissioner." Dina leaned into the door frame, crossing her arms and sulking. "Another boring dinner with the mayor, I suppose."

"No, Di, not a dinner with the mayor, thankfully, and don't be rude about it. I'm talking about someone much more important than the mayor, much more important to you." Claude Jordan reached into the darkness by the side of the door, guiding a nervous Miranda into the light. He pulled her in close. "This young lady has deemed her evening with you to be more important than my own, and I concur emphatically. She is ravishing, captivating beyond simple words and delightful. We spent the entire day together. She is quite, shall we say, special. Please do not give me cause to regret having surrendered my evening for naught."

Dina's shock could not have been more expressive. She stared wide-eyed with her mouth agape as Claude kissed Miranda's hand, then her own, and walked away whistling without so much as another word. He stood for a brief moment at his car, grinning widely as most of Miranda disappeared behind a wall of roses. The two women couldn't have squeezed each other any harder before Dina broke loose and pulled Miranda into her home.

"I guess we know some pretty important people, huh, Green Eyes."

"Chérie, I can't believe this. How did you do this?" She shook her head. "Never mind. What I said on the phone was true. I do love you, but we can't. You're a Pearl."

"Yes, we can, Dina. I'm an orphan too, since yesterday, not to mention unemployed." Miranda looked at the little box in her hands. "You asked once what you would have to do for a bracelet. Do you think we can we find out?"

Miranda tore the ribbons and wrapping away from the box herself, too agitated to wait for Dina. Inside the velvet box was a glittering sliver bracelet with a single ruby.

"Chérie!"

"There's more, Dina, something very special. Before your message I was going to keep it to remember you and I'm not sorry, but now I don't have to, I have the real thing."

She handed Dina the box. The ribbon pulled away strand by strand, the paper fold by fold. The pearl-handled stiletto was wrapped in silk.

"Miranda I don't understand. I received my MOP this afternoon."

"Pearl sent you mine. This one is yours, the one I used. I didn't think I would see you again. I needed something I knew meant a lot to you, not just these." She raised her cuffed wrist.

"Thank you."

"I was already removed from active facilitation, Green Eyes, that Sunday in Montreal when we met Pearl at the hotel. Then they asked me as a special favour and I knew I was acting for Nancy. I never expected my last one would be so significant."

Tears welled in Dina's eyes. "It's finally over."

"No, Dina, it's finally beginning. I could never be an effective Enabler. I've known all along and Mother understands I had to leave the family."

Dina wiped her eyes and eased the bracelet over her wrist. "Tomorrow I'm having those cuffs dipped in gold. So far this gift-giving thing of yours has been a little one-sided."

Miranda didn't hear or didn't care to hear. She was too busy taking in the décor of Dina's home. "What's for dinner? And I want to hear about this villa of yours."

"Home-made boeuf bourguignon and they'll begin construction on our villa next week."

"Oooh, Green Eyes, we're really going to live in a villa on the coast of France?"

"Oui, Chérie. God help the French. They have no idea."

Dina and Miranda held hands walking into the dining room when Miranda abruptly stopped.

"What's wrong, Chérie? Second thoughts so soon?"

Miranda was visibly upset. "No, my first thought. I heard what you said on the phone, and I listened to Claude talk about you all day, still I had to see you to be sure you wanted me. I didn't want to say goodbye a third time with a suitcase in my hands, so I don't have anything to sleep in."

Dina ran a hand down the back of Miranda's dress, squeezing a firm mound of flesh beneath a thin layer of silver and gold-coloured silk. "I think you do, Chérie, and maybe a little too much."

Green Eyes and Chérie laughed in each other's arms until their eyes and cheeks sparkled with tears. They hadn't kissed in three weeks and suddenly dinner could wait.

Mother of Pearl

Other Mystery – Suspense - Thriller Novels
By Doug Booth:

Split Verdict
The 4th Man
The Madam
Family Lies
Mother of Pearl
From Inside Her Bedroom
The Feast of Tombola
Deferred Prejudice
The Hunt for Gilligan Rose
The Fatal Diners' Club
Silent Conviction
A Christmas Killer, Comfort and Joy
Pariah In the Mirror

***

No One to Tell (Creative Non-fiction)